THE
POET
EMPRESS

THE POET EMPRESS

SHEN TAO

BRAMBLE

Tor Publishing Group
New York

This is a work of fiction. All of the characters, organizations, and events portrayed in this novel are either products of the author's imagination or are used fictitiously.

THE POET EMPRESS

Copyright © 2025 by Storygoose, LLC

Designed by Jen Edwards
Ink stroke by marukopum / Shutterstock
Rice illustration by Yauheniya_Bandaruk / Shutterstock
Endpaper illustration by Elena and Olivia Ceballos

A Bramble Book
Published by Tom Doherty Associates / Tor Publishing Group
120 Broadway
New York, NY 10271

www.torpublishinggroup.com

Bramble™ is a trademark of Macmillan Publishing Group, LLC.

EU Representative: Macmillan Publishers Ireland Ltd, 1st Floor, The Liffey Trust Centre, 117–126 Sheriff Street Upper, Dublin 1, DO1 YC43

The Library of Congress Cataloging-in-Publication Data is available upon request.

ISBN 978-1-250-40681-1 (hardcover)
ISBN 978-1-250-40682-8 (ebook)

Our books may be purchased in bulk for specialty retail/wholesale, literacy, corporate/premium, educational, and subscription box use. Please contact MacmillanSpecialMarkets@macmillan.com.

First Edition: 2026

Printed in China

10 9 8 7 6 5 4 3 2 1

For my family, near and far

THE
POET
EMPRESS

CONTENT NOTE

FRUIT FROM NOTHING

House of the azalea, where thorn meets bud;
Brother betrays brother, blood forgets blood.
—UNKNOWN LITEROMANCER, AZALEA DYNASTY, YEAR 607

My sister Larkspur was the fifth child we buried.

It was a cold and misty dawn as Ma and I climbed the hill out of our village, towards the Ancestors. We carried with us only some incense and a bamboo casket small enough I could tuck it under one arm.

The fifth time had been the easiest. She had been so little when she left us, only three days old. When Ma wept yesterday, when Larkspur's tiny chest had stopped rising, I suspected that she mourned not her daughter but all the extra bowls of rice she'd consumed during her pregnancy, nutrition that was now wasted. Ba didn't even weep. He might have wept, I thought, if Larkspur had been born a boy.

My brother Bao was still young enough to believe dead girls became kittens in their next life. He liked kittens, so he did not weep either.

So it happened that, of all of us, I was the one who mourned Larkspur the most. Not as much as the other times, but I did cry as we lowered the casket on a bed of poppies at the crest of the hill. As I knelt next to the box on the damp soil, I remembered how I had already nicknamed her in my head. Little Lark. I remembered how I had pictured us chasing each other down the drying rice paddies, her delighted laugh as I showed her the best corners to catch catfish. I remembered how I had imagined braiding her hair, as I thought big sisters ought to do, as we giggled and gossiped about the village boys.

After we lit the incense, I kissed the cold crate. I told the Ancestors to take Larkspur to a place where she would never be hungry.

A place, or a time.

I asked the Ancestors to let her be born again earlier. Perhaps when the Azalea Dynasty was not withering and a dying emperor did not sit the throne. I asked them for a time when the people who ruled over us were still good, and children newly born did not die of a famine nobody knew the cause of.

An earlier time, or perhaps even a later one. When dynasty and emperor and thrones and famine became all a distant memory. I should like Larkspur to be born again then, in a time when all children could learn to read, even poor ones, even girls.

It was not long before the land took her.

Ma and I watched, silent, as tendrils of vines snaked up from the soil and wrapped themselves around the crate. Little white flowers blossomed on the bamboo, and from the canopy above, a nightingale crooned. The country might have forgotten people like us, but the Ancestors still remembered.

For New Year's there was no meat on the table. There was only half an extra bowl of rice porridge for everyone—a whole bowl for Bao, since he was growing—and as many preserved bamboo shoots and spiced radishes as we could want. Bao and I got two prunes each from Ba, who had traded some eggs to one of our neighbors, Uncle Gray.

"Take me to the city," Bao said after lunch, tugging at my skirt as I washed the dishes. "I want a Blessing! Please, I want one!"

I smiled as I ruffled his hair. He was only seven to my sixteen, and the gap in our ages meant I was almost a second mother to him. "It's a far walk, Bao-berry. We could play together at home if you'd like."

I was too hungry to want to make the walk to Guishan. The energy required for the half day's journey could have been spent gathering extra food—foraging for dandelion leaves or catching frogs in the paddies—or resting. But that was not the only reason for my refusal. The more important reason was that I did not want Bao's heart to be broken.

On New Year's, supposedly, representatives from the palace would come to our cities and share their magic with the people. A proverb or two that would help the fields grow lush and fertile, ward our huts from mosquitoes, or heal a child from the gray fever. It was said that an Azalea

House prince had once raised a lake in a drought-stricken town with a poem, and that another, with a ballad, had carved a valley road from Duerlong all the way to Cloud's Landing.

Those were the stories, anyway. I had gone to Guishan every New Year's since I was Bao's age, and I had never seen them come by once. Perhaps another place or another time, the Imperial Houses might have given out Blessings, but I had given up hope for ours.

Bao was not giving up, however. He snuggled up against my side, his brown eyes wide in a way that he knew would move my heart. So I sighed, kissed him on the forehead, and said, "All right, Bao-berry. But you'll have to stay close to me."

I then looked for permission at Ma, who was sitting on a bamboo mat on the floor, mending Ba's trousers. She said, without glancing back at me, "Change into a clean shirt, Wei. And remember to walk like a city girl, the way we've practiced."

I didn't miss the hint in her voice. It was every village mother's dream for her daughter to marry a city boy.

Our knees were aching by the time we felt, through our worn soles, the dirt path turn into the paved cobble of Guishan. But as soon as we were through the gates, I felt myself infected by the excitement of the city, and promptly forgot my hunger and pain.

Though the shadows had turned long, it was so much busier here than back in Lu'an. Festive red lanterns blazed from the sloped eaves of every roof. Vendors hawked dumplings, fried mantou, and clacking wooden toys from every street corner. As we wandered into the city square, we found it so packed with people there was almost nowhere to walk.

It smelled of firecrackers everywhere.

"*Streets of powder and red,*" Bao sang cheerfully, "*means a girl will soon be wed!*"

As we passed through the crowd, my brother's hand in mine, I tried to walk the way Ma taught me to, purposeful and coy. I tried to smile sweetly. Ma might be the one who had the dream first, but she had taught me to have it too.

If I married a city boy, then he might have money. If he had money, then Bao and I would no longer have to feel the dull ache of hunger in our bellies. And maybe Ma would not be sick so much and Ba would not limp with pain as he carried bushels of rice on his shoulders. Maybe the city boy would even have some money left over and Bao could go to school. If Bao went to school he could learn to read, and if he learned to read, he could be anything he liked.

A minister, a merchant, a literomancer.

I realized suddenly that Bao was no longer holding my hand. Panicking, I searched the crowded plaza, and was relieved to find him near a stall that sold glazed hawberries on sticks.

When I came to take his arm again, I saw that his eyes were wide with longing. But he was a smart boy. He knew we had no money, and so he did not even ask.

"Would you like a prune?" I asked him in a hushed, secretive voice, as I pulled him away from the vendor.

His eyes went even wider. "You still have some?"

I gave him my best conspiratorial smile and pulled out one of the dried fruits from my pocket. I had saved both of mine for Bao, knowing how he loved sweet things.

Bao made an excited noise and took it. The precise moment he bit into the prune, a gong shuddered through the city square.

Everyone went very still.

Merchants stopped crying their wares, customers stopped haggling, passersby stopped their conversations. Another ring of a gong startled a flock of sparrows into the sky.

And then the voice of a herald: "Prince Guan Isan! Bringer of Spring, Overseer of Feasts, and Third Son of the Azalea House!"

Bao almost dropped his prune in surprise. My own heart was pounding fast. Prince Isan?

It seemed like a dream, like something that only happened long ago and far away. It was unexpected enough that someone from our Imperial House had actually come to give New Year's Blessings at all. But it wasn't even just any representative.

It was a seal-bearing son of the emperor himself.

The look of wonder on Bao's face was as if he'd just found proof that all magic was real and all promises were true ones. I was so shocked myself that I didn't even stop to question why a prince hadn't sent a servant in his place but had come to Guishan in person.

The crowd parted to make way for the procession, and I stumbled stupidly back with them. Bao started to climb me to have a better view, and I helped him to sit on my shoulders. I myself could barely see through the layers of people in front of me, all jostling each other to have a look.

When the procession did come into view, there was no mistaking who they were. They were all dressed in a striking red, a red so true it was almost radiant against the brown of the common people and the gray of the city.

It was not just the color that made them stand out, but the sheer *life* they brought with them. Blossoming green vines crawled over their bodies in place of jewelry, lilies unfurled on their hair and their sleeves, and magnolias bloomed along the swords on their backs.

I felt Bao's hand pull at my hair. "Look, sister," he paused sucking on his prune to whisper. "Back there. That's him, isn't it?"

A horse-drawn carriage had appeared from behind the gong, surrounded by eight men on either side. It was made of mahogany wood and draped with wisteria and spring briar. The carriage stopped in the middle of the plaza. A bowing servant reached out and pulled the curtain open, and out stepped Prince Isan into the reverent silence.

I did not know what I expected. In the stories, the children of the House were beautiful and valiant, filial and generous. And though I did wonder where the stories came from, and who had a vested interest in telling them so, I did know them all by heart. If I believed the stories, I might have expected Prince Isan to be beautiful.

If I didn't, I might have expected him to be ugly. The Imperial House was supposed to protect the people from famines. They were supposed to make sure babies were not born small and malnourished and promptly buried. People who were rotten at their hearts, like the sons of the Azalea House, ought to be ugly.

But now that I was seeing him—really seeing him in the flesh—I found that I hadn't the attention to judge his appearance. I was too busy staring at the House Seal, glowing on his left cheek. It was the only thing I could focus on, and no doubt it was what everyone else was staring at too.

The outer ring of the sigil was circular and bore the flower pattern of the Azalea House. There was a single character inscribed within. I could not read, of course, but everyone in Tensha knew the seals of our imperial sons.

"果/Guo," a man standing beside me whispered to his wife, and a similar murmur spread through the crowd. "The Ancestors' word for fruit."

As if in confirmation, Isan raised his hand.

The earth responded right away. The cracks in the cobble beneath our feet groaned and widened as bushes and vines began unfurling out from the dust-trampled ground. Blackberry bushes, mulberry trees, plump grapes on vines all sprang up from the earth. Branches heavy with pears poured out from under the eaves of a nearby store. Peach trees erupted from the gutters, blossomed, and bore fruit, all in the span of a breath.

Bao squealed in delight, then climbed off me to make a dive for a small haw tree. Around us, everyone else was scrambling to pick fruit of their own.

I helped myself to a peach. As I bit into it, it occurred to me that it was the sweetest thing I had tasted in my entire life. It went into my empty belly like fire filling a cold hearth.

And I started weeping uncontrollably.

I wanted to keep hating Isan. I wanted to keep hating the Azalea House for the years that they never came to give their Blessings, for not stopping the famine that killed Larkspur and four of my other siblings, that might possibly still kill Bao. But I found that I could not. I tried very, very hard to summon hatred, but found myself unable to feel anything at all, except for the taste of peach juice in my mouth.

"I have come to Guishan to celebrate the Year of the Dragon." Isan's bright voice rang through the plaza, pulling the crowd's attention back to him. "I am here to give Blessings to the people, and make one request. First, the Blessings."

At his command, the officials and servants in red livery all produced strings of firecrackers and lit them. They burst into deafening crackles, and through the smoke, tiny red papers fluttered over the city square like quince blossoms in spring.

"Catch one, sister! Catch one for me!" Bao cried, and then I was scrambling, like everybody else, to get my hands on one. But I didn't have to fight for it. There were plenty to go around.

I managed to catch two slips in the end, each inked with a glowing four-character proverb. I gave both to Bao, who laughed like a toddler and bounced up and down. He shoved them into his pocket and threw his arms around me in a hug.

"What do you think they are?" he asked, eyes so shiny with excitement that I couldn't help but smile back.

"I don't know. We'll have to find out when we get home, won't we?"

He looked about to burst with impatience. "We can ask someone here. Someone in Guishan will know how to read. I don't wanna wait—"

"Now the request," Prince Isan announced, sending the crowd into a renewed hush. "As you may be aware, my father has recently changed his chosen successor. The heir of the Azalea House is no longer my eldest brother, Maro, but my second brother, Terren. As part of his new duties, Prince Terren has begun a search for concubines. All interested candidates between the ages of fifteen and nineteen should gather in this square for appraisals, one week from now at noon."

This announcement, even more so than the Blessings, sent the crowd into a chattering frenzy.

Everyone here knew of Isan and his Guo seal, but there was not a soul in Tensha who did not fear Prince Terren and his Dao sigil. Prince Terren, whose affinity for blades made him the most powerful man in the nation. Prince Terren, terrifying and ruthless and cruel, who was to inherit the throne after his father's death.

Nobody knew for sure why the ailing emperor had suddenly named his second son heir, but it was certainly not for Terren's character. I had heard that he would have a servant flayed for merely spilling his tea. I had heard that he would have a dog slaughtered if it so much as barked at him as he passed, that he would have a maid's tongue cut off if only she forgot to address him by his proper title.

I had heard that he killed his own mother.

But watching the crowd, it was clear that nobody was thinking of those whispers. Or if they were, they did not care. All they had heard in that speech was an opportunity.

"Sister?" Bao tugged at my arm.

And, it terrified me to admit, so had I. I ran my hand through my brother's hair absently as I stared at the retreating procession. It terrified me that I was not thinking of Prince Terren's cruelty, of flayings or slaughtered dogs or cut-off tongues.

I was thinking of full bellies, and nights on soft beds, and little sisters who did not have to be buried.

I was thinking of Ma's hollow cheeks filled in and of Ba's pain getting fixed. With the gifts I might receive as a favored concubine, we could buy anything we wanted, even prunes on days that were not New Year's.

"I wanna go home," Bao pressed. He was tugging at my arm again. "I wanna try the Blessings. Please please please?"

I was thinking of Bao going to school. Going to school and learning to read. I was thinking of Bao leaving the famished village life behind and becoming whatever he wished.

My hand closed around my little brother's, and for a brief moment, I let myself imagine a future as sweet as the peach juice lingering on my tongue.

2

POWER AND GREATNESS

Ma took to the idea right away, and even got the whole village excited.

For the next week she collected gifts from everyone in Lu'an. New shoes from Aunt Lien, necklaces of beads and daisies from Grandpa Cai's sons, more dried prunes from Uncle Gray. They would all go in my basket of offerings, the day I was to get appraised to be Prince Terren's concubine.

In Tensha, one did not borrow. One gave what one could, always. The idea was that if I became a concubine, I would have so much more to give. The whole village was counting on me for that.

For the next week, I learned and learned again how generous my neighbors and friends were. I was managing pretty well to hold in my tears until the two Rui sisters showed up at our door with their goat on a leash.

"Myrna gives great milk," said Rui Fan, her sun-leathered cheeks tugging into a smile.

"Fresh and sweet," said Rui Shina. "I think Prince Terren will love it."

Then I couldn't keep it together anymore, because I knew Myrna's milk was not supposed to be for me. It was supposed to be for the Rui family's youngest son, because we all knew that the milk was the only reason Rui Dan had so much energy to run around and play. "I can't accept this," I said between sobs. "Keep her for Dan, I beg you, for him to grow up lively and strong."

But they kept shoving Myrna's lead into my arms, and in Tensha when somebody insisted three times it became rude to refuse.

The evening before I was to go into town for the appraisal, all the villagers from Lu'an gathered on the hill where the Ancestors lived, where Larkspur and the other siblings and so many others were buried, where ghosts sometimes roamed. We sat together in the clearing in the larch grove on the hill, where wild poppies grew, and we all lit red lanterns and let them float into the sky.

For the moment, we forgot how hungry we were. Bao wrestled with the other kids, with Obe and Sangka, and even Ma was all smiles as she chatted with Aunt Raia and Shu Monshu. Ba was sitting solemn next to Uncle Gao, but I was not solemn, I was laughing and dancing. I danced first with Rui Fan, our bare feet stepping in rhythm, and then with Cai Xi'er, my farm-hardened hands entwined in his.

I felt powerful.

The only other time our village had gathered together like this was when we were sending off the Har family's youngest son, ten years ago. Har Asori had always been a bright child. He had snuck into the city more than once to steal lessons from behind the school's fence. Everybody had given what they could to send Har Asori to study in the capital.

Asori wrote us letters every year. None of us could read them, but the Har family kept them all still, and passed them around every so often so that we could all have a look at the beautiful calligraphed characters. Asori held that kind of power, the power that allowed others to believe there was a life beyond death and hunger. And now I had it too.

Later that night, Bao declared, "It's literomancy time!" and we all stopped our festivities and turned to look at him.

His grin was as wide as a young moon as he pulled out the two slips of paper Prince Isan had given us. As impatient as he had been to see what Blessings they contained, I'd managed to convince him to save them until tonight, when we could cast them in front of everyone. When one had magic, it ought to be shared.

Grandpa Har did the honors. His grandson was the one who had gone to school, after all. We all leaned over as the old man traced the four characters from one of the slips in the damp soil with a stick. His handwriting was shaky, unpracticed and uncertain. But he was very careful about it. I could hear everybody else hold their breath, just like I did, as Grandpa finished the last stroke.

Was his penmanship good enough? Was Prince Isan's intent strong enough? Would our Ancestors accept the words?

My doubt only lasted a heartbeat, because the effect was immediate.

The slip of paper Grandpa had been holding dissolved into dust. The characters on the earth flashed with light. The flash coalesced into a tiny spark, and the spark streaked across the ground, through the dirt and grass, all the way to the edge of the hill to where we had buried my youngest sister.

From that spark in the earth, something started to grow. Just a sapling at first, but soon a young tree. We all laughed and yelled like little children once we recognized its leaves as those of a peach tree. A Blessing was not *pure* magic, the kind Isan had demonstrated in the city earlier, so it did not immediately bear fruit.

But our hearts still soared. We knew that this tree was magic enough, at least, to withstand the blight. We knew it would bear fruit for us in the years to come and that we needed only be patient.

"The next one!" Bao yelled, delighted. "The next!" He held out the other slip.

Again Grandpa Har traced the characters into the earth. Again there was a flash.

This time, the glow traveled, unexpectedly, to Bao. We all fell into hushed silence as we watched it climb up his leg, to his heart, stay there for a brief moment, and vanish.

Everybody was staring. My brother was staring at *himself*, his chin resting right against his collarbone, his eyes bug-wide.

"The Blessing went to Yin Bao," said Shina. She was stating the obvious, of course, but that was fine because that was what we were all thinking.

"Well?" Ma said after a while. "Do you feel any different?"

Bao, who looked still very surprised, shook his head.

"It's a sign," Ba announced decisively, standing. When something strange happened in a small village, whichever interpretation was stated with the most authority tended to stick. And Ba put much authority in his voice as he proclaimed, "My son will grow up to be a great man in the future. Perhaps one who will change the world."

Later that night, Ma surprised me by coming to my bedside. I had been asleep, but my eyes fluttered open when I felt somebody's hands fold over mine.

"Ma?" I whispered.

I was surprised to find her crying softly.

I sat up and cupped her thin cheeks. "Ma, everything will be all right. I promise." I had no idea why she was weeping on a night of celebration. We had Isan's peach tree, and Bao had the other Blessing, and I was possibly going to be a concubine.

She was too sad to speak, but finally she swallowed and whispered, "What if he hurts you? What if he kills you?"

I blinked. "Prince Terren?" All the stories of cruelty, of death, tied to his name. "I'll be careful, Ma. I was raised by you and Ba, after all—and you have made me very clever." I hoped the praise directed at her would please her.

"You don't have to go, you know," she said, voice as fragile as fallen petals. "You can still change your mind."

It was then that I realized Ma loved me.

I mean, I did know, but I had always thought she loved me the way any mother in Tensha loved their daughters. They loved them, then they sent them away to marry somebody from a better family, then they loved them a little less.

But I didn't know she loved me in *this* way. In a way that, if it meant I could be hurt, she would not wish me to be a concubine of Prince Terren's, or join the palace, or bring our family wealth with his gifts. I had no idea she could ever prefer that I stay.

And she was right. I could still change my mind. I could try to marry a city boy instead and bring my family out of poverty slowly instead of all at once, one copper or bowl of rice at a time.

But then I remembered all the people of my village gathered earlier, on the hill, their eyes glittering as they reflected the lanterns in the sky. I remembered feeling powerful. I imagined all the things Bao could be if he could go to school and learn to read, and I knew at once I could not choose anything else.

I kissed Ma on the cheek and lied. "I am not afraid of Prince Terren or of the Azalea House. I am not afraid of anything."

3

THE JOKE OF GUISHAN

I may have felt powerful that night, but when the sun was high the next day, when we entered the city square with our basket of gifts and Myrna on a leash, I felt a fool.

I was far from the only candidate there vying for Prince Terren's attention. The fact should not have surprised me, but it did. The whole plaza was filled with young women, at least several dozen. And they were all far better than me—this was the truth, not false modesty.

They were city girls, not girls brought up on the rice paddies. Their skin was not sun-leathered, their cheeks not hollowed, their lips uncharred. Their baskets were filled not with baked buns and prunes, but with flowers, precious stones, and silk cloths.

How could I have ever thought Prince Terren would want me for his court?

My family, who was with me, seemed to have the same worries. Especially Ma. Ma's lips went into a thin line as her eyes traveled over the other candidates' clean, dyed gowns, their sturdy shoes, their painted nails. I had done my hair in braids for the occasion, but their hair, pinned up in the fashion of the city, made mine seem crude by comparison.

One of the girls near me, who had clearly darkened her brows with ink, actually laughed at us as we passed by.

"He stinks," her companion said, jabbing a finger at Ba. Everyone around her burst into giggles so falsely dainty that I felt my blood heat.

Bao's hands balled into tiny fists, but I held him firm. I was angry myself—it nearly broke my heart, watching Ba limp with his shoulders hunched so—but I knew that starting a fight would only make us look even worse.

I joined the end of the line. My family retreated somewhere into the shadows, waiting unseen. I sent a silent prayer to the Ancestors. *Let me help my family. Let me help my village. Let Bao go to school.*

Let me be chosen.

It was not so long after that the selection began. First, a few local officials arrived to oversee us, and then came representatives from the Azalea House itself.

There was less fanfare than on New Year's, especially without a prince in a procession. Only two representatives had ridden in, but we still drew in a breath anyway when we saw their red livery, stark and vivid. We all stared at their horses, who had leaves for manes and flowers for tails, and smelled not of beasts but far gardens. They pulled a carriage behind them, which was wreathed in carnations.

One of the representatives descended. He was a smile-faced man with soft features and a singsong voice. "I am Li Ciyi—a eunuch serving under Prince Guan Terren, the Winter Dragon, The One Who Cannot Die, and the Second Son and Heir of the Azalea House."

The other representative, the one wearing a large sword on his back, did not dismount his horse.

Ciyi went down the line of young women. To the apparent surprise of almost everyone, he did not look into our offering baskets, which were silently collected by the local officials. The only thing he seemed interested in were our bodies. He examined our ears, our eyes, our breasts, our teeth. He got us to take off our shoes so that he might look at our feet.

When he got to me, at the end of the row, his laughter was even crueler than the women from earlier. "You smell like village," he said.

I kept my eyes on the ground. Ma had told me that city boys preferred girls who were docile and did not speak up, and I thought that possibly Prince Terren, and therefore his representative, might prefer the same.

Ciyi carried on. The appraisal process did not take very long. After two passes down the line, Ciyi pointed at the girl who had laughed at Ba earlier, the one with the painted brows. "You. Let's go."

It was as perfunctory as purchasing cabbage from the market.

It did not quite register that I wasn't chosen until Ciyi was helping the other girl into the carriage. When it did, I was no longer thinking. I left the line where I was standing and raced all the way to the eunuch.

"Please." The words came pouring out of me before I could stop them. "She doesn't need it. She's not hungry. Not the way I am."

Ciyi regarded me the way he might consider a fly on his rice. "And what does it matter what a peasant like you needs?"

"I know I'm nothing, but please." I fell onto my knees. It was so unlike me to beg, but at that moment, I was so desperate I would have done anything. My stomach panged with hunger, and my muscles still ached fire from the half-day walk. But I couldn't think about anything but Bao. I wanted him to grow up tall and healthy, and I wanted him to go to school in the capital, just like Har Asori, and I wanted him to become the great man that the Blessing said he would. "I have a brother. He's young. He's thin."

I did not want to mourn him like I did Little Lark, as I feared I might if the famine continued. That would absolutely break me.

"Is this some kind of a joke?" Ciyi's disgust deepened. "A village girl, an ugly one at that, dreaming of becoming concubine to the Imperial House."

"Then let the prince laugh," I said, without thinking.

The eunuch had been in the process of remounting his horse but stopped.

I stood up now, and the words came out angrier than I should have dared. "If it's a joke as you say, then let His Highness Prince Terren laugh at my expense. Bring me back and see if it will please him to show everyone how ugly I am, how filthy, how thin. Let him laugh at this poor village girl and then behead her—it will be no loss to you."

When I said all this, I did not expect him to actually listen to me. I only said what came to my mind out of anger and desperation.

I definitely did not expect him to smile a pearl-toothed smile or wave me into the carriage.

There was hardly any time for goodbyes.

Bao threw himself around my leg and cried and asked me to come back and visit soon. Ma wept.

Ba stood stone-silent; it was his own way of saying he would miss me.

4

AZALEA HOUSE

The girl in the carriage with me was named Zou Minma. She was eighteen and the daughter of a literomancer. It had taken a while for us to speak—we did not much like each other, for clear reasons—but there was nothing else to do while the carriage rocked us over hills of famine-starved land, and so eventually we relented.

Her father wrote spells for mending clothing and blankets, which they sold in Guishan's archives. Both her older and younger brothers had gone to school, so I gleaned her family was moderately well-off. I wanted to ask her if she had taught herself how to read in secret, but I knew that she would not tell the truth even if she had. Girls did not speak of learning to read, not if they wanted to keep their lives.

And besides, she was very suspicious of me.

"How did you get the money?" she kept asking, one inked eyebrow raised. "There's no way you could have gotten in without bribery—you don't even know the first thing about being a concubine."

"And you do?" I said. When she didn't reply, I tried to figure out how to get more information from her and settled on flattery. "It's very impressive that a girl in Guishan should know what life is like in the capital."

"Of course I do," she snapped. "I'm not a dumb village girl like you. I know politics. I keep up to date with the succession war."

"Succession war?" I played with my hands, trying to seem embarrassed that I was not aware.

Her lips curled up, clearly smug that she knew something I didn't. "Do you think Prince Maro is *happy* his brother was chosen instead of him, when he had been heir all his life? Do you think with all his power and allies, he would let Prince Terren even close to the throne? The two have been fighting for the Crown since they were old enough to know what it stood for. If it were possible to kill Terren, Maro would have done so long ago."

Brothers fighting brothers. Brothers *killing* brothers. I tried to imagine Bao hurting anyone, even a sparrow, and could not.

"Is it really true?" I asked in a small voice. "That our prince has a spell that makes him unable to die?" As with all rumors about our princes that made it to Lu'an, I had no idea if this was the truth or an embellishment.

Minma glared daggers at me. "The Aricine Ward? You best *hope* it is true. If Terren does not live to become emperor, then what is the point of us serving as concubines? What is the point of us letting him plant us, over and over again, for the small chance that just one of the seeds will take?" She looked out the carriage then, at the hills barren of anything edible. "What is the point of suffering if we have nothing to gain?"

It was towards the evening that I had my first glimpse of the Azalea House. The carriage had crested a hill, and because I smelled flowers, I thought to open the curtains and have a peek outside.

For a moment, I couldn't even breathe.

The Azalea House was beautiful in a way that made me understand why scholars wrote poems. Some kinds of beauty were too large to hold with simple prose.

The palace, vermilion and striking, sat between two lush peaks through which the setting sun bled its light. It was enormous and sprawling, with many-tiered pagodas and walkways and courtyards that were all visible only because I was still far enough away. Around it, flowers bloomed on the hills in ten thousand colors, red poppy and yellow rapeseed and blue hyacinth, and many others I did not know the names of.

A huge red dragon was unfurling in the sky like a ribbon, chasing its tail with the slowness of clouds. I had not noticed it at first, because its colors had blended in with the setting sun, but as soon as I knew it was there, I could not look away.

"That dragon," said Minma conspiratorially, "is the Crown of the Aza- lea House. He serves whoever the emperor is, and amplifies his magic a thousandfold. Guan Muzha now—but soon, Terren." And then, with a calculated amount of threat in her voice, she added, "And after Terren, my own son."

I tried to imagine *my* son with the Azalea Crown at his command and found that I could not. It terrified me. I should have been more afraid of Prince Terren's knife, the one that cut off tongues, but all I could think about was how much I did not want to be planted by him and have to hope that something magical would grow. And if by some miracle of Heaven it did, I did not want to carry it in my belly for nine months.

But then I thought of my family, who needed me. And Bao, especially Bao. And so I hugged myself to keep warm and tried to imagine it anyway.

I tried to imagine becoming a high-ranking concubine in the court, sharing tea with the prince in those beautiful pagodas. I tried to imagine bearing a son for Prince Terren, one with a seal. One that would please him enough that he would not hurt me, and instead send Blessings all the way back to Lu'an.

I closed my eyes and held on to that image, because if I didn't, I thought I might cry. Why had I told Ciyi to bring me so I could be the prince's joke? Why had I told him it was fine for me to be laughed at, to be beheaded?

Later, when the air grew cool and the stars winked into view overhead, the carriage, at last, pulled to a stop.

I thought I would see Prince Terren as soon as I stepped out, the sigil for Dao glowing stark on his cheek. I imagined him pointing his sword at me and having me cut up on sight when he saw how unsuitable I was.

But he was not there. It was a quiet night, with only a sprinkling of guards at the arched gate. It had to be a side entrance, for how unassuming it was, tucked away behind branches heavy with blossoms and whistling nightbirds.

Of course he wouldn't be here, I realized. The heir was too important to see two of presumably many candidates on arrival. I was ashamed of how much it relieved me.

Ciyi whispered something to one of the guards, who went inside. A moment later the door opened, and two young girls came outside in flowing robes.

"These are attendants from the House," Ciyi said pleasantly. "They'll wash you up and make sure you look presentable." At the word *presentable*, his eyes flickered unsubtly to me.

I tried not to stare too long at everything as I was led inside. Everything in the palace was so intricately made, from its ancient walls, brilliantly red, to the fountains and sculpted osmanthus trees. As we went down a hall, along a courtyard, I noticed that even the smallest pillars had carved gold etchings on them, depicting ancient seal-bearing men fighting demons and moguei and more horrifying things. Even the red lanterns lighting the walkway held stories, lines of verse inked on their papery sides.

At last, we arrived in a far, tucked-away wing of the Azalea House.

"This is the Hall of Earthly Sanctity," said Minma's attendant. "Where the candidates will stay." Hundreds of occupied chambers all faced a huge, peony-filled courtyard, candlelight flickering from every window. "Selection Day is one month from now. If His Highness chooses to retain you as one of his thirty concubines, you will move to his East Palace, the Palace of Blades. If not, you will be sent home."

"This way," my attendant said, and pointed in the opposite direction that Minma's attendant was about to lead her.

Before we became separated, Minma grasped my wrist without warning and leaned into my ear. "You may be a village prude, and ugly, but you are also from Guishan. I do not wish for you to die. So let me warn you: do not trust any women in the court. We may not fight with swords and poems like the men, but we have other ways of fighting. You may think the women here are your friends, but we are all competing."

"For the prince," I agreed, because I thought what she said was obvious.

"For power," Minma corrected. "Those who are starved are most desperate. And even the Ancestors know that women have long been starved for power." We went our separate ways.

5

THE FATE OF CONCUBINES

O Tensha, Motherland!
The birthplace of culture. The resting place of great men.
All the world fears the poem written in Tenshan pen.
—TANG GEWEN, AZALEA DYNASTY, YEAR 589

I wish I could say I listened to Minma's warning. That I kept on being afraid of the Azalea House women, or the prince and his knives, or even of Prince Maro and his plans to regain the Crown.

But when my attendant led me to where I would be staying—a warm, lantern-lit room, nestled deep within the rustling peony bushes—all I could manage was a childlike awe. Vivid rugs, curtains, and tapestries blooming with live flowers covered every surface. Paper lanterns sitting on every table guarded against the chill of night. I saw things I had only ever heard about in stories: bronze mirrors, and porcelain cups, and lacquered furniture made of what I guessed was sandalwood.

By one of the latticed windows, a cat with holly leaves for fur sat watching me, tail flicking as it soaked in the moonlight. It was yet another sign of the magic inherent in the Azalea House. I felt like a little girl again under its gaze, knowing nothing about the world.

Connected to my chambers was a basin-room. When I went inside, looking for a place to wash myself, I found a bath already drawn, still warm and scented with hibiscus petals. For a long time, I worked on scraping the thick layer of mud off my body—from my brittle black hair to my calloused soles, to beneath my bit fingernails. I wondered if it was enough for me to be clean, or if there was some ineffable part of me that was and would always be *village*.

When dinner came, there was enough food to feed a whole family.

The cook named each dish as he set it down. "Braised chicken with mung bean. Shrimp and abalone dumplings. Egg flower soup. Thousand-year fig cakes, to promote beauty and longevity. . . ." By the time he left, there were more than a hundred plates on the table.

At first I just stood there numbly, as if I had forgotten what food even was. Even the rice here was different—white and pristine. I had rarely ever had a bowl of pure rice like this before, without mixing in bran or tree bark or plants we foraged from the hills. Even on New Year's, we could have only watery porridge.

New Year's had not been that long ago. I still had the image of Ba giving the one extra bowl to Bao burning in my mind. I still remembered how he had eaten his own portion slowly, one grain at a time, so that he would finish at the same time as his son.

Now I had all this for only myself.

I should have resented the Azalea House for it. Instead, I ate so quickly that the soup burned my tongue. For the first time, the constant ache in my belly vanished, like a shadow scared away by the sun, and that was when I understood—really understood—why village girls wanted to marry city boys and city girls wanted to marry princes.

I wanted to stay here forever.

I would want it even if I had to fight the women in the palace and dodge Terren's knives. Even if I had to be planted, over and over again, until I grew them a son. So long as I was never hungry again, I thought, they could do to me anything they pleased.

But wishing was not enough to make something so. If that were the case, Larkspur would still be alive.

I was reminded again of how little chance I had to be chosen when I glimpsed the other girls the next morning. They were milling under the courtyard's pear trees, in the haze of dawn, walking gracefully and speaking gently. When they laughed, they covered their mouths so that only their eyes showed.

"I am from the province of North Lan," I overheard one of the girls say. "My family owns three tribute houses near the prairies. We hold feasts for several city officials each month."

"That's impressive," her companion replied, in a tone that suggested it was not. "My unworthy family only owns an entire fleet of merchant ships. Sadly, we only get to hold feasts for hundreds of foreign dignitaries every week."

It was from these overheard conversations that I learned who the other candidates were: daughters of ministers, scholars, and high-ranking officials. There was even a niece of the empress here, the Sun Clan's Jia. The more I learned about them, the more foolish I felt.

How could I have ever thought the prince would choose me? I had already been unsuitable compared to the candidates in Guishan. Compared to the women here, I felt like a weed trying to flower among lotuses.

There were other things the women whispered about, from speculation on the succession war between the five princes to rumors about how ill the emperor truly was. It was said that he had not spoken a coherent word in months, that switching his heir to Prince Terren had been one of his last lucid decisions.

Mostly, there was gossip about the concubines from previous generations.

They were so envious of each other.

They were all so spoiled by their emperors.

They fought each other so viciously. Most imperial concubines do.

The more of it I heard, the more uneasy I grew. It was said that of Emperor Muzha's Inner Court, which had once been full of thirty women, only the empress and one other remained. Some had been deemed unworthy and dismissed; some had fled of their own accord. Most had died.

The girls spoke of knives, and poison, and drownings on moonless nights.

The palace eunuchs, always smiling with smugness or pity, informed us that the deaths were only accidents.

On the third day, our lessons began.

A gong woke us up at dawn, before birdsong. I joined the hundreds of candidates in the courtyard to sit in tidy rows, on grass still wet with dew. While the pear trees showered down blossoms, the House brought in a rotation of instructors to teach us how to be proper concubines—how to dress, and walk, and speak to people of rank.

There was even a senior concubine, the last remaining from the emperor's court, to teach us how to please a man.

Lady Chara, a frail woman with jutting cheekbones, spoke quietly and without smiling. "It is important that you never skip to the main activity." Her voice was like a wind's whisper. "You must first cultivate desire in your prince, for as long as he permits you. This allows magic to build up in him, so that his seeds will come out as potent as possible. The difficulty of an imperial child being conceived, you must understand, is far higher than that of an ordinary one. It is vanishingly rare for a seed to be viable—only male seeds are strong enough to hold Heaven's magic, and even so, only the tiniest fraction of them survive to be born."

She explained that our emperor had to plant many, many times to get our five seal-bearing princes—Maro, Terren, Isan, Kiran, and Ruyi. And even so, five was unusually high. In many eras past, it was considered lucky to receive even two, to guarantee the line of succession.

I supposed that was why they needed so many of us.

"That is why techniques are so important. They help us improve our chances. It is a lot like literomancers and their poetry. Pleasing rhythms can draw out magic no matter its source—Heaven, the Ancestors, or our prince. The one I will teach you now was developed in the early years of the Sun Dynasty, by a mistress of the Wenning Emperor. It is called the Allure of the Snake." Two maids held up a bamboo pole, and Lady Chara demonstrated.

My eyes went wide as I watched. Ma had told me the childmaking activity was only natural, that every girl in Tensha was born knowing how to do it. I had never even considered that she might be wrong, that it was something that had to be taught.

Beside me, the other girls practiced on imagined bamboo of their own, and I tried clumsily to mimic their motions.

When Lady Chara finished teaching us this technique, she moved on to others. Moth's Flutter, Crane's Glide, Twirl of the Calla Lily. They all seemed very similar to me, but a furtive glimpse at the other concubines told me they had a much more intuitive grasp of the lesson. Possibly they had all learned their duty already, long before they had come to the palace.

Minma, I noticed, was not following her own advice.

Instead of being careful of the other girls like she told me to, she was trying to befriend everyone. Her father must have given her spells to use here, to copy onto the earth and mend palace gowns, because I saw her offering slips of paper to the others, to gain favor. During breaks, I saw her whispering with Tu Yan, a general's sister, and later that morning, trying to form an alliance with Aika and Tiron, both daughters of scholars.

Once, she even tried ingratiating herself to Sun Jia.

But the empress's niece only looked at her with disgust, like Minma had done to Ba back home. "A literomancer's daughter," Jia sneered, kicking mud onto Minma's gown. "If your father's spells are worth anything, how come he has not been brought to the palace, to work for the emperor?"

Minma didn't react. She simply brushed it off and moved on. Not even ten breaths later, she had seated herself by one of the trellis tables under the pear trees, to share tea with Yuan Lily and Liru Syra.

Maybe, I thought uncertainly, I ought to make alliances of my own. I decided to forget about our prior enmity and approach Minma. "May I sit with you?"

Her sharp eyes flicked up to meet mine. For a long time, she only looked at me in silence.

It was Syra, with a face powdered like a moth, who broke it. "Do you know her?"

Instantly Minma scowled. "Her? Why would I know *her*? I have never spoken to that unsightly creature even once."

"Look, she's even tied her sash on the wrong side," Lily chimed in. "Has she never worn a gown in her life?"

They were still laughing when I ducked out of sight.

I tried to make more alliances, but was met with the same scorn. Whether it was because the other girls could tell, at a glance, that I was *village*, or because the quick pace of gossip had ensured that everyone already knew who I was, nobody wanted anything to do with me.

The only candidate who showed friendliness was a short, pale girl named Ciera. She found me, on a clear, breezy afternoon, watching the swallows flit about under the eaves. "Wei," she drawled. "What an interesting name. What does it mean?"

It was not an unreasonable question, since the same sound in the Tenshan language could have multiple meanings. "It means *tail*," I told her, more than a little embarrassed. "And *end*, and *last*. When I was born, my parents thought I would be their final child." Except my two older brothers had died soon after, both in quick succession, so they had to keep trying for more sons.

Ciera gave me a cat's smile. "Maybe you are meant to end something bad, so that you might begin something good."

It was a kind thing to say, and I thought I had at last made an ally. But the next morning, I woke up to the bloody tail of a swallow staining my windowsill. Huge flies were crawling all over its tiny, delicate feathers, and it was already beginning to reek something awful. Its body was nowhere to be found.

I tried my hardest not to care. I told myself that it didn't matter if nobody liked me, because I was not here for them but for Bao. But even so, I could not help but cry a little that night, curled up on a bed too silk-soft to fall asleep in. I had never met people like this before, people who were cruel like villains in a story.

I wondered if they were born like this, or if something about the palace made them this way, like a cliff pine bent by strong winds.

Our lessons continued. On the fifth day, an imperial doctor came, dressed in swishing robes of black. "There are several known places where magic lives in a man," he intoned, and bade a eunuch undress himself except a cloth around his groin. He used a stick to point at various locations on his naked body. "If you wish to increase the chance of passing that magic to his son, then you must know how to touch and engage these pressure points. Here—here—and here."

On the seventh day, an apothecary came in from the capital Xilang. He wore the tasseled headdress of scholars and carried a large crate with him, from which he drew several pouches and clinking jars. "These are aphrodisiacs, made for stoking the pure magic of Heaven." There were all kinds of them—from ginseng tea to toad's venom to jujubes, to something dark and bitter he called "Red Bean Brew." After we had a look, he made us memorize a long list of fragrances made from wildflowers and herbs, emphasizing how important it was to match the aphrodisiac to the prince's mood. "Like pairing dim sum with exotic tea."

On the tenth day, the palace manager Lü Hu taught us the inner workings of the palace. "The House was first built two dynasties ago, following the reunification of Tensha. It is the largest palace in history. There are four thousand servants working within its walls, eight principal palaces, six hundred pavilions, and two hundred and forty gardens." He was a jolly, enthusiastic young eunuch, with huge sleeves that waved around as he spoke. "Unfortunately, not all are accessible to you. You see, the House is divided into the Inner Court and the Outer, and the two sections are strictly separated. Women are not allowed to leave the Inner Court, just as men cannot enter it. Only your prince and eunuchs may visit, to ensure the sanctity of the concubines."

Each night, when we all returned to our chambers, I tried to go over each lesson in my mind, lips moving as I recited new terms. It was difficult for me, since everything was so unfamiliar, but I wanted to do the best I could. I had come to bring gifts back to my village, and I did not want to go back empty-handed.

The night before the selection, we had our very last lesson.

"There are approximately thirty days in the lunar cycle," said an astronomer in starry robes. His voice was like a singing kettle. "The female energy rises and wanes with the moon, and so the prince's nights must be scheduled accordingly. The highest-quality nights are saved for his future wife, the Empress-in-Waiting. He may choose to bed her at any time, including the full moon . . ."

He went on to explain the concubines' ranking system, and how it related to when they could bed the prince. If the prince did not wish to see the empress, he could summon one of two Noble Consorts—on any night except for the full moon. The first-rank concubines could only be given nights on gibbous moons and below, the second-rank on half-moons, the third-rank on quarter-moons. The even lower-ranked companions, the astronomer said, would only be considered when the moon was crescent or new.

A current of anxious murmurs passed through the girls. It was a grim reminder that competition between us didn't end on Selection Day. Even after we were chosen for the prince's Inner Court, we would still be competing to share the imperial bed—just like concubines of generations past. We would fight each other for the small chance to use Lady Chara's techniques and the even smaller chance to become mother to a seal-bearing son, the chance to become powerful.

The astronomer frowned at us with disapproval. "A proper concubine," he said, turning his nose up, "must never envy those who receive more time with the prince. After all, are we not all here for the same purpose? The Azalea House is only as strong as our seal-bearing sons. We must pray for each other's success tomorrow during the selection, so that our nation will be great and lasting!" He said it like there was nothing more important in the world.

But that seemed to do little to allay the candidates' worries. By the time Selection Day came—a gray day, the sky heavy with the promise of rain—the candidates were no less competitive than the first morning.

And, I was ashamed to admit, I felt the same. As I fell into line among them on the long walk to the East Palace, I allowed myself a thin flame of hope.

If by some miracle, I thought, Terren didn't kill me and instead chose me, I would perform the very best I could. If he allowed me just one night with him, I would show him that I could grow a seal-bearing son, just like the girls from the cities.

6

SELECTION DAY

The day of the selection itself was not auspicious. We did not see a phoenix in the sky, or a jade serpent shedding its scales, or a plumeria tree flowering earlier than expected. As eunuchs herded the hundreds of us to the East Palace, the Palace of Blades, the sky stayed as heavy and quiet as stone.

It was cold in the Hall of Divine Harmony. On the ceiling hung ten thousand lichen-covered blades, their tips all facing down; on the far walls, swords sat in rows among white lilies, like the jaws of a flowery beast. As we walked the length of the great hall, towards the throne at the back, I felt as if I was entering a night-story—the kind Grandpa Har used to tell us, awful and impossible, to scare us from wandering too far from home.

Why had I told Ciyi to make me the prince's joke?

The candidates lined up behind the dais, which held a row of golden seats, two couplet-bearing pillars, and a throne forged from lilies and even more swords. The servants, eunuchs, and guards around us tried, without succeeding, to pretend they weren't staring at us. Their whispers echoed in the hall. *That one looks a little thin. That one's pretty as a leaf. That one looks dainty upon first glance, but her feet are very big.*

The girl in front of me was crying.

The candidate next to her gave her an impatient look. "Keep it together, Zhen. He is going to behead you if he sees you like this."

Soon, guests began to arrive. As each filed through the open gates, they were announced by a solemn herald with a twitching mustache. "General Cao Myn, the Evening Tide! Jun Li, Minister of Rites! Inspector Cyrun of Chong'an! . . ."

They seated themselves on the carpet, behind the rows of cherrywood tables facing the throne. Cold dishes and clear wine were already set up. The guests picked at them while they socialized and laughed *oh ho ho* from their bellies. I had seldom seen men like these before. Men with soft plump faces, shaven chins, and gowns as bright as a bee-eater's feathers. They were as different of a creature from the men of my village as the city girls were from me, and I could not stop staring.

Each brought their own servants with them, who carried poles draped with tasseled, rectangular banners. On them were huge characters and sigils, which I could not read, but guessed they contained their ranks, titles, and clan affiliations.

"Empress Sun Ai!" announced the herald, suddenly loud. "Matriarch of the Sun Clan! And her son, the Fifth Prince Guan Ruyi!"

As the first members of the imperial family entered, the crowd fell into a hush. I craned my neck over the other girls to have a look myself, at the woman who had survived to be empress when so many of her competitors had died of *accidents*.

She had cunning eyes, long nails, and lips painted in sharp vermilion. A golden gown trailed behind her like daylight, shimmering like it was hot to the touch. She was not monstrous looking—rather very elegant—but even so, I could not help but wonder what wicked things she had done to get where she was.

In her arms was a sleeping infant, whose cheek bore half a seal. Though the floral outer ring was present, no character gleamed from within.

Prince Ruyi, I knew, was too young to have magic. Though a prince was always born with that half-formed seal, it was not until he was nine or ten, the age a boy first started to become a man, that he came into his power.

Last autumn, when our fifth prince had been born, everyone in Lu'an had gathered to guess at his powers. Ma had bet it would be a military one like Terren's Dao, but stubborn Aunt Lien had insisted it would be an economic one like Maro's Lu. *Commerce runs in the Guan Clan's blood,* she'd said with a huff. *Just look at our emperor and all his dead brothers.*

The little ones, Obe and Sangka and Rui Dan, had all hoped for something spectacular. *Like the Yan power of the First Emperor, whose pillars of flame can be seen a thousand li away.*

"The emperor isn't coming, then," whispered a girl behind me. She had a moon-pale face and cautious eyes. "If he was, he would have been with his empress."

The girl behind her, with rosy cheeks, scowled. "If he can't even make it to his own heir's selection, he must truly be as ill as the rumors say."

The empress took a seat on the dais, her son like a doll in her lap—right as the herald announced another imperial guest.

"Prince Guan Kiran! Bringer of the Storm, and Fourth Son of the Azalea House!"

A gust of wind swirled into the hall, rustling the lilies on the walls. Thousands of heads turned towards the gate, watching as a procession of men in blue ribbons set down a cloud-white palanquin. Out stepped a boy, bony and dark and with ruffled hair.

Other than his 風/Feng power, I knew little about the thirteen-year-old prince. Few stories about him had reached Lu'an, perhaps because his reputation was far outshone by his elder brothers.

"I heard his mother is a commoner," whispered the moon-faced girl, as Kiran and his men took their seats by a cabal of South Sea sailors. "That our emperor, while on a military campaign, had planted his seeds all over the nearby villages. Heaven must have smiled on the nation that day, because one of them turned out viable."

The rosy-cheeked candidate scoffed. "No wonder he's not half as pretty as the rest of them."

I still could not decide if the Azalea House sons were ugly or beautiful, though everyone else seemed already convinced. *Born marked by Heaven,* the ladies in Guishan sighed—and even the radish sellers at the wet market would have a wistful shine in their eyes. *From a father with imperial blood and a mother handpicked out of millions. Is it so surprising that they are all as lovely as legends?*

But in the end, ugliness and beauty were traits that belonged to people. And no matter how hard I tried, I could not make myself see them as *people.*

The next prince to enter was Isan; I caught the scent of ripe fruit before his palanquin even appeared. He and his men wore gowns of blossoms, and carried with them baskets heavy with mandarins and apricots. When they sat, it was next to the River Province's governor, the Minister of Revenue, and several palace literomancers in black. They were gifted a fruit basket each.

"Now that one looks more like a prince ought," the rosy-cheeked girl said. "Though I hear he is cowardly and overly soft. Bends to people as easily as reeds in the wind."

The moon-faced girl snorted. "It's not like he has a choice. You know already how unthreatening his magic is."

I thought of the sweetness of that peach on New Year's, of Bao's delighted laugh as he picked a hawberry from its bush. I could not decide whether I was grateful to the third prince for having gone to Guishan at all, or if I resented him for having only gone once.

"But where is *our* prince?" the rosy-cheeked girl muttered. "Shouldn't Prince Terren have been the first to—"

She hardly finished her sentence when the earth began to rumble, making us all jump.

Plates and teacups rattled on tables; swords clattered on the ceiling. Everyone turned to stare as stone and moss burst out of the wooden floor, alongside blooms of yellow chrysanthemums, and a path paved *itself*, like a rolling carpet, from the gates all the way down the length of the hall to the still-unoccupied throne.

"Prince Guan Maro!" The herald wasted no time with the announcement. "Carver of Rivers, Builder of the Salt Road, and First Son of the Azalea House! And his wife, Lady Song Silian!"

With hair that swept past his waist, robes of shimmering white and gold, and a cloud-etched staff tied at his back in place of a sword, Maro looked every bit the Azalea House prince of stories. His 路/Lu sigil, of roads and passageways, shone even brighter than his brothers'.

And then I thought, maybe I did know what they meant when they said *as lovely as legends.*

Guan Maro: the eldest, the most honorable, the one who should have been heir. I had heard the most about this prince. All through Guishan, and even farther away, the common people sang about the roads he had paved, the rivers he had carved, and the remote villages he had connected to bustling cities. It was said that at the young age of eleven, he had even built the Salt Road—the most important trade route in all the nation.

"I have heard," whispered the moon-faced girl, "that he never took concubines of his own back when he was heir, so deep was his love for his wife."

"Or perhaps he is simply a prude," the rosy-cheeked candidate replied, apparently equipped with a jab at every prince. "I hear he has spent many years of his youth wasting away in the temples. Perhaps he is so religious he cannot spare a single thought for us girls."

My eyes drifted to the woman walking beside him, whose hair was frost-white, as I knew was common for members of the Song Clan. Her dress was woven from lotuses and glowed like the moonlight. *She* was beautiful, I decided. Though as with its men, I had not yet understood the palace's powder-faced and ink-browed idea of *beautiful*, I did admire her smile, which made it seem like she was afraid of nothing. It was no surprise that she had caught a prince's attention, I thought, with a smile like that.

The first son, his wife, and their servants took their places near the dais. And then there was only one prince left.

We waited a long, long time for Terren.

We waited so long that the gray skies outside gave way to gray rains, and storm winds battered at the windows. The crowd had become as restless as Heaven, and the candidates just as agitated, when a figure finally did appear at the gate, alone and drenched all the way through.

7

MERCY

The hall was silent as the second son entered, dripping water with every slow step. There was no palanquin to carry him, no servants to tend to him, no allies for company. His gray robes were entirely plain. The only adornment he had on his person was an unsheathed sword, which he used as a walking stick.

He was shorter than in my nightmares.

There was no scowl on his face, but he did not need one. There was enough menace in his black eyes to fill the entire room. Beneath his rain-slicked hair, his 刀/Dao sigil burned like fire, though it was not the only part of him that was magic. Around his whole body, a stream of Tenshan characters, arcane-white, swirled like glowing chains. I wondered if it was the Aricine Ward I'd heard so much about, the legendary Blessing that made him unable to die.

"Something's wrong with him," the rosy-cheeked candidate whispered.

I blinked; she was right. The prince was not walking normally but stumbling with every step. Several times, he had to use his sword to stop from falling.

As he passed us, I caught the stink of rice wine, strong and sour and sick-making.

"Prince Guan Terren." The herald's voice was uncertain. "The Winter Dragon, The One Who Cannot Die, and the Second Son and Heir of the Azalea House."

He had a hard time getting up the steps to his throne. He actually tripped and fell—*twice*—but nobody went to help him. Not the banner-men in the audience, not the hundreds of servants and guards stationed around the hall, not any of his half brothers. The empress remained motionless in her seat, though she almost seemed like she was pleased.

"May you live a thousand years," the guests said in unison. The standard greeting for an empress or a prince.

Terren barked out a laugh as he sank into his throne. "I doubt any of you actually wish that." Even slurred, his voice was dark and dangerous. "I doubt any of you wish me to live even a day longer."

A scared knot formed in my stomach, unbidden. I had tried to prepare myself for the selection by imagining all the ways he could have been terrible, but this was one I could never have conceived of. The few times I had seen men drunk like this, in Guishan's gambling houses, they were always angry and throwing things. And the only things near Terren were knives.

A stooped, white-haired eunuch stepped up to the dais. "If it pleases Your Highness, we will begin your selection now."

"It does not, Hesin, but I am told we must anyway." Terren produced a gourd flask from his belt, took a long swig, and wiped his lips with a draping sleeve.

The look of hate on Maro's face could have burned steel.

The old eunuch named Hesin bowed and waved the first girl forward, who stepped onto the dais. "Then, on behalf of the Second Son and Heir, and the Mother of the Inner Court, we begin." He unfurled a scroll and read, "Kang Rho. Daughter of the Scarlet General Kang Zhulun, of Angxi City. Seventeen years old."

"Discard her," Terren said immediately. I did not think he had even looked at her.

From beside him, the empress's mouth twisted. "We will do no such thing." She stroked her sleeping son's head with a nail and turned to Rho. "I understand, my dear, that your grandfather has given his life for the empire during the War of the Highlands. This sacrifice has not been forgotten. We will retain you as a concubine. In addition, we grant you one of two positions of Noble Consort."

Rho's eyes widened. The only rank higher than Noble Consort was Empress-in-Waiting. I knew it must have been a tremendous honor.

Hesin glanced warily at Terren, as if waiting for him to protest the empress's decision, but the prince didn't seem capable of speaking. His head kept tipping forward, eyes growing increasingly unfocused.

The eunuch swallowed and turned back to the crowd. "The House has made our decision. We thank Lady Kang for her family's military achievements, and we grant her the title of Noble Consort."

Whispers began immediately from every corner of the hall. Everyone seemed as shocked as I was. Prince Terren was powerful. He was the bearer of Dao magic, after all, the heir to the empire, the wearer of the mythical Aricine Ward.

Why was he not even choosing his own concubines? Why leave it to the empress?

The selection continued as Hesin moved to the next candidate. "Bi Lou. Daughter of Bi Byrou, governor of the East Valley District. Age sixteen." A thin girl stepped onto the dais to await her judgment.

Terren's head had slid to rest on the iron arm of his throne, his body gone still as ice. For a brief moment, I didn't think he would respond, but at last he murmured half-coherently, "I tire of this. We already have one consort. Let us end the selection."

"My dear prince." The empress's voice was gentle, as if speaking to a disobedient child. "As Mother of the House, I must remind you of your duty to fill your Inner Court entirely. It is hardly auspicious for so many pavilions to remain empty now, is it?"

One of Maro's allies audibly scoffed.

Terren forced his head up until his eyes rested on Lou. "Women," he said tiredly. "They're all the same to me. We kept the last one, so let us get rid of this one." He punctuated the pronouncement with another drink from his flask.

The ugly way he said *women*, like how Ba cursed the rats in our kitchen, sent a shudder through my spine. Something was desperately wrong. The House had told us we were all here to be planted, to bear a magical son for Tensha and bring glory to the nation. But if so, why was the prince so uninterested in us?

This time, the empress didn't speak on the girl's behalf. Hesin waited for a while longer, and then he said, "The House has decided. We thank Lady Bi for her willingness to serve the empire. We dismiss her with a reward." At his word, two maids stepped out of the shadows to hand Lou a red azalea pin and a small but bulging sack. She wept all the way to the doors.

The selection continued. As each candidate stepped onto the dais,

Terren tried to turn them all away. The empress, for her part, mostly let him. Very occasionally, she stepped in like she had for Rho, retaining them and giving them titles. Virtuous Beauty. Honored Companion. Second-Rank Concubine.

She only did this for girls from important families, I noticed. It seemed far more politically motivated than for Terren's benefit.

Minma was not chosen. When she stepped up to the dais, Terren dismissed her handily, in less time than it took to draw breath. I was not surprised. She might have worked hard in the past month to make allies, might have spent the whole morning inking her brows, brush by brush, but none of it mattered when it was not the prince choosing but the empress. And the empress chose only based on our family names.

Zou Minma might have been a city girl, but compared to everyone else here, her background was still unremarkable, a bonfire swallowed by the brilliance of suns.

As she was escorted out by guards, azalea pin scrunched in one fist, she turned back and searched the remaining candidates. When she found me, her eyes lingered. For a moment, there was an unreadable expression on her face, and then she turned around and was gone.

I swallowed something bitter in my throat. I should have felt vindicated—for how cruelly she had laughed at Ba, how she had called me ugly and treated me like I was nothing. But instead, I could only feel sorry for her. I still remembered the light in her eyes, on the carriage ride here, when she had spoken of becoming mother to a prince. Now that dream would never come true.

If Minma wasn't chosen, I thought, *then surely I have no chance at all.* At once I felt foolish, for coming here at all, for staking all the hopes of my village on an empty wish.

The line of candidates before me was dwindling. As my turn approached, I was not sure if I felt relieved or disappointed. Maybe the reward for coming would be worth something nice. Maybe it could be traded for haw candies on New Year's.

"Sima Zhen of the Inner Sea District." Hesin was now introducing the candidate right before me, the girl who had been crying earlier. "Daughter of Sima Emian, Distinguished Merchant of the Inner Sea. Age eighteen."

By now Terren hardly seemed awake. He had been drinking wine without stop as the selection carried on, commanding Hesin to fetch a fresh flask every time he had finished his previous one. As Zhen stepped onto the dais, his head hung forward. His eyes stayed shut.

He did not notice her drawing a knife. Did not see her plunging it towards—

A knife. Half a gasp escaped my mouth before I could stop myself. By the time I had the sense to react, he should have already been dead three times over. But he was still sitting there, still alive, because Zhen's blade *never touched him.*

The Aricine Ward had stolen his death. The band of Tenshan characters around him had lashed out, coiled itself around Zhen's blade like chains, and stilled it mere breaths away from his heart. I thought I saw the faint outline of a white tiger flash behind the throne, but I blinked and it was gone.

Impossible, I thought, still half in shock. How could magic so powerful be true?

The crowd reacted all at once. Guests crying out, servants screaming, the remaining candidates huddling together like frightened geese. "Take the assassin away!" Hesin cried above the clamor. "Protect the prince!"

"No. Nobody move." Terren's voice was surprisingly lucid. His eyes fluttered open, as if waking from a long sleep.

The hall stilled. Zhen let go of the hovering blade—the ward coiling around it keeping it afloat in the air—and dropped onto her knees. "Your Highness," she gasped. "Forgive me. My father made me do it . . . it wasn't my idea . . ."

The way Terren looked at her, as if she had told a joke nobody else in the room found funny, made my blood turn to frost. Hesin must have seen that look too. "Your Highness, please," he said hurriedly. "Let us take her to Heaven's Worship, where we may question her according to procedure."

"No need. I shall deal with her myself, here and now."

For the first time all morning, the prince was alert. His dark eyes fixed intently on Zhen, as if he had not had trouble keeping them open mere moments before. "I had thought my selection would be a torturously boring piece of theater, but it seems the Ancestors are kind today. They have sent me entertainment."

Zhen let out a choked sound and shuffled backwards.

"*Terren.*" Maro stood from where he was seated by the Salt Road merchants. "Do not forget yourself. This is the Azalea House, and there are procedures to be followed. You must not dishonor our father and our Ancestors."

Terren's eyes flicked to him. "Ah, Maro. You plead on behalf of an assassin. An ungenerous interpretation would be that you also wish me dead."

Maro's hands clenched into fists. "The only thing I am pleading on behalf of is the Crown's dignity. Whatever you are about to do, don't do it. Not in front of all these honored guests. Not in front of Ruyi!"

The fifth son had awakened sometime during the selection and sat blinking at us with big eyes. With a shaking hand, and a look of pure enmity at Terren, the empress turned the infant's head away.

Terren's eyes never left Maro. "I do what I please. I am the rightful heir, after all." His voice was calm, not argumentative, and that seemed to rile his brother even more. "And besides, I had only planned to be more merciful, not less." His gaze traveled to Zhen, who whimpered. "Surely you are aware of the usual punishment for what you have attempted. The Extermination of Nine Relations."

Tears streaked through the powder on the girl's face.

"Though it is an inconvenient process, I must admit. To hunt down so many grandparents, siblings, and cousins. It is much simpler to let you go." With a flare of his sleeve, Terren gestured to the open gates, beyond which the rain still poured—a dozen pillars away, all the way across the length of the hall. "Leave, Zhen. Once you make it to the doors, I will see to it that we spare your family too."

My chest seized with terror. There was not a chance this wasn't a trick. Zhen seemed to realize it, too. She stayed on her knees, shivering like a leaf in the wind.

"What are you waiting for?" the prince said, becoming impatient. "Do you not wish to live?"

"Terren," Maro warned again.

He ignored him and leaned closer to the assassin. "Don't worry," he said, as if telling a special secret to a child. "My aim is not very good. As you can see, I am quite drunk at the moment."

That finally seemed to startle her into motion. She climbed hesitantly to her feet, took two slow steps along the moss path that Maro had made. Then, as if making a quick decision, she bolted for the gate.

Terren waited until she was halfway across the hall before raising an arm. There was a flash of his 刀/Dao sigil, and then the blades on the ceiling rattled like chimes.

Instantly, everyone realized what was about to happen. Guests, servants, and candidates all screamed as they leapt out of Zhen's trajectory, and I cried out as I dove after them. Half a heartbeat later, the knives rained down. Clattering against the wooden pillars, plunging through the tables, shattering porcelain plates, cutting through carpet. A sword caught Zhen in the arm, then another in her leg. She screamed and dropped to all fours, but kept crawling forward, a smear of blood emerging in her wake.

Terren watched her progress silently from his throne. When she drew close to the gate, he sent down a second shower of swords. One of them clipped her shoulder. A second plunged into her back and out her belly, its tip glistening red.

Zhen collapsed onto her side, sobbing incoherently.

I was close to crying myself. All the rumors were true. Prince Terren really *was* as wicked as all the stories—maybe even more so. During my month in the palace, a small, childish part of me had still been hoping that the crown prince wasn't really cruel, that they had only said he was. I had even hoped he might turn out kind.

I should have known better than to indulge in such foolish fantasies. None of them, not even Maro, were *kind*. I had gone to Guishan all those empty New Year's mornings. I had known what they were all like.

Terren's sigil had stopped glowing now, the blades lying on the ground motionless. In the lingering silence, I could hear only the rain—and the *scrape, scrape* of Zhen dragging her body forward by her arms. With each movement, she grew slower, feebler.

Let her suffering stop, I begged of the Ancestors, sick to the pit of my stomach. *Let this end quickly.*

She was so close to the gate now that for a brief moment, I thought she might make it. That she might really feel the rain on her cheeks before death took her, save her nine levels of relations from a similar fate. But at only an arm's length away from the gates, she spasmed and went still.

Nobody said a word.

Isan sat statue-silent among his men in blossoms; across from him, by the South Sea sailors, Kiran had taken a sudden interest in his tea. Even Maro seemed subdued, his face a dark mask of defeat.

It was Terren who broke the silence. "A pity. It seems we must exterminate her family after all." When nobody responded, an uncanny smile appeared on his face. "Shall we resume, then? I believe we were in the middle of my selection. Say, Empress Sun, didn't you mention I must fill my Inner Court completely?"

The empress clutched her son tighter, her scowl deepening.

Terren turned to the old eunuch. "Well, Hesin? I am not used to repeating myself, but I will if I must."

"Your . . . Your Highness." Still half-dazed, the eunuch returned to the dais, bowed to the prince, and turned to the next candidate in line, which was me.

I did not know how I made it to the dais, with how much I was shaking. I could hear every thump of my heart as I forced myself to stand in front of the prince.

In Guishan, when I'd prayed to the Ancestors, it had been *Let me be chosen.* And maybe if I was braver and more worthy, I could have kept praying for the same. But after all that had happened, with the air redolent of wine and blood, with the knives strewn all over the ground, with Zhen's body cooling in the same room, I found I could not make myself brave.

When I sent a prayer into the earth, it was only *Let the prince spare me. Let me return to Lu'an alive.* I prayed that I could marry a city boy like Ma wished for me originally, and that the Azalea House might exist only in stories once again.

"Yin Wei of Lu'an," Hesin announced, "of the Guishan District. Daughter of Yin Huang, Rice Farmer. Sixteen years old."

I prayed desperately and with as much heart as I had left to give. I told the Ancestors that if they helped me this once, I would never ask anything of them again.

"Rice farmer," Terren echoed, and the contempt in his voice was so great that I braced myself for the worst. But he didn't kill me. Instead, he said, "I choose her. And I grant her the title of Noble Consort." The entire room stilled with shock, but he kept speaking. "No, I change my mind. I shall make her Empress-in-Waiting. I shall wed her."

8

TO SHOOT DOWN SUNS

Pity the fish confined to its pond.
It cannot play in the grass. It will never feel the breeze.
How can we claim to have suffered enough?
Pity the fish. It will never swim among trees.
—TSAO TE SHU, LIANG DYNASTY, YEAR 445

I didn't cry as eunuchs dragged me through the cold rain and deposited me somewhere deep in the East Palace, but only because nothing felt real. It was like everything was still a continuation of that night-story, embellished to be as frightening as possible.

I was not the prince's betrothed, I tried to tell myself. I was still a girl in Lu'an, dancing with the rest of my village under a clear evening sky, and I had only dreamed the palace.

The pavilion they put me in was huge and empty. I sat in one corner as servants busied themselves around me—moving furniture, carrying in rattling towers of silver plates, hanging up rain-soaked bundles of embroidered cloth. For the most part, they ignored me. Only once or twice did one cast a glance over my way, as if to wonder how a village girl had tricked her way into becoming the prince's betrothed. The one who would receive the majority of his nights, anything from the full moon to the new. The one who would, after a betrothal period of three hundred days, wed him.

The one who would—should Terren survive his coronation—become empress.

"Lady Yin, how fortunate you are! I am baffled as to why you are not dancing and singing."

I looked up, surprised to find a familiar face. It was Li Ciyi, the eunuch who had brought me here from Guishan. "Why are you here? What do you want from me?"

The eunuch ignored my questions and made a grand gesture

encompassing the entire room. "Ah, is this place not a true marvel to behold? Fit for an empress, I daresay! Look how the hydrangea bushes sprout from the base of the walls; see how the orchids peek their shy faces in from the lattice windows. And the ceilings! Hanging with a thousand blades, just like the main hall! Our prince has put such *thought* into decorating your new home."

"What do you want from me?" I asked again, running out of patience. I could not look at him without remembering how he had gone down the line of girls in the city square, like picking cabbages at the wet market.

He cleared his throat theatrically. "I hope you will not be offended, Lady Yin, when I say it is clear you know little of palace politics. But it need not be that way. Everyone knows that all great empresses past have had a trusted chief eunuch advising them. An ally who can slip, like an eel, between the Inner and Outer Courts, who can help you navigate the palace's intrigue and vicissitudes."

"You want my employment?" I was stunned into saying. I had never met someone so shameless. "I thought you said I was a joke."

His eyes narrowed into crescent moons. "That was when you were nobody, Lady Yin. Now you are to be an empress! The currents of the palace flow faster than a white river; alliances in the House change hands quick as currency. You asked what I want from you, so I will answer you simply and truthfully: I wish to rise with you in station. Should you survive to become empress, *I* will be the most powerful eunuch in the palace."

I couldn't believe we were speaking of currency, as if Zhen had not been cut apart that very morning. As if the prince would not do the same to me without the slightest hesitation. "Why have you let me come to the palace anyway?" I demanded. "Did you know the prince would choose to wed me?"

"Of course not." He gave me a strange look. "You think that I predicted the assassination? That I could have guessed at the prince's fickle whims? Lady Yin, I brought you in to collect a gift from the candidate who went after you—no other reason."

So that was all. A bribe. Someone on Selection Day had wanted to seem better in contrast, and had arranged for the most unworthy candidate to go before her. I could not even remember if that moon-faced girl had made it. Terren choosing me had been such a shock that the rest of the selection had passed in a blur.

"See?" Ciyi warbled. "I have been nothing but truthful to you. Now you see you can trust me."

"I do not want your services," I said, not kindly. "Even if I desired a chief eunuch, which I do not, it would not be *you*."

"Ah, but you have little choice. You underestimate the danger you are in—how insulted the other concubines feel now that a rice farmer was chosen over them, what dreadful lengths they would go to to remove you from your position. I may benefit from this arrangement, but make no mistake: you benefit far more. Without you I will not have my promotion, but without *me* you will be dead." The wider Ciyi's smile grew, the narrower the crescent moons. "And if you die, what will become of your brother? The one who is young and thin?"

Anger surged through me like wind in a storm. "Go away. I do not wish to speak to you any longer."

"You still do not trust me, then. I shall prove myself to you with a gift." He pulled from his sleeve a long, metallic object and offered it to me. When I didn't take it, he let it clatter onto the wooden floor. "This needle, made of mountain silver, turns black in the presence of poison. I suggest you use it on anything another concubine brings you." He whistled a cheery tune as he left me.

As much as I despised Ciyi, he was not wrong. My purpose was to help my brother and others waiting for me back home. I could not keep standing here feeling sorry for myself, not while the famine was still ravaging Lu'an's rice paddies and starving its people.

I had to use my new position to save them. Each moment I delayed was a chance that another sister, like Larkspur, could die.

The rain had stopped now, leaving behind a heavy stillness. In the languid afternoon light, I could see that my pavilion was no longer empty. The servants had filled it with ornate rosewood tables and elm benches, reed mats and cushions for guests to sit on. Vases of beautiful porcelain, depicting immortals on misty mountains, held young trees of olive, mandarin, and fig.

The Cypress Pavilion was far bigger than the guest chambers in the Hall of Earthly Sanctity. It boasted a huge parlor, a crafts room, two bed-chambers, a dining area, a sunroom, and a courtyard. It had both a front garden and a rear garden, which extended deep into the cypress grove. In the rear garden, I found a maid and a eunuch, sweeping stray leaves off the cobblestones.

When I stepped outside, they dropped their rakes in a hurry and bowed.

"You don't have to—" I began, but the maid interrupted me.

"May you live a thousand years." She was young and bright-eyed, and wore her hair in two buns; her shawl bore the red, white, and black coloring found on cranes. Behind her spray of freckles was a gentle blush, behind her smile a shyness. "I am Lin Wren, the head attendant for the Cypress Pavilion."

"And I am your scribe, Tel Pima." The eunuch had startled-looking brows and a braid that reached his waist. He kept a quill pen tucked behind one ear.

Women might have been forbidden to read, but the more distinguished ones kept male scribes for correspondence. It should not have surprised me that I was assigned one myself.

"I'm glad to meet you both," I said, and meant it from the heart. Nobody had spoken to me this kindly in a month. Then, remembering my purpose, I lowered my head. "I have a favor to ask. I come from a small village, and the famine has not been kind to it. Are there any provisions I can send back home?"

Instantly, Wren's face darkened. "I am sorry, Lady Yin, but what you ask is beyond the abilities of this humble servant. Everything in the East Palace is accounted for. Everything that comes in and goes out must be approved by His Highness."

"You ought to ask the prince himself," Pima said. "He is, after all, betrothed to you."

There was no mockery in his tone, but it was hard not to interpret it as so. They picked up their rakes and began sweeping again, signaling the end of that conversation.

For the rest of the afternoon, I tried to speak to the other East Palace workers. As I wandered through the cypress grove, I made my plea to several others. But no matter who I asked—from the youngest maid feeding the holly-cats to the oldest eunuch trimming the azalea bushes—their answers were the same. One of the older maids mending a scarf by the creek, with gray-streaked hair and a face sagging with age, did not even look up or acknowledge me once.

Did they hate me? I wondered, despairing. Did they spurn me for being a lowly villager?

Or did they resent me for being Empress-in-Waiting?

Daylight was fading by the time I made it to the end of the garden, where a plain pavilion sat tucked away between the cypresses. Warm firelight flickered from its windows.

As I approached, I heard laughter and excited conversation, punctuated by what sounded like a story being passed around. "*Long ago, in a world burning with heat, the Archer shot down nine of the ten suns.*" When I looked inside, I saw at least twenty maids and eunuchs gathered for dinner. *The servants' quarters*, I thought.

I did not dare enter. Once, I might have thought myself one of them, but now I was not so sure. I was not an empress, certainly, but I was not quite a villager anymore either. I didn't know *what* I was. I stayed outside, close enough to hear their conversation, but not close enough to feel the warmth of their hearth.

It was there, pressed up against the cold wood and hugging my knees, that the prince's eunuch found me. "Lady Yin," Hesin said, "His Highness calls you to his bedside."

9

THE ONE WHO CANNOT DIE

By the time we arrived at the Tower of Mental Tranquility, the sun had halfway set, painting each tier of the pagoda with the color of blood.

Hesin led me up the stairs wrapping around its exterior, up a dizzying height, and from it I had my first look at the palace's surroundings. Two sides ended at the base of lush peaks; beyond a third side, what must have been the capital, Xilang, lay sprawling over a shrouded ridge. On the fourth side, the mountain plunged into a jaw-droppingly deep valley. I tried to avoid looking that direction.

"Your Highness." Hesin knocked on the wooden door. When there was no response, he simply opened it.

I stepped into the prince's bedchamber. Like the Hall of Divine Harmony, where the selection had taken place, this room was also covered with swords from wall to ceiling, white wisteria floating between their hilts like clouds. In the center of the room was a table large enough for twenty but set for two. At one end of it, Terren sat with his legs crossed and his gray robe pooling on the carpet, reading from scrolls sprawled messily on the ground. His ward of glowing characters hung motionless around him.

I felt my breathing quicken, that awful knot of fear returning.

"I will leave the two of you to your duties now." Hesin gave me a look that I could not interpret, then left us. He did not slam the door behind him, but it sounded loud anyway, like a cage door shutting.

The silence lingered. Terren did not look up or acknowledge me. Finally, I forced myself to say, "May you live a thousand years."

"Formalities irritate me. It is only the two of us, so there is no need to waste perfectly good silence on vacuous words. Sit. Eat."

I sat at the other end, as far away from him as possible. The enormous length of the table between us teemed with at least a hundred steaming dishes, soups and braised meats and stir-fries, but I could not bring myself to feel hungry.

Terren wasn't eating either. He finished the paper he was reviewing and stamped a red seal at its bottom. The next one he crinkled up and tossed aside, and then he did the same for a third. "Maro's allies. Some try to switch sides now that I am heir. What would you make of this?"

I was too afraid to think of a proper response, so I blurted out what Lady Chara had taught us to say. "I'm afraid I have no opinion, Your Highness. This humble servant knows nothing about the men's side of the palace." And anyway, it was the truth.

Terren made no further comment. He set down the paper and picked up another. The silence drew on, the sunlight through the window becoming redder.

"Your Highness," I said, before I could stop myself.

He kept his eyes on his paper.

I should have kept my mouth shut and my head down, the way Ma always said that city boys liked. But perhaps it was the creeping darkness giving me urgency, or because part of me knew that when Pima had said, *You ought to ask the prince himself*, he'd been right—I knew I had to at least try.

I owed it to Ma and Ba, and to the Rui sisters who had given me their only goat Myrna. I owed it to everybody in my village who had released a lantern that night on the hill, who counted on me being brave enough to bring gifts back.

"I would like your help." My voice came out tiny and frightened. "To send my brother to school. Bao is very clever, and learns things quickly, and if he goes to school he can become anything. And . . . I would like to send some food home. The famine has torn my village apart, and we are all suffering. I have seen how much abundance there is in the Azalea House, and thought that perhaps . . . perhaps a few barrels of rice can be spared."

"There is no greatness without suffering," Terren said. He set down his paper at last and met my eyes. "Our dinner is getting cold, Wei. You should eat."

My palms began to sweat. It was the same almost friendly voice he had used on Zhen, and it told me that this was a trick.

"What is the matter? Are you afraid of me?"

No, I tried to say, but the lie was too large to make it out of my throat.

He leaned in with interest, his ward beginning to swirl like a winter gust. "Was it what I did to Zhen, during my selection? Or was it something you heard about me even before? Tell me, was it the slaying dogs, or the bloodying servants, or the cutting tongues like snipping roots off bean sprouts?"

The worst part was that his curiosity didn't even seem feigned. It was like he truly wanted to know.

"Perhaps you've even heard about the time I cut a scribe's body into twenty pieces and laid him in the sun to dry." When his mood shifted, it shifted suddenly, like storm clouds that had sprung from nowhere. "And yet you came to my selection anyway, greedy thing." He jabbed his chin at the food on the table. "Eat."

With trembling fingers, I picked up my chopsticks. He did not pick up his. Instead, he watched me intently, dark eyes following every hesitant bite I took.

By the time I had finished my bowl of rice, he still hadn't touched his own.

"Surely that can't be all you're having," he drawled into the lingering silence. "The cooks in the palace work very hard. The food they prepare is among the best." His sigil gleamed as he floated a knife from the ceiling towards us and used its tip to scoop more rice into my bowl. He watched me until I finished it. When I was done, he filled my bowl again.

My stomach stretched with a fullness I was only beginning to get used to. "Have you eaten yet, Your Highness? The food is getting cold."

"I would rather my betrothed get her share first. My mother has taught me how a man ought to take care of a woman."

"I . . . I am satisfied, Your Highness."

"I am disinclined to believe that. After all, this is what you have come for, isn't it? You were starving, and you imagined there to be a bounty of food in the Azalea House, and so you attended my selection. Most of your kind don't make it all the way to the capital. But somehow, like a rat into a kitchen, you've slipped through." He filled my bowl again.

I stared at him, my blood running cold. I was beginning to realize how dangerous he truly was. The last time I had seen him, he had been hideously drunk, to the point that his violence could almost be excused as a wine-induced whim. But now, seeing him with lucid eyes and a cutting smile, it was clear how much intent there was behind his cruelty, how much intelligence.

He was still watching me expectantly. I could not stomach another bite, but I had little choice. I ate the third bowl and shuddered as a wave of sickness swept through me. He gave me a fourth.

"If I have any more," I said in a small voice, "I fear I may be sick. And I do not want to disgrace Your Highness with such unpleasantness."

He waved a hand. "I have seen plenty of body fluids, most of it spilled by me. I am not squeamish."

I felt his eyes burning into me as I ate the fourth bowl, bite by slow bite. It was like swallowing stones. Halfway through, I felt my insides churning. I threw down my chopsticks and rushed to the basin-room, where I sicked everything I had eaten into a bucket. For a moment I just sat there shivering, my gown soaked through with sweat.

Then I took a few deep breaths, wiped my face with a cloth, and returned to the table.

This time, I didn't wait for him to prompt me. I picked up my chopsticks and kept going. There was a fifth bowl, a sixth, and I was sick twice more. By the seventh, there was a change in Terren's demeanor, a darkening, as if the joke had turned sour. There was an eighth and a ninth. I swallowed it all down and sicked it all up. I ate until there was no more rice in the basket, and then I sicked one final time, hunched over the bucket on all fours, heaving and heaving until I expelled only acid and burning air.

I was so weak after that I could barely stand. As I made my way back to him, step by agonizing step, I had to use the walls as support.

While he waited, he had been polishing a sword from off the wall with a different one. When he saw me again, he said the last thing I wanted to hear, the thing I had been dreading all day: "I am tired. Let us abed."

Servants came in to empty out the bucket and clean the basin-room. Then they prepared a hot bath for me infused with ginseng and pomegranate blossoms, both aphrodisiacs the apothecary had shown us. Listlessly, I scrubbed the soft red flowers over my bare shoulders. *Pomegranate will make the night calm and tranquil,* I could hear the apothecary saying. *In the calm, Heaven's magic gathers.*

When I was clean again, I stumbled to Terren's bed, cold and shaking with dread. But he wasn't waiting to take me. He was already turned on his side, fast asleep.

I couldn't believe it.

While washing myself, my mind had run through a hundred ways he could have forced himself on me, each more horrible than the last. Wasn't the whole point of this ill-fated selection for him to plant me? To produce an heir for the nation?

Maybe he'd been telling the truth when he'd said he was tired. Maybe the Ancestors hadn't entirely forgotten me after all, and they were looking out for me still, even now.

I climbed into the bed next to him, quietly so as not to wake him. I could smell the soap left on his sheets, hibiscus and the nauseating sweetness of ripe plums, and it was all I could do not to heave.

I didn't sleep that night. How could I, when I was so sick I could barely move? When there were all those white wisteria knives on the ceiling, all pointing straight down at me? When I could feel his every stirring, every breath beside me? My eyes traced his figure, limned in the net of moonlight pouring in from the lattice window. I wondered if he bled like the rest of us. If underneath those gray robes, inside the cage of his chest, there was a beating heart just like mine.

The One Who Cannot Die, they called him.

It was forever until dawn's light came stuttering in, and another until Terren stirred awake. The first thing he did was float one of his swords down from the ceiling using Dao magic. He looked disappointed that I didn't flinch or protest as he hovered its point towards me.

His seal flashed as he cut a shallow gash under my rib, then tilted the blade so that my blood dripped onto the sheets. "If you tell anyone what happened last night," he said, "I will kill you. If you try to escape the palace or get out of our betrothal, I will kill you." Then he sent me away.

10

CONCUBINES AND EMPRESSES

Concubines Anyë and Ruchen, two beautiful peonies;
They loved each other like a valley its river.
The Dongwu Emperor plucked them, petal by petal,
Till, root by leaf, they wither.
—UNKNOWN LITEROMANCER, ASH DYNASTY, YEAR 12

When I returned to my chambers, I was so weak I couldn't leave my bed. My throat was burning from all the sickness yesterday, my stomach like it had been set afire. The taste of bitter bile in my mouth would not go away no matter how much chrysanthemum tea I drank. When Wren knocked on my door around noon, she took one look at me and said, "Perhaps we should powder your face before the guests arrive, Lady Yin."

"Guests?"

"Last night was for you and the prince, so the Inner Court has left you alone. But now that the selection has been consummated, everyone will be arriving to offer their congratulations. It is palace tradition."

I forced myself out of bed. I sat like a stone as I let Wren powder my face, ink my brows, and stain my lips the color of azaleas. The dress she had me put on was a mix of cypress green and gold, its hem brimming with trumpet flowers no doubt grown by palace literomancers. Since gold was the imperial color, my attendant explained, only emperors and their empresses could wear it in full. But people of high enough status like mine ought to wear it in part, to boast their power.

I did not feel like I had power.

The parlor of the Cypress Pavilion was already set up for guests. Low tables were arranged in a circle, between the hydrangea bushes, their surfaces brimming with hot tea, dried dates, and colorful mung bean cakes. There was an elevated seat at one end, not quite a throne; it was there that Wren directed me.

As each guest arrived, their scribes announced them. *Lady Liru, Third-Rank Concubine. Lady Cinna, Honored Companion. Lady Sun, Noble Consort.*

The higher the rank a concubine had, the more exquisite the embroidery on their phoenix gowns and the thicker their perfume. Flowers of all kinds—trumpet vines, morning glories, bougainvillea—adorned their necks and sleeves. At least one attendant accompanied each of them, more for the higher-ranked guests.

If they were afraid of Terren or of what he'd done to Zhen, their demure smiles didn't let on. Possibly they believed their families and clans would protect them.

"May you live a thousand years," they said, and gave me practiced bows.

Sun Jia didn't bother with formalities. As she entered, in a gown heavy with a thousand stones of jade, she only *hmmphed,* rolled her eyes, and pointedly never looked at me. I vaguely remembered Jia going to the dais sometime after I'd been chosen and receiving, at the empress's suggestion, the remaining position of Noble Consort.

She must have loathed me to her core. As niece to the empress and a member of the great Sun Clan, everyone had expected her to be sitting where I was.

I kept my eyes averted, my lips silent. I was too exhausted from Terren's torment to play her games, and it was taking up all my energy to not be sick.

Empress Sun came in last. When she arrived in a full gown of glimmering gold, the first thing she did was have her six servants bring out an elevated seat like mine. When she sat on it, she rose even higher than me. "I hope you don't mind," she cooed. "I have joint problems, and my knees are not fit for sitting on the ground."

"My only wish is for Your Majesty's comfort," I replied, having learned etiquette during my month in the peony courtyard.

"A pity you would not afford yourself the same comfort." She peered at me sideways. "You do not look well, my dear. Are you ill?"

Some primal instinct made me lie, the way a deer might hide a limp from a fox. "I am only tired. It was difficult to sleep last night, with the excitement of being chosen. And besides, you know how stimulating the childmaking activity can be."

The girls in the room giggled. At once, like a dam breaking, the questions came flooding out. They wanted to know which techniques he liked, the compliments he gave, even what he smelled like. "All the maids were gossiping about the blood on the sheets," Qi Nere said excitedly. "Please, tell us about your night!"

I thanked the Ancestors I had spent so much time memorizing all those techniques, and recited what Lady Chara had taught us. I told them I had begun with Setting Mountain Sun, which had drawn out of him delighted noises, and then I had accelerated the night with Cascading Waterfall, which had made his sigil radiant with pleasure.

I did not tell them how scared I had been, how helpless I had felt. *If you tell anyone what happened last night, I will kill you.*

As the afternoon drew on, there came time for gifts. The concubines brought out earrings of jade, necklaces of clattering pearls, and perfumes that smelled of rose honey and fig. One concubine had brought in fine teas imported from as far as the Eriet Mountains, and another a live peacock in a cage, which I had not the first clue what to do with.

"These are lucky buns—made of sesame and lotus paste," said a short-haired girl called Jiang Rovah. "They are specialties from my home in the Jiangtu District—please, try one."

"Oh, do try some of this plum wine too." The skinny, tan girl called Jin Veris held up a golden jar. "My uncle runs a winery near Xuen, and each jar can sell for a thousand coppers."

It was rude to decline, but I did so anyway. There was not a chance I could stomach anything at the moment. Even the mere thought of eating, even the faintest scent of food, made me want to be sick all over again.

Jia didn't give me anything. The longer the afternoon went on, the more agitated she became. Finally, she stood and pushed her table over. "Are we not going to talk about the fact that this witch"—she jabbed a finger at me—"tricked and ensorcelled her way into the Inner Court? How village *filth* has somehow clawed its way into our ranks?"

When nobody responded, her scowl became terrible. She tried to lift the nearest porcelain vase—which held a mandarin tree—and couldn't. She then went to a smaller vase, lifted that one high above her head, and smashed it onto the ground with a shattering *klink*.

Everyone in the room went silent at once. Even Chua Yan and Liru

Syra, the two concubines who had been whispering by themselves all the way in the corner, had stopped to look at Jia.

"How did you do it?" she demanded. "It was supposed to be me. It was always supposed to be me! If he had not chosen you first, *I* would have been the most powerful woman in the Inner Court!"

My face burned like hot coals, but I kept my eyes on the ground. *If only I knew.*

The empress was watching me closely. As Mother of the House, she should have stepped in to make peace, but she showed no intention of moving.

"Rice farmer," Jia snarled. She must have taken my silence as an invitation to continue. "I know your kind. Dogs bred from the dirt, tracking mud everywhere they run. Hideous, mangy things—even powder and finery can't hide your true nature." Her voice was as sharp-edged as the porcelain pieces scattered at her feet. "Mark my words, village cur: you are going to die. And once you die, I am going to take your place."

It was the fact that she had swept everyone else into those awful words that made me angry enough to speak. That she had insulted all the hardworking people of Lu'an, who were much more deserving than any I had met in the palace.

I lifted my chin, unwisely, and looked her straight in the eye. "No, Jia," I told her. "I am going to live. I am going to become empress."

After everyone was gone, I sent for Wren and Pima. "There was a silver needle yesterday on the ground. Did you happen to find where it was?"

Wren brought it to me at once, so quickly that she must have kept it somewhere close at hand. I went through the gifts by lanternlight, plunging the needle into the honey sweets and the lucky buns, the fig candy and the tea. When I got to the golden wine from Jin Veris, the entire length of it went stain-black.

For a long time I stared at the needle, uncomprehending. When I'd tested the food, I hadn't really expected it to turn black. Some subconscious part of me had done it only to prove Ciyi wrong. To say, *Look, nobody wanted to kill me after all.*

To prove Minma wrong. *Look, the women in the palace are kind.*

"Lady Yin," Wren said, and there was something almost like sympathy in her voice.

They really did want me dead. They really did want to be Terren's wife in my stead, despite knowing what kind of monster he was.

It was so absurd that if I were not so afraid, I might have laughed. Instead, I could only envy the upbringing all those city girls must have had, to believe themselves so invincible.

I looked up and met Pima's eyes. "Please send a message to Ciyi. I would like to see him."

11

THE CURRENCY OF THE PALACE

The eunuch was already smug when he entered my pavilion, but when he saw the black needle, his face lit up with a beaming smile. When I told him that I would accept his offer to be my chief eunuch, his smile turned positively radiant.

"But there are two conditions," I said from my raised seat. I was finally beginning to feel better. At the very least, my head was clearing. Behind us, under the light of a scarce moon, the peacock battered its wings furiously against its cage.

Ciyi's smile was gone. Clearly, he had not expected a simple rice farmer to know to bargain.

And I wouldn't have, had it not been for him and the other women of the court. They had finally taught me that power was the currency of the palace. That, even if it didn't feel like it, I held some of that currency in my hands.

"First, I'd like you to teach me to read."

His expression turned instantly to horror. "But that is treason, Lady Yin! Surely you know what happens to women who are found to be literate!"

I did. Of course I did. I had seen those who tried in Guishan, strung up in the city square with lash marks bloodying their backs, dead or in the process of dying.

But this was not Guishan, this was the Azalea House, and my life was already in danger. From the prince, from the other concubines, from all those who would oppose Terren's claim to the throne.

If I had to be in danger, better it be that of my own making.

"Why?" Ciyi pressed. "You already have a scribe. Why take such an unnecessary risk?"

It was not because of what I told Jia earlier, about wanting to be empress. Those had only been words said in the heat of anger.

When I had summoned Ciyi, having decided that I wanted to learn literomancy, it had only been because it was the last option I saw left to accomplish my real goal: to send Bao to school, and gifts to those who waited for me at home. A goal that was not so easy, as I'd once thought, as simply becoming concubine. The servants' hesitancy, Terren's cruelty, the smashed vase, the blackened needle—I had finally learned that if I wanted to send Blessings to Lu'an, the only way was to write them myself. Even at risk of being strung up.

That was the true reason, but it was not the one I said aloud.

"Because I have always wanted to learn," I told the eunuch, lifting my chin. "Ever since I was little. And now that I am in the palace, now that I am Empress-in-Waiting, now that I have power and influence to trade, I intend to do what I never had the option to before."

I hoped it was a plausible lie. I tried imagining a different version of me, cleverer and more daring, who had as a girl knelt beyond the fence of the school in Guishan and stolen lessons there, just like Har Asori. Maybe she would have dreamed of going to school in the capital herself, instead of merely dreaming it for her brother.

Ciyi's eyes bore into me, as hungry as when he'd entreated me the day of the selection. I could almost see him weighing the possibilities in his head. If he reported my treasonous words, no doubt he would gain a small reward. He could even take his chances with whoever replaced me—Sun Jia, likely—by making a similar offer.

But somebody as powerful as the empress's niece would not be half so easy to manipulate. She would already have knowledge of the court. She'd have her own opinions, allies, and political ties. He would not be able to control her as completely as a helpless village girl, one whose life he believed depended entirely on him.

"We must keep it a secret," Ciyi drawled at last. "If they find out I am teaching you, they will undoubtedly have my head too. Now, what is the second condition?"

I gestured at the cage sitting by the moonlit wall. "I'd like you to help me find somewhere to release that peacock. Somewhere safe and free."

We started early the next day in my bedchamber, the dawn outside cold but gentle. I had told my servants to give us complete privacy, claiming that I needed time to strategize with my eunuch.

"Reading need not be daunting, Lady Yin." Ciyi set down several empty papers and ink jars on the table. "The characters are not random, but pieced together from smaller units of meaning." He was a surprisingly patient teacher. Though the language of our Ancestors had more than twenty thousand characters, each with their own set of strokes, pronunciations, and meanings, he knew how to break them down for me in a way that made sense. "Some characters even look like what they represent. Let us begin with those."

He wrote for me the word 鳥/Niao, like the spring swifts playing outside among the eaves. 山/Shan was like the peaks rising in the distance, and 木/Mu the cypresses swaying in the wind. In Ciyi's lively brushstrokes, I could see his 魚/Yu swimming in one of the palace's many ponds, as slippery and free as the real thing.

When he wrote for me the character 女/Nü, I could see several different women in its gentle figure. I saw, in turn, Ma washing our clothes in the creek; I saw Song Silian, elegant in her lotus gown, as she swept into the Palace of Blades. 女/Nü was Minma with the dangerous dream, and the empress with her sharp vermilion smile.

It was Sun Jia, lips twisted, calling me *village filth*.

It was Jin Veris, blinking innocently as she insisted I try her plum wine.

"What have you done with your poisoner?" Ciyi asked, during one of our dawn lessons.

I looked up from the inked paper spread out all over the floor. "What do you mean?"

My words must have revealed something like cluelessness, because my eunuch gained a sudden scowl. "Lady Yin! How could you let something like that go? You should have punished her! The crueler and more public the better!"

Punish. It had not even occurred to me that I could *punish*.

"You are soon to be empress," Ciyi chastised me, the same way Uncle Rui did his young son Dan, whenever he ran too far into the woods. "You have power. It will do you good to wield it."

"What should I have done?"

"Summon the entire Inner Court. Present the gift and the blackened needle as evidence. The usual punishment for an attempted assassination of a concubine is a painful death. Pick something gruesome and public— like Thousand Cuts or Slow Dismemberment."

I stared at him in utter horror. What he had suggested was so different from what Ma had taught me that for a moment, I had no idea how to respond. Ma had always told me to avoid trouble when I could help it. To keep my head down and smile gently. Ma would have said that as long as I kept quiet about the poisoning, it would not happen again, because when Veris saw I was still alive and her ploy had not worked, she would simply give up.

"Or, at the very least, have her flayed to death in the courtyard and her body left for the sparrows."

"No," I said.

Ciyi's brows knotted in frustration. He stood abruptly and started pacing the study, startling the willow-cat napping on the windowsill. "Don't you know why they dared to poison you so openly and shamelessly? It was precisely because they knew they would succeed. And even in the small chance they didn't, they knew you would not retaliate! They think so little of you because you are an ignorant villager. They do not know that you have *me*." He swiveled sharply to face me, the syrup-sweetness in his voice gone. "It is not too late. Tomorrow you will use your authority to call a meeting. We will do as I say."

"No," I repeated, firmer now. My heart beat faster as I stood to face him. "If I have power as you say, then you cannot make me do anything. Least of all *kill* someone." It took all I had to keep my voice from wavering. A real Empress-in-Waiting would not let her chief eunuch overrule her own desires.

"*Lady Yin*—"

"Veris may have stooped low enough to poison me, but I will not be like her. I will not be like anyone in the Azalea House. I refuse to be made cruel."

I would not be like Empress Sun, who had sabotaged her competition to get to where she was. I would not be like the seal-bearing princes, who had fought their brothers for the Crown ever since they were children. Nothing the House could offer me could ever tempt me to be so heartless.

"You are still thinking like a villager, not an empress," Ciyi snarled. "If you refuse to be cruel, someone will be cruel to you first. If you refuse to make others suffer, then you will be made to suffer first." He was so angry he left before our lesson was finished.

12

NIGHTS

Not long after the first night, Terren summoned me again. Before entering, I paused at the top of the tower to take several deep breaths, willing my pulse to steady and my hands to stop quivering.

There was no food on the table this time, only stacks and stacks of paper. A hundred lanterns sat flickering on the rug around the prince, and the room smelled of burning candles and fresh ink.

He was writing spells. I knew because every time he finished inking a line, the characters glowed, like the Blessings from the firecrackers did on New Year's. They were as beautiful as the Azalea House was terrible. I imagined myself writing one just like it, for Bao and Rui Dan and all the other children.

It was going to be a harvest song, I'd already decided. A harvest song that could be heard all the way in Lu'an, one that would bring gifts to everyone.

Hope stirred through my fear, watching the prince work. Ciyi might have been teaching me how to read, but even he could not teach me *literomancy*. If I wanted to learn how to write my own Blessings, could I learn from a skilled literomancer himself?

Though I wanted nothing more than to squeeze my eyes shut and disappear, I forced myself to speak. "Your Highness." I tried flattery, which had worked on Minma before. "You must be quite skilled, to write Blessings so quickly. I see there are already three completed verses at your side."

His reply was calm, almost reasonable. "As Azalea House sons, one of our primary responsibilities is to contribute spells to the House's stores. Unlike other literomancers, our seals can help us. Poems relating to our own affinities are the fastest and easiest, and it is no feat to compose three of them in a night." He finished another spell and unrolled a fresh scroll before him. "You should know that the more you speak insincerely, the worse I will torture you. I receive enough flattery during the day that I grow impatient with it at night."

His tone was not a threat, but his words were. My breathing became as fast as in my nightmares, and something deep in my stomach started churning.

If this night was anything like the last, or like the selection ceremony, then it was only a matter of time before the prince's calm vanished and those storm clouds of cruelty came. I had to hurry if I wanted to get information out of him. "How do you know when you've come up with a spell?"

"Poetry is truth and emotion. Even a small child can recognize both those things instinctively. If you've ever heard an affecting poem, you would have felt that stirring in your heart. Magic, waiting to free itself." He paused to write a fresh character on his scroll with a water-brush. "But some truths are easier to come by than others. Dao Blessings to me are like second nature. Ever since I was young, my blades have always been whispering to me, telling me what they know, guiding me towards their truths. Wei, would you like to see a spell?"

My heart sped up. Even trapped in a room with a man I was terrified of, what remained of the child inside me still remembered how to yearn for magic. ". . . Yes, Your Highness."

He nodded. His sigil flashed, and the next moment a sword had drifted from the ceiling to hover in front of me.

It was an old sword, darkened with rust. Terren took one of the poems he had written from his stack and retraced it onto his rug—which was embroidered with a dozen fearsome, cloud-dancing dragons—with the tip of a second sword. I could not tell what the characters said, and he did not read them for my benefit.

The Ancestors accepted the words. The entire poem flashed once, then became a flurry of sparks that shot up to embrace the rusted sword. The sparks became white lilies, which folded delicately over its blade, and when they unfurled again the next moment, all the rust had vanished. The sword had become as shiny as if freshly forged, reflecting the hundred lanterns in the room like a mirror.

"Fascinating, isn't it?" His smile had become dark and terrible. "This one can go to Ji Province, perhaps. The ministers there keep pestering me for new weapons." The paper in his hand did not disappear, I noticed, unlike the Blessings we had cast in Lu'an. He let it fall back onto the table.

"How many times can a Blessing be reused?" I hurried to ask, still not knowing when his cruelty would begin. I had previously thought each Blessing could be cast only once. But if the paper had not vanished, perhaps it could be given to the earth once again.

"Mmm. It depends. It could be once or hundreds of times, depending on the quality of the spell, its complexity, its length. But all literomancy has its limits. Each poem can only be used so many times before it loses its magic, before the Ancestors no longer find meaning in it, before its words become wiped from everyone's memory." The hovering blade turned in the air until its hilt was facing me. "This spell has at least five or six casts, but since it is one I just wrote, I do not yet know if it is good. Shall we test it out?"

He kept looking at me, as if he meant me to take the sword.

I reached for it hesitantly. It was lighter than I might have guessed, its grip brazier-hot.

"Make a cut," Terren told me.

I searched the room for something to cut. My gaze swept over the scrolls and lanterns splayed out around the room, the roses seeping out from beneath the moon-brushed windowsill, the young cathaya trees sprouting near the pillars and wall corners. It did not seem prudent to destroy any of the prince's belongings.

In the end, I cut the sash of my own gown. A band of green silk fluttered onto the rug.

Terren's eyes never left me. "Wei," he said, voice suddenly steel, "this is a sword, made for combat. We ought to test it on its intended target, not some arbitrary object."

Intended target. My whole body turned to ice as I realized what he wanted. The storm clouds, the violence, they had come just as I'd predicted.

"Make a cut," he repeated, louder.

Shaking, I pressed the sword's glistening edge to the palm of my spare hand, wincing as it sank into my flesh. A red line welled where steel met skin.

"Not there." He sounded irritated. "On the battlefield, do you suppose fighting men would aim for the hand?"

I tried to hold back a sob but could not, and a tiny sound struggled out of my lips. I had no idea where fighting men aimed on battlefields.

"Don't worry," he said, after I still had not moved. "My magic's affinity is blades, and that also extends to mending wounds made by them. Now, go on."

It was the same almost encouraging tone as he had used on Zhen. *Don't worry. My aim is not very good.* Still shaking violently, I brought the sword tip to the softness of my stomach. Was this what he wanted?

Every part of my mind was screaming *no, no, don't do it,* but I forced all my terror aside, squeezed my eyes shut, and shoved the sword towards me in one decisive motion.

It would not budge.

When I blinked open my eyes, I saw the prince's seal was glowing. He must have used his magic to prevent the sword from moving.

"Not there either. A stomach wound is fatal, Wei. We are only testing my magic, not trying to have you dead. I said I can mend wounds, not work miracles."

My heart pounded so hard I could feel my pulse against the grip. Swallowing, I brought the blade to my leg instead. When I thrust it into my thigh this time, nothing held it back.

The pain seared like hot iron. Something like a sob, or a gasp, found its way out of my throat—then another, then another.

"Deeper," the prince said.

It hurt so terribly that my eyes went blurry with tears, and I was now crying uncontrollably. But still I obeyed. I did everything he asked, just like the first night, because what choice, really, did I have?

He did not plant me that night either.

Before we went to bed, he mended my wound with a spell from his stash, just like he'd promised. Then he lay down and did not speak to me again.

As I sat on the corner of the bed, watching the Aricine Ward swirl languidly around his sleeping figure, I wondered if he was hiding some terrible secret. Maybe he was sick. Maybe someone had put a curse on him, one that made him unable to father a child. Maybe he was really a demon beneath that wicked face, with the legs of a goat and the scaled belly of a snake, and nobody knew because nobody had seen him unclothed.

The skin on my leg was intact, as if nothing had happened, but I was not intact, I was broken and scared. Even with magic, he could not put back all the blood I lost, and my head kept throbbing and throbbing. Why was it not enough, I asked the Ancestors over and over, that I had lost Larkspur and all the others, that I had been born a girl worth nothing? Why must someone also have to hurt me?

Terren called on me often. Not every night, not even every week, but often enough that every day, when the afternoon light waned and the shadows of my windows' lattices grew long on the floor, I would begin to breathe fast. My chest would tighten with the panicked hammering of my heart. I would taste bitter bile in my mouth just anticipating Hesin's knock on my door, which would surely be accompanied by the dreadful words *His Highness calls you to his bedside.*

What the astronomer had told us earlier, about the lunar cycle, was all a lie. The prince did not spread his duty out among his Inner Court, according to the patterns of the moon. He did not even call on his two Noble Consorts. The only one he ever summoned was me. And when he did, it was never to do his duties and plant me, only to torture me cruelly.

One night, he filled a tub full of mudwater and sedges, the kind that grew wild in rice fields. He then forced me to drink as much of it as possible without allowing me to a trip to the basin-room. "I heard that a paddy needs flooding for rice to grow. As you are a paddy creature, born from the mud, I have supposed you must need to be similarly watered."

Another night, he brought in a barrel full of a hundred starving rats. "Since you have traveled so far from your village, I have brought for you a piece of home." With a floating knife he smeared a stew of rancid meat all over me before forcing me into the barrel. He then let the piece of home swarm all over me until I would never again forget their moist bodies, their pittering feet, or that gagging, gutter stench of fur and rot.

Another night, he took me to the Palisade Garden, the biggest garden in the East Palace. "As you are not used to the House's splendor, Wei, I wish to share with you all its beauty." He led me to the pond within the garden, swathed with mist and moonlight. "Please, do admire the carp," he said, as he floated three dozen swords to make a cage around me, force me underwater, and hold me there amidst the fish. When I coughed or struggled, he told me that I was not appreciative enough, and had me admire the carp once again.

At first, I tried to figure him out. If there was a logic to his cruelty, I reasoned, possibly I could learn to avoid it.

But soon it became clear there was none. If I spoke to him, he hurt me. If I refused to speak, he took it as a slight and hurt me. He hated it when I acted terrified, and he hated it when I acted resentful, and he hated it when I tried to pretend I was neither and spoke kindly. My ignorance provoked his knives, as did any hint of cleverness. The days I cried, he hurt me worst of all.

Maybe hurting people was an itch for him. An itch that kept digging and digging until he scratched it. Maybe that was why he'd chosen me as his Empress-in-Waiting, the one person he could summon exclusively without raising eyebrows in court. I had no powerful family backing me, no political ties. He could hurt me and hurt me, and there was not a thing I could do but bear it.

Terren's nights with me infuriated the other concubines. Everywhere I went in the Inner Court, I was met with tense smiles, whispered comments, and probing remarks.

It was not hard to guess why. The prince's choice to summon me exclusively had robbed them all of what they had come here for. During my month in the palace, I had come to learn what favors a concubine could pull in a prince's bedchamber. Ministerial positions given to fathers, money sent home to mothers, a brother promoted or an uncle pardoned. I had even heard the legend of Wang Li, who had snuck into an enemy state during the War of the Seasons, attended *that* state's selection, and become consort to its king. After gaining his favor, she had charmed him into ending the invasion of her homeland.

"The only one he ever calls on is you," Liru Syra reminded me during tea in the mornings. "You must feel very lucky." Her words were kind, but she spoke in the same tone Aunt Lien did, the year Asori got into school and her own son didn't.

Noble Consort Kang, during our afternoon strolls in the Palisade Garden, kept bringing up the fact that I was the only one the prince had chosen for himself. "Everybody else was chosen by the empress, Lady Yin. Surely that means he loves you dearly."

"How did you charm him?" Xu Mie demanded one night. The concubines had gathered together on a candlelit evening to embroider. Mie's fingers moved deftly as she wove an ibis flying over a misty mountain. "You must tell us your secrets."

I kept my eyes on my own embroidery and whispered that I did not know. I was hoping the conversation would end as soon as possible. Every time I paused to think about Prince Terren, or his tower, or the knives on the ceiling, my head would not stop throbbing.

But later that week, when Sun Jia asked me that same question, I looked her hard in the eye. "Perhaps it is because he likes farmers. Perhaps it is because our prince values hard work and strong arms. Perhaps it is because even a future emperor is not above enjoying a bowl of fresh-steamed rice." With Jia, I seemed unable to help myself.

During the days, Hesin held court on the prince's behalf in the Hall of Divine Harmony. All of his concubines were expected to attend. While Hesin discussed with distinguished guests affairs pertaining to the Outer Court, we would stand neatly by the white lily walls like decorative vases. During breaks we sang for them, played our instruments, and danced using fans water-brushed with azaleas.

The other girls did everything they could to humiliate me. Sometimes, when it came my turn to serve tea, they tripped me. Sometimes I would find my fan painted with rats instead of flowers. Sometimes when I picked up my erhu—a pear-shaped instrument that I was only beginning to learn—I would find the bow frayed or a string broken.

"The future of Tensha's imperial family," one of Hesin's guests would exclaim, "in the hands of one who would bring a broken erhu to court!"

"That hideous, clumsy woman," another would cry. "Is she truly our prince's betrothed? How doomed shall we be if she becomes empress!"

They said things they would never dare to someone like Sun Jia or even Jin Veris.

If Hesin noticed I was being targeted, he said nothing in my defense. He only bowed politely to his guests. "This unworthy servant is most sorry for your troubles. I will bring up your concerns to the prince—and see to it that Lady Yin corrects her behavior."

Ciyi told me, during our twilight lessons in my bedchamber, what the concubines were hoping to accomplish. "If the prince's political allies hated you enough, Lady Yin, it would force him to choose a different wife. Even somebody as powerful as our prince is not immune to political pressure."

Political pressure. I had only a vague idea of what it meant, knowing little of the men's side of the court. Even so, the thought of anything pressuring Terren seemed absurd.

I do what I please, he had said to Prince Maro, so matter-of-factly. *I am the rightful heir.*

Still, I was careful. I had not forgotten Terren's threats from the first night. How if I escaped or got out of our betrothal, I would be killed. If the concubines somehow did manage to depose me, I was under little illusion that Terren would show me mercy.

So I did what I could to survive. I bore the humiliation at court as silently as I did Terren's nightly torture. I apologized for spilling tea on the guests and breaking the instruments, for being a source of shame to the Azalea House. On days there was no court, I stayed far from the other concubines. I did not join them when they gossiped under the summer sun or on strolls through the Palisade Garden. When I felt compelled to accept their invitations—to take tea under the magnolia trees, to feed the carp, to work on embroidery—I made sure to stay only where there were guards or eunuchs to keep watch.

Some days, I wondered if I should have punished my poisoner like Ciyi said.

If Terren was a tiger who displayed its fangs bare, if the other concubines were coiled serpents waiting to ambush me, then Empress Sun was a spider, spinning careful webs to trap me.

"She might be our emperor's wife," Ciyi warned me, "but she is also the matriarch of the Sun Clan, the greatest of the Great Clans." He explained to me how Sun men were stationed everywhere in the capital, occupying various positions of power. The most illustrious of them might have been governors and generals, but even the minor clansmen served as managers or capital officials. "As for the Sun Clan women, many have been favored consorts or empresses in eras past. So be wary of the empress. She desperately wants her niece in your position, to carry on her clan's legacy."

The empress, however, was impossible to avoid. As Mother of the Inner Court, she held no shortage of gatherings for all of us. "Being a concubine is meant to be an extravagant affair," she would say grandly. "We ought to all be having the time of our lives!"

As concubines, we were not permitted to leave the palace, so the empress had guests brought to us. She hired hoop-dancers from East Hu, sword swallowers from the coast, and traveling minstrels from Duerlong. She invited renowned poets from the capital, who wept as they recited ballads about lovers losing each other in the darkness. Once, she even brought in two snake handlers from the desert. They placed a knot of mean vipers in a fenced-in arena and had them fight to their deaths before our eyes.

It was an ugly form of entertainment, but everyone laughed anyway, because the empress had laughed first.

During one of the feasts she held—for no other occasion than to celebrate the waxing of the moon—she had me sit immediately beside her.

"I do not like goji berries," she told me.

Her servants had laid out rice cakes, to go with clear wine, and Empress Sun picked at them relentlessly. With sharp nails, she scooped out the orange berries one by one, until they lay in a mushy pile at the base of her plate.

Nobody was paying us any attention. In the background, the concubines were chatting among themselves about two handsome dignitaries at court earlier. One of the older girls, Wu Zhao, was joking with a guard stationed by the door.

I had no idea what to do with the empress's information, so I remained silent. Once again, I had the feeling of being a deer trying to hide a limp.

"Here, try some. See if it isn't better without them."

She handed me one of the rice cakes, pocked where she'd dug out the berries with her nails. I had no choice but to reach for it. When I did, she grabbed my wrist without warning and held it high in the air. My loose sleeve slid to my elbow, and her eyes scoured my skin as if checking for cuts.

There *had* been a cut. Several of them, truthfully, made over the many nights of torment. But there was no trace of them left. Terren had mended them all.

A few weeks later, Empress Sun brought in an opera performer and twelve accompanists, and again had me sit near her. We watched the performance from the shadowed rear of the Hall of Even Temperaments. The opera singer's face was painted paper-white, the lids of her eyes red as cranberries. Her hair was wrapped in a bejeweled headpiece twice the size of her head, which glittered under the spotlight as she danced.

"Pity the fish confined to its pond," she sang.

As the other concubines admired the skit, the empress leaned in close to me. "Did you know that if Terren died, all his concubines would get to go free?"

My heart leapt to my throat. I did know this, of course, but I did not like it coming from the empress's mouth. Her tone was casual, but her gaze was probing.

"It cannot play in the grass," the opera girl sang. *"It will never feel the breeze."*

"Not to mention that the House will give you a sizable bride price," continued Empress Sun. "More than enough to pay whatever you came here for. Food for your village, perhaps? Money to buy shoes without holes?"

I looked around, panicked. Nobody was near enough to hear us over the music. I could run to one of the guards by the door and tell him the empress was speaking of treason—but who would believe my word over the Sun matriarch's?

"Your Majesty," I said hesitantly. "I do not wish my prince to die."

"Truly?"

"I . . . I love him very much."

"Is that so?" Her smile was like a barbed hook.

The accompanying zithers crescendoed, the light dimmed. The concubines gasped with excitement as the singer belted out a poet's question: *"How can we claim to have suffered enough?"*

The empress ignored the performance and peered at me closely, as if I were made of glass and she could see inside me. "Have you heard of the heart-spirit poem, Wei? If you pay a literomancer enough, it is said that they can write even the most powerful of killing spells." She leaned in as her voice dropped to a whisper. "And they can cast it during his coronation, when he has to fight the dragon. He will not be invincible then."

My heart raced. I had no idea what the empress wanted. Was she trying to convince me to assassinate Terren? Was she merely trying to fish treason out of me, to use against him politically?

Either way, I could not take the bait. I put as much despair into my voice as I said, "Your Majesty, I cannot bear imagining the death of my beloved. Have mercy on me, I beg of you, and do not force me to speak of it anymore."

I must have passed her test, because her smile vanished. Lips pressed into a tight line, she turned her attention back to the opera.

"*Pity the fish,*" the singing girl lamented. "*It will never swim among trees.*"

14

WORRYING OVER LIGHTNING

The empress might have spoken of Terren's death only to trap me, but her words lingered long after the opera show, like mosquito bites. I could not stop thinking about them.

That night, I tried to get more information out of Ciyi. I phrased it carefully, pretending like it came from a place of concern. "Is there any way our prince can fall to an assassin?"

The eunuch set down his brush, the lanterns casting his frown in their flames' light. "Women. Always worrying about things they should not. Do you forget he has the Aricine Ward, which makes him unable to die? Did you not witness Zhen's foolishness on Selection Day with your own eyes?"

"That may be so, but he will not be invincible during his coronation."

I had known that even before speaking with the empress. *Taming of the dragon*, went the children's chant, *when empire changes hands*. On Dynasty Day, in Guishan, little boys would run loose in the streets, pretending to be crown princes fighting their dragons. Their friends would light fire-crackers in the background, adding to the drama with smoke and noise, or join in the action as allies armed with swords of mulberry branches and pine.

Even the youngest children knew that princes could not use Blessings when taking the Crown, for the dragons accepted no literomancy in the taming process. Terren would have to rely only on the power of his sigil.

Ciyi gave an exaggerated sigh. "Yes, his ward will be down. But I assure you that he will be *very* well protected, just like all the other princes in eras past. There will be guards. He will have an army with him. Literomancers will put up a magical barrier between the spectators and the arena—one that no dagger or arrow can pass through."

But what about a spell? "The empress said something about a heart-spirit poem," I whispered. "I was really frightened."

The eunuch made an impatient noise, the same one as when I'd refused to flay Jin Veris to death and leave her for the sparrows. "Lady Yin, a heart-spirit poem is *not* something any literomancer can write. It is one of the most complex spells ever discovered. A killing spell, yes, but one that takes the form of a love poem. One so heartfelt it can only be written for someone whom the composer knows deeply. Tell me, do you think anyone can get close enough to our prince to write a *poem of love?* You might as well worry over lightning."

Over the weeks, I tried to probe Ciyi for more information on the heart-spirit poem. Even though I knew it was foolishness. Even though I was not capable of writing one yet, even though I might possibly never be.

It is only out of curiosity, I told myself. *I am not really considering slaying the prince.* My body still ached with the shadows of the pain Terren inflicted on me when I was not even his enemy. I could not begin to imagine what he would do to me if he suspected me of treason.

Ciyi was always begrudging when I asked too many questions, but since he served me, he had to answer me.

"That Blessing was developed in the early Ash Dynasty," he explained, "as a potent derivative of the more commonplace healing spell. It is the only killing poem that can find its way directly to the heart from afar—no physical barrier can stop it. But they are rare. Only a handful of them have been written successfully over the years."

"Because of their complexity?"

"Because they are love poems," Ciyi corrected. "The Ancestors are fair, after all. To be the judge of whether it is necessary for someone to die, one must love them first. But once there is *love,* it becomes very hard to still want them dead, does it not?"

"Is there a specific form the poem must take? Any rules for it to be written?"

The eunuch gave me a strange look. "It is the feelings that matter, and the bareness of the recipient's heart on display. I am no literomancer, but I do know that heart-spirit poems in the past have all taken different forms. The only thing they had in common was being emotionally powerful enough to move the Ancestors." A pause as his look became searching. "Lady Yin, surely you are not fool enough to think of writing one yourself?"

I pretended to be frightened by lowering my eyes. "Of course not. I only wanted to be assured that our prince will be safe."

From the mixture of disdain and twisted satisfaction on Ciyi's face, I knew what he deduced from my words—that I was growing fond of the prince. Falling for him like any unwise concubine might, once she had experienced the pleasures of his bed.

I did not care what Ciyi thought of me.

"Let us continue with our lessons," he said at last, face settling closer to satisfaction. "You are upholding your end of the bargain, so I shall make good on mine."

As much as Ciyi and I argued, our lessons were the one respite I had against the tiger and the serpents, against the spider spinning her web. They were the only times when I did not feel helpless.

With every character I copied, hot summer wind drying the ink, I felt in control. The words on the page were mine. Nobody could take them away. Even if they burned these papers, I could simply write more.

Two months into my studies, Ciyi brought me my first book.

"These are from the palace archives." He dropped a bamboo crate onto the desk, the *thump* of it startling the robins nesting on the windowsill. There were more than twenty scrolls in the crate. "*The Annals of the Four Seasons*: mandatory reading for any schoolboy wishing to become a scholar. It chronicles the period of history from the beginning of the War of the Seasons to the First Emperor's unification of Tensha. If there is any character you do not recognize, ask me."

He put the first volume into my arms. The scroll's lacquered dowel was smooth, the ribbon tying it soft. I marveled at its beauty as I unraveled it.

The hardest part about reading, I was surprised to find, was not the characters themselves. It was the sheer number of new concepts. *Tariff, vanguard, vassal state.* Growing up on the rice terraces of Lu'an, I had no concept of trade or diplomacy, no understanding of bureaucratic systems or titles given to officials. I had not heard of all the historical names and places referenced, ones that the author assumed the reader already knew.

As I went through the volumes, I had to pause many, many times to ask Ciyi questions. *Where is the Caeyang Corridor? How vast is the Inner Sea? Who was the explorer Mei Xian?* Images I had never seen before swam through my mind. Images of wind-flattened steppes, and valleys carved by ancient rivers, and mountains so high their tops were bone-cold with ice. I saw bustling cities, and empty deserts, and vast and violent oceans; I witnessed as three-masted junks braved their hungry waves, shipping salt and jade to faraway nations.

The Annals might not be literomancy, I came to realize, but they were still magic all the same. They allowed for the impossible: to take someone, even a concubine trapped in the palace, to another place, another time. It was a warm and beautiful feeling. Like the world had only been for other people before, but now I was a part of it too. As if this country, this dynasty, they could also belong to people like me.

15

CHESS PIECES

Towards the end of summer, something strange began to happen: I began to understand the men's conversations at court.

"While it is true we must obey the Mandate of Heaven," said a clan leader with a face long like a horse's, "even you must agree that the emperor's change of heir was rather sudden. If His Majesty woke up from his illness, are you so sure that he would not change his mind again? The Gaoping Emperor of the Liang Dynasty changed his successor *three times* while in the grip of death. Those who pledged early were the biggest losers."

"That is not always true," Hesin replied evenly. "Those who supported the First Emperor from the very beginning, for example, were rewarded in multitudes for their loyalty. Those who joined him later saw no such profit. It is an Aolian teaching even the youngest schoolboy has memorized: *an even temperament and a steady heart shall win in the end.*"

The clan leader's face darkened at the subtle chastising, but shortly afterwards, he agreed to continue his allyship with Terren.

After he left, the next guest was sent in.

This time, it was a red-faced soldier, who sighed much more than he spoke. "We *would* aid the East Palace during the coronation," he lamented, "but it is a shame that my army is unworthy. Many of my men are still using old, worn-down swords from our last campaign. Hardly weapons fit for taming a dragon." A sigh. "Your Highness deserves a much better army to support him than mine."

Hesin took the hint. "I will speak with the prince, Captain Zhu, and ask him to outfit four hundred of your men in time for the coronation.

Once we are successful, and he has his magic amplified by the Crown, we can discuss the rest of your army." It was a different tactic entirely than what he had used with the clan leader, and I marveled at how quickly the eunuch was able to adapt.

"What are you staring at?" Sun Jia hissed to me from where we knelt by the wall. "Ogling the captain, are you, village filth? I heard your kind breeds with anything that moves."

I kept my eyes on Captain Zhu. "I thought you said we are dogs that breed with dirt," I whispered back. "The last time I checked, dirt does not move."

After the captain left, a governor from one of the western provinces entered. His brows were thick and perpetually furrowed. "The West Palace, I'm afraid, is offering us a greater boon. The province of Nanbo stretches deep into the Eriet Mountains, where few roads lead. Prince Maro promised he would build us a route straight to the capital."

The old eunuch put on an expression of false sympathy. "Ah, Governor Yuan. I understand the burden of being near the mountains. Few roads for trading men, but plenty of open space for raiders. I have heard that two of your border cities have been pillaged by the Cividí since spring. It is unfortunate that Prince Maro would not arm you with sharp weapons, and instead promises only more dirt and stones."

Governor Yuan turned firecracker-red. After a few more rounds of verbal sparring, he was persuaded to back Terren's Dao seal over Maro's Lu.

Each meeting, I noted the words I didn't know. *Treaty. Expansionism. Global policy.* I memorized the figures they mentioned and the scholars they quoted, so that I could ask Ciyi about them later.

I should not *want* to understand these things, I knew, things which were meant for the minds of men. But poetry was truth and emotion. Terren had confirmed it himself. I suspected that only men got to be literomancers because only they knew the truth. Perhaps if I were to write a Blessing myself, I needed to know the truth too.

"Who are the factions that support each prince?" I asked Ciyi one evening.

We had finished with *The Annals* by then, and even *The Classics of Heaven and the Ancestors*, which was the book he had me read next. Now we were in the middle of *Myths of the West*—a fictional epic about demons and men who fought them riding clouds. The scroll lay open on the table. We had encountered a break in the story, and I had found my mind wandering back to court.

Ciyi frowned at me, the way he always did when I asked questions I was not supposed to be asking. "You keep pushing the boundaries of our agreement."

"I am growing concerned for our prince, that is all. His brothers fighting for the throne might pose a danger to his life. I wish to understand just how strong their bid for the Crown is." *And how much hope I have of one of them deposing Terren.*

I was not sure if Ciyi believed me anymore, when I pretended my questions came from anywhere but my own curiosity. But to his credit, he did not berate me. Instead, he sighed and excused himself. When he returned, it was with a chess set.

"The emperor has produced five seal-bearing sons, each with a different mother."

The eunuch removed five ceramic tiles and, with a brush pen, inked characters on the backs of four of them. Maro's *roads*, Terren's *blades*, Isan's *fruit*, Kiran's *wind*. The fifth tile he left empty, for Ruyi's unknown sigil.

Dit, dit—he set the tiles onto the board one by one. "Do you know what happens to a prince's magic when he becomes emperor?"

I nodded. "The one who holds the Crown will have his magic amplified a thousandfold."

"Right. So as you might imagine, the question of who wins the throne has major implications on the people's future. Will the coming years be ruled by economy and trade routes, as will be the case if Maro inherits"—Ciyi moved the 路/Lu tile to one end of the board—"or by military power, if Terren does?" The 刀/Dao tile went to the other end, on the opposite side of the chessboard's river.

I thought about Isan and his 果/Guo magic, and the peach tree he grew back in Guishan. "Why did the emperor not choose his third son for heir? It seems an obvious choice. His fruit power can help with the famine."

Ciyi shook his head. "It is not so simple, Lady Yin. When it comes to choosing which seal to amplify, the emperor must balance many external forces. Will the Great Clans approve? Will the magic be strong enough to contest foreign powers? Will it grow the nation's legacy, so that the next generation will be more prosperous than the last? And, perhaps most important of all, will it maintain stability *within* the country? The last Ash Dynasty prince did not have strong enough support, and the nation was burned from inside by all the infighting and rebellions."

I remembered the crowd of men on Selection Day, each gathering next to their allied princes. "Prince Maro has a lot of support. He was popular among the merchants."

"Right. There are many who back the first son with their coin and army, in hopes of a more trade-oriented future. The merchants, as you say." Ciyi withdrew a blank tile and slid it towards 路/Lu. "But there are others, as well."

He drew a handful of fresh tiles. "Since we are in a harsh famine, many of the provinces languish. For their governors, new routes means the ability to connect the poorer districts to the wealthier ones, so that aid and prosperity can be spread faster." He slid some of them towards 路/Lu. "But of course, the wealthier provinces—like Chong'an and Sial—don't *want* to share." *Dit, dit*—he slid two new tiles towards 刀/Dao. "Then there are those who want to expand the Salt Road westward, in hopes that more trade with foreign powers will strengthen our nation. Then there are those who wish to fortify our existing borders instead, to ensure that nobody can destroy us while we're weak." Tiles moved to both sides of the river.

Ciyi continued in this way until almost all the blank tiles had been divided. When he was done, there were far more pieces on the *roads* side than the *blades*. A few tiles were nestled next to *fruit* or *wind*, but not enough to make much of a difference. A lone tile, which stood for the Sun Clan, went to Ruyi's piece.

"So now you see," said Ciyi, gesturing at the board. "The third and fourth sons have few allies, so they do not make ideal choices for heir. Neither does little Ruyi, though the Sun Clan would certainly try."

I stared at the board a long time before speaking. "But the first son still has more supporters than the second. Why did the emperor remove him as heir?" It had happened so suddenly, only a few months ago. "Why choose someone so—" I stopped short of saying *detestable*. "Why choose someone less favored?"

Ciyi sighed. "Nobody knows for sure, as His Majesty has long been too ill to speak. But if I were to guess, it is because war is on the horizon once again. The Lian in the north have been a sore spot in Tensha's side for several dynasties, and tensions have risen to a fever pitch. Prince Terren's power amplified can finally conquer our enemies, once and for all."

War. It seemed so obvious in hindsight, but without having spent all this time in court, how could I have guessed? Lu'an had been nowhere close to the border, and everyone there had been far too preoccupied with survival to think of nebulous threats like *war*.

Slowly, everything was fitting together. The books, Ciyi's lessons, the conversations overheard at court. I was beginning to understand the truth.

And the truth was more horrible than I thought. Terren's violence didn't just end at court. It was going to affect the whole nation.

I was about to ask another question when a wail tore into the study, sharp and heartrending.

It had come from the back garden. I ran to the window to find Wren, sobbing as she stumbled into the cypress grove. By the light of the lanterns hanging from the eaves, I could see a figure slumped over her shoulders.

The scribe, I realized with horror. *Tel Pima.* Knife wounds bloomed across his back like poppies.

16

MALICIOUS INTENT

I sent Ciyi to fetch a doctor and rushed out the back door. Wren had laid Pima down beneath the cypresses, between two old roots. His blood pooled dark on the nest of daisies beneath him. "What happened?" I demanded.

It was hard to understand Wren through her sobs, but eventually I pieced it together. Terren had been in a bad mood walking home from the Hall of Scholarly Cultivation. Something about an ally withdrawing support, to favor his brother in the West Palace. When he'd passed by Pima, who was on his way to deliver a message to me, he had taken it out on the scribe.

"Taken it out?" I bellowed. The scribe was almost *dead*.

Wren clutched her friend close to her and sobbed into his gown. I stared at the unconscious eunuch as panic seized my own chest. I didn't know much about medicine, but even I could tell that by the time Ciyi brought back a doctor, Pima would have bled to death. The cuts on his body were deep. One under the other, in tidy rows, making it clear they were no accident. Each bloom of blood bespoke malicious intent, an intent I had experienced firsthand.

"Wait," I whispered, an idea springing to me. "I can help."

Wren stared at me as I found a cypress branch and traced a poem in the grass quick as I could. It was the same poem I had seen Terren draw on his dragon rug, every night he had made me cut myself.

My magic's affinity is blades, and that also extends to mending wounds made by them.

I didn't even have time to doubt myself. The instant the last stroke was finished, the characters erupted into a spray of orange sparks. The sparks swarmed like fireflies onto Pima's wounds, which closed like petals furling.

Wren gasped and shuffled backwards. A damp wind rustled the canopy above.

Only then did I realize what I had just revealed. I had drawn those characters so quickly, so confidently, the way only someone who knew how to read could have done. And the spell I had written was a Dao mending spell, one of the prince's. Only someone who had been tortured by him could have known it.

There was no time to think about that now. "Wren, is there anywhere we can hide Pima while he recovers?"

"The servants' quarters," she replied in a tiny voice. "Nobody goes to the cellars except for me and Duan, and I trust him."

I lifted one of Pima's arms and draped it over my shoulder. "Help me, then. Before Ciyi returns. We'll tell him that Pima died, and . . ." The palace was built into the mountains. Much of it was bordered by a sheer plunge into the valleys below. "And we were afraid of the body, and didn't know what to do, so we threw it off a cliff."

There was no way Ciyi could know about the mending or the torture. A literate woman was a crime, but a woman who cast *spells* was a danger to thousands of years of tradition. There was no telling how Ciyi would react. He might suddenly become afraid of me or decide I was not worth the risk.

And if he caught even the slightest hint that Terren tortured me—if he so much as *suspected* I had a reason to not want to wed the prince—he would betray me in an instant. He was only my ally because he wanted to rise with me as I became empress.

"Do not tell anyone what you learned tonight," I pleaded to Wren.

She took Pima's other arm and we lifted him to his feet. "That you can read? I already knew that."

I was caught by surprise. "You did?"

Her voice became quiet, even bashful. "The scent of ink lingers in your bedchambers, Lady Yin. Even if you leave the windows open, it still stays on the silk. When I wash your bedsheets, I always make sure to wash them three times."

With Pima supported between us, Wren and I slipped into the servants' pavilion through a side door. The cellar was filled with barrels of rice, grains, soybeans, dried fruit, and sweet wine. We laid him on the wooden floor in the far corner, hidden behind a shelf. Wren retrieved a blanket from it to warm him.

I checked the scribe's breathing and thanked the Ancestors it was steady. "Once he recovers, find a way to sneak him out of the palace, into the valley. The capital is nearby. Since Pima will be presumed dead, none of Terren's men will look for him."

At this, Wren laughed—a soft, bitter sound. "He won't look for him regardless. I don't even think the prince knows his name. He had only wanted to hurt someone, anyone, and Pima was unlucky enough to be near. It is not the first time he has done something like this, you know." She wiped at her eyes with a sleeve. "Oh, Lady Yin, he has killed so many of us. I am so afraid of him. We are all so afraid of him."

My own eyes welled with tears. Now I realized with certainty how foolish I had been. The day I moved into the Inner Court, how quickly I had decided all the servants hated me. But it had never been about me at all. They were just as afraid as I was. All those rumors of flayings, of cut-off tongues—hadn't I heard the stories even before arriving in the palace? Hadn't I experienced his torture myself—concluded that he was a monster beyond logic, born to hurt things?

"The heart-spirit poem," I whispered.

A love ballad on its surface, one so heartfelt that it could only be composed for someone whom one knows deeply. But beneath, a spell that killed its subject. One that could find its way straight into a heart, even one guarded by allies and spearmen and literomancers, even one belonging to a man with the powerful magic of blades.

They kept telling me it was not possible for Terren to die. But I had read all of *The Annals*, as a girl and a commoner, and now I had cast a Blessing too. I was beginning to believe in the impossible.

"Lady Yin?" Wren said, a question in her voice.

If he died, there would be no Dao seal amplified.

If he died, the nation would not become ruled by military, by war; the throne would fall to Maro, who could then begin a prosperous economic reign. The House would send my bride price back to Lu'an. My family would be saved.

If he died, there would be no more torture, no more pain, no more people cut apart by knives. The Cypress Pavilion servants would never have to be afraid again.

I would not have to be afraid.

When I spoke again, my voice was so dangerous I hardly recognized it. "Don't worry. I am going to kill him."

17

LOYALTY

How to write a love poem for someone I hated so deeply, with every drop of blood in my veins? How to do it so convincingly that even the Ancestors believed it?

Those were the questions I had to grapple with if I wanted to kill Terren, questions that had no easy answer. But I had to find them, for both my own survival and the nation's, and I had to find them fast.

Emperor Muzha, I knew, lay gravely ill on his bed. As soon as he joined the Ancestors, Terren's coronation would be scheduled. The Taming of the Dragon was the one time his ward would come down, the one time he would be vulnerable. The one chance I had to kill him.

Before the emperor died, I had to finish my spell.

Since Pima was dead to everyone except me and Wren, I had to appoint another scribe to replace him. I went with the obvious choice of Ciyi, which had the added effect of pleasing him so much that he stopped asking about the strange way I'd dealt with the "body."

"A *very* prudent move," the eunuch told me, with no small amount of smugness. "It was about time you and I worked together more closely."

The message Pima had been delivering was an invitation. The empress wanted me to attend the Mid-Autumn Parade, a festival where all the women of the palace would enter the capital and dole out gifts to the common people.

The first task I gave to my new scribe was to deliver my acceptance. I did not *want* to; spending time with the empress was like swallowing poison.

But it would not have been proper for me to not attend, given my position in court. And besides, Mid-Autumn was one of the few opportunities for me to leave the palace. I knew I would regret it if I didn't take the chance.

The second was to send a message to Terren's eunuch.

Ciyi raised a brow. "Yong Hesin?"

"Yes. Him." The old eunuch, as far as I could tell, was the only one Terren trusted. From what I'd heard, he'd served the Azalea House for three generations—first the Yonghuan Emperor, then the Yongkai Emperor, now Terren. I might not know how to write a love poem for the prince, but speaking with his closest advisor—and, as far as I could tell, only—seemed a promising start.

We met on a quiet, fog-heavy dawn in the Palisade Garden. Instead of trees, the garden was filled with thousands of giant swords, half-buried in the grass like gravestones. Everything was entirely still, except for the ghosts. Ghost rhododendrons blooming into the cold, their glows reflecting against the steel; ghost cuckoos fluttering about their hilts, weaving nests of ethereal petals. I had seen ghosts before, back in the rice terraces at night, but never so many as here. Possibly it was another sign of the magic inherent in the Azalea House.

"You wanted to see me?" Hesin said. His voice was old and tired.

I had thought long about what to say. The obvious option was to deceive him like I had everyone else. *It is my duty to learn all I can about my betrothed*, I could have said, *so that I may better love him.*

But Hesin would not have fallen for it. He was a manipulator himself, and clever; I had seen how he had handled the men in court. And besides, if he knew the prince half as well as I'd hoped, he would also know his true nature. He would never believe that Terren and I shared a benevolent relationship.

I said instead, "He tortures me at night."

For a while he did not reply, instead stared at the sword spokes in the fog. Then he sighed. "I know."

The words stung like thrown stones. The night of the selection, he had given me such a knowing look before trapping me with Terren. He had known how I had suffered, all this time, and he had not done a thing.

"I'm sorry," he added, surprising me. The mask of deception he wore at court was gone, replaced by only deep and weary helplessness, and suddenly he looked even older than Grandpa Har. "There is nothing I could have done to help you, and I wish there was. Wei, truly, I am sorry."

Wei, not *Lady Yin*. In Tensha, calling someone by their given name instead of their title was done out of disrespect or familiarity—or sincerity. There was no question which one he meant to convey. Hesin wanted me to know his apology was earnest.

But still, there was something I couldn't understand. "Why are you so loyal to Prince Terren if you know what he is truly like?"

He shook his head. "I am not." He stepped forward and rolled up his sleeve, revealing a single scarred character on his palm. "忠/Zhong—the Ancestors' word for *loyalty*. It is not so common anymore, but when I was a boy, it was tradition for eunuchs to swear to Tensha instead of individual princes or concubines. So, to answer your question, I am loyal only to the nation. It just so happens that Prince Terren is his father's chosen—the one to receive Heaven's Mandate—the rightful heir of Tensha. Even if I despise him as much as anyone, I am oathbound to help him become emperor."

My eyes traced the scar, black like it had been charred by a fire. "Does our prince know this?"

"That I am not loyal to him, or that I despise him?" A quiet, humorless laugh. "Well, it does not matter. The answer is the same: he knows. That is why he trusts me."

I understood at once. Terren *knew* how much everyone loathed him. He would not have believed for an instant if someone claimed to be loyal to him. But someone who followed him only in service of the Crown? That was something even Terren was capable of believing.

It is a lot like how I trust Ciyi, I thought bitterly. I was under no delusion that the eunuch worked for me because he liked me. But he was hungry for power, and ruthless in his ambition, and those things I could trust like the sun rising.

"You did not come here to talk about me," Hesin pointed out.

I shook my head. "I came because I wanted to understand why the prince is the way he is. To hear any stories you have, if you would share them." Poetry was truth and emotion. If I wanted to kill Terren before he became emperor, I had to find both. "My Ba told me once that all children are born kind, it is only later that they learn to be otherwise."

"Kind." Hesin's eyes welled with tears. "Yes, he was, wasn't he? Such a gentle and sensitive child, and extraordinary in his talent for poetry. One who loved his brother dearly. The relationship he and Maro shared was so close, so tender, that even their father could scarce believe it. It is nothing like now, when they hate each other so bitterly."

I recalled suddenly what Minma had told me, on our carriage ride here. *The two have been fighting for the Crown since they were old enough to know what it stood for.* But that was not true after all. Maybe even the city girls didn't know everything.

"Then what happened?"

His smile was sad, wistful. "I shall tell you—if you would bear with my digressions. I will start not with the last prince I served but the first. To understand the whole truth, Lady Yin, we must start from the beginning."

18

SANCTUARY

The decline of the Azalea Dynasty began with our prince's grandfather. The Joy Emperor, they called him. His era name was Yonghuan: *everlasting merriment*.

I knew him as Jinzha.

I met him shortly after I came to the palace, after having been castrated at the age of six. He was a year younger than me, a bright but spoiled child. As a second-rank prince—the son of the emperor's deceased brother—Jinzha had no interest in either his studies or the affairs of the court. Instead, he spent all his days playing with me and the other young eunuchs.

One of his favorite places was a lake hidden halfway up the mountain. Lush and warm, with a huge waterfall plunging into it from one side, it was the perfect place for a prince to visit without being bothered. He called it his Secret Sanctuary. When we became older, it became simply Sanctuary.

"Hesin, come swim with me," he would call to me, from where he treaded water deep in the lake. "It is a most magnificent summer day. Don't tell me you plan to stay on those rocks all afternoon."

If I refused, he would tease me relentlessly.

"Oh, *Hesin*." He would laugh as he splashed cool water on me. "Does your deficiency make you less buoyant? Is that why you are so afraid of the water?"

Jinzha's sigil was Qin. That was immediately obvious if you ever came near the palace during that era, because there was music everywhere.

Zithers constantly chorused from every pavilion and hall. Nobody was there to pluck them; their strings danced on their own. Bamboo flutes hanging from the eaves blew by themselves, playing joyful odes and mournful ballads in turn. Even the magpies in the pines sang like they were larks. The only time the music stopped was when Jinzha slept.

Once we came of age, I began to serve as his advisor. I handled all the court affairs he loathed—similar to what I do for Terren now. I managed all of Jinzha's correspondences; I spoke to his guests; I made secret alliances and promised covert favors on his behalf. Since he was only a second-rank prince at the time, his disinterest in politics did not concern me. There was already another seal-bearing prince, the emperor's heir Han, who was benevolent and could call down lightning.

Then Han and the emperor died, both on the same day.

They were fair deaths, no foul play involved. Deaths on the battlefield. The Shouyuan Emperor had been leading a military campaign for the past decade, and he and his son had conquered most of the Highlands by then. But before they could defeat the last of the Civid kings, an avalanche came crashing down the mountain and wiped out their entire camp.

"I am going to run away," Jinzha told me, the night we received the news.

We were sitting on the rocks at the edge of the Sanctuary, bare feet dipped in the cool, clear water. Jinzha had tucked in his arms a mandolin, as round as the full moon above, and he was plucking at it absently.

"Your Highness," I replied, "you know you cannot. You are the world's last seal-bearer. If you do not take the Crown and rule the nation, who will? If you do not spread your seeds and produce sons, who will keep the magic of our dynasty alive?"

His plucking became more agitated. "Must there be someone commanding the Crown? Must there be more sons with Heaven's magic?"

"Yes," I said, baffled. "That is how our nation works, and has since the time of the First Emperor."

He kicked the water angrily, and the ripples chopped up the moon's reflection. "I do not care. I am going to run away, and I command you to come with me."

"I cannot, Your Highness. If you must leave, then someone has to remain in the palace and clean up the mess you make of our nation."

He was nearly in tears. "You really won't let me go? After all you claim to care about me, you would force me to fight that ugly dragon? To take *concubines?*"

"I am not forcing you to do anything, Your Highness. You are the heir. You can do whatever you please."

He threw his mandolin across the pool. It smashed apart on the rock, wood splintering into sharp pieces. A pair of mandarin ducks, screeching, took off into the sky.

He did not run away.

A few weeks later, we gathered in Heavenly Square to watch the coronation. Ten thousand onlookers crowded all of its three terraces to cheer as Jinzha—and his archers, cavalry, and swordsmen—took down the dragon.

After that, he filled his Inner Court. Beautiful women were carted in from far provinces, which he took two or three at a time. He took them in the courtyard under the shedding magnolia trees, and he took them in the Sanctuary behind the waterfall, and he took them on the sloped rooftops of his moonlit pavilions. Eventually, he would produce seven seal-bearing sons. It would be the most of any Tenshan emperor in history.

Jinzha had followed my advice in the end. He had taken the Crown and spread his seeds.

But that was the last time he listened to me. Shortly after his ascension, he demoted me to a low-ranked palace manager and filled his Outer Court instead with sycophants. "Your beauty is as profound as your music," the men would say in melodic voices, and Jinzha would laugh and laugh.

So it was that the Azalea Dynasty began to wither, like magnolia blossoms past their season. Jinzha's father might have reopened the Caeyang Corridor, and *his* father might have begun the golden age of literomancy, but the young emperor lived up to neither of those legacies. The only thing he lived up to was his own era name. *Yonghuan*. He threw extravagant parties, of music and nonstop feasts; he siphoned money from taxes to shower those who flattered him with lavish gifts. From the northern borders, he pulled young men from defending the wall to have them dance for him instead.

He had changed. He was no longer Jinzha, the generous-hearted and spirited boy I knew, but the Yonghuan Emperor. He was corrupt and insatiable, imperious and proud. He was, above all else, merry.

It should come as no surprise to you then, Lady Yin, that his sons decided he needed to die.

If the dynasty had not been so strong to begin with—the strongest any had been in Tenshan history—then it surely would not have survived the Joy Emperor's reign. But an old and sturdy redwood takes many ax-cleaves to fell, and despite the constant raids in the Caeyang Corridor, despite our weakening border in the north and the invasions on our southern coasts, Tensha remained standing. All this is to say that, when the civil war finally began, there was still some semblance of a nation to fight for.

I had tried to warn him.

I had tried to tell the Yonghuan Emperor that his eldest son was conspiring with his second to overthrow him. That his sixth was courting one of the princesses of South Meir, an enemy nation. I tried to tell him to be especially careful of his fifth son Muzha, whose conniving intelligence frightened even me. "I have never seen some-one so hungry for power, Your Majesty. He is a serpent waiting for a chance to ambush."

He clapped me on the back and laughed uproariously.

"Ah, Hesin. Hesin Hesin Hesin. You've been this way since we were boys—always worrying over every little thing. But why worry when you can be merry?" He turned to one of the women draped over his shoulder. "Bixiu, sweetheart, fetch my mandolin for me, will you?" To the one on his other arm, he said, "Find some strong wine for my anxious friend, Nina-dear. The stronger the better." To the third, with her head in his lap—"Are there any sweet gao from last night's feast left? Please, Aellan, do find us some."

When they were gone, I found myself alone with him for the first time in almost thirty years. "Jinzha." I spoke with all the anger and urgency I could summon. *"Your life is in danger."*

He only leaned back on his throne. That faraway smile never faded. "Let me tell you a secret, old friend. A secret that I have told nobody else."

"Please," I begged him, "listen to me. Your sons—"

"The secret is this: the dynasty will not fall so long as I am emperor. So long as I hold the Crown, nobody will kill me."

"You cannot know that!"

"But I do. I made a deal."

"Jinzha—"

"I spoke to Heaven."

"Please—"

"I borrowed from the future."

"*What?*"

But he never explained, because his concubines had returned. They brought his moon mandolin—a new and bejeweled one, since his old one had broken; wine that smelled as strong as poison; and pastries that looked too colorful to be edible. He asked me if I would stay and hear a new ballad he'd composed, but I was too angry so I turned and left.

That night, the coup happened.

The first son lit the palace on fire, and moments later, the second son betrayed and killed the first amidst the chaos. I fled with Jinzha and his men down the mountain, the hot smoke choking us, all the way to the old capital. We hid there as the Azalea Civil War raged on, as battle after battle erupted between the remaining seal-bearing sons. We waited out the Siege of Long Peace, the Moonlight Maneuver, the Deception at Orchid Gate. We bided our time, disguising ourselves as monks to hide from searching armies, as Guan blood was shed and the heads of fighting men fell like rain.

Muzha, as I'd predicted, came out on top. After he killed all his remaining brothers—with the support of the Sun Clan's massive army—he sent a battalion to the old capital. He checked every man on every street until he found the one with the Qin seal, and then he marched his father—now gaunt and thin after his long exile—back to the palace.

"I will not kill you," he told him, "for patricide is not the Aolian way." He laid before the bound emperor a vial of nightshade, a white cord, and a blade so sharp it gleamed. "So you will do it yourself. Choose."

The Yonghuan Emperor looked from the items to his remaining son to me, who was tied up at his side. "Actually," he said quietly, "I would like to go for a swim."

When I went with Muzha to fish his body out of the water, I found the Sanctuary tranquil and moon-flooded, just like the night we'd received news of the Shouyuan Emperor's death. Mandarin ducks, bobbing in the calm water, made gentle circles around Jinzha's pale corpse.

After we pulled him out, I knelt for a long time by his side. I gripped his cold hand, thinking about how stale and lifeless the palace was without all that music, how strangled it had become under all that heavy silence. A cowardly part of me wanted to go echo-step with him, to follow him into the afterlife, but Muzha would not let me.

"You have sworn an oath, Hesin," he said. "You will live and serve me. Round up all our allies and remaining patriots, and help me tame the Crown."

I did. He did. The dragon was subdued without complications, and Muzha became the Yongkai Emperor. Then the famine began.

19

RUMORS

I asked for more stories, more meetings, after the first. Though I had begun speaking to Hesin from an inkling, the mere beginnings of a plan, I had gained a suspicion that I was on the right track.

As we met each morning in the fog, Hesin told me about his days serving the Yongkai Emperor and, after Terren and Maro were born, their shared boyhood; I listened in solemn silence, knowing it was my duty to capture truth and emotion. If only I captured enough, I could turn his stories into a prince-killing poem, the way a weaver spun silk into yarn.

One evening, after I'd returned to the Cypress Pavilion, Wren surprised me by running to me at the gate. "Lady Yin, Lady Yin!" Her voice was as excited as a young child's. "Tel Pima, my friend, he has awoken!"

Joy and relief blossomed in my heart. "Wren, that is terrific news."

She grinned and took both my hands. "He would want to see you before he leaves the palace. Will you join the servants for lunch? The others don't know about Pima, of course, but I told them you are a friend . . ." She was bouncing up and down, as if nervous to even ask the question, as if I would not be overjoyed to accept. As if it would not be the first meal in the palace I shared with someone who did not point knives at my throat.

"I would love nothing more," I said, and meant it.

It was bright and cloudless in this corner of the palace. The cypresses waved to us with their branches as we passed under their canopy; hidden within their rustling leaves, Hwamei birds sang their bright *ju-wee, ju-wee*. In the far distance, by the lush peaks rising out of the mountainside, I could see the Crown of the Azalea House beginning its midday flight. Its serpentine body unfurled with ancient slowness.

A fond smile appeared on Wren's face. "When I was little, you know, I had a chance to ride it."

My eyes flew wide. "You aren't joking?"

"Of course not. It would be poor form to joke with the lady I serve. I was sold into the Azalea House when I was four and nameless. Long before I worked in the East Palace, I was in the South as an attendant to the emperor's magical menagerie. My first charge was to take care of a little orchid-wren; it was then that I received my name." Her smile widened. "Soon, I moved on to the turtles and the monkeys, the ivy-maned horses and the soaring phoenixes. I did such a good job that I was soon given the privilege of attending the Crown itself. Once a month, I would climb onto its head and clean its horns of dirt and trapped leaves. Oh, what I wouldn't give to be up there once more . . ."

I had to admit I was envious. I imagined how the dragon's red horn must feel under my fingers, rough and hot with magic. "Why did you leave the South Palace?"

"It wasn't by choice. My superior—an irritable maid by the name of Bairon"—a scowl on Wren's face told me what she thought of Bairon— "had wanted to climb the palace ranks for as long as I can remember. As the emperor's illness grew more dire, as his heir came closer to taking his place, Bairon believed that serving the East Palace would be more fruitful than investing in the South. She bribed some people, and we moved here."

How often was it, I wondered then, that the path we took was one forced upon us?

Not long after, we arrived at the servants' pavilion. Lunch was already set up outside, among the azalea bushes. Soups, sweet plum juice, and rice in bamboo steamers crowded the cypresswood tables, and around them sat the pavilion's twenty-three servants. They bowed to me as I neared, and I bowed back, though etiquette did not decree I needed to.

Wren introduced them to me in a playful, conspiratorial voice. "That's Duan, the bookkeeper—he's brilliant with numbers, but will forget his own age. That's Aron, the oldest and most experienced gardener, but he's terrified of cats. If one so much as nears the flower bush he's trimming, he'll yell like a boy until one of us chases it away! And that's Aunt Ping, who cleans the windows. Gentle in the heart, yet foul-mouthed, verbose. All of us younger maids avoid her, because she won't stop telling us not to slouch, or to keep up our nutrition, or to drink hot water three times a day . . ."

It was true. As we ate, in the company of cicadas and sparrows, Aunt Ping had no shortage of words for me. "*Ayah,* Daughter of Huang, you must eat more," she complained, piling more and more pork dumplings into my bowl. "A young girl like yourself must grow plump, like geese, heh? But you are more like the bones of chicken!" She prodded at my elbow with a chopstick.

She reminded me so much of Aunt Raia, from my village, that I could not help a grin. But that only made her frown deepen—and the number of dumplings in my bowl grow larger.

For the past few weeks, eating had been hard for me. After that first night with Terren, I could hardly spend a meal without feeling nauseous— especially when the scent of warm rice was in the air. But somehow, this time, it was easier. This time, when I reached for the rice, I was reminded less of that night with the prince and more of my family's table back in Lu'an.

After lunch, the twelve-year-old maid Teela leapt onto the table, yelled, "I want to show Lady Yin a new song I composed!" and played a tune for us on her bamboo flute. As she did, the elderly eunuch Mo repeated a well-loved story. "Nobody had thought it was possible to shoot down the nine extra suns," he said toothlessly, "but the Archer believed and did it anyway. It was thanks to him that the world was saved from its burning and fiery fate."

It was that afternoon that I noticed the scars. Knife lines everywhere— slashing across brows, splitting lips. Duan was missing a finger; Fern, an ear. Du Hu, the old maid with gray-streaked hair, the one who had been mending the scarf, was missing her tongue.

That was why she hadn't spoken to me the day of my selection, I real-ized with aching guilt. What I had been so arrogant as to have taken for dislike had been simple inability.

She was not sitting at our table, but on a stool at the edge of the clear-ing by herself. "Come join us," I asked of her, but she only kept her head down and her shoulders hunched, and did not look at me even once.

After lunch, Wren and I went to the storerooms. Pima was where we had left him, tucked away behind barrels and shelves, reading a scroll by the light of a paper lantern. I recognized it as a treatise by the Sun Dynasty explorer Mei Xian.

When he noticed me, he prostrated himself at once. "Lady Yin, I cannot thank you enough for saving me. I leave the palace tomorrow."

His words were joyful, but his expression was somber. "Pima," I said, bewildered, "what is the matter?"

His shoulders hunched. "When I go, it will be without my wages, without the honor of a palace position. How will I face my family? I may have escaped with my life, but what will become of my grandfather? Or my sister, who is too sickly to marry? Lady Yin, I do not mean to sound ungrateful, but going home will only be a source of shame."

Wren bit her lip and turned away, as if to acknowledge the ugly truth in his words.

I hardly knew what to say myself. I had fancied myself so noble when I saved his life, forgetting that sometimes living was not enough.

That was why none of the East Palace servants could leave, I realized. They might have been intimately aware of the prince's cruelty, but many of them had others who depended on them. And even if they did not, it was still shameful to leave a prestigious position in the palace, even if the palace did not care if they died.

A knocking upstairs interrupted us.

I left Wren and Pima for the door—only to find Jin Veris, my poisoner, on the other side.

"I was told you would be here," she said, and peered at me. "Why are you in your storerooms like a lowly servant?"

"Why are *you* in my storerooms?" I replied, because I felt like being rude.

"Because, Lady Yin, your life is in danger."

It surprised me so much that for a moment, I forgot to be angry. "Danger? What kind of danger?"

"There are rumors. Rumors of the sort that, if found true, will see you executed." She took me aside, deep into the cypresses and outside the hearing of my servants. "Sun Jia is trying to kill you. I know this because she told me to help her spread them."

My head was spinning. "What are the rumors?"

"That you have not done your duties with the prince. That is, the childmaking act." She produced an edict from her jacket, a short letter stamped with the phoenix seal of the Inner Court, and handed it to me. "I stole this from Lady Sun's pavilion: it is an edict given by the empress. To-morrow, they will send doctors to examine you. And if they find that you have *not* been planted by him, then . . ." She trailed off, intentionally coy.

"Then what?" I demanded.

She exhaled. "If a crown prince is found not dutiful, then he would be removed from his position, and all the concubines he has spent even a single night with would be executed."

I went very still.

"But there is nothing to worry about, is there?" Veris continued, too carefully. "After all, you have told us all about the techniques you have used with our prince. You have spent many fruitful nights with him."

"Yes, indeed." My voice came out strained. "Thank you for letting me know, Lady Jin, but your warning was not needed."

She nodded and turned to leave. On her way out, she paused and said, "Jia told me to put the poison in the wine. I did it, because back then I thought an alliance with her was the most valuable one to make. I no lon-ger think that." She left without waiting for my reply.

As soon as she was gone, I went back to my parlor and summoned Ciyi at once. "Send a message to Prince Terren. I must meet with him tonight."

His mouth fell open. "Lady Yin, it is not proper for a woman to initiate—"

"Did I make a mistake promoting you to scribe?"

To his credit, he arranged his frown back into a smile at once. When he spoke again, his voice was once again sugar-coated. "How should we phrase our request?"

I lifted my chin and hoped he would not see my hands trembling. "Tell him that I miss him. Tell him that I cannot bear to spend another day without him. Tell him that I must see him tonight, or I shall weep so hard I go blind."

20

A TRAVELER'S TALE

Terren was absolutely delighted when I entered. He even looked up from the dead peacock he had been skinning, by the blood light of the sunset, to meet my eyes. "How presumptuous of you, to think that you can see me whenever you please."

No doubt he was so pleased because he saw, from my unusual request, an opening—to newer and even more creative torture methods.

I could not look at that horrible smile without remembering the feel of a knife in my thigh, or the burning in my lungs as I was held underwater, or the bitter taste of bile in my mouth. Or Pima, bleeding to death on that bed of daisies.

That peacock. I wondered if it was the same one I had released, and he had somehow tracked it down.

"You miss me so much that you are trembling," he continued, almost giddy. "With excitement, I presume. This is one form of flattery I can appreciate."

"There are doctors coming tomorrow, Your Highness. They will examine me to see whether we have been dutiful."

His smile vanished at once. His eyes flashed something dark and terrible.

"So that is why I had to see you tonight. For our mutual benefit. Me to keep my head, and you to keep your position as heir." I set the empress's edict on the table.

That was the only thing I had in my favor: for how wicked he was, Terren was no fool. If he did not desire the throne, he would not have been so angry as to punish Pima when one of his allies withdrew their support. If he did not want to be heir, he would have ceded the position to Maro long ago.

His eyes brushed over the letter. Then he set down the peacock and rubbed the black blood off on his gown. In a voice chillingly calm, he said, "Shall we eat first?"

He didn't even hurt me during dinner. Just sat across from me silently as he watched me pick at my bowl of pork-and-cabbage dumplings.

I had little appetite. And for the first time, it was not because of looming torture, but the childmaking activity itself. I might have prepared for it for a whole month, with all those lessons and demonstrations, but now that I was on the precipice of actually doing it, I was terrified.

What if it hurt?

What if it didn't hurt, but Terren found a way to make it hurt anyway?

Terren was not eating either. He went only for his wine. He finished a whole jar, then went for another, and when that was done, he went for the next. Soon, the entire room reeked of fermented rice.

"Your Highness," I ventured to say. "Perhaps you might consider—"

A knife flew by my ear, slamming into the wall behind me. I went ice-still.

He opened another jar of wine.

Perhaps I really was that undesirable, I thought. He could not even be himself when he took me.

At last, as the sun went down to a sliver, he wiped his drool with a sleeve and pushed himself unsteadily to his feet. He summoned a sword from the wall and tried to use it to walk, but it wasn't working. The first step he tried to take, he fell to the ground with a *thump*. I rushed to help him, but a hovering sword point stopped me from touching him.

"Go to my bed," Terren slurred from where he was sprawled on the ground. "I will join you shortly."

There was nothing to do but obey. I went to his bed, peeled apart its gray canopy of curtains, and sank into the cold sheets. Around it, servants had already lit candles scented with cardamom and cacao. *An intoxicating night*, the apothecary's voice droned in my head. *One conducive to slow and sensual love, the kind that ripens magic like a flame-oven ripens a bun.*

I untied the sash of my gown and let it fall loose in a pool around my bare knees. Then I glanced at my hips. For a moment, I worried he would find those jutting bones unattractive and decide not to bed me after all. Then I laughed. I was possibly going to die tomorrow, and I was worrying about whether he would like my hips.

When Terren finally joined me, he was somehow even more drunk than before. He threw himself heavily on the far side of his bed and lay there, not moving.

"My prince," I whispered. "Your robes."

He made a noise that didn't sound like words.

Maybe he was incapable of undressing himself. I crept closer to him on my knees, the bed creaking beneath me. That wine smell made me even sicker than earlier, but I ignored it as I reached for his gown. "Here, let me help." The ward coiling above him glowed white, but did not stop me as my hand went trembling to the top knot. He lay still as a corpse as I undid the first button, then the second, the third. The silk fell loose, exposing a bare chest full of bizarre, three-pronged scars. I could not fathom where they could have come from, unless a bird made of fire had trampled all over him.

But as I fumbled for the fourth and last clasp, his body jerked suddenly, making me flinch. "Don't touch me. *I'll kill you.*"

His eyes had flown open. His ward had lashed around my hands like a chain. I could not move them at all.

Belatedly, I realized there was a blade pressed against my throat.

"My prince—" I began, but cut off when I felt the sting of its edge in my flesh. I did not want to know how close it came to splitting open my life's vein. For a moment, we stared at each other. I didn't dare breathe.

It seemed like forever before he let the blade go.

It left my neck and dropped limply to the bed, flicking dark droplets onto the sheets. At the same time, the ward swirled loose. Abruptly Terren got up, stumbled towards the door, and *left*.

For a while I just sat there, stunned. I wiped at my throat with the back of my hand. It came back glistening wet.

What under Heaven had I done wrong?

If even giving myself to my torturer wasn't enough to save me, what was I supposed to do?

"*What am I supposed to do?*" I screamed. I grabbed the knife from the bed and threw it as hard as I could. It bounced off the wisteria-covered wall and clattered uselessly to the ground.

I grabbed for my gown, threw it on, and went looking for Terren.

I found him deep in the Palisade Garden. He was crouched in the alley between two pavilions, amidst bushes of thistle. His head was buried in his arms.

"Your Highness." It hurt to speak through the wound in my throat, but I forced the words out anyway. "I know you do not wish me to die, or you would have killed me by now. I also know that you wish to keep your position as heir, because if you did not, you would not try so hard to keep up appearances. So please. I don't want to do this either. I am terrified of you, and I am bleeding from your knife, but we don't have any choice. I'm begging you. Just give me one night. *Please.*"

He didn't respond.

He didn't even seem awake.

For a long time, I could only stare at him, uncomprehending. It must be some sick joke from Heaven, that my life should be in the hands of a man too drunk to even look at me. That I should have to beg someone who had *tortured* me to avoid execution.

And the worst part was, when the doctors came tomorrow, it would be only me who died. Terren might lose his throne, but that was all he would lose. I was a girl, and replaceable, and once they found me undutiful, they could simply throw me away and find another. And I hated and hated that they could.

I left him there and ran, a choked sound escaping my throat. Maybe this was what the Ancestors had decided for me. Maybe I had been born only to suffer and then die, and that was why all this was happening to me.

Larkspur had been born to suffer and die. Even Ma, holding her tiny body in her arms, listening to her feeble puffs of breaths, held no hope in her gaunt eyes. Even Ma knew that there was nothing she could do when the Ancestors had already made their decision.

I didn't know how far I ran, under the darkness of night. How many turns I made, how many bridges I crossed, how many beautiful and indifferent pavilions I passed. When I looked up again, I found myself in a bamboo grove at the edge of the palace, towering silver in the moonlight.

I slumped against one of the trees, tired to my bones.

My neck ached terribly.

When I had been young enough to believe I could become anything, I had imagined myself a traveler. One with a rickety wagon and a thin but dependable horse, with no other purpose than to bring sundries and stories from afar. Wherever I stopped, I would pass them around, both the sundries and the stories.

There are monsters in the bamboo forests, I would say to all the village children, as we all gathered around a warm fire. *Fanged demons with a face like an eyeless monkey's and a body like a carp's. I have seen them myself: swimming through the air, tail moving back and forth as they weave through the dark trees.* Maybe some of them would be scared enough that they'd sleep holding their ma's hand. Maybe some of them would take it as a challenge and venture into the forest themselves, that very night, looking for the truth.

A wind shuffled the leaves overhead.

I looked up, at the canopy and the stars beyond, and that was when the idea came to me. A foolish one, but I was desperate enough that I would have done anything.

When Lady Chara had demonstrated all those techniques to us, she had used bamboo.

I didn't know what the doctors would be looking for tomorrow when they examined me. Maybe the childmaking act made a girl magic inside— and they would check to see whether I glowed. Maybe they would stab a silver needle into my belly and see if it sprouted vines and blossomed flowers. Maybe they would press their ear to my chest, listening for the hum of the act between my frantic heartbeats.

Whatever it was, I was not going to get it from Terren.

It did not take long before I found a stick about the size of the one Lady Chara had used. I used a rock to saw it to the right length, then I lay on the cold soil and pushed it beneath my gown.

It wouldn't go in at first. I repositioned the stick and pushed some more. When it still would not budge I pushed even harder, biting my lip against the pain. I had no idea whether I was doing the right thing. They had spent a month teaching us how to please a man, but nobody had ever mentioned how it was supposed to feel for a woman.

Ma had told me that the childmaking activity was only natural. That every girl in Tensha was born knowing how to do it.

Tears leaked from my eyes with every push. She had been lying. I knew that for certain now. If she had been telling the truth, it would not hurt as unbearably as it did.

I was not sure how much would satisfy the doctors—how much of it would make me glow, or make the needle blossom, or make my heart hum—so I kept shoving the bamboo inside me for as long as I could bear it. I did not stop until my insides burned like fire, until my hands were sticky with foul blood.

I couldn't walk afterwards. I couldn't even stand. For a long time I just lay there, curled in the dew as the night passed me by, crying softly enough that nobody could hear me.

21

BEACON IN THE STORM

"What caused the famine, exactly?" I had asked Hesin, during the second of our dawn meetings. As always, cold fog blanketed the Palisade Garden; ghost flowers bloomed soft and pale around us. In the distance, I could hear the cries of cuckoos, though what they grieved for I could not say.

"Nobody knows, other than the fact that it is magic. It cannot be solved by ordinary means." Hesin shook his head, rueful. "But that didn't stop Jinzha's successor from trying anyway."

The Yongkai Emperor looked so much like his father. Rigid cheekbones, clever eyes, long dark hair that fluttered loose past his shoulders. The only thing he did not have was Jinzha's irreverent smile.

Muzha never smiled.

My oath did not require me to love him, and I did not. He had killed his kin to claim the Crown, and had forced me away from the release of echo-step and into his service. But even so, I served him to the best of my ability. He was the only seal-bearer left, just like Jinzha had been, and the future of Tensha was once again balancing on a needle's tip.

For the first few years after the civil war, it was a mad scramble to stabilize the nation. I organized what remained of our allies, promising them double and triple what we had in years past; I did another accounting of our palace's resources, scrounging every leftover Blessing from previous princes I could manage.

"We need more magic," I told Muzha urgently. "Debts from your father's reign are piled high, our armies are weakened from war, and the provinces are divided. You need to make sons."

He only looked at me with hard eyes. "And have them grow up to covet my position? To compete with me for a place in history? To potentially *kill* me? Hesin, I am not a fool."

"If you do not have sons, Your Majesty, what happens to the nation after you die? Who will inherit the Crown?"

"Let it go to someone with merit. Whoever is capable of seizing the throne will be the most qualified person to occupy it. And if he must rule without magic, so be it. Heaven knows that men have been doing so long before the First Emperor."

That is not to say he did not use his own magic while ruling. Muzha would not have killed his brothers without having a plan for the nation's recovery, and his plan involved making generous use of his 鹽/Yan seal.

Salt had been a scarce commodity before his reign. It had been so expensive that Caeyang Corridor merchants used to disguise barrels of it as wine, so as to not be targeted by bandits.

And after? Well, perhaps you have seen the effects of it even in your village, Lady Yin. I heard that, even far from the capital, there was a time when flakes of salt fell from the sky like snow, and white crystals of it bloomed out of the ground like wildflowers.

The first thing Muzha did upon his ascension was pull out all the Yan Blessings he had written in his youth, Blessings he had hidden from the rest of his family, and use them to make salt. When he ran out of them, he began using his seal magic, riding the dragon every day to amplify his power. Soon, ships heavy with barrels started setting sail for Orsagh, Seen, and Moonshadow Bay, to even farther places where snow covered the ground all year long. Caravans went northwest in droves. Traders returned with bars of gold and jade, to be exchanged for the loyalty of mercenaries and stone to build walls.

It worked for a while. It might have worked for even longer had it not been for the famine.

Nobody saw it coming. The rice crops failed first, paddies drying all over the nation's south. Then everything else edible—wheat, millet, pepper, and soy—began dying as well. Tensha, once the greatest nation in this corner of the world, was quickly on its way to becoming the poorest.

The Yongkai Emperor made more salt to compensate, and when everything was sold, he made more still. But it was not enough. Salt prices were decreasing rapidly, because of oversupply, and at the same time, his health was failing. He had drawn so much magic from himself that he'd become frail and sickly. Some days, he could not even rise from bed.

"Why did you do it?" I asked him.

With great effort, Muzha propped himself up on his pillow. I passed him a cup of hot medicine, which the imperial doctors had prescribed, and his fingers shook so hard he could barely hold the porcelain.

"I suppose you mean the manner in which I took the throne," he said.

"Your brothers could have helped you, had you not killed them."

"I had to kill them to ensure the Mandate of Heaven is mine."

"Or you could have forced the eldest to name you heir, killed only him, and spared all the others. You did not have to rule a nation by yourself."

"If that is truly the case, why is there only one emperor, one Crown? Why is there only one—" He dissolved into a fit of coughs. A moment later, he cleared his throat and took a sip of the herbal concoction. "Why is there only one name passed down in history," he finished, weakly.

"Plenty of names are passed down in history, Your Majesty."

"But only a few so often as the First Emperor's. Or the Wenning Emperor. Or my father's father. There is only so much room for names like those." The more agitated he became, the worse his rasp. "What other chance did I have, being born the fifth son? Tell me, Hesin, what could I have done besides what I did?"

"Your Majesty," I said quietly, "you will have no legacy if your dynasty falls. If Tensha ceases to exist, nobody will be left to write your history or sing your name."

He was a wise emperor, all things considered, and did not behead me for speaking difficult truths. But still he did not listen to me. No matter how dire the situation became, he refused to take concubines and try for sons.

Stubborn: it was another way he was like his father.

One day he fell off his dragon.

It was a dark autumn evening, the sky torrenting with rain and the mountaintops flashing with lightning. I had been holding meetings on the emperor's behalf all day, and had not known he was going to ride the Crown. But even from the Hall of Supreme Merit, I could hear the dragon's blood-churning roar when it came, a sound so loud it rumbled the walls. I knew immediately something was wrong.

Outside, a brilliant light went to the sky like a beacon. The Crown was signaling to us.

"Please pardon me," I said to our guests hurriedly, and then I sprinted out the door towards the light, along with just about everyone else in the palace.

I reached him first. Halfway down the mountain, in the thick of the forest, he was lying face-down beside the Crown's claw. His body was half-submerged in the torrent of rainwater rushing downhill.

"Your Majesty!" I raced to his side and turned him over. As soon as I saw the empty barrels next to him, barrels he had intended to fill with salt, I knew exactly what had happened. Despite all the doctors' warnings not to use his seal magic, he had tried to ride the dragon anyway.

I shook him in desperation. "Muzha. *Muzha.*" If he died, there would be no more seal-bearing sons. Nobody to inherit the throne. And I knew enough of history to know that when thrones sat empty, nations crumbled to dust.

Soon others arrived too. Doctors and literomancers in the darkness, casting spell after healing spell to try to save the emperor. For a long time, we didn't know whether we were too late—but at last, Muzha stirred and gave a weak cough. We took him to his bed. He slept for many days, during which more doctors, literomancers, and apothecaries from distant provinces came to heal him.

I never left his side, and neither did the rain, which kept falling out the window in cold bouts.

"Hesin," he whispered.

I stirred awake; I had fallen asleep against the table next to him. The storm winds coming in from outside had blown the lanterns out, and we were completely engulfed in darkness.

"Tell me the truth," he continued. I could not see his face. "If I had died, would I have gone down in history as a fool?"

"Your Majesty," I said, through the lump in my throat.

"The one who killed his father to save his nation, but ended up destroying it. Tell me: is that what they will say about me?" The desperation in his voice was the most emotion I'd ever heard from him.

I was silent. I did not want to tell him what I truly believed, which was that nobody would say anything at all. When the Azalea Dynasty fell, new rulers would write new histories, and the old ones would be forgotten or revised.

"I don't want to die," Muzha said. His voice was small and broken, like a child's. "Not if that is the way I will be remembered."

By a flash of lightning, I found a lantern near us and managed to light it. Warm light spilled into the damp darkness, and by it I could see how gaunt his face was, how old and tired, though he was still young for an emperor.

I said softly, "It is not too late. Cease using your magic immediately. I will keep hiring the best doctors to look after you. I will put out a search for concubines, and they will give you sons."

"I cannot stop using my magic, Hesin. The nation needs it."

"No, we do not." I found his hand and held it, the way I will always regret never having done for his father in life. "We'll cede the southern territories to the Islanders. We'll make treaties with the mountain kings and give back Duilin and Lok-Cividí. We'll turn over the Corridor to the desert states, and we'll set up tribute houses at the northern border to broker peace. And if the provinces in the east keep crying for independence, we'll give that to them too. We will let our enemies walk over us for a while, and we will be weak but still alive, and everything will be all right." I gripped his hand tight and repeated, "Muzha, everything will be all right."

He did not say anything more, and I guessed he had fallen asleep again.

That brush with death was what made him finally listen to me. He did not use his magic anymore after that; instead, we paid what we had to pay and ceded what we had to cede. Soon, his health recovered enough to lie with the concubines I'd brought in, and Heaven was kind and gave him sons. Maro and Terren, two years apart—to Lady Sky and Lady Autumn. Four years after that, Isan, to the empress at the time, Qin Rong. When each of them was brought to his bedside, he held the child once before giving them back to their mothers.

"Take care of it," he said, almost the same words each time. "Make sure it does not gain treasonous thoughts against me when it's older. And make sure it does not die before we get to use its magic." Then he sank back into his pillow, lids closing heavily.

The rain came often, those days. I spent my time by his bedside, feeding him bitter medicine as we watched the sky batter the valley beyond his window. We hoped for the only thing left for us to hope: that those who came after us would fix the mess we had created. We hoped that the next generation would be a little less foolish, a little less wicked, and that it might be enough to save a nation.

22

WET MARKET

My whole body was still aching by the time they marched me to the main hall for my trial. There was already an examination table set up by the dais. Two Azalea guards shoved a cloth in my mouth before pushing me onto the cold wood.

The room was already crowded with spectators, almost as many as there had been on Selection Day. I could read their banners now, peeking out from between the pillars. There was a literomancer named Bi Xuan and a city official from Dusu. There were merchants of the Nian Clan, in glimmering silver, and sailors of the Qi Clan swathed in blue ribbons. The prince's half brothers were all present, scattered throughout the room with their allies. 路/Lu. 果/Guo. 風/Feng.

The emperor was absent. Empress Sun stood on the dais with her son Ruyi in her arms, but the throne of blades and flowers sat empty.

Terren was standing alone by a shadowed wall. His expression was unreadable.

"On behalf of my husband the emperor," declared the empress, "I call upon Imperial Doctor Wu." A man in flowing black robes stepped forward from the crowd. He was not the same doctor who had taught us about pressure points earlier. "He will determine whether Lady Yin—chosen wife of Prince Guan Terren, the Winter Dragon—has committed treason of the highest degree: falsifying the childmaking act."

Hundreds of eyes fell on me then. Some of the men wore malevolent smiles, as if hoping I would be found guilty. Perhaps if I were not so afraid and in pain, I might have realized it was because they wanted Terren deposed, but lying splayed there for everyone to stare at, with my heart pounding in my ears, I could only interpret those smiles as them wishing me dead.

The guards strapped me to the table, and it took all the self-control I had not to thrash and fight back. I squeezed my eyes shut. I tried not to be aware of the rough way they tore off my clothes. Of the feel of their hands on my body, the coldness of their instruments prying me open.

In Guishan I had seen a pig once. A whole pig. It had lain on the table at the wet market, crammed between the sugar cane vendor and stacked cages of live chickens, on display for whoever chanced to pass by. Flies as big as mulberries buzzed in the air, vying for places to land on its pink flesh.

Every so often, a customer would stop at the table and haggle with the butcher behind it. After some arguing back and forth, the butcher would saw off a piece of it, wrap it in brown paper, and exchange it for a bundle of old coins.

"She is bleeding," the doctor said. "There are many recent tears and ruptures, and damage to her internals. When was the last time she visited the prince?"

I was six or seven then, and had never seen an animal so big. I had no idea there could even be so many pieces inside it, twisting and bulging and reeking. I tried to touch the pig—to wake it and ask it what it was doing, sleeping in the market with so many people around—but before I could, the man behind the table yelled at me and slapped my hand away.

"Just last night, Doctor Wu." Hesin's voice, far away. "I was the one who let her in. I swear it by the Ancestors."

"It must have been a rough night," the doctor said matter-of-factly. "And there is a cut on her throat."

Several of the men in the audience snorted. "It makes sense that the prince would enjoy those kinds of games," someone near the front whispered, "given what his magic is."

The empress and the doctor were the only ones who did not laugh. The doctor continued his examination, scraping me in a way that should have hurt even worse than the bamboo stick. I should have felt the pain, except I was pretending I was not in the Azalea House. I was pretending that I was back in Guishan that windy afternoon, by the pig, being yelled at by the butcher. The yelling had gone on for so long that all the customers around us had stopped their business to stare. By the time Ba finally came to fetch me, I was already in tears.

When the butcher saw Ba, he stopped yelling at me and started yelling at him instead. *You should have raised your daughter better. You should have taught her respect. How can you let a girl run wanton like this, without anyone to keep her in line?*

I felt awful for getting Ba in trouble, but he hardly seemed bothered at all. He only put a gentle hand on my shoulder as he led me away. *Don't worry*, he said. *Let's go home.*

Someone far away said, "Lady Yin passes the test. We have determined her to be dutiful."

Later, my scribe barged into my basin-room while I was still washing myself. "I told you," he said venomously. "I *told* you."

I threw my hands over my breasts and sank further into the bathwater. I was too tired and too hurt to argue with him.

"I told you it was a mistake not to punish Jin Veris. Because you did not, the other concubines have grown bold. Because you did not, your enemies have learned they can hurt you without consequence. And now look, they try even baser tactics in an attempt to kill you. You have only yourself to blame. You and nobody else . . ." He went on and on.

If I had punished Jin Veris, I would have never known about the rumors in the first place. But Ciyi could not know that.

I let him yell at me, pretending Ba had one strong hand on my shoulder. *Don't worry. Let's go home.* After Ciyi left, I kept washing myself. I kept scrubbing and scrubbing at any place the doctor touched me, but it wasn't working, I still felt dirty.

23

NOT MAGIC

Terren summoned me that very night.

He was not doing anything when I entered—neither reading letters, nor writing spells, nor skinning peacocks. Instead, he greeted me directly at the door, as if impatient to see me. "Who was it?"

I didn't understand his question at first. "Your Highness?"

He gave me a glass stare, as if he thought I was deliberately playing dumb. "Who did you perform with. To pass the test."

I hesitated. I knew what happened to concubines when they were suspected of bedding a man other than their prince, when their sanctity was found not to have been preserved. But I was not sure how to tell the truth in a way that he would believe me.

"Don't worry," he surprised me by saying. "I am only curious. I will not punish you for it."

Probably he wanted to know so that he could kill the other person, for knowing his secret. "There was nobody, Your Highness. I did it to myself."

Only saying it aloud did the significance of what I'd done hit me.

The childmaking act had been so valuable that they had recruited hundreds of girls from all over the country. So valuable that they'd spent a whole month teaching us how to do it, that they would have a girl executed—and a prince deposed—when it was *not* done. It was an act worth everything to the Azalea House, and I had faked it.

Perhaps it was not magic after all.

Terren considered me for a moment longer, but he must have believed me in the end, because he didn't kill me. For the first night ever, he didn't even hurt me.

He was already up by the time I stirred awake. He sat at his window, the one overlooking the autumn valley, sipping at hot pu'er tea. "Hesin says the rumors were started by that Sun girl," he said, without looking at me. "What was her name again?"

"Sun Jia."

"Yes, her." His smile became twisted. "Now that you are awake, shall we go punish her?"

Punish. The way he said that word chilled me and made me instinctively want to protect her. *Actually,* I imagined myself saying, *I do not know if Hesin is correct. Rumors could have come from anywhere, Your Highness.*

But then I thought of the humiliation I had suffered during court. The smashed porcelain, the awful words, the poison that she had told Veris to slip me.

I thought of the rumors meant to have me executed, which had led to the bamboo forest and the blood on my hands. The rumors that had led to the cold instruments crawling all over my body, a feeling I could not forget no matter how much I tried.

"Yes," I said softly. "Let us punish her."

Everyone was staring at us when we entered.

It wasn't unusual for me to hold a gathering in the Cypress Pavilion, but it *was* unusual for me to be accompanied by Terren. It might have been the first time he'd stepped inside his Inner Court at all.

The concubines stood rigid as we made our way to the dais. "Your Highness," they said in unison, not taking their eyes off the prince. "May you live a thousand years."

There was awe in their voices, mixed with envy, with fear.

I was ashamed at how thrilled I felt. For the first time, instead of cowering from my monster, I was walking at its side. For the first time, when it opened its foul, bloodthirsty jaws, it would not be to bite me but someone else.

Let them be afraid, a wicked part of me thought. *Let them tremble at those raised knives.*

Let them realize that even girls from the cities are not invincible.

We got to my dais. Terren gave a disdainful look at the elevated cushion I'd been sitting on during my meetings. Without a word his sigil flashed, and a bouquet of new swords erupted from the polished wood, hilts tangling with white lilies and flowering ivies, edges interlocking to form two makeshift thrones.

He sank into one of them. I sat on the other, cold and uncomfortable. He said to his concubines, in a slow drawl, "Surely, you have all heard what happened by now."

They shifted uneasily. Liru Syra looked on the verge of tears, and the two oldest girls, twin sisters Nere and Rai, had found each other's hand and gripped it until their knuckles went white.

"Sun Jia." His eyes flicked to the empress's niece, standing by one of the pillars. "I hear you have started this."

Jia actually looked *pleased* that her name was called. She was still wearing that haughty smile of hers as she stepped forward, as if delighted that the prince was finally paying her attention. "Of course it was me," she said. "You see, I was very concerned about Your Highness and the future of our imperial sons. I had my suspicions that *this creature*"—she jabbed a finger at me—"was lying about her duties. So of course I had to discuss it with others and find out if it was true. I did not mean for you to be caught up in the rumors too, Your Highness."

The sad part was, I believed her. Sun Jia had no reason to want Prince Terren deposed. She was still playing the game. She still wanted to become empress.

Terren didn't deign to respond to her. He merely floated one of the blades from my ceiling into my hand. "The punishment for spreading untrue rumors is a tongue cut off. As it is you she has wronged, Wei, you should be the one to do the honors."

Jia paled. "Wait. I didn't mean—you can't be serious—"

I turned the knife over in my hand, and again that shameful thrill shuddered through me.

"Do you know what my last name is?" She was panicking now. "The Sun Clan is the greatest in all of Tensha! We've been allies to the Crown since the days of the Lixi Emperor!" Her terrified eyes darted to the prince. "Have you forgotten how many martial men my father has pledged for your coronation? Aren't you afraid that he'll withdraw support? *How will you fight the dragon without us?*"

An amused smile crossed Terren's face. "Let me tell you a secret, Jia. A secret I trust you will never spill, considering that soon you will have no tongue." He leaned forward on his throne and said, so quietly only Jia and I could hear it, "The coronation. I plan to do it alone."

Jia's lip began to tremble. I could tell the exact moment when she realized that everything she thought protected her—her family name, her clan's political support—did not matter. Not for this prince.

She had been playing the wrong game.

"I do not need allies to tame the dragon," he continued, in a voice like dark syrup, "seeing as only the weak need help. But, as you are aware, I am not weak. I am very powerful." He made a broad gesture encompassing the Cypress Pavilion, and—I guessed—the entire palace beyond. "All this is a charade, Jia. It's theater."

She tried to bolt.

She flung herself towards the exit, but the guards stationed there blocked her path with outstretched swords. She stumbled backwards and fell to her knees before one of the concubines at the back. "Suwen, help me. We are friends, are we not?" She tried to cling to her legs, but Wang Suwen gave her an indifferent kick.

Jia's panicked gaze then went to Jin Veris. Sobbing, she crawled towards her. "Say something, Veris. We were working together to kill that peasant girl, weren't we? We are allies!"

Veris did not even look at her.

"Guards," Terren said. "Bring her to my betrothed."

They did. Two Azalea guards in red pushed her forward with unsheathed swords, like herding a dog, until she was on her hands and knees before me.

"The empress will avenge me!" Jia screeched, only half-coherent. "She is not going to let this go, village cur. She is going to chop you into pieces and bury you in the mud where you belong." But when her threats didn't sway me, she turned to begging. "Please, Lady Yin. I'm sorry. I'm so sorry." Tears dribbled down her cheek. "Please have mercy on me. If a man loses his tongue, at least he can read and write. But a woman without a tongue is no more than an animal!"

Animal. I thought of that pig, splayed out on the table in Guishan, and suddenly had trouble breathing. Sweat loosened my grip around the blade.

Don't do it, I could almost hear Ma saying. *Keep your head down and stay out of trouble.*

Her coarse voice fought with Ciyi's oily one. *If you refuse to be cruel, someone will be cruel to you first.*

"Please, Lady Yin, mercy," Jia sobbed. She knocked her forehead to the wood before my feet over and over.

I remembered how I felt, kneeling on that hill where we buried Larkspur, wishing for a day that all little children could learn to read, even poor ones, even girls.

Your mercy will cost you your life.

I remembered Bao's wide eyes as he clung to me on New Year's. I remembered the Rui sisters, believing in me, giving me the leash to their goat. I remembered Ba's strong hand on my shoulder at the wet market, shielding me from the butcher's yelling, guiding me home.

You are still thinking like a villager, not an empress.

I raised the knife. The guards held her mouth open for me, muffling her screams, and the blood was dark and warm.

24

EVERLASTING SPRING

Like his father and grandfather, Terren was not born wicked. He was born tiny, frail, and not breathing.

The birth had nearly killed both mother and child, but as Lady Autumn lay bleeding out on the bed, the doctors paid no attention to her. Instead, they all crowded around the seal-bearing infant, desperately trying to get him to gasp out his first breath, to save the magic trapped within his fragile body.

After she recovered, Lady Autumn would not look at her son. She left him in the arms of his wet nurse and spent all her time with her friend Sun Ai instead, strolling in her gardens, catching up with all the gossip she had missed.

"Hesin," she asked me once, "why are women always expected to love those who would hurt us? To take care of those who would use us, however they please, without the slightest regard for whether we lived or died?"

He was a strange child, quiet and easily frightened. Even a snap of a twig or the clinking of glass could startle him into tears. When he did speak, it was only a few stunted words at a time. *Hungry. Scared. I'm sorry.*

He had three toys that he took with him everywhere—Tiger, Niu Niu, and Little Sparrow—and if we tried to take any of them from him, he would run to the nearest corner, cover his face with his hands, and hide there until we gave it back.

While everyone adored his older brother Maro, whose personality was bright and fierce, few took a liking to the second prince.

The concubines of Muzha's court mocked him in public. The servants of the House did the same in private. *Heaven's pure magic,* they whispered when they thought nobody could hear, *wasted on a child like that.* I am ashamed to admit that for a long time, I held the same opinion.

The only one who seemed to like him—genuinely like him—was his brother.

"My brother is the cleverest," Maro declared proudly, to anyone who would listen. "He's going to be the best literomancer Tensha has ever seen. Just you wait!"

They did not see each other very often—ever since the days of the Wenning Emperor, princes have always been raised separately—but the whole court did gather during festivals like New Year's or Sweeping of the Dead. On those occasions, Maro and Terren were inseparable. Like a lost duckling, Terren toddled after his big brother all over the halls and gardens.

"I think we should let them play together," I told the emperor, the year Terren turned four. "As often as possible."

It was not a suggestion I made lightly. Throughout Tenshan history, imperial brothers killed each other for the Crown as often as nations waged wars. *You cannot keep two angry bulls in the same pen,* the poet Jiang Le writes. Farther from the capital, they say, *You cannot keep two roosters in the same cage.*

"Hesin, you always try me," Muzha said, amused. "Your ideas grow more and more unusual every year." He sat hunched over his dining table, drinking his bird's nest soup. Every time he spilled a drop, the young maid standing behind him would hurriedly dab it away with a cloth.

"Maro is the only one who I have ever seen make Terren laugh, Your Majesty."

"Does it matter? Laughter does not grow a prince into a ruler. Jinzha laughed more than anyone we knew."

"Your Majesty, if your sons grow up happy, their magic will be stronger as well. Are we not counting on them to help us with their powers? How will we regain all the territory we've lost without them?"

It was that argument that made him relent. With a sigh, he said, "The Palace of Everlasting Spring is empty at the moment. There is a peach garden there where the boys can run around, and several pavilions where your eunuchs and scribes can work. Move your office there. You can help watch after the children while you review my memorials."

I did. The Palace of Everlasting Spring was even more beautiful than I remembered. Thousands of enormous peach trees blossomed in its garden year-round, the air forever sweet with the scent of beginnings.

The boys loved the garden as much as I did. With all the space to run, Maro and Terren played together tirelessly. They flew kites, caught geckos, chased swallows, invented games, and generally found creative ways to get themselves into trouble. My colleagues and I watched them from our pavilion's window while we organized memorials or copied scrolls, smiling whenever their laughter broke up the monotony of our work.

Soon, the peach garden began to fill with visitors.

Drawn by the young princes' energy, the servants, scribes, cooks, gardeners, and doctors all began to gather in the Palace of Everlasting Spring during their breaks. Even the emperor's concubines came by to watch them play.

On bright, sunlit afternoons, Empress Qin would regale an enraptured audience of several concubines about an opera skit she'd seen. Companion Tang would work on her embroidery with Mingyue, Lady Chara, and Lady Sky, as Lady Autumn napped next to Noble Consort Sun plucking absently at her zither. After Isan was born, he was raised in the garden too, accompanied by his wet nurse and tutors.

Those days were some of the most peaceful I can remember. Days when both the Inner Court and the Outer Court did not fight, and the future of the dynasty seemed prosperous.

I miss those days so desperately, Lady Yin.

One morning, Terren let himself into my office. Without a word, he placed a stuffed animal, white fur matted with mud and leaves, on my desk next to the ink and open scrolls. *Tiger.* Then he set down the shell of an enormous, petrified snail. *Niu Niu.* Then a whistle made of cherrywood, carved to resemble a young bird. *Little Sparrow.*

Maro burst through the door behind him. "He wants you to keep his friends safe," he explained. "We're going to play hide-and-seek by the carp pond, and he doesn't want to accidentally drop them."

I watched as they left giddily out the door. It was the first time Terren had ever let go of his toys willingly, and I felt a deep and indelible stirring in my heart.

After that, the little prince asked me to look after his toys more and more often. One day, he didn't even come back for them. Tiger, Niu Niu, and Little Sparrow stayed on my desk, forgotten.

"You can't just stand there," Maro declared with a huff. "You have to fight back!" He picked up the oakwood sword his brother had dropped and pushed it into his arms. "Come on. Again."

Terren had to use both hands to lift the blade. His tiny fingers barely closed around its hilt.

"Ready? I'm going to come at you again. This time, raise your sword. Strike."

I was sitting under a peach tree not far from where they were playing, pretending to read a scroll while watching them with one eye. Maro charged forward again—and this time, he bowled Terren over, sending both of them rolling in the grass.

"No, no, no!" Maro shook his head. "You're playing the game wrong. Haven't your tutors taught you anything? It's easy. Just swing it like this." He leapt to his feet and demonstrated.

Terren propped himself up and rubbed at his temples.

Lady Sky looked up from her embroidery. "Go easy on your brother. He's a lot smaller than you. You could hurt him."

"Don't worry, Mother." Maro grinned, pulled Terren up with both hands, and brushed off the blossoms still sticking to his gown. "Look, he's fine. He's not even crying."

It was true, but the young prince did seem a little tired from Maro running at him all morning. I was relieved when his mother said, "I don't think he knows how to fight yet. Maybe you should play a different game."

Maro pinched his lips into a pout. "Fine. A different game." He swept his gaze across the garden—at the pavilions, the visitors sitting under the gazebos, the pond full of shining carp—and brightened when it fell on the biggest tree in the garden. "Hesin's not looking," he whispered to Terren, presumably believing I was out of hearing range. "That means we can climb the Century Peach."

Terren's eyes widened with excitement, which pleased Maro so much he laughed and grabbed his hand. "Come on!"

He led him all the way to the edge of the garden, by a pagoda with eight golden-roofed layers. Next to it stood the biggest and oldest peach tree in Tensha, huge branches spidering wide and into the sky. Its magic, according to an ancient legend, was what made it spring in the garden year-round.

It was not difficult to climb, and provided easy access to the top roof of the pagoda, with the view of a thousand li. I had made it there myself, with Jinzha and the other palace boys, when I had been young enough to be reckless. I did not forbid them, though I knew that the emperor would have wanted me to.

Instead, I pretended not to notice as Maro hoisted Terren onto his back. With his little brother clinging tightly to him, he climbed onto the lowest branch, then the second, then the third, until they were out of sight, somewhere safe above the canopy of blossoms.

Their close relationship filled me with unspeakable joy. The Yongkai Emperor might have killed his brothers to seize the throne— like so many other princes in eras past—but for the first time, it seemed the cycle would be broken. Perhaps the two Azalea princes, I thought, were the ones Muzha and I had been waiting for. The ones who would clean up the mess we had made of our dynasty.

A little less foolish, a little less wicked.

But I had no idea just how quickly things would fall apart.

It all started the day Terren wrote his first spell, at an age before most boys could even read.

He was—is—brilliant. That is no exaggeration, Lady Yin. All the
Azalea House sons are gifted, necessarily—born to fathers who were
emperors and mothers selected among millions, taught by the nation's best tutors on everything from classics to calligraphy, to state-
craft and music. But even so, even among the shining legacy of the
Guan line, Terren was exceptional.

We did not know it for a long time. *My brother is the cleverest,* Maro
kept telling us, but none of us believed him. How could we, when
the prince spoke little, hid often?

"He-sin." That wet and gray afternoon, Terren had wandered over
to where I was sitting. Maro was ill and convalescing in his mother's
pavilion, and I supposed that was why he had come to me.

I looked up from my scroll. "Your Highness. What is it?"

His eyes glistened with tears. "He-sin." He pointed to the pond.
"Come see."

I trudged after him as he led the way towards the water, mud and
blossoms sticking to the soles of our shoes. He stopped over a bridge.
Under it, a carp floated on its side, a bleeding gash across its golden
scales. An animal must have gotten to it, perhaps a hawk or one of
the palace's many cats.

The young prince crouched down, poking at its feeble body with
a willow branch. He looked at me expectantly.

I understood at once what had upset him. "Ah, Your Highness—
this fish is about to pass on." I saw an opportunity to teach him an
important lesson, one every child must learn. "It is only natural. All
things that live must die."

"No." He buried his head in his knees.

I knelt beside the boy, on the damp wood, and made my voice
gentle. "You need not mourn it, Your Highness. This fish will return
to the Ancestors, where it will join all the ones it has ever loved. And
one day, perhaps in a different place and a different time, it shall
be reborn again. As a peach tree, maybe"—I gestured at the garden
around us—"or a different creature"—I pointed at a family of ducks
parting the blossom-covered water—"or even a little prince." I lifted
Terren's head up gently and gave him an affectionate rub under his
chin.

He stared at me with big black eyes. For a moment, I thought I had been successful in teaching him the lesson. Then he said again, "No." He stood abruptly and began tracing a poem on the bridge with his branch.

I could not believe what I was seeing.

Since it was a literomantic spell, I cannot repeat for you the words he used. But I still remember the sentiment behind it, the empathy, the love—*It is not a curse to be confined to water.*

Although to an onlooker, the poem argues, a fish might seem trapped in its pond—although to you and I, it may seem to know nothing of the world on land—it is not so. A fish can still admire the reflection of spring clouds on the water. It can still taste the blossoms that dapple its surface and imagine itself swimming among the trees. It understands more than we will ever realize.

His words were so beautiful, so vivid, that I could almost hear that injured fish speaking to me from amidst its suffering: *Do not pity me.*

My life might be smaller than yours, but it is full of joy and worth living.

Do not assume that I dream of greatness. Do not assume that I wish to be reborn in a different time or a different place, in a different life. I wish only to admire the blossoms in this one.

Do not pity me—for I am exuberant!

The characters on the wood glowed. Sparks shot up from them and arced into the water, growing lotus flowers wherever they landed. The petals wrapped delicately around the golden carp, and a moment later, the fish righted itself, wiggled its fins, and darted away into deeper waters.

Terren seemed just as shocked as I was, staring wide-eyed at the ripples it left behind. A moment later, everyone else in the garden arrived, drawn by the light and commotion.

"The second prince wrote a spell," I confirmed, and the crowd instantly erupted into excited whispers.

Even the First Emperor had not been so precocious. Even the Prince of Eria, who had moved mountains, could not have written something so complex as a healing spell only by instinct.

The only one displeased was Lady Sky. Her son, who was two

years older and heir, had not yet written his own first spell. It must have been a deep source of shame, for her son to be outshone by his younger brother, even if Prince Maro was still very young himself. She turned and left without a word.

For many months after that, Maro did not come to the peach garden. I heard from my informants that Lady Sky was keeping him locked in his bedchamber to compose his own spell, not to be disturbed except for one meal a day.

With his brother gone, Terren grew subdued. On days he came to the garden, he would sit alone, silent as he watched the swifts play in the branches overhead. Once, he tried to climb the Century Peach—but some time ago, the lowest branch had broken off from a storm, making it difficult for him without his brother's help. Even when I put out a stepping stool for him, he still could not make it very far up.

It took many months for Maro to write his first Blessing. He cast it at the emperor's birthday celebration, in front of many distinguished guests. But despite his success, it was like something in him had broken irreparably.

He never came to the peach garden again.

25

A WICKED THING

Long after his brother stopped showing up, Terren still came by. Every day, I would find him sitting in the same spot, under the shadow of the Palace of Everlasting Spring's arched gate, hugging his knees as he waited for his brother to return. But the longer Maro remained absent, the more agitated Terren seemed to become. As the days passed, he cried even more than usual and spoke even less.

He began hiding from us. When he was not by the gates, I could not guess at where he was. The other scribes and I would search every corner of the peach garden, only to find him crouched deep inside a thornbush or a shadowed alley.

One afternoon, he creaked open my office door and poked his head inside.

"Your Highness?"

He flinched at my voice, as if he thought I was angry at him—but I was not angry, only concerned. "Is there something you need?" I asked.

His gaze drifted to my desk.

"Ah," I said quietly. "Your friends." He was seven now, far too big to be playing with his old toys, but I blew the dust off Tiger, Niu Niu, and Little Sparrow and handed them to him anyway. He took them into his arms without a word and retreated deep into the peach trees.

One of my subordinates, Taifong, looked up from the scroll he was copying and scoffed. "An Azalea prince nearly grown, yet he still acts like a baby. Even young Prince Isan doesn't cry half as much as he does. Lady Autumn should be ashamed, for giving His Majesty such a disgraceful son."

"Taifong," I snapped, not knowing why I was suddenly so angry. "Terren is an imperial prince. The next time you speak ill of him, I will inform the emperor, who will behead you for it."

Not long after that, Terren must have given up waiting for his brother, because eventually, he stopped coming to the garden too. With both the eldest princes having outgrown the palace, the visitors stopped coming and my colleagues moved out.

The years passed. The peach garden stood empty. Its blossoms fell with nobody to admire them.

The only one who came by was Isan. On windy, muted days when I went to feed the carp, I would sometimes catch the third son wandering the garden, alone. Long after his brothers were gone, he would still climb the Century Peach, sit atop the golden pagoda, and watch the world turn from amidst the flurry of an unending spring.

Maro was ten when he came into his power. When his sigil was revealed to be Lu—a much-needed one—the whole palace feasted and celebrated for three days. Then the emperor sent him away to make use of it. For weeks at a time, Maro was off in some remote province or another, building roads. He carved navigable rivers through valleys, canals to connect cities to ports, and winding trails through dense and formerly impassable forests. Trade slowly began to revitalize, the nation reawakening from its long recession.

One day, Muzha told me his most ambitious idea yet.

"My son will re-establish trade with the West," he said. "We will be as wealthy as when we still controlled the Caeyang Corridor." The summer in the valley outside his bedchambers was lush and green, and a fresh wind came in through the lattice windows. "He will carve a tunnel through the Fallen Sun Pass, which we shall call the Salt Road."

I was not sure about the plan. It seemed overly bold; the terrain of the Eriet Mountains was known to be bitterly cold. The campaign would take several months at the very least, the work harrowing and at high altitude, and I worried for Maro's safety.

But the emperor was right that it would breathe new life into our nation. It would give us a new route to the West, one that was not so far north that it could be contested by the desert states and the Lian. A route that would be all our own.

I said carefully, "Prince Terren is almost of age."

The emperor responded to the reminder as I'd hoped. "Ah, yes. We should send my second son as well, in case he comes into his power during the campaign and can help."

That was not the main reason I had suggested Terren go with Maro. I still remembered the laughter and the love they shared in the peach garden, the days when the second prince—and everyone else in the palace, truthfully—seemed at their happiest. I had hoped that by putting the brothers on a campaign together, they would become as close as they had been when they were younger.

But my plan did not work. The second son did gain his own sigil sometime while in the mountains, but it turned out to be Dao. A power that pleased the emperor far more than his brother's Lu, a power far more useful for our weakened empire, surrounded by enemies on all sides.

Perhaps Maro envied his brother. Perhaps Terren, having finally tasted power, had no more use for his brother's companionship. I would never know why, but after the Salt Road campaign, they split apart. Maro returned to the capital to rest, while Terren continued northward to fight a war in Tieza.

They never spoke to each other kindly again.

When Terren came back from Tieza, he was no longer the gentle child he had been, the one who cowered behind loud noises. He was fearless, vicious, uncompromising. There was a new contempt in his eyes, I was horrified to find. He listened to no reason, answered to no one.

He'd begun to hurt things.

It started with birds, which he delighted in shooting out of the sky with his new magic. Then it became ground creatures, squirrels and moonflower-rabbits, their dying squeaks making him cackle with laughter. Then it was people. He found any excuse he could to torture or to behead, punishing servants for the smallest of faults. When he was out on military campaigns, he would win battles for his father— but he won them by decimating armies and raining blades on streets full of civilians.

The summer he turned sixteen—just days before he finished the Aricine Ward and made himself invincible—he poisoned all the carp in the peach garden.

It had been a wet morning, the beeches and willows still trembling under the weight of recent rain. *"Hesin."* Taifong had burst into my office, face red with fury. "The entire palace reeks of fish."

When I arrived at the pond, I saw hundreds of carp bodies floating on the surface, all bent at unnatural angles. To this day I have no idea where he had gotten the poison from, to have killed so many at once.

I was shaking all over. I tried to tell myself they were only fish, even if they were the same ones I'd been feeding all these months. There were many ponds in the House, and it would be no effort to replace the ones in here. But there was no such thing as *only* fish. Terren himself had taught me that.

That little boy on the bridge, the one who had refused to let a carp die—where had he gone? The one who had written his first spell to save a small and exuberant life?

He-sin. Come see. My heart seared with the memory.

Taifong came up beside me. "This is the child you were so intent on defending," he spat. *"Do not speak ill of him,* you once told me. Now you finally see what a monster he truly is."

We had spoken in private, but Terren must have found out about our conversation somehow. The next day, I found Taifong's body in front of my office, cut into twenty pieces and arranged neatly so that they caught the sunlight. A terrible wail escaped my throat. I dropped to my knees, cradled my colleague's severed head, and cried until the sky turned dark.

That night, I pleaded with the emperor to stop this madness.

"Everyone is terrified, Your Majesty." I fought hard to keep my voice from quivering.

Muzha only waved a hand to dismiss me. "Good. We have many enemies. It is about time that the Azalea House is feared again."

"Your Majesty, he *killed*—"

"Some fish, is it? A few servants? A handful of people while fighting a war for me? The First Emperor killed many more in his quest to unite the nation, and we all revere his name."

I was stunned into silence. I had always known how ruthlessly utilitarian Muzha was, but I had never thought him *heartless*.

After I left him, my hands in fists, I went to the West Palace.

"Do something," I begged Maro. "Your brother has killed my colleague of twenty years. Your father might not care, but I know that you are the kind of prince who would protect the innocent."

Maro stood tall and graceful, his white-gold robe pooling in the moonlight pouring in from the window. "He is not my brother any longer. Do not call him that." Gone was the excitable boy he had been in his youth; in his place was a young man who looked every bit the future emperor, as noble as he was judicious.

"Whatever he is or is not, he must be stopped!"

"How? You know what his power is. I cannot win against him in a fight anymore." His voice was calm, but a slight tremble of his lip betrayed his own helplessness. "If there was something I could have done, do you not think I would have done it already?"

I pointed at Taifong's blood, still smeared all over my gown. "So you plan to just stand aside and do nothing? While he keeps on *killing?*"

"Not standing aside. Waiting." Maro turned to face the moonlit lake outside. "Remember: I will be emperor one day. When I gain access to the Crown and the imperial armies, I will be strong enough to make a move against him. I am biding my time until then."

"And you would bet everything on that?" I snapped. "Are you so sure the emperor will keep you as heir?"

His expression turned solemn. "For years, I've done everything he asked of me. I carved all those canals. I diverted the Aricine River. I built the Salt Road. He knows how much I've suffered for the nation."

Maro might have been content to wait, but I could not. The emperor was sick, it was true, but even so, it could take years or decades for him to finally die and pass down the Crown. Who knew how many more loyal servants would be dead by then, at the second prince's blade? How many more cities brutalized?

I went to the last person I could.

Deep within the cascading gardens of the Maple Pavilion, Lady Autumn was sharing tea with Sun Ai and Mingyue. Her cloak fluttered with red leaves as she rose to greet me. "Hesin. I have not seen you in the Inner Court for a long time."

I fell onto my knees, weeping as I told her everything. "You are the last person he still loves." He still invited her on his missions, still visited her in her pavilion. "He listens to you. Help guide him back onto the right path."

Lady Autumn set down her tea and looked at me intently. "I'm curious, Hesin—what do you suppose the right path is?"

The question caught me off guard.

"Never mind," she said, as I was still formulating my answer. "I will speak with him."

She did. He killed her for it. Cut her across the throat and left her to bleed out on the blossoms.

When the Yongkai Emperor heard about what happened, he gave only a grunt of annoyance. "Now that the mother is dead, we need someone I trust to look after the son. Hesin, I appoint you to serve as his guardian and advisor."

"So you see now, Lady Yin, power is such a wicked thing. Razing everything in its path, consuming all, leaving none untouched. Not even the kindest of souls among us are spared, once they have had so much as a taste."

26

A WOMAN WITHOUT A TONGUE

It did not take long for the thrill from punishing Jia to fade away, leaving behind only a cold emptiness.

As I sat in my garden, watching the fireflies dance in the autumn evening, I kept thinking about that tongue. I thought of its wetness in my hands, its slipperiness, the warmth of its blood. I kept hearing Jia's gurgling, "*Urrh, urrh,*" as she was dragged out of the palace, the only sound she would make for the rest of her life.

A woman without a tongue is no more than an animal.

Holding that thought, I stepped onto my tiptoes and carefully unhooked one of the paper lanterns from my roof—the character on its side was 福/Fu, for Blessing—and carried it through the cypresses, towards the servants' quarters.

Many of them were still awake. "Good evening," said Bing Mu as she looked up from washing the dishes with Elia. The bookkeeper Duan was still awake too, and playing a game of Go with Aron. "I can't believe he beat me *again*," he complained to me as I passed. "Losing to someone frightened of cats—can you imagine it?"

I smiled as I greeted them, though really I was here for someone else.

The old maid Hu was outside on her usual stool, mending a scarf that belonged to Wren. She did not look up in my presence, much in the same way she did not look up the first day I saw her or any of the other days. I set down the lantern and knelt across from her, in a position indicating respect for an elder. "Hu, would you like to learn to read? Li Ciyi usually gives me lessons at dawn, in my bedchambers. And evenings, too, when the prince does not summon me. Only Wren knows about these lessons, so it will be safe for you to come." I reached for her arm and held it gently. "Please, Hu. Join me."

She did not answer me, not even when I asked her three times.

But two days later, when the morning was still young and golden-gray, she opened the door to my bedchamber, very carefully, her head hanging and her shoulders hunched.

Ciyi jerked his chin up from the scroll we had been reading. "I didn't know you were serious, Lady Yin." He turned the shade of hawberries. "I thought you'd been joking about bringing a servant."

I laughed. "Don't stand so far away, Hu. Come join us." I used some of the scrolls Ciyi had prepared for me to write for her a few beginner's characters, teaching her the same way my eunuch had taught me. "Reading seems more daunting than it actually is. Even though our Ancestors have given us more than twenty thousand characters, they are not random. Some characters look like their meanings—watch." I wrote for her 鳥/ Niao, then showed her how it could be seen as a spring swift.

Soon Wren began coming to learn too. She had been the one to ask.

"Lady Yin," she had blurted out one morning as she was changing my sheets. "I keep smelling the ink on these, and I was thinking . . . well, Pima used to read to me. But he is in the capital now." She spoke quickly, as if she felt the words too dangerous to be said one at a time. "But I miss those stories and poems, Lady Yin. And . . . and it would be nice to be able to write him letters too, and have him write me back."

Ciyi's eyes widened when he saw Wren enter that night. "That is *not* part of the bargain." His eyes bulged even wider when Wren then brought two of the other maids a few days later, Fern and Eli, the latter holding an oak-furred kitten in her arms. When Teela, the rambunctious flute player, also joined in, he looked as if he was going to positively burst with anger.

"Don't worry," I reassured him, grinning. "I am going to be empress soon. I will do the hard work; all you have to do is provide us with ink and scrolls." He mumbled something under his breath as I produced a fresh paper and began to write for the newcomers.

Soon, enough of my servants knew about this arrangement that we no longer had to hide in my bedchambers. The storyteller Mo began to come, and so did the old gardener Aron; both of them were men, but they'd never had the means to go to school. We turned the Cypress Pavilion's parlor into a study, filled with the sounds of people reading aloud at night. *Niao. Mu. Shan. Yue.* We all knew that if one person told, everyone would be punished equally—even the servants who were not part of the lessons—so we all trusted each other to keep the secret.

As Mid-Autumn approached, moonflower-rabbits started coming out in droves, chirruping quietly as they played among the cypresses. We could see them outside the window, their fur glowing softly in the night.

The court had grown quiet. The concubines stopped trying to humiliate me. There was no more spilled tea, or broken strings on my erhu, or rats painted on fans. Perhaps the others had finally learned that with a prince like Terren, they could no longer play the game they had come to play. Perhaps they had grown afraid of me, just as Ciyi had predicted.

I found I did not mind it.

Terren still hurt me at night. In fact, he hurt me worse than before. But somehow, the pain felt lessened, because now I was not alone and not without power. I knew now that one day there was going to be an end to all this suffering, like the sun erasing the cold of night. All I had to do was finish my poem.

Wren was the only one who knew I was writing it.

"I have three pages completed," I told her one night, after all the other students and Ciyi had left. I lifted one of the floorboards in my parlor and unfurled the scroll I'd hidden there. "Remember Hesin's stories that I relayed to you? I've written my spell based on them. But I'm stuck. I don't know where to go from here."

"Let me see." Wren held up the paper to the moonlight by the window, above one of the mandarin trees. She asked me about a few characters—she still could not read as well as I could—then laughed a little. "This is an angry poem, Lady Yin. When you were recounting Hesin's stories to me, I don't remember there being so much anger."

Poetry was truth and emotion. When I'd written the lines down, I had not thought too much about the words, only followed the stirrings in my heart like Terren described. I'd written about the full moon in the Sanctuary, the smashed mandolin, the mandarin ducks in the water. About the pillar of light in the storm and the Yongkai Emperor's scared voice in the darkness.

The heartbreak, the helplessness, the fear—those had all been in Hesin's stories.

But the anger had been mine.

"When Hesin told me the story about serving the Yonghuan Emperor," I said, "he mentioned something that I have not been able to forget. *I have borrowed from the future.* I don't know what that means exactly, but it felt . . . selfish. Selfish and shortsighted. I can't shake the feeling that Jinzha is responsible for everything." My older brothers dead, Larkspur buried, Bao not able to go to school. "It made me very angry, and I felt the urge to put it into writing."

My eyes moved to the verse below, and I heard the thunder in that unending storm again, felt the cold rain outside the emperor's bedchambers. "And I was angry about what Muzha said as he was dying, too. When his country had been torn apart by famine, when the people were starving outside his walls, he had not thought of helping them. Not once. All he cared about was how to defend his country and maintain his legacy." I exhaled, suddenly doubting myself. "Do you think I should not have poured all that anger in? It is mine, after all—not Terren's."

Wren shook her head fiercely. "No. It is a good thing, I think. Whenever Pima read me poems, he'd tell me a bit about the scholar who wrote them. *Everyone who tells a story leaves a part of themselves inside it,* he'd say. *That is what gives it power. There is the feeling from the story, and the feeling from its teller, both working together.*" She knelt next to me and held my hand. "But that also means, Lady Yin, that sometimes even the teller does not know the truth. They only know what they perceive. Perhaps you have not been able to finish your poem because Hesin does not know everything."

"Doesn't he?" He had served three generations of princes. He knew more about the country than any of us.

"Do you truly believe Hesin's theory? That our prince has been corrupted by power?"

"I don't know. Maybe they all have." The magic of a Heavenly sigil, the gift of whispered truths and easy literomancy, the possibility of the Crown—how could one gain all that and remain the way they were?

"Or maybe," Wren said uncertainly, "there is more to the story. Maybe Hesin's experience with the first prince he served has colored his perception of the last. Maybe there is someone else you must speak with."

Prince Maro.

I knew her meaning at once. In Hesin's accounts, Terren's brother had been the one person who stuck close by his side, the one person who knew him intimately. If there was anyone who could help me complete my poem, it was the first son.

But . . . it was not possible. Maro was of the Outer Court, a place someone like me could never go. He was also Terren's enemy. Even if I did have a means of passing messages to the West Palace, I could not do so without arousing suspicion. How would the House punish me when they found out? How would the empress? How would *Terren?*

When I glanced out the window again, all the rabbits were gone. Whether they were hiding only for the night, or a predator had come, there remained only darkness in the courtyard.

27

GENEROUS GIFTS

By Mid-Autumn, the beginnings of an idea had come to me. It was a risky one, and foolish. If it failed I would likely be executed.

But time was not unlimited. The emperor lay dying on his bed. The Crown was about to pass on to a tyrant, and Terren was still hurting people. The heart-spirit poem was all I had. If I did not take risks for it, how else could I change my circumstances?

The palace's main entrance had five gates, each as tall as three stories, and it was there we waited to begin the festivities. The main entrance, in the middle, was for the emperor only; the two on either side were for princes and distinguished guests. The gate at one far end was for the palace staff and lesser guests, and the gate at the other, the women.

It was at that last gate that the women of the House and our servants clustered, in preparation for the parade in the capital. The air was lively with laughter and excited chatter; even girls from the city must look forward to leaving the palace, after having been confined to it long enough.

"Lady Yin!" Wren announced. "Everything is ready!" She and Fern, Mo, and Duan from the Cypress Pavilion wheeled in a carriage, which was draped with autumn flowers.

Everyone else's carriage was adorned in their own clan's fashion. Silian's was overflowing with Song lotuses; Veris's carriage was curtained by the Jin golden plum. The Qi sisters, Nere and Rai, draped their carriage of nettle and sage with the seaside clan's double fish emblem.

I did not have a clan of my own, so did not carry any emblem. Earlier, Ciyi had suggested that I use the Guan red azalea—*You are betrothed to*

one of their sons, so it is not inappropriate, he'd said—but I had declined. To
do so would have made me one of them.

I was not one of them.

"My distinguished dears," the empress silenced the chatter by announcing, "it is time for one of the palace's oldest traditions: the Mid-Autumn
Parade. While the men fight battles and handle affairs of state, we have our
own duties to perform." She made a grand gesture with her sleeve, encompassing the valley beyond the gate. "My husband, the Yongkai Emperor, has
permitted us to leave the palace. Tonight, let us all enter the capital and give
our gifts to the people of Tensha."

He must have prepared that edict a long time ago. Since as long as I'd
been at the palace, the emperor had been too sick to leave his bed.

The empress gave us the order of our procession. The few who remained from His Majesty's Inner Court—herself, Lady Chara, and Lady
Tang—would make up the front. Silian of the West Palace would be at
the rear, and Terren's twenty-eight remaining concubines would make
up the middle.

"Except for Lady Yin," she said suddenly, sweetly. Her eyes fell on me
for the first time since I'd cut off her niece's tongue. "Since she is Empress-
in-Waiting, I invite her to ride next to me."

Azalea guards led our horses, which had manes of oak branches and tails
of golden larch, down the road to the capital, their hoofbeats muffled by
autumn's shed leaves. I was silent as I rode next to the empress, our servants and carriages trailing us. No doubt she had something she wished
to say, to have wanted me next to her, but I was not about to begin that
conversation.

Xilang, nested on the cloud-laced ridge yawning before us, was the
biggest city in the nation. The August Emperor, who had built the palace,
had founded the city at the same time. For years he had incentivized people to move there with subsidies, governmental positions, and carefully
cultivated myths, in hopes it would grow as populous as the old capital.

It did, quickly. The rivers carried into its walls the magic of the House,
and the lush winds from the nearby peaks brought in fertile rains. Whispers
of opportunity in the new capital spread throughout the nation. Before long,

Xilang blossomed with music and poetry. It grew so much over the centuries that even the mountain could not contain its sprawl. Like rainwater, its sea of gray roofs spilled downwards, towards the valley.

Now, it was home to more than two million people. So many that, as our procession made its way to the heart of the city, imperial guards had to hold back the crowd.

"Over here, Azalea ladies!" a girl laughed from atop her father's shoulders, waving a sprig of crocuses in the air.

"No, no, over here!" a group of boys yelled from the opposite side. They raised their zodiac-shaped lanterns—monkeys, roosters, dragons—to compete for our attention.

Lanterns. There were more here than I could count. They hung colorful and tasseled from roof eaves and bridge railings, from the arms of red maples and elms. The smell of street food mingled with the crowd of thousands, sizzling chive pancakes and spicy lotus root and tripe, and mountain dumplings drenched in Nanbo broth.

I understood now why poets sang about this city. *Xilang, my heart*, wrote Lao Shan; Ciliet called it *the crossroads at the top of the empire*. Tsao of the Liang Dynasty named it with fervent passion *the childhood dream and final resting place of scholars*.

The parade continued. While the ladies of the palace proceeded on our horses, our servants helped distribute our gifts. Plum wine from the Jin Clan, colorful mooncakes from the Qi, fig candies that changed flavor the longer they stayed in our mouths from the Cao. The Jiang were giving out lucky buns, decorated with the faces of zodiac animals; the Sun, prosperity candles. Enchanted by clan literomancers to never burn out, each pair bore an auspicious couplet on their red stems. *Long live the Emperor Yongkai*, one candle said; the other, *May the sweet azalea never die*.

"Do you like them, dear?" the empress said, speaking to me for the first time. We rode close enough that nobody else could hear our conversation. "Perhaps we should save a pair for you, to light up the dreary Cypress Pavilion."

"They are very generous gifts, Your Majesty."

Singing yellow orioles, little echoes of the large one on the Sun emblem, delivered them into eager hands. I wondered if, when the recipients burned those candles, they were meant to remember the red azaleas or those yellow birds.

"Not as generous as yours." She glanced back at my own carriage, where Wren and Duan were handing out heavy burlap bags. "Rice and soybeans, is it? I hear there is even a pinch of dried fruit scattered in there, like pigeon feed."

I had never heard a voice so sweet drip with so much disdain.

They were hardly impressive gifts, I knew, but it was not like I had any choice. I had no clan to endorse me, no family to lend me help, and Prince Terren would have sooner gouged out my eyes than have provided me with anything to give away.

My servants and I had improvised. For the months leading up to the festival, we had all eaten less than our usual share. Whatever we could scrounge from our storerooms, we saved for the parade. Duan, who was in charge of our recordkeeping, had risked himself to inflate some numbers; Wren had used her connections with other attendants—and her old supervisor Bairon—to collect leftovers from their pavilions.

"This humble servant does not deserve such praise," I replied, struggling to keep my voice pleasant.

"I am curious, though." The empress leaned in. "I would have supposed that since the prince loves you so dearly, he might have offered you something pretty. Perhaps even some spells. His skill with literomancy is known throughout the capital, after all. I should think the people would be *heartbroken* when they receive, in place of Blessings, something so disappointing as rice."

Rice. I thought of Ba and the other uncles in Lu'an, stooped under a harsh sun, sweat shiny under their cone hats as they labored over a harvest. My blood was so hot it was hard to think straight. "He did offer, Your Majesty. But I talked him out of it. Since we are in a famine, I had thought the common people would not appreciate Dao magic so much as they would something to eat."

If she sensed my mounting anger, she gave no indication. "How considerate of you, my dear. There is no famine in the capital, being next to the House and all its magic, but I suppose I cannot fault a village mind for not knowing better." Her gaze brushed over my carriage. "It is only a shame that people will not know who to thank for such thoughtfulness. After all, you carry no emblem."

"I am not doing this for thanks, Your Majesty."

"Oh? Then, what for?"

We turned a corner, onto an even larger street. The crowd erupted with bickering laughter as they fought for wines and jostled each other for crates of mooncakes. There were not so many who were reaching for the Cypress Pavilion's rice, but I did spot Wren going to a small boy under a willow tree, dirty and hollow-cheeked. When she placed a sagging bag in his thin arms, he clutched it like it was precious jade.

There is no famine in the capital, the empress had said, but how could that be true? There were people who suffered everywhere. It was only that here, they were easier to look past.

"What for?" she pressed, when I had not replied. "Why fight so desperately to keep your position of empress? Why let yourself be planted night after night, like wet soil, for the small chance at an imperial son?"

I could no longer keep my fury in check. "Perhaps you might know that reason already, Your Majesty," I snapped. "After all, you are empress yourself."

Her smile only sharpened. "You're right," she said, completely calm. "I do know." She nodded behind us, at the second-rank concubine Wang Suwen waving at the crowd. Her servants were handing out chess sets of glazed ivory.

"The Wang Clan—pitiful. A shadow of its glorious Liang Dynasty days, when fifteen of its sons sat the throne, fat and sumptuous. If Suwen became empress, it would restore at least a little of her clan's lost honor. No doubt that is why her father signed her up for the selection."

She gestured towards Veris, whose servants were doling out jars of plum wine. "The Jin are equally sad. They might be wealthy, but wealth is all they have. Though they control many districts outside the heartlands, they have never had much success inside the palace. They are desperate for prestige, like starved wolves. If the Jin girl ever became mother to a seal-bearing son, imagine how much they could raise the price of their wine."

She then pointed a nail at Lady Chara, whose carriage bloomed with azaleas. From it, her servants were doling out jars of salt and spice.

"Chara may not have a clan, but she is a royal of Hai, a kingdom

surrounded by enemies. I hear one of her brothers recently died in a battle. Heartbreaking." She did not sound heartbroken. "If Chara had given
the House a prince with magic, she would have leverage to ask Tensha for
military aid. But she did not, so she cannot."

She turned back to me, her smile like a honed edge. "Now you understand, my dear. Power might be useful to the few of us, but it is only
wasted on the likes of you. It seems you have cut off the tongue of a young
girl—one with her whole life ahead of her—for no reason at all."

But it wasn't for no reason, I thought, panic rising. The empress did
not know that if I ever tried to escape or get out of the betrothal, Terren
would kill me. And I had to punish my enemies to deter them. Ciyi had
told me so.

I had only been trying to survive.

Even as I told myself this, I could not stop myself from hearing Jia's
tongueless burbling, feeling that dark blood again on my hands.

"Or perhaps," the empress continued sweetly, "you did it simply because you wanted to. Because it felt good. How warm was that blood?
How soft was that tongue? You must have liked it very much."

We turned a corner again. The sky had darkened now, the full moon
enormous in the sky. Two men in the crowd were fighting each other over
a porcelain tea set Liru Syra was giving out, pushing aside a girl with the
head of a pig.

Not just her, I realized with horror. Everyone else, too. Pink and
speechless and naked, flies skittering across their pale flesh.

I blinked and they were people again, limned by the moonlight. Stooped
grandmothers, laughing children, husbands with a gentle arm around their
wives.

I was going to be sick.

Empress Sun leaned closer, and her horse brushed right up against
mine. When she spoke, I could feel her warm breath on my neck. "It seems,
dear, that you are harder to kill than I thought. But I have no doubt that
you will end up dead, one way or another. Girls like you, they never survive
long in the palace."

28

A THOUSAND LOTUSES

The parade ended when the gifts were gone. The concubines spent the rest of the evening wandering the markets by the slow river, laughing as they ate street food or admired the moon overhead. It was round, yellow, and so bright I could not see any stars.

"Lady Yin, you do not look so well." Wren arrived with a plate of mooncakes. She offered one to me, but I did not take it.

"It was her." I stared at the maple leaves drifting on the water. "The empress. She was the one who told Sun Jia to spread the rumors." *It seems, dear, that you are harder to kill than I thought.* "It makes sense. Jia never wanted to hurt Terren. She wanted only to have me dead so she could become empress in my place. But Sun Ai? She has motive enough to also want to ruin the prince."

Wren seated herself on the boardwalk beside me. Bulbul birds, white-crested, played above us from atop garlands of colorful lanterns. "Perhaps she is eyeing the throne for her own son. With the second son deposed, there would be one fewer prince between Ruyi and the Crown."

"Perhaps. Perhaps it was also to avenge her friend, Lady Autumn." It was only a guess, but in Hesin's story, they had been close. Strolling in the gardens, sharing tea in the Maple Pavilion, sitting together in the peach garden on sunny days. "Perhaps after all these years, she has still not forgiven him for killing her."

There could have been other reasons, too. Maybe she wanted to weaken the Guan Clan so that the Sun might sit the throne once again. Maybe she was working to remove Terren for the same simple reason I was—because he was wicked, violent, and unfit to rule.

It could have been anything, but the fact remained the same: she had no qualms about killing me for it then, and she had even more reason to want me dead now. I knew she would not kill me outright—not while retaliation from Terren was a possibility. But still, I could not shake the memory of my neck's skin tingling, when she had whispered to me her threats.

"Did you get to see him tonight?" I asked Wren, to take my mind off the empress.

She brightened, nodded eagerly. "Pima was with his grandfather and sister, right where we'd agreed to meet. I gave his family two bags of rice."

"Is he well?"

"I think so." Then she hesitated. "Well, I should not hide anything from you, Lady Yin. To tell you the truth, he is not very happy. His neighbors find him so shameful they will not let their sons near him."

I felt a heaviness settle in my chest. "Oh."

"His neighbors say that a man ought to provide for his family—never mind that Pima is only half of one. They say it would have been more honorable to die in the palace, and let his family collect grave-money for his service, than to have run like a coward."

I didn't know what to say. It was hurting my heart, to think of Pima as half of anything.

Wren didn't seem to have much to add either, because she ate the rest of her mooncake in silence. Around us, everyone else continued to celebrate. Fern and Mo were sharing a lively conversation with the guards, and Veris, Suwen, and a few other concubines were enjoying a street performer's melancholic song.

It was later that I saw an opportunity to speak to Silian. She had been admiring the wares at the riverside market with her own servants and Lady Tang—brushing her fingers over textiles, agate hairpins, and palm-sized bronze mirrors—but was now breaking off from the group alone.

I went after her. She walked upstream, towards an emptier part of the city. It was darker here, the street lanterns sparser. The only light came from the moon, which spilled onto the ground so brightly that I mistook it at first for frost.

Silian knelt by the river. From her sleeve, she produced a lotus flower about the size of her hand and set it gently onto the water.

"Lady Song," I said.

She did not look up. "The Mid-Autumn Festival is a day for remembering home, Lady Yin. The ancient poets say that when we look at the same moon as the ones we love, our hearts are connected through Heaven. No matter how far away we are."

There was surprisingly little hatred in her voice, which was soft like silk. Just as Terren had stolen Maro's position of heir, I had taken Silian's position as future empress. I was shocked she did not push me into the river.

"Lu'an is not far from here, is it?" she continued. "Though I suppose when one cannot leave the palace, everything seems much farther."

The drifting flowers broke up the moon's reflection. In the ripples, I thought I could see my family, huddled around a sparse dinner table, Bao laughing as he clutched a prune in his hand. I missed them all fiercely.

I will see you soon, I thought. *At the end of all this.* When I had first begun learning to read, it had been to write a Blessing to send home. Now it was to kill someone who needed killing. But either way, the result was the same. The bride price I would receive would pay for Bao's schooling, and I would marry a city boy. Nobody in Lu'an would be hungry again.

"Where do you come from?" I asked Silian, searching for an opening.

Her smile was polite but distant. "Yoor, in the Northeast."

"That is a two-month journey from here, maybe three." I knew a river from the capital led to it; I wondered if it was this one. "You must miss it a lot."

"The palace is decadent enough to distract me."

A light pulled my attention back to the water. Her raft was magic. I did not know until I saw a new lotus flower curling into life, glowing even brighter than the moon's reflection. White sparks arced outward from the petals, to land in the surrounding waters, and from each of them sprouted new rafts and new flowers.

I sucked in a breath of awe. "Did Prince Maro write it?" There were other literomancers in the House, to make practical things, but this spell did not seem practical.

Her eyes shone—the first genuine emotion she'd shown all night. "Every year, for this very festival. It is the one thing I've ever asked of him. Every year, he asks me why I wish for them. Every year, I tell him it's because they are lovely."

They were. For a while, I sat next to her by the quiet river, watching the flowers multiply and multiply. A thousand shining lotuses, twice that if you counted their reflections, journeying somewhere far from the capital. Then I said, "How do you suppose I knew how far Yoor is?"

An arch of a brow told me she had wondered it herself. "Perhaps you heard it from a eunuch."

"And if I have seen it on a map? If I have read about it in a book?"

Her face darkened with suspicion, but there was no turning back now. I had to push forward with my plan.

I had already thought it all through. Even if Silian outed me for my treason and managed to have me executed, Terren would simply replace me with someone else in his court and nothing would change for her. But if she worked with me and I succeeded, the Mandate of Heaven would fall to her husband. Maro would become emperor, Silian his empress.

If there was anything I'd learned at court, it was that I could rely on few things more than power and ambition. I told her everything.

29

THOSE WHO ARE HEARD

"My husband's goals are aligned with ours," Silian said, from beneath the night's shadow of her cloak. "He would do anything, give anything, to save Tensha from Prince Terren's violent reign. He wants his brother dead as much as anyone. But still, he would never work with us."

Our secret meeting took place two weeks after the Mid-Autumn Festival. In the West Palace, where she resided, on the shores of the Thousand Lotus Lake. The moonlit waters to our side teemed with lotus flowers, which were interspersed with the occasional floating lantern.

"Why not?" I asked, trying not to despair.

"Well, suppose you are a prince. Suppose you have seal magic, and armies at your command, and Blessings that come at the calling of your pen. Suppose you are a peer to Tensha's most influential scholars, its most renowned literomancers. Would you stake the fate of the nation on a girl from the rice fields? On one who has only just learned to read?" Silian shook her head. "He would not make the time to meet with you, Lady Yin. And even if he did, he is far more likely to report you for your literacy— out of respect for tradition and duty to uphold Tenshan law—than collude with you."

She was right, of course. As soon as she had said the words aloud, I knew just how foolish my plan had been.

How could I have expected Prince Maro to believe in me, when I hardly believed in myself? I was a girl, not a poet, and somehow I had fancied myself taking down the Winter Dragon. The One Who Cannot Die. Succeeding where the eldest prince—who had magic and wealth and armies—had failed. It seemed a special kind of arrogance, held by the worst kind of fools.

My success in getting Hesin to speak with me had made me forget my place.

Silian turned onto a bridge, which crossed a narrow stretch of the lake onto an island. "But *I* would stake it on you," she surprised me by saying. "Men never think much of people like us—we are not the ones sitting on thrones or holding court, after all—but their underestimation, I am convinced, is our strength. Our names may not be in the bylines of poems, but we still have power to change things from the shadows, in our own way. It has been the case since the first dynasty."

Has it? I thought uncertainly of all the classics Ciyi had shown me, that detailed only the deeds of men. But perhaps the women were there too, between the lines, not visible. "You think there's a way for me to finish the heart-spirit poem without speaking with Prince Maro?"

"The men who authored the books you've read, the poems you've memorized—you have never spoken to them either. Yet have they not made themselves heard all the same?"

We arrived at the other side of the bridge. On the island was a single pavilion, half-hidden in the shadows between stooped and ancient willows. Silian produced a key from her sleeve and opened the door.

"Maro's study. He keeps all his private documents here, where even his closest advisors cannot access. After we were married, he gave me the key. *Silian, I trust you with my most intimate secrets,* he told me. Sweet words on the surface, are they not?" A soft laugh, tinged with the bitterness of winter. "But if you think about it, they don't mean much at all. How can I ever know his secrets if I do not know how to read? If I did, I doubt he would have ever let me anywhere near this place."

It smelled of dampness inside, of old paper and fresh flowers. Silian fiddled with some lanterns, and a moment later, the room was bathed in a warm glow. Stacks of worn books—volumes of classical poems and histories, judging by their titles—sat piled on desks and bookshelves and windowsills, which teemed with huge yellow chrysanthemums. There were Blessings here as well. I could identify them by the intermittent flickering within the calligraphy, lightning caged within each stroke of the brush.

On one wall hung a toy oakwood sword, and on another, a

battered-looking kite in the shape of a dragon. A few dried peach blossoms still clung to its paper teeth.

Silian pushed aside a cabinet, revealing a dust-covered hatch in the floor. From it she retrieved a mahogany chest. "Maro has kept a journal since he was old enough to write. I remember being in here with him one day, watching him remove some entries from his collection. When I asked him why, he told me that they were the pages concerning Terren, from their youth. Pages he wanted out of his sight. He has not reviewed them for a very long time, so I trust he will not miss them. It will be safe for you to borrow them for a few months."

The chest was carved with ornate tortoises and beautifully lacquered, and was heavy with scrolls and loose pages. I took it with solemnity, met her eyes, and tried not to be intimidated by the courage in them. "Lady Song, thank you."

She smiled. "Do not thank me, Lady Yin. There are no altruists in the palace. We all work for ourselves." And I left her thinking of another way that words were magic— *You have never spoken to them, yet they have made themselves heard.*

As autumn dissolved into winter, as my fateful wedding day loomed closer, I went through Maro's journal, foraging for pieces of his brother. And the more I read, the more I realized Wren was right.

Hesin did not know the whole truth.

30

THE CAT, THE TREE, AND THE WIND

At first, when I'd heard Hesin's story, it had not been clear why Maro took such a liking to his younger brother. But after reading his journals, it became obvious: everyone else expected something from him.

His mother and Master Ganji made him study all the time, expecting him to become a prodigious literomancer. Master Len trained him relentlessly in sword and strategy, expecting him to one day lead armies and conquer nations. Officials and clan leaders cornered him during festivals to offer him toys and sweets—long before he was old enough to understand what a bribe was—with the expectation of future favors.

His father wanted him to save Tensha.

"Our great nation is dying," he told Maro, the day he had first learned to read a map. "Here are our country's borders in the days of the Shouyuan Emperor." He pointed to a mural that took up an entire wall of his strategy room, then to a second on the opposite wall. "And here is what they are now. Pitiful. We are even smaller than we were during the Sun Dynasty. My son, my heir—you must correct this as soon as you can."

But Terren never expected anything from him. Terren was harmless, affectionate, and easy to please. Make the right silly face, and he would squeal with laughter. Hug him the right way, in a way that made him feel safe, and he would cling to you like a rescued kitten. Sneak him a mung bean cake during a banquet, and his entire day would be made.

Maro loved him ferociously.

He loved him so much that he kept sparring with him in the garden, even when Terren kept losing. In Hesin's account, the eunuch had made it seem almost like Maro was bullying Terren, with how handily he kept winning. But Maro had not seen it the same way.

Mother and Hesin think I've hurt him, he wrote in his journal—and I could almost feel the hot indignation through his words—*but he isn't hurt. He wouldn't want me to stop sparring with him just because he's still little.*

That would be like giving up on him.

But the grown-ups forced him to play a different game anyway, and Maro was still young enough that he had to obey. So he took Terren to climb the Century Peach instead.

One branch, then the next, then the next. Terren clung tight to his back as they climbed. Maro liked the weight of him. Carrying him made him feel powerful and big, like a river dragon.

"Ma-ro!" Terren chimed brightly, as soon as they were out of earshot of the grown-ups. "Wanna play 'dueling couplets'? I have a first line."

Maro grunted as he dropped from a branch onto the roof. He set his tiny brother carefully on the eaves, then took a seat next to him, legs dangling over the steep drop over the garden. "I'm still mad at you, you know."

"Why?"

He crossed his arms and pretended to be fuming. "Because you're boring. You keep not fighting me. You keep playing the game wrong."

"I'm sorry."

"Say it three times and I'll forgive you."

"I'm sorry. I'm sorry. I'm s—"

"Okay, I forgive you," Maro blurted out. "What's the line?"

Terren produced a slip of paper from his pocket. It fluttered in the wind, which came cold from the mountains.

His calligraphy was beautiful. Maro envied it. "*The cat lives in pursuit of the mouse,*" he read. "*The tree grows in pursuit of the sun.* Hmm. Let me think."

It was a game literomancers often played with one another, to practice their art. A poet would come up with the first half of a poem, and their opponent was challenged with completing it. Some of the most famous classical poems had been written as a result of "dueling couplets."

Maro looked out at the valley as he thought—at the thousand-li view, the far peaks, the Aricine River making its slow way towards the sea. Another wind from the mountain came rushing in, sending blossoms from the Century Peach swirling absolutely everywhere.

He brightened. "Ah! I've got it!"

> *The cat lives in pursuit of the mouse;*
> *The tree grows in pursuit of the sun.*
> *Are we the cat or the tree, pursuers?*
> *Are we the wind, born only to run?*

One day, Terren showed up to playtime very hurt. He often got himself hurt—he was little, Maro reasoned, and fragile—but this time, it was much worse than usual. There were bruises all over his neck and collar, and when Maro rolled up his sleeve, he found patches of blue and purple there too.

"What happened?" he demanded.

It took a lot of questioning, but eventually Terren admitted he fell off a tree.

"Show me," Maro said, his hands balling into fists. When his brother didn't move, he repeated, *"Show me the tree."*

The fury in Maro's words must have startled him into obedience. Terren led him, limping, to the Century Peach at the far end of the garden.

That one. Of course it's that one. Maro looked up at the giant tree, taking in its towering height and ugly flowers, and then he started hitting the lowest branch. Hard. When that didn't seem to hurt it, he jumped up and hung himself from it, kicking and kicking at its trunk. He didn't stop until he heard a *snap,* and the next moment both he and the branch had thumped onto the ground.

"Ma-ro." Terren blinked at him, looking very confused.

"I wanted to teach it a lesson," Maro explained, still panting. "I wanted it to know what happens when someone messes with my little brother." He extricated himself from under the branch, wiped his bleeding knuckles on his gown, and kissed Terren on the forehead. "We're family. Family is for keeping each other safe."

"He is not really your family," Master Len said, correcting Maro's fighting stance with a steady hand. "He may seem harmless now, but he is still young enough to not covet your throne. There will come a day when you are both older, and things will not be so simple."

The Dawn Pavilion, where Lady Sky resided and Maro was raised, was always lively with birdsong. Bushes of golden trumpet flowers blew lush in the earth-winds of summer. At the far side of the courtyard, Maro's friends—Mei Clan's "Little Rain" and Song Siming—were sparring with their own tutors.

It was difficult balancing in the Crane Pose, but Maro was getting better at it. "Even when we're older," he said defiantly, "we won't care about thrones. We'll still play together even when we have white hair like you."

The corners of his tutor's eyes crinkled with smile. "Grown-ups don't play, Maro."

"*We* will. And we won't stop until we've played ten thousand games. And written ten thousand poems!" Maro lost his balance, flailed his arms, and fell flat on the moss. "Oof."

Siming picked that precise embarrassing moment to run over to them. "Your Highness! Master Gu said I just did a perfect Arc of Rising Sun." He hopped from one foot to the other in excitement. "Want to spar? I'll show you."

Maro peeled himself off the ground, rubbed his sore elbows, and looked for permission at Master Len. He didn't like sparring with Siming—Siming didn't fight fair and cheated at every opportunity—but he was glad for the distraction anyway. It meant he didn't have to hear awful words about his brother anymore.

Master Ganji's warnings were far more direct.

"He *will* go after you," he said one afternoon, in Maro's study, during a break in memorizing classics. "It is inevitable. He is the second son, which means that you are all that stands between him and the position of emperor."

"So? He'll never win against me in a fight." Maro tried to open his scroll again, to read one of Tsao Te Shu's poems, but his tutor snatched it away.

"Maro, you aren't taking my warning seriously."

"I am. Can I have my book back?"

"He and his advisors will first try to gain your father's favor, so that he will switch his named heir. If that doesn't work, they will depose you by force. And if that still doesn't work, they will kill you."

"Please. I want my book back." Maro reached for it, but Master Ganji held it high over his head.

"Or perhaps they will skip the first two steps. Perhaps they will go directly for your throat."

Maro was frightened almost into tears. His hands went protectively to his neck as he stared out the window, trying to bite back a sniffle. Mother said a prince should never cry.

"You know what they write about the Azalea House already. *Brother betrays brother, blood forgets blood.* The August Emperor, who began the dynasty, killed two of his brothers on his path to the Crown. Your second uncle Nisin killed your first uncle Anzha—even after they'd spent years working together to overthrow the Joy Emperor. And don't forget your very own baba. You know what he has done for the good of the nation."

Of course Maro did. It was a story he'd heard many times. Father killing his own kin to save Tensha, sacrificing blood for country. There was nobody in the world Maro admired more than his father, and he had never grown tired of that story.

But it was not the *only* story he'd heard.

"In the villages," he said sulkily, "and other places far away, families live in the same house. Sometimes even in one room, all together. I read all about them in books. Babas and mamas eat at the same table and hug each other lots, and brothers take care of each other even when they're all grown. And sometimes there are sisters too." He had always wanted a sister, but Mother said that even if the Ancestors gave him one, they wouldn't be able to keep her. Mother said girls were like water, for helping their brothers grow into flowers.

"That is *there,* Maro. Not *here.*" Master Ganji's voice had become iron, nonnegotiable. "You are not some lowly peasant. You are heir to the dynasty! For you, the word *blood* does not mean family but country. Your veins are Tensha's flowing rivers, your beating heart its capital, your flesh its mountains and fertile valleys. Do you understand?"

Maro watched the bee-eaters darting about the trumpet flowers outside. Every so often, one would catch an insect in its beak, killing it. "I don't wanna be heir to the dynasty. I wanna be a peasant."

Master Ganji hit him. With the hard rod of the scroll, right on his seal-bearing cheek. It stung terribly.

"One day you will grow up, Maro, and you will finally understand how good you have it. Men have fought long wars for the kind of power you hold. You will learn to value it. You will learn just how easily it can be taken from you. And you will be grateful."

Maro *was* grateful. He might throw tantrums sometimes, or act childishly on occasion, but most of the time, he was the prince everyone expected him to be—filial, hardworking, and dutiful.

On days he was not in the peach garden with Terren, he stayed in his mother's Dawn Pavilion, practicing his swordplay until he was too tired to stand. He studied classics long into the night, until the candles in his lanterns burned to stubs, and the replacements burned out too. Even when he was too sick to read, even when he was confined to his bed with his eyes shut, he still memorized poems by running them over in his mind.

One day, as he was bedridden with a cold, he heard his mother coming in. "I have brought some herbal medicine," she said, setting a tray at his bedside. "It will help with the cough."

She was crying. She was trying hard to hide it, but Maro noticed anyway and sat up, alarmed. "Mother, what is the matter?"

"Terren has written his first Blessing," she said, sobbing into her sleeve. "A powerful one." She recounted to him the events of the day, about the carp and the healing spell, the admiration on the faces of everyone present. "What if the emperor names him heir instead? All that grueling training, all that arduous studying—and he still ended up better than you. I am frightened, Maro, that we have both sacrificed so much for nothing."

Her words stung worse than Master Ganji's rod. Seeing her cry—because of *him*—was the worst feeling in the world. Maro left his bed in shame and fell to his knees before her. "I'm sorry. I'm an unworthy son. Forgive me."

His apology seemed to cheer his mother, at least a little. She gently cupped his cheek, the one with a seal, and said, "You must not let your brother get any further ahead. You must write a Blessing too. I will tell your masters to relieve you of your lessons for now, and you will spend all your time composing instead."

He dipped his head. "Yes, Mother." She gave him a kiss on the top of his head and left him.

Worthless, he scrawled into his journal that day, his calligraphy messy and anguished. *Worthless worthless worthless. Why can't I be smarter? Better?*

News of the second son's Blessing spread through the palace like pollen in spring. Soon, even the lowliest maid was gossiping about it while washing sheets in the river. The same people who had called Terren *a waste of Heaven's magic* were suddenly praising him nonstop.

"I knew it all along," said one gardener to another as they trimmed the trumpet flowers right outside Maro's window. "The second prince is the one Tensha has been waiting for, a child extraordinary enough to change the fate of dynasties. His older brother, on the other hand? He is competent but nothing special . . ."

Maro hid under a blanket and blocked his ears until they went away.

Soon, an imperial edict arrived from the South Palace. "The emperor's birthday is in three months' time," the messenger read off a scroll. "He invites his eldest son to demonstrate his literomancy in front of the leaders of the Great Clans and other distinguished guests."

Maro knew exactly what the edict meant.

Father was disappointed in him. Father wanted him to write his own Blessing, as soon as possible, to avoid the embarrassment of his first son and heir being outshone by his second. Father had set him a deadline.

Worthless, he wrote again, in huge characters that took up an entire page.

He didn't leave the Dawn Pavilion after that. In Hesin's account, it had seemed as if Lady Sky was the one who'd kept him there—*not to be disturbed except for one meal a day,* the eunuch had said—but that had painted her as unfairly cruel. In truth, the resolve had come from Maro himself. He forbade himself from doing anything except study, and he did so from dawn to high moon. When his own mother knocked on his door any fewer than three times, he did not answer. When servants entered for any other reason than to refill his inkpots and paper supply, he would yell at them to go away.

Every day, in his journals, he tracked his progress. *I think I'm close,* one entry would say. *I can feel the warmth of magic under my pen.* The one after it might declare, dejected, *No, everything is still awful. I'm not close at all.* As the emperor's birthday drew nearer—as the three months turned to weeks, then days—his entries became more and more frantic. I could tell exactly which days he cried, because the ink would be blurred and the paper wrinkled.

Two days before the deadline, Maro heard movement outside his window.

When he opened it and saw who it was, he felt sick in the stomach. "You can't be here! What if someone sees?"

Terren had to stand on tiptoes to reach the windowsill. He rested his chin on the ledge, between all the golden trumpet flowers, and his eyes were wide and pleading. "Ma-ro. Play with me."

"I can't."

"Please?"

"Leave me alone."

"Please?"

"Find other friends."

"Please!" He produced a crinkled-up paper from his pocket and held it out over the windowsill. Its characters shone lively as fireflies, and Maro's breath caught right in his throat. *A Blessing.*

Terren knew. Of course he knew. He was far too clever to not have figured out why his brother had stopped going to the garden.

Maro took the spell with a shaking hand, eyes tracing over that beautiful, familiar calligraphy. There was so much magic in those words. Words that, in two days, would *save him.*

Words that would impress not just the emperor, but all his distinguished guests too. Words that would finally make his mother and his tutors proud of him. Words that would make all the people of Tensha respect him at last, instead of seeing him as a source of shame.

His brother's words, but it wouldn't matter, because nobody would ever know the truth.

"Thanks." He smiled and gave them back to him.

Terren's eyes widened with surprise. "You don't like it?"

"Of course I like it!" Maro laughed as he pressed his own cheek to the windowsill, watching the bee-eaters and the golden flowers, the hazy peaks in the distance. "But I'll be emperor one day, remember? I'll have to lead the nation. And when I do, I'm going to do it with integrity. With pride." *Your veins are Tensha's flowing rivers, your beating heart its capital, your flesh its mountains and fertile valleys.* "I can't begin my reign by cheating, you know. I can't make my people believe I wrote a Blessing that I didn't. I would rather fail with honesty than succeed without honor. Better the whole world be ashamed of me than for me to be ashamed of myself."

"Ma-ro."

"Hmm?"

"Catch it!"

When Maro blinked in confusion, Terren only kept tugging at his sleeve excitedly. "That feeling," he squeaked. "Catch it! Catch it in a poem!"

I will lead the nation with integrity, with pride.

Better the whole world be ashamed of me than for me to be ashamed of myself.

My veins are Tensha's flowing rivers . . .

In the two remaining days, Maro spun his emotions into a poem, and the poem turned out to hold magic. When he cast it in the banquet hall, in front of the emperor and all those important men, the entire floor began to burst at its seams with grass and wildflowers. Mountains and valleys sprang up between banquet tables, rivers curved into life around the pillars. Miniature forests bloomed into existence, tiny tendrils of mist weaving through their canopies.

The entire room had turned into a living map of Tensha. And standing at its capital, at the crossroads at the top of the empire, was Maro, holding his brother tightly. "I did it," he whispered. Then louder, laughing, "I *did it.*" And Terren grinned just as wide and hugged him just as tight.

The emperor rose from his seat and smiled for the first time Maro remembered. "This map is quite accurate," he said. "It pleases me. I shall make this my new strategy room." He then nodded to his advisor. "Hesin, make the appropriate arrangements."

Except it didn't happen like that, not exactly.

31

WORTHLESS

That last part, about the emperor's birthday banquet, had all been made up.

It was what Maro had written in his journals, so it was what I had believed at first. But a few pages later, he wrote, *It is what I wish had happened. I was really upset that day, so I didn't want to write the truth.*

Here is the truth.

He *had* cast that Blessing, and it *had* turned into a map of Tensha. But Terren had not been standing next to him. Instead, he had been with his mother and his other advisors from the Maple Pavilion. The emperor had not been watching attentively. Instead, he had sat sick in his throne, his eyes barely open. When Maro had finished his spell, his father only grunted in acknowledgment and said nothing more. Some of the guests in the audience had begun to clap, but they were quickly interrupted.

"Please, everyone, your attention. I have something important to say."

It was the empress, Qin Rong. Her swan-feather gown haloed around her as she made her way down the hall to the dais. She was accompanied by Lady Autumn and Long Shan, one of Terren's tutors. Her own son, baby Isan, began crying in the arms of his wet nurse, but nobody was paying attention.

"As Mother of the House," she said when she reached the front, "I am obligated to investigate any reports concerning the Inner Court—including any princes not yet of age. I have reason to believe the first son did not write the spell he'd shown us."

Maro felt like he was falling.

"Several witnesses have informed me that they believe the second son was its real author. Prince Terren, you see, has been spotted in the Dawn Pavilion. Some gardeners have even witnessed him passing a slip of paper to Prince Maro—one with a Blessing on it."

No. No no no.

He wanted to hit something, to scream, but all he could do was stand silent as a statue.

Lady Sky's face had gone completely red. "It is our emperor's birthday. Qin Rong, have you no respect for your husband?"

"Of course I do. That is why I do my duty, even if it is unpleasant."

Father was angry. Maro could tell by the way his eyes burned and the corner of his mouth turned down. But he was very sick by then, and when he tried to rise to stop the accusations, he coughed and sank back into his seat. He didn't even have a chance to speak. Two of the empress's eunuchs rushed him back to the Inner Court to rest. "Your Majesty," they said as they retreated, "we must not overtire ourselves on such a happy occasion."

As soon as the emperor was gone, the fighting began.

The people of the Maple Pavilion repeated the empress's accusations. "Maids saw Terren sneaking out of his bedchamber," they cried. "Where else would he be going but to see his brother?" The people of the Dawn Pavilion shouted angry words back. "Maro has shut himself in his room for months to write that Blessing. He didn't even allow himself to break for supper." Throughout it all, Maro felt barely there, like he was living in someone else's dream.

No, not a dream. A night-story. The kind that churned stomachs and made blood run cold.

It felt like forever before the accusations were finally put to rest, and only when Hesin arrived with a letter from the emperor. "*I understand where the accusations came from,*" he read off the scroll, "*but my eldest son has integrity and would not lie about such a thing. And in any case, you have all felt that Blessing and seen its effects. How can such an ardent, patriotic poem be written by anyone other than the true heir?*"

But by then, it was too late.

The guests were already whispering horrid words, and Mother was weeping again, and Master Ganji was pushing one of Terren's tutors into one of the fake rivers. The story of tonight, Maro knew, would spread like the gray fever. Rumors would reach even the farthest walls of Tensha, each telling more exaggerated than the next, and everyone would have it in their minds that the first son was a liar and a cheat, even if neither of those things were true. It would take years and years for him to restore his honor. He might not be able to do it at all.

Worthless.

He felt ashamed. So ashamed that he wanted to bury himself deep in those useless mounds of dirt he'd made. Master Ganji had tried to warn him, hadn't he? *He and his advisors will first try to gain your father's favor.* He had tried to warn him and Maro hadn't listened. *If that doesn't work, they will depose you by force.* And now everything he and Mother had worked for was ruined. *And if that still doesn't work, they will kill you.*

"Ma-ro." A timid tug at his sleeve.

Maro looked down at his brother, an awful lump forming in his throat. "Did you set me up?"

Terren tried clumsily to climb onto his back, but Maro shook him off like the autumn wind a leaf.

"*Did you set me up.*"

His eyes grew huge and brimmed with tears. "No."

So little, but so much cleverer than he let on. So timid, but that sigil shone so bright. Maro considered him for a long time, feeling like crying himself.

"I believe you," he said at last, very quietly. "But I have to stop playing with you anyway."

32

FOUR PLEDGES

It snowed the day of my wedding: sparse and scintillating, each flake a fleeting glimmer in the sun. If it had been another man I was marrying, I might have found it beautiful.

If it had been someone else, I might have jumped for joy when Wren and Teela came in with my wedding gown, heavy with azaleas and moon-season roses, or when Fern came bearing a shimmering headpiece that was crowded with leaves of polished gold. When Aini came in with a phoenix shawl, so elaborate it must have taken a thousand days to embroider, I might have felt aflutter as I ran my fingers across its silk. And maybe Aunt Ping would not have said, "Don't frown so much, heh? Unless you want wrinkles like me," and would instead have told me to straighten my posture.

If it had been anyone but Terren, I would have laughed with delight when I saw just how extravagant my wedding was. As they paraded my palanquin through the gates to Heavenly Square, I would have counted the lucky lanterns hanging from the balustrades, the banners across the pillars, the tasseled fortune lions with fearsome teeth dancing amidst the audience. And the pots of smoking incense—emblazoned with flying dragons, filling the open square with the aroma of longevity and fortune—I would have counted them too.

But not the guests. There were too many of them. Thousands, at the very least, all bearing banners as they stood amidst red azalea petals, white snow.

My scribe, however, was laughing enough for the both of us. "I have never had such a good view of an imperial wedding!" Ciyi exclaimed, from where he marched beside my palanquin. "When Prince Maro wed Lady Song, I was only standing back there!" He pointed at a far corner of the square.

The square was surrounded by three terraces. Envoys led me out of my palanquin and escorted me up the marble steps towards the portico of the Hall of Heavenly Supremacy. On the bottom level sat the distinguished guests. Clan leaders, relatives of the House, and renowned literomancers in black sat on the second. On the highest, overlooking everything, sat the imperial family—the five princes and their entourages, Lady Song and the empress, the other East Palace concubines. Both Jin Veris and Kang Rho nodded to me as I passed, but none of the others would look at me. I took my place next to the prince.

Had it been a different man I was marrying, I might have felt shy.

I might have been as giddy as a young girl as I tried to glimpse my new husband from behind my fan. A husband who would—well, not *love* me; I was not that greedy. A husband who would take me into his home and treat me kindly.

He would smile at me in the mornings. "I am off to work in the Administrative District now," he'd say—because he would be at least a minor official, Ma wanted at least that for me—and then he would give me a polite and perfunctory kiss on the cheek. "Please have dinner ready for me when I come home," he would say, and then he would not cut me or torture me.

At least once a week, he would take me to the wet market, not far from our home in the heart of Guishan. We would buy a head of cabbage, an inexpensive cut of pork, some flour. "This week, I'll make dumplings," I would say, and his eyes would crinkle with delight. Once a month, he would send money back to Ma and Ba, and Bao would be able to eat as many prunes and sweet things as he wanted. When he got a bonus, it would go towards my brother's tuition. "I support him going to a good school wholeheartedly," he'd say, because he would believe in the value of education. "Perhaps one day, he will attain an even higher post than I have."

I would have been so happy during that wedding.

Even if it was a small one, even if it had only the villagers of Lu'an in attendance instead of several thousand bannered men, I bet I would have laughed and danced with everyone there.

"You may now perform your pledges," the Minister of Rites intoned from behind us.

Terren and I knelt on the top terrace, three steps apart. He was not looking at me. His eyes stayed on the rug, which was embroidered gold with dragons, matching his ceremonial robe.

It was the first time I had seen him in anything other than gray. His dragon gown was striking in its redness, its silk gleaming as bright in the sun as the sigil on his cheek. His hair did not fall wild but was instead kept neat, in a top knot, by a gold pin in the shape of yet another dragon.

I had no idea how Hesin had convinced him to look so presentable.

Or to hold back on his wine. He was only a little drunk today—even I could barely tell. If not for the barest whiff of rice wine in the air, and the slightest bit of unsteadiness in his posture, I would not have known at all.

We performed our ceremonial kowtows. Four of them, to four beats of a gong, our foreheads pressing all the way onto the cold snowdust on the rug. They symbolized the same four pledges every new bride and groom in Tensha, even villagers, made on their wedding day.

For each other and our children, care.

For our parents and the Ancestors, piety.

For our community and our nation, duty.

For the emperor and Heaven, obedience.

"Rise," the minister said.

We got to our feet again, but still Terren did not look at me. It was like he was afraid someone would hurt him, if he took his eyes off the rug even once.

"You may now begin the service of tea," said the minister. "To Chancellor Inly, who will act for His Majesty the Yongkai Emperor. To Her Majesty Empress Sun. Together they will bless the union of the Inner and Outer Courts—and, on behalf of all those who have come before, make the marriage official."

Servants came forward to bring us teacups on plates, decorated with lacquered red and shimmering gold. I took a plate in my hand, and so did Terren. The tea was scented softly with jasmine and lotus seeds, and steamed through the lid.

Not far from us, a pale and fragile-looking eunuch—the chancellor—was seated next to the empress. I knelt on the snow-coated carpet before them. Terren hesitated a moment longer, the Aricine Ward flickering fast. Then he took his place stiffly beside me.

I held myself very, very still. We had not been this close since the night of the rumors, so close I could feel the warmth radiating from his body. I was terrified that if I took a wrong breath, I might accidentally touch him.

He was still not looking at me, but the empress was. As I met her eyes, she gave me the smallest of private smiles. *Girls like you*, it said, *they never survive long in the palace.*

She was planning something.

My heart thumped even faster. It suddenly made sense why she had not antagonized me as of late; she must have been waiting for the right opportunity. A wedding in front of the Great Clans and thousands of important guests? It would be the perfect moment for her to strike at both me and Terren.

Terren served the chancellor first, looking like he would rather swallow poison than be this close to me, kneeling for someone else. I raised my own plate towards the empress. She did not reach for the cup. Instead, with one sweeping motion, she brushed the entire plate with a golden sleeve—sending the porcelain set shattering onto the ground next to us.

I would have flinched, had I not been trying so hard to not move.

"I wish I could bless the marriage," she said, standing. "But unfortunately, there is a matter to settle first."

Terren seemed just as caught off guard as I was. His eyes flicked to the empress, and in them I saw the murderous intent of a pit viper. "Sun Ai. You are ruining my happy day."

"On the contrary, my dear. I am only trying to look out for you. It is my duty as Mother of the House to ensure the integrity of the Inner Court. Every report must be thoroughly investigated—including the one I am about to bring to your attention."

He rose to meet her gaze. "You might have had the courtesy to investigate beforehand. In private."

"There was no time, I'm afraid. I only received it this morning." A twitch of a smile laid bare her lie, but only to those close enough to catch it.

"Then it can wait until after."

"It cannot. It concerns your bride, and therefore the sanctity of your marriage."

My throat became dry. I could almost touch the tension in the air, feel the silence that rose from the crowd of thousands to greet the falling snow.

The look on Terren's face, it was like he was going to kill the empress, right there and then.

But he wouldn't, I thought. Not without a reason, so publicly, on such an auspicious day. That would turn all of Tensha against him. The empress seemed to know it too, because her posture was smug and unconcerned.

"Guards," she said. "Bring in the witness."

Two Azalea guards led a terrified maid up the stairs, skinny and no older than thirteen.

"This is one of the maids in the West Palace. She came running to me right before the wedding, poor anxious dear." The empress turned to the girl. "Maya, would you like to repeat to everyone what you told me?"

There were tears in Maya's eyes and all over her cheeks. She fell onto her knees on the top step to face the crowd of bannermen below. "I . . . I saw Lady Yin going . . . going . . ."

"Louder," said the empress, sweetly. "So that the whole hall can hear."

"I saw her going to the West Palace," she cried. "At night. Alone. Dressed in nothing but bedrobes."

33

SUSPICION

Bedrobes.

For a long time, I could only stare at the maid, uncomprehending. I had no idea where the lie could have even come from.

I had only gone to the West Palace once, to obtain Maro's journals, but that had been in secret. And even if someone *had* seen me, I had not been wearing anything near so dishonorable.

"I see," said the empress with mock somberness. Her gaze swept the entire audience—the princes and the concubines on the terrace, the thousands of guests in the square below. "If I understand the implication correctly, it means our bride's sanctity has not been preserved."

Then I realized that I did know. I knew, with nauseating certainty, that the lie had been planted by the empress. I could even imagine the exact words she used. *If you do this one favor for me, I will set you free. With a sizable reward, more than enough for what you came here for.* The empress was practiced at offering temptations and making threats; I was well acquainted with both. *And if you don't . . . Well, that would be a shame, dear. If a lowly maid died without explanation, who in the West Palace would even notice?*

Terren was breathing fast. His sigil flickered like coals, like he was trying hard to hold back from summoning knives. But it was one of Maro's entourage who spoke first.

"*Your Majesty.*" He was young and sharp-chinned, and red with fury. "You would make such ugly accusations against the first son's honor."

"I did not mention Prince Maro's name," the empress said lightly.

"But you implied it!"

"I am merely investigating a report. There is no need to be so angry—especially if you do not believe the accusations to be true."

It was an insidious way of wording things. She had somehow managed to make herself sound perfectly reasonable, while only making Maro seem guiltier the angrier his allies grew.

Maro seemed to realize this, too. He put a steady arm on his friend's shoulders. "Our empress is right, Mei Yu. She is simply doing her own duty to the nation. We must let her carry on." He wore a courtier's impenetrable calm, but I did not miss the dark edge that flashed in his eyes.

Efficient of her, I thought, *to target two of her son's competitors at once.* Did the empress have plans to tarnish the reputations of Prince Isan and Prince Kiran too?

The third and fourth sons stood close by, with their own allies. They must have been taught well by their advisors, because neither of them said a word. Prince Isan, in a gown of plum blossoms, stood straight and solemn as he looked out at the crowd. Prince Kiran, draped in a ribboned cloak, was surreptitiously playing with a maple-cat. The furry tassels of his boot, which the cat seemed to delight in pouncing on, were hidden behind a pot of incense—out of view of anyone looking from below.

"She is only one witness." Hesin's voice.

All eyes were drawn to the old eunuch. He had been standing on the lowest terrace, but was now making his way up the snow-dusted steps to the rest of us.

He inserted himself between Terren and the empress, and repeated, "Maya is only one witness. If it is her word against Lady Yin's, then we must take the word of our prince's chosen over a maid without status, must we not?"

"Ah, you." The empress's smile never faded, giving me the sickening feeling that the eunuch was playing right into her hand. "After all these years, you remain as wise as when you served the Joy Emperor."

A backhanded insult, but Hesin said nothing. I had seen him use the same tactic in court, wielding silence like a weapon.

Empress Sun waited a little longer for him to speak, and when he didn't, she turned to me. "What the eunuch says is, of course, true. It seems that all you have to do, Lady Yin, is deny the accusations and we can get along with our merriment. It is only right that the House takes your word over a maid's—even a young one. *With her whole life ahead of her.*"

Those words crept up my spine like frost. I knew they were meant just for me.

Now I understood her game. If I denied the accusations, it would mean that Maya was lying. A lie that implicated a prince might have meant a cut tongue for the likes of Sun Jia, but for a mere maid? She'd be lucky if her death was quick.

Decide, Wei, the empress's smile seemed to say. *Deny the accusations and let an innocent girl die—or confirm them and die yourself.*

No matter how things turned out, Empress Sun would still come out ahead. In her husband's absence, she would have managed to flaunt her power to an audience of thousands—while taking a stab at both the eldest princes. A rumor like this, even dispelled, could still blossom into something more sinister. I knew the power of rumors by now.

And the price was very cheap. Either Maya's life, or mine.

My cheeks burned with shame. I already knew what I was going to do. Which was the obvious thing, which was save myself.

As much as I wished I could be like the martial heroes in the myths, I was only a village girl who knew nothing. I did not want to be here, facing the empress and the Great Clans, about to marry a prince who tortured me. I did not want to be in the palace at all. I wanted to be home, alive, safe.

If I died, I would never feel Ma running her hands through my hair again. If I died, I would never get to see the great man Bao was going to be, how he was going to change the world.

I rose unsteadily to my feet. I looked from the empress to Terren, whose face was a cloud of violent intent, and then to Mei Yu, Maro's friend, staring at the ground with his hands in fists. Hesin looked pensive. Maya looked terrified—just as terrified as I was—and it was then that I made my choice.

"The maid's allegations are true." I blurted out the sentence before I could stop myself, the words tumbling out all in a rush. "I do not deny them."

There were a few audible gasps from the crowd. I sensed the guards closest to me tense, as if readying themselves to seize me. My hands were shaking at what I had just done, but there was no choice now, I had to keep going.

Because maybe there was a chance I could save us both. Maybe.

I drew in a breath, made my voice as steady as possible. "But that is not the *whole* truth."

Terren lifted his chin and narrowed his eyes. He was reassessing, re-calibrating. I knew that if I lived through this, he would no doubt punish me for what I was about to say. We had our wedding night ahead of us, and two weeks' retreat after that to spend alone. There would be plenty of opportunities for him to hurt me.

I could not worry about that now. I only had room in my mind to save one person at a time.

"Explain," the empress said.

"Perhaps we should let Maya go first, Your Majesty. She has told the truth, after all. It takes remarkable bravery, to report something as dangerous as she has."

She nodded to the guards, who took the maid away. "Explain," Empress Sun repeated, turning to me. "Why *have* you gone to the West Palace at night, dressed so dishonorably?" She looked absolutely delighted, likely believing I was about to be executed—which I would be, if my gamble did not work.

"Your Majesty, I was going to see my teacher." I glanced over at Silian. "Though I had learned some techniques to please a man, I knew I had room for improvement. Since my wedding day was nearing, I wanted to surprise my prince with new techniques, to please him during our retreat. And I . . . I knew that Lady Song had more experience than me. So I asked her to . . ." I trailed off and lowered my head, trying to seem too embarrassed to speak.

Empress Sun gave me a poisonous look. "If that is the case, why have you asked Lady Song—and not a concubine in your own prince's Inner Court?"

"Your Majesty, I was thinking of feasts. I was imagining that I had invited a very important guest to a banquet, and had served him a hundred dishes. But if none of them appetized him, I do not think I would double the quantity of an existing plate. I should think a gracious host would look elsewhere, for new flavors."

A few men in the terrace below laughed, then coughed to disguise their laughs.

Please, I begged Silian silently. *Work with me. Corroborate my story.*

My heart drummed so loud I heard it in my ears.

"It is true," Silian said with a smile. "In Yoor, in the northeastern districts, the ladies receive a different education than in the heartlands."

Now it was Maro's turn to look suspicious. Beside him, Mei Yu had turned an even deeper shade of red, matching the azalea petals strewn all over the ground. I wondered how Silian would handle her husband's questions once they had a chance to speak in private.

"What different education?" the empress demanded. I could tell her temper was rising. "What different techniques?"

I looked at my feet, trying to seem uncomfortable. "Must I demonstrate for everyone on the day of my wedding, Your Majesty? In front of so many other men? I had intended to save my learnings for the wedding chamber, as a surprise."

There was a chuckle from one of the Great Clans' leaders, and this time, he did not even bother to cough over it.

The empress went quiet. She must have sensed the sentiment shifting against her, known that if she kept pursuing the matter, it would only be herself that she embarrassed. "No, that will not be necessary," she said in a strained voice. "I am glad we have clarified that minor misunderstanding, so that we may now resume our celebrations."

She said the ceremonial words alongside the chancellor, to officiate the marriage.

I didn't even have a chance to feel relieved. As she said those words, I felt Terren's eyes bore into me. He wore the same thoughtful look he did whenever he was thinking of new torture methods. I may have lucked my way out of the empress's trap, but who knew what he was going to do to me tonight? He was one of two people on the terrace—other than Silian—who knew for certain that I'd been lying.

The other was Hesin.

In the break after the ceremony's end and before the beginning of the feast, the eunuch found me. "Lady Yin, you are quite lucky that Lady Song has helped you."

I picked a safe thing to say. "The Ancestors are kind."

The two of us were the only ones left on the terrace. Below us, the square had cleared of the less distinguished guests, leaving behind trampled red azaleas, discarded paper cutouts, and dropped lanterns. The snow was falling in earnest now, each cluster as large as a blossom.

The more important guests were already gathered in the Hall of Heavenly Supremacy behind us. Music, warm light, and the smell of feasts and flowers poured from its gates.

"I must tell you the truth," Hesin said. "I am growing suspicious of you."

I was completely caught off guard. My heart raced fast, but I forced my voice to be steady. "Is that so?"

"I know of one way, at least, that the prince we serve can be killed. Despite his invulnerability ward."

I knew the interrogation tactic he was using. I had seen him use it on the men at court, in the blade-filled Hall of Divine Harmony—guessing at motivations to see whether they would react in a telling way.

I tried to imagine I had never heard of the heart-spirit poem, had never even tried learning to read. "Really?"

"It requires stories. The very kind you have been asking me about."

A wind blew a flurry of wet snow down my collar, and the biting cold of it made me shiver. "I did not know that stories could kill a prince."

"I would not have expected someone like you to." Hesin looked out at the square. We could see quite far into the palace from our vantage, the roofs of pavilions, pagodas, and watchtowers covered in white. "But now that I see you have been in contact with the West Palace, it is only adding to my suspicions."

My mouth was so dry it was hard to speak. "Ah, you mean Lady Song. I admit that we are friends. We bonded at the Mid-Autumn Parade."

"An interesting match."

"Isn't it? I have thought so myself."

His gaze lingered on me. It was the same measuring look he gave all those men in Terren's court. My daring lie in front of the empress—in front of all those courtiers and guests—must have changed his opinion of me. If he knew me only as a scared victim of the prince's cruelty before, he now saw me as someone worth *measuring*.

Had I not been so afraid, I might have felt flattered.

"Forgive me," he said at last. "I am old, and my thoughts have grown unruly with the passing years. The cold only exacerbates it." He rubbed his hands together and exhaled a cloud of air. "Shall we go back inside?"

34

A CONCUBINE'S WEAPON

You must be more careful, Wei.

What you did today was not very wise.

All this time, I had been focused on defending myself from the other concubines, not knowing that with my wedding, I would enter a much bigger den of beasts. Empress Sun. Maro. Terren. Hesin. They had all been playing the game far longer than I had, and I felt a lark foolish enough to fly among hawks.

Hesin. I had not seen it coming at all.

I am loyal only to the nation, the old eunuch had told me once. *I must help the one who holds the Mandate of Heaven become emperor.* As long as Terren was heir, he was oathbound to keep him alive. My intent to kill him meant Hesin was my enemy. Why hadn't I realized it sooner?

"*The Aricine River flows east,*" sang the opera girl, "*without so much as a glance behind it.*"

With a painted face and a dress clattering with beads, she twirled from table to heaping banquet table inside the Hall of Heavenly Supremacy. More dancers in flowing skirts trailed behind her, flitting among the wedding guests, weaving between the gold-engraved pillars, incense pots, and pomelo trees growing out of the ground.

"*A long pilgrimage to the seas, where no more canyons would bind it.*"

Was Jin Veris still scheming against me, too? Were any of the other concubines still trying to overthrow me? Prince Isan and Prince Kiran— what moves were their advisors pulling from the shadows?

Terren. What was he going to do to me once we were alone again? How was he going to punish me for my ties to Silian? I had not forgotten the malevolent look he'd worn today, or the fact that I had to enter his wedding chamber tonight.

"My dear friend's sailboat drifts down its misty shore. He does not glance back either, and his shadow becomes no more."

One of the generals laughed and raised his glass. "A farewell poem by Lao Shan—how classic. But why such a sad song on such a joyous occasion?"

"Yes, yes!" clamored a group of men around him. "Sing a happier song next!"

Had I even done the right thing, I wondered? I might have saved the life of one maid, but in doing so, I had revealed to everyone that I was more than just an unassuming village girl—that I was capable of lying, scheming, and making my own allies. I had just announced to an audience of thousands that I was a real player in the grand game of the palace.

Saving Maya might be what led to me getting caught—and thus the heart-spirit poem not finished, and Terren not killed. Saving her could mean a wicked man becoming emperor.

Maybe, I thought uneasily, *I should have let her die.* It frightened me that I was even in a position to choose.

A hand fell on mine. "Eat," said Silian. She kept her eyes on me as I picked up a piece of gao made of rice and jujubes. "People like us only get married once. Regardless of whether you are happy with your husband, you ought to try to enjoy your wedding."

"O Tensha, motherland!" Pressured by the guests around her, the singing girl had chosen an upbeat, patriotic song for her next piece. *"Mountains echo with our poetry. Seas carve our songs in sand."*

The gao was sweet in a gentle, barely noticeable way. "What was yours like?"

"I do not know, Lady Yin. I am ashamed to say that I spent most of it weeping under an ormosia tree."

"Weeping? Do you not love him?" My eyes went to Maro, who sat across the hall, drinking with his merchant allies and other influential friends.

All the Azalea sons might have stood near each other during the ceremony—the closest they had ever been to seeming like a family—but now they were separated again. Isan and Kiran were fraternizing with their own courts. The empress, with the little prince Ruyi cradled in her arms, had taken up an entire quadrant along with her Sun-bannered allies, and they were all laughing about something secret. Their glasses clinked.

Even a snap of a twig or the clinking of glass, Hesin had said, *could startle him into tears.*

And now he was afraid of nothing.

My husband—even thinking the word made my stomach twist with revulsion—sat alone on the dais, one hand cupped around an open jar of wine, the other holding a military treatise. The Aricine Ward circling him like white chains—and the eight unsheathed swords he kept hovering around him—seemed to deter people from bothering him with platitudes.

"O Tensha, all under sky! *The greatest nations will never fall. The greatest empires will never die.*"

There were three empty jars of wine on the ground next to him already. *Good,* I thought. The more he drank, the less of a chance he would be awake when I went to our wedding chamber.

"I mean, I do now." Silian gave a small laugh. "But then? I was only fifteen, and so far from home. I didn't even know what he looked like until I was standing up on that terrace, about to do my four pledges. Every girl is a little frightened, I think, when they give themselves to a man. Even a kind one. Even one she expected to marry since she was old enough to know what the word meant."

"You were expecting to marry him?"

"My cousin is a childhood friend of his. Just after I was born, my father paid a lot of money to my uncle, in hopes—"

"O Tensha, motherland! *Enemies tremble before our might. Kingdoms fall at our command.*"

Silian looked at the singing girl with distaste, even as the military men around her laughed and downed wine in praise of her performance. "I tire of this song. Shall we take a walk?"

We passed by Terren's other concubines and my servants on our way out. Ciyi had been in the middle of tearing into a chicken leg, next to Jin Veris's scribe, Ah Ronta, but looked up when we passed by on our way out. "I have never had such exquisite food before, Lady Yin! The last imperial wedding, I had not even been invited to the banquet!"

I could not help but smile, relieved that somebody, at least, was enjoying my wedding. "Take note of the dishes you like," I told him. "I will have our cooks try to replicate them in the Cypress Pavilion."

Day had passed into night. Outside, the snow had finally stopped, leaving behind only a coat of it on the ground that glowed pristine in the moonlight. Silian liked its softness. I could tell because she shuffled as she walked, leaving longer footprints than she needed to.

We went around the portico of the hall, towards the back gardens.

"Have you ever been in love?" Silian asked, after we were out of hearing range of everyone.

If the empress or anyone else had asked me that, I might have been on edge. But Silian already knew enough about me to convict me. She must have been merely curious. Possibly she wanted to know how much like her I was. I would have wondered too, had I been in her position.

"I think so," I said, after a pause. Even now, I was not sure if that had truly been love, though I hoped it had. "I had a friend called Cai Xi'er, in my village. Sometimes we walked to the market together, just the two of us, to sell peppers and rice." I remembered thinking that he was funny and kind. I remembered deciding that if he ever asked me to run away with him, into the clouds, I would have said yes in a heartbeat. "But he was not a city boy," I hurried to add, without really knowing why. "His family didn't have much money."

"Was he sorry when you left for the palace?"

"He . . . will be pleased to know I have made it, I think. He has given me necklaces to put in my offering basket, after all." That cold morning in Guishan, the local officials had taken our baskets and promptly vanished. I did not think the offering had even made it to the Azalea House. "And I think he would be doubly pleased I returned with gifts." The more I spoke, the more embarrassed about my inexperience I grew. "What about you?"

"Maybe a few martial heroes, from the stories." She gave a sheepish smile, one that made her look young. "When I was a girl, I owned a fan with a water-painting of Li Zhi the Lionheart. I spread it so often to look at it that the silk folds had become smooth over time. It didn't matter that the heroes weren't real. In fact, it made marrying one seem even more possible. *If I were also not real*, I remember thinking, *I could fight demons with them all day long.*"

We both had a laugh at that, because it was true. There was not a child in Tensha who had never dreamed of being a hero, before we had learned to be practical.

"Thank you for corroborating my story today," I told her.

"There are no altruists in the palace," she replied modestly. "I needed to clear Maro's name."

"Allies come rare enough in the Azalea House. Altruists or not, I am still grateful for them."

Her smile deepened as she turned onto another walkway, her lotus dress trailing behind her. Under the frosted balustrades, a pair of pine-feathered larks played in the snow. "Speaking of allies—how far have you gotten in your poem, now that you have Maro's testimony?"

I was glad she asked. "A lot further, actually. His journals have given me a far more complete picture of Terren, from his childhood all the way to when he was sixteen." The year the carp was poisoned, Taifong was found dead, and his mother had been killed—all in quick succession. The year the brothers met in the peach garden for the last time. "But my words are not magic yet. I am not sure what's missing."

I had poured myself into reading and composing over the past month, writing and rewriting each verse. On some days I swore I could feel *"the warmth of magic under my pen,"* as Maro had put it; on others, the ink remained cold and lifeless. Working on the heart-spirit poem had made me empathize, viscerally, with Maro's long struggle to write his first Blessing.

Especially since, like him, I had a deadline.

The emperor lay in bed, gravely ill. So ill that he had not even attended his own heir's wedding. His absence on Selection Day could have been explained away—the duties of the Inner Court were not in his domain but his empress's, after all—but the dragon throne sitting empty today, in front of thousands of distinguished guests, confirmed just how serious his condition was.

Once the emperor died, the coronation would follow immediately after. It was the one opportunity I would ever have to kill my prince. The heart-spirit poem *had* to be ready by then.

"Hmm." Silian had taken me to an empty courtyard, the sounds of the wedding far away. Not even a single guard stood watch here. Instead, there was only a huge ormosia tree, still green with leaves despite the winter. It was a small form of magic, the kind the palace had no shortage of.

She stood under it and looked up at its snow-laden branches, where clusters of shiny red beans peeked through a coat of white. "You know, Maro tried to write a heart-spirit poem for him too."

"He did?" I should not have been as surprised as I was.

"He had the same plan as you—to kill him during the Taming of the Dragon. But he never managed to finish his spell. Do you know why?"

I shook my head. My mind was suddenly spinning with the implications, and they were hardly encouraging. Maro was a gifted literomancer, and he really *had* loved Terren. If even he could not write the prince's heart-spirit poem, what hope did I have?

I had only learned to read a few months ago. I had only ever despised him.

"I do." Silian turned sharply to me. "My husband is prideful. He has always assumed he knew his brother well enough, from their shared boyhood, to compose his poem. But seasons pass, people change, and Terren is not sixteen anymore. I do not think Maro has spoken an earnest word to him since then. I think he failed because he wrote the poem for who Terren was before, and not who he is now."

A torturer, I thought reflexively. *There is no more to him than that.*

But at the same time, I knew with certainty that he was more than something that caused pain. I knew because while a hundred floating knives could hurt me just as badly, I could never hate those knives like I did Terren. I did not hate the hurt he inflicted. I hated the person he was.

"You think . . . I must speak earnest words to him." Even the idea of it made me feel drowned.

"More than that. I think you must get him to speak them back. I think you must wield a concubine's weapon."

"A concubine's weapon?"

"Wang Li became consort to an enemy king to end the invasion of her homeland. Empress Chena felled a corrupt dynasty and founded a new one with her paramour. Virtuous Beauty Tang manipulated two rebel generals into killing each other by claiming to love each of them. They have all used this weapon." She took a step closer to me, eyes catching the moonlight. "Here. I'll show you." And then she kissed me.

It was very gentle, not at all like the needle-precise techniques Lady Chara had taught us. It was more like a butterfly landing, a petal on the wind. Silian was sweet gao and lotus tea, she was moonlight and new snow. It did not feel like a weapon. But I tried to learn it anyway, and kissed her back.

Nobody had ever taught me how. I just did. Maybe it was only natural, an act every girl in Tensha was born knowing how to do.

35

BEYOND THE FARTHEST CREST

I think he's doing well, Maro wrote in his journals. *I hear from Master Ganji that his own studies are progressing quickly.*

Maro never knew how much his absence, after the incident at the emperor's birthday banquet, had affected his brother. He never knew how many years Terren kept waiting for him in the garden, how often he hid from everyone, how he had begun clinging to his old toys again.

I hope that one day, I can be as good as he is at literomancy.

I miss him lots.

His own studies were going well, too. He had written several more Blessings after the first one, which he had contributed to the House for paying off its debts. He had memorized several more classics under the tutelage of Master Ganji. He had grown closer to his training partners, Little Rain and Song Siming, and had even won a martial tournament with them in Cloud's Landing.

When he turned ten, he gained his 路/Lu seal. The whole palace feasted and celebrated for three days, but Maro barely had time to attend. The first afternoon, the emperor immediately summoned him to his strategy room. "There's not a moment to lose," he said, making a gesture encompassing the entire living map of Tensha, all its mountains and fertile valleys. "The nation has been waiting too long already." Then he sent him away.

For more than a year, Maro traveled on a harrowing schedule, working even harder than during his studies when he was younger. Day and night, he channeled the magic of Heaven through his sigil, spinning it into roads, canals, and passageways. He worked through rains and harsh winds; he worked through exhaustion, fevers, and headaches. He was re-lentless.

But saving Tensha was not the only reason he did his duty with such urgency.

I must recover my reputation, he wrote, over and over again. *I must, if I want the respect of my people.*

The rumors from when Maro was younger, that he had cheated at writing his first Blessing, had mostly died down—but there were still some who believed them. There were still some who would question his honor, his competency, his patriotism. Maro would prove them wrong once and for all.

His mother wrote to him while he was on the road. Lady Sky's scribes penned many letters on her behalf, bearing pleasing news from the capital, wishing him good fortune or reminding him to eat well. Sometimes, they were accompanied by a handmade scarf, a jar of plum juice, or little candies.

The letters her servants sent told a different story. The emperor was growing sicker by the day, they said, and in his absence, unrest had be-fallen the Inner Court. The concubines' fight for power had only grown more desperate, petty bickering escalating to active sabotage. All of the concubines were becoming frightened.

Come back, Your Highness, I beg of you, read a letter from Lady Sky's head attendant. *Your mother would never tell you, but she asks after you nearly every day.* One of her eunuchs sent him a letter, too. *Please, Your Highness, you must take her with you on your missions. She is no longer safe in the Inner Court, which has become full of scorpions.*

Those letters made Maro feel awful, but there was nothing he could do. Even if Father and Master Ganji allowed him to go home—and they would never—there would not be time. He had to keep working, because Tensha was waiting. For him, *blood* did not mean family but country.

And bringing his mother with him wasn't an option either. He could only imagine the shameful whispers that would come out of doing so. *Eleven years old already, heir to the nation, and he still needs his mama by his side.*

Maro continued his work. He built roads from the capital to Ru'en.

He built new bridges in Lie City to replace the ones destroyed in a fire. He created a diversion in the Aricine River, at Snake Bend, to prevent the annual flooding of several nearby towns.

Then an edict arrived, summoning him to the Eriet Mountains.

"*His Majesty calls the first son to the Tuyun Fortress*," read the messenger. "*He calls him to build the Salt Road.*"

The air is so thin in the mountains. Every breath feels like a gasp. The winds here bite no matter how thick my cloak!

I hate how cold, cold, cold it is.

A few hundred men had come with him—soldiers and strategists, doctors and cooks, advisors and longtime tutors. There was even an astronomer to interpret omens from Heaven.

Nestled between the two looming peaks of Long Peace and Fallen Sun, the Tuyun Fortress seemed almost small amidst the endless snow and dark rock. Inside its stone walls, it was not much warmer. Even when Maro was snuggled deep in his fur blankets, he found his nose was still freezing and runny.

I miss the palace. I miss Mother. I miss my friends. Is it unprincelike to admit so?

He dreamed of Mother at night. Of Song Siming and Little Rain, laughing as they wrestled him amidst golden trumpet flowers. He had not been home, or spoken with anyone his age, since the day he'd received his sigil.

Every night, after a long day of forging the Salt Road, he would spend the night in his room, freezing and alone. He was often too tired to read or study, but he would make the time to huddle by a lantern and write in his journal. Sometimes, he composed poems.

> *In the mountains, no sound but the wind;*
> *No leaf-stirrings or songs of the cuckoo.*
> *How long until I can talk again with a friend?*
> *Even some rain-patters at my window would do!*

About one month into the campaign, a delegation from the capital arrived.

Master Ganji came into Maro's bedchamber, where he was wolfing down a supper of lukewarm noodles and cured ham. "It is not good news," the tutor said, stone-faced. "Your brother is here with his mother and advisors. I can only assume the Maple Pavilion has come to sabotage our work."

Maro barely even heard the rest of the speech. He'd dropped his chopsticks at the word *brother*. A moment later, he was laughing as he ran outside, across the snowy interior of the fortress. "Terren! Terren!"

The second son was standing at the gates, his cloak shining red in the sunset. He was accompanied by his own traveling party of about a hundred men, but Maro didn't care about anyone else. He made straight for Terren and pulled him into a crushing hug. "I missed you. I missed you more than anything."

Well, it was not *exactly* true. During those lonely nights, it had not been Terren he dreamed of, but his friends he used to play with, Song Siming and Little Rain. But, Maro thought, maybe it was the playing that he missed. With anybody, it didn't matter. Those gentle days under the sway of magnolia trees, sparring between the trumpet flowers, chasing cats and bee-eaters—maybe it was those he missed most of all.

In any case, Maro had never been so happy to see anyone as he did his brother.

"Does that mean you'll play with me?" Terren blurted out.

He had grown in the time they'd been apart. His sigil was brighter, like bayberries newly ripening. He was still small for his age, but he no longer looked so tiny he could break at any moment. He had accumulated a few new scars too, around his collar and his ears, and Maro wondered how many trees he had fallen from over the years.

Maro drew back. "Maybe. We'll see. I don't know how much time I'll have, with the Salt Road needing to be built." When his brother began to look crestfallen, he took both his hands and said, "How about this? I'll ask Commander Remi if you can stay with me, if you'd like. My room is too big and too cold for one person."

Just like in the stories. Families eating at the same table, sleeping under the same roof.

Terren kept his eyes on the snow beneath his boots. In an almost whisper, he said, "I would like that."

He hadn't brought much with him from the capital. When the servants helped add a new cot to their room—along with a swathing abundance of warm furs—they brought in only one chest, mahogany and carved with tortoises. As soon as they were gone, Terren left the corner he had been hiding in and crawled over to it, his eyes shiny with excitement. "Maro, I brought something for you."

"Yeah?" Maro seated himself on the rug across from him.

"Mung bean cakes!" From the chest, Terren drew a smaller box full of the colorful flower-shaped desserts. They weren't flower-shaped anymore—mung bean cake was brittle, and the journey rough and long—but he arranged the pieces as neat as possible before presenting the box to Maro. "Since you've been far from home for so long, I thought you would want some treats from the palace."

Maro took them. They smelled a little stale. "Thanks! That's nice of you."

"Remember?" Terren said, when Maro didn't eat any. "When we were really little, I was never tall enough to reach the banquet tables. You would help steal them for me."

"Oh, yeah, I think so." It did sound like something he would have done, when he had been younger and more of a troublemaker.

"You don't like them?"

He gave the cakes back to Terren. "No, I do. But Doctor Shu says I can't have sugary foods. I've been getting headaches, see. He says that I need to eat healthy to support all the important work I've been doing for the nation." He gave his brother a playful jab on the shoulder. "And besides, you like them more. You should have them."

"Okay." He sounded disappointed. But he brightened again when he dug further into his chest. "I brought our swords, too. In case you want to spar. You always liked sparring." He fished out two oakwood swords, still crusted with mud and dried grass, and set them onto the fur rug as carefully as if they were made of porcelain.

"Oh, neat!" Maro picked one up and turned it around in his hand. It was tiny and far lighter than he was used to. "I haven't used a wooden sword in a long time. My friends and I have been fighting with steel for years now." He threw it in the air and caught it by its blade. "Master Len said my swordplay was really good, so he graduated me at the same time as Siming, even though he's a year older."

"Oh."

"Why didn't you bring your steel sword? You should have one by now, even if you've been progressing at a normal pace."

Terren blushed. He said nothing, just kept unpacking. He took out some nightclothes, some books, a second winter cloak. Then he drew out a stuffed tiger, a stone snail, and a wooden whistle in the shape of a bird.

"Hey, I remember those." Maro leaned in with interest as he watched him set the three of them on his bedside table. "They were your favorite toys when you were a little baby."

Terren had been in the middle of arranging them but froze.

"I had no idea you still played with them!"

He scooped them back into his arms, turning an even deeper shade of red. "I can keep them under my blankets. That way you don't have to see them."

Maro blinked. "Wait. I didn't mean it like that."

He began shoving them under his blankets anyway.

"Terren, your friends are welcome here."

He made all three of them disappear under heavy layers of fur, and then he began piling pillows on top to bury them further.

"*Hey.*" Maro ran over to him and caught his arm. "Didn't I say your friends are welcome here? Leave them out."

He kept staring at the bed, breathing fast.

"Please. I want to see Tiger's toothy smile too. And I want to hear Little Sparrow sing at night. And Niu Niu, with his beautiful crystal spirals—are you going to keep those to yourself, too?" Maro tore the blankets and pillows off the toys, took them gently into his arms, and arranged them back on the bedside table, the way Terren had it before. "Tomorrow, I'll tell Commander Remi I want a break in the morning." He had never asked for a break before, but somehow, it felt important to do so now. "I'll show you around the fortress. And your friends should come too." When Terren still said nothing, he made his voice conspiratorial, teasing. "Unless they're afraid of the cold?"

He finally looked up. "They are *not*. Well, maybe Little Sparrow is, just a bit. But she'll be fine as long as I keep her safe under my cloak."

Maro grinned. They readied themselves for bed after that, and then he tucked him into bed, climbed into his own, and blew out the last lantern. "Good night, Terren."

"Good night, Maro."

". . ."

". . ."

". . ."

". . ."

". . ."

". . ."

"Psst. Terren. You still awake?"

"Yeah."

"I've come up with the first half of a poem. Want to help me complete it?"

"Yeah!"

> *In the mountains, where there is only wind,*
> *A little sparrow flies far from her nest.*
> *A thousand li traveled, braving the cold,*
> *For one look beyond the farthest crest.*

36

A BURNING STAR

The next morning, Maro took Terren around the fortress. They bid hello to the cooks and the sentries, the men repairing its stone walls. They lit incense at the shrine dedicated to the Shouyuan Emperor and Prince Han, who had retaken the pass on the same campaign they had lost their lives on. Then they climbed up the guard tower, so that Terren and his friends could have a look at the Eriet Mountains' jagged peaks and stunning vistas, at all that unending snow under a red-scorched dawn.

Maro drew his brother under his cloak and pointed towards the horizon. "That peak over there—I've always thought it looked like the head of a dragonhorse."

Terren leaned his cheek on his brother's shoulder, breaths coming out in white puffs. "It does!"

"And that one next to it—that's the titan hero who rides it," Maro said, conspiratorially, the way they used to whisper secrets to each other from atop golden pagodas. "And look over there, across the snow, the big one. That's the demon king they're about to fight. Those craggy overhangs are its brows."

Terren's eyes widened. "It has horns, too! Scary ones, rising out from just behind its head. Ones he intends to use against the titan hero."

Maro laughed. "I see it! I see it!"

"Do you think he'll win? Can he really slay the demon king?"

"'Course he will. Evil always gets defeated in the end, doesn't it?"

They shared a quick lunch after that—of steamed wheat buns, mountain grouse, and white radish soup—and then Maro took him to the Salt Road.

"It's about a quarter of the way done," Maro declared, proud. They stood at the east side of the Long Peace Mountain, not far from the fortress, where a tunnel had opened up like a long, verdant dragon. Willow leaves and ivies draped lush over its stone walls. Flowers bloomed, impossibly, from amidst the ice and frozen stone—anemones and orchids and lots and lots of chrysanthemums.

"You did this?" Terren's eyes went wide with admiration, which made Maro feel like he was glowing.

"Of course! Who else?" He led the way inside.

Lanterns lit the path at regular intervals, the character for 鹽/Yan flickering gold on their round bellies. The first commodity to be traded once the tunnel was completed, the imperial edict had mentioned, was scheduled to be salt. It would be an homage to the early days of the Yongkai era, as well as an auspicious sign for the dynasty's future. Barrels of it stood waiting in the palace's storerooms for the Salt Road's grand opening, alongside shelves full of the emperor's Blessings, to make even more.

We await news of your success was the edict's concluding sentence. Meaning the nation was counting on Maro.

At the end of the tunnel, his support was already waiting for him. His tutors and Doctor Shu, a few trusted servants from the Dawn Pavilion, some high-ranking soldiers. Commander Remi frowned when he saw Terren there as well, but upon seeing how Maro clung to him, he reluctantly let him stay.

With his brother around, Maro was the happiest he had been in a long time. I could tell from the way the journal entries shifted in tone, the word choices becoming more joyful, the brushstrokes light like clouds.

Terren is my equal, he wrote, during one of his many moments of sentimentality. *My tutors, my elders, Mother, Father—I must look up to them. Everyone else must look up to me. Even Little Rain and Siming call me "Your Highness"!*

But my brother, with a sigil like mine—he is my only equal.

For the next few months, Terren went with him to the tunnel as Maro carved through the mountain, bit by harrowing bit. Terren was not there every day—sometimes he had to study with his own tutors, or perform filial duties for his mother, Lady Autumn—but he went whenever he could. Maro was far too focused on his own work to engage in conversation, but just knowing Terren was by his side, reading a book or practicing calligraphy, made everything better. Even his headaches became easier to ignore.

He was reminded of peach trees and sunlit afternoons.

After a long day of using his magic, Maro was usually too tired to play. Sometimes he was even too tired to eat dinner and went directly to bed. Those days, Terren was the one to tuck his older brother into bed and blow out the last lantern. "Good night, Maro."

"Good night, Terren."

I should have known something was wrong. My headaches have always felt different than the ones I got before.

The fifth month working on the Salt Road, Maro was in the tunnel, channeling his magic as usual, when yet another headache began. But this time, when he tried to ignore it, it didn't go away. It grew. It grew and grew, and soon it hurt so bad that it felt like somebody was taking an ax to the inside of his skull. His vision blurred. He fell to his knees, fighting for breath.

When he woke again, he was in his bed and it was dark.

". . . overuse of magic . . ."

". . . he's still young. It's still reversible . . ."

He pushed himself up to a sitting position and blinked open his eyes. Lanterns lit up the faces of Doctor Shu and Master Ganji, talking in hushed voices not far from his bed.

"Maro," said Doctor Shu, when he noticed he was awake. He placed a bowl of herbal medicine into his hands. "Drink this while we talk."

It tasted absolutely awful. It was even more bitter than the stuff Mother used to make him drink when he had a cold.

"You have always been a bright and discerning boy," said Doctor Shu. "I can speak to you as a child and mince words, but I would rather speak to you like an adult and peer. Can you handle it?"

His tone was frightening. Maro felt his pulse race, but he forced himself to nod anyway.

"Today confirms something I have suspected for a long time: that your capacity for magic is not as high as most seal-bearing sons. It has not even been two years since you've received your sigil, and you are already suffering from Heavenly Fatigue." He heaved a sigh. "Then again, most princes rarely use their magic with such intensity, and at such a young age."

Worthless.

That was the only conclusion Maro could draw from the doctor's words. First, he had to lag behind his younger brother at literomancy. Now, it turned out that his magic was weak. How was he supposed to save Tensha when he was so much *worse* than what they needed him to be?

"Okay," he said.

"You know about the Fatigue, I presume. You have seen your father go through it."

"Uh-huh." It was hard to keep his voice steady. He was trying very, very hard to keep being an adult and a peer, but he just wanted to throw something and scream.

"Well, your case will be even worse. The trajectory of your decline is far faster. You are a burning star, Maro. Brilliant, but fleeting."

In other words, *worthless*.

"But the good news is that, at your current stage, recovery is almost guaranteed. If you stop using your magic at once and return to the capital, and rest for a few years, all the damage will become undone. You will be as healthy as the day you received your seal. After you inherit the Crown from your father, your magic will be amplified, and you will find that everything will become much easier. It is not too late to wait until then to accomplish things."

Maro stared at him.

"Do you understand?"

"The Salt Road. I need to finish it." It was the *doctor* who didn't understand. Maro had been in the mountains for five months already, and at the rate he was going, he only needed about two more. "The sooner it's done, the sooner we can control trade with the West again and replenish our depleted treasury. Tensha is a nation holding its breath. We cannot wait to save it, in the same way we cannot wait to save a drowning child."

The doctor and Master Ganji exchanged glances.

"And what about the missions that come after?" Maro pressed. "Father has already planned the next few years. We need to widen the Grand Canal. We need to add new mountain roads to make Ji Province more defensible. We need to rebuild the harbor in Tian City, to replace the ones our enemies destroyed." The more he spoke, the more panicked his voice became. "Everything is urgent. The nation needs me. I can't hide in the capital like a coward."

"Maro, let me put it more simply: you are dying."

"*Tensha* is dying!" he screamed.

So everyone kept telling him, from his first breath, his first words. So his father kept reminding him, over and over again. *Pitiful. We are even smaller than we were during the Sun Dynasty.* So he had seen for himself, in all the reports he'd read about the famine-stricken cities, the raids near the borders, the people impoverished. It was one of the first truths he'd ever known.

The room echoed with his outburst. In the silence that followed, Maro heard only his own breathing, very fast.

Then Master Ganji laughed. It was chopped and without humor. "I told you, Doctor Shu. I told you the boy would side with me."

Rare emotion broke through the doctor's mask of gravity. When he spoke next, his voice even wavered a little. "Maro's stubbornness I can at least sympathize with. But yours, Master Ganji, is reprehensible."

"These years are more important than ever, and you know why. The emperor does not have long to live, but he still has time to change his mind about his heir. If Maro lacks accomplishments during these critical years—"

"You would risk his life?" Doctor Shu snapped. "Just so you can rise with him in status?"

"I am thinking of him, not me." Master Ganji was completely calm. "Besides, I am not convinced it is as bad as you say. Maro is tenacious. When he was younger, he used to study even through his worst fevers. Minor ailments and little pains do not bother him."

"Little pains," Doctor Shu echoed, disgusted. "Since you find yourself qualified to make diagnoses, then I do not know what you need *me* for." He turned to leave, but Master Ganji blocked his exit.

"Remember my instructions earlier." The tutor's voice was full of menace, and Maro wondered what he had threatened the doctor with. "You will tell nobody the true nature of his illness. You will tell them he's sick because he's not sleeping well, or because he's skipping dinners, or because he's working long days—but you will not mention the words *Heavenly Fatigue*."

"I do not answer to you." Doctor Shu looked past Master Ganji to Maro. "I answer to my prince and future emperor."

Maro understood at once, and rose from his bed. He was only in his sleeping robes, and still exhausted, but he tried to put as much dignity in his voice as he could. "Doctor Shu, it is my will that you do as my tutor says. Tell nobody the truth of my condition, and dispel any rumors as they come."

The doctor's eyes lingered on him a long time, but at last he gave a resigned sigh. "If that is your will, my prince, then I will follow it. But know that you are running straight for a cliff's edge. You may find yourself falling suddenly, fatally, without warning."

"I understand, Doctor."

"Monitor your symptoms closely. If you faint again, or if there is blood-cough, inform me at once. That will tell us you are close to the edge."

"I understand, Doctor."

The moment the doctor left with Master Ganji, and the door had closed behind them, Maro threw himself face-down onto his cot. He pounded both fists into the bed, so hard that it sent Niu Niu's shell rattling on the bedside table. "Worthless," he screamed into the blankets. "Why am I like this? Why can't I be better? Why why *why?*"

"Maro."

He whipped his head to where the timid voice came from. Cold horror seeped into his chest when he saw his brother crawl out from under his own cot, beneath a swath of fur blankets that had been hiding him.

"You were spying on me."

"No." Terren was crying. He must have been doing so for a long time, judging by how red his eyes were. "I stayed because I wanted to make sure you were okay."

Horror turned to fury. *"Why wouldn't I be?"*

He flinched. "Because the grown-ups can't be trusted. I didn't want them in a room with you while you were sleeping and helpless."

Maro wanted to pick him up and throw him against the wall. Terren was still small enough that he bet he could.

He didn't. Instead, he swallowed a painful lump in his throat as he let his brother climb onto the bed beside him. A moment later, little arms wrapped around him, warm and unconditional. "Family is for keeping each other safe," Terren said, barely a whisper, and a moment later Maro was crying himself. Hot, shameful tears came gushing out, and even when he tried to hold them back, they kept coming anyway.

They stayed holding on to each other for a long time. Then Maro said, through his sniffles, "Promise me. Promise you won't tell anyone."

"I promise."

He cried even harder. "I'm still mad at you."

"I'm sorry."

"Say it . . ." He could barely choke out the words through his tears. "Say it three times and I'll forgive you."

"I'm sorry. I'm sorry. I'm sorry."

37

A VILLAGE GIRL'S DREAM

When I arrived back at the wedding banquet, Hesin came to tell me Terren had already retired for the night. "His Highness calls you join him in his wedding chamber."

"Did he?" I asked.

Hesin seemed surprised. "Lady Yin?"

"Did he really ask for me?" I was thinking of every terrifying night in the palace he had supposedly called me to his bedside. Every night he had used instead to hurt me, to keep me as far from him as possible.

Hesin did not look my direction as he began leading me down several side hallways, each adorned with bronze lion statues and silk tapestries. "There are certain appearances that need to be kept up in the palace, as you surely have noticed. Duties that need to be upheld as decreed by Heaven and the moon. Our prince has many enemies who watch him, looking for an opening, the first sign of weakness. And that includes his Inner Court."

Any sympathy he may have had for me once was gone. He gestured me coldly into one of the back rooms, where he left me as summarily as the first night, chest tight and heart heavy.

The wedding chamber was decorated with red-tasseled curtains, pillars full of auspicious poetry, and countless joy lanterns. Azalea petals were strewn all over the floor. A generous helping of incense hung as dense as syrup in the air—burnt rose and jujube and cinnamon.

Passionate, explosive love, the apothecary's voice echoed. *The sparks of which are sure to ignite Heaven's magic.*

There was one bed at the very back, hidden behind another thick layer of curtains. I crept towards it like a mouse navigating a viper's den. Except I was not a mouse, not really. More like a hawk, I thought, or something else that could both be hurt by vipers but also hunt them.

Speaking with Silian had changed me. Before, I might have been more frightened, as frightened as I had been the day I was selected. I might have prayed that he would be asleep, so that I could be safe for one more night.

Now, I had the concubine's weapon.

All this time, I hadn't really bothered getting closer to Terren himself, having already decided long ago he was not really a person but something that doled out pain, the way a fire was made of nothing real but still seared whatever it touched. But Silian was right. I could not write his poem without looking into the heart of the fire, even if doing so meant getting burned.

I drew a deep breath, then peeled apart the curtains with a trembling hand.

Terren was somewhere between sleep and wakefulness. He was lying in his bed, face-up. His eyes were closed, but the way his ward swirled told me he was still conscious. There was a Liang Dynasty scroll tucked under one arm, which I supposed he'd been trying to read, containing poems about mountains and rivers. But he must have had too much wine to have focused for long. By the pillow next to him was another jar of it, half-empty.

The instant I made my presence known, he was going to torture me. I was sure of it.

But I had to finish the poem.

I sucked in a deep breath and made myself brave, just like I'd done before the empress and the Great Clans earlier that day. It was the hardest thing I had ever made myself do—even worse than the night I'd had to use the bamboo on myself—but I knelt before the bed and said, softly, "Terren."

His given name, not his title. The way a wife would address her husband. Just the dangerous sound of it made my stomach knot with terror.

His eyes fluttered open. His sigil flashed, and my body instinctively tensed. But there must have been no blades in the room, because none flew my way. He opened his hand and a new, crude one began to form within his palm, in a nest of sprouting vines and blooming lilies.

"Wait!" I said, panicking. "If you kill me, you'll never know the truth! Of why I'd been going to the West Palace."

The appeal to his curiosity must have worked, because while he finished making his knife, he did not cut me with it. Instead, he pushed himself up, with difficulty, to face me. "I imagine it is something inane. But tell me anyway."

"I will." That thin thread of curiosity was the only thing keeping my blood inside my skin. I had to stretch the moment out as long as possible. "But first, I have something to say. Now that we are wed, I wish for a fresh beginning. I . . . wish for us to forget the path we have taken so far and forge a new one, together."

His expression darkened, his sigil flaring with mounting anger.

It took all I had to wring the fear from my voice. "I have made a vow today. *For each other, care.* You are my husband now, so I wish to care for you. I wish to . . ."

Out of the corner of my eye, I saw that he'd gripped his knife so hard his knuckles turned white.

I hurried to change my approach. "In the villages, do you know what every little girl dreams of?" It was hard to breathe, let alone speak. "It is different than in the cities or in the palace. We do not dream of power. We do not dream of ambition. We dream of marriage."

That was not true. We dreamed that the constant ache of hunger in our bellies would vanish. We dreamed of having enough food on the table so that our mothers did not have to give their share to our fathers, our fathers to our younger siblings. We dreamed that one day we, like our brothers, could become anything.

Marriage was only a means.

"Every village girl wishes to stand at her husband's side, supporting him in his every endeavor. So now that we are forever bound, let me stand at yours. Even if said endeavor is as large as dynasties." *Earnest words,* Silian had said. *You must get him to speak them.* "Terren, now that you have an empress, you need not take on the burden of the Crown alone."

He laughed, ugly and terrible. "*Forever* is an interesting choice of word, seeing as I can kill you at any moment."

"It may not be forever for you, but it is for me. You may have many concubines in your Inner Court, as many as you please, but I only get one husband. One person to care for. One person to"—I had to bite out the word through my teeth—"*love.*"

He stared at me a long time. I could see him working to figure me out, why I was debasing myself so in front of someone who had tortured me. I knew he knew I was not being truthful, but I also knew he couldn't see through me completely. If he understood me wholly, he would have cut me like he'd cut up everything else and been done with it.

He was brilliant, I thought, but he was the wrong kind of brilliant.

He might know poetry and words, but that was not the same as knowing the hearts of people. Especially people like me, who could never make themselves heard in books. Why bother to know our hearts when it was far easier to make us afraid?

I supposed that was why he needed Hesin.

"This past year," I said quietly, "I've kept your secret, haven't I? I have always lied for you against Sun Jia and the other concubines. The empress keeps prying and threatening me, but still I have not told her a thing. And don't you remember in summer, when the rumors came? I saved us from the doctors then."

It was obvious now why he'd chosen me as his wife, the one person he could call upon exclusively without raising eyebrows. He hadn't wanted the position to fall to Sun Jia, or Kang Rho, or anyone else from a distinguished family, been forced to summon *them* according to the whims of the moon.

He couldn't threaten anyone else to keep their mouths shut about his condition—not without risking retaliation from a Great Clan—but me, he could torture however he wished.

And besides, with my low status, nobody would believe me even if I did tell.

"None of the things you mention were for my benefit." His voice dripped with disdain. "Each time, you were only trying to save yourself."

"Maybe so, but they still prove that I am capable. Capable of helping you, defending you. Fighting for you. And I will continue to do so from now on, even if I don't need to save myself, because you are my husband and I have made a pledge."

He started to reply but swayed forward suddenly, unsteadily. His hand flew to his temple as he grimaced. "Ahh . . ."

"Terren." I made my voice gentle. "Do you need me to get you something to eat?"

He shook his head, though there was a sheen of sweat on his face.

"Some tea might help." I thought of all the drunk men I'd seen in Guishan late at night, in the gambling houses, their wives coming with ginger tea and angry words to drag them home.

"No. I only need . . ." He looked around, found his half-empty jar of wine, and downed the rest of it in one long, disgusting gulp. Then he sank heavily onto his pillow and closed his eyes.

I went to get him the tea anyway. I would have prayed that the wine would kill him while I was gone, except I was pretty sure the Aricine Ward protected him from that too.

By the time I was back, he still hadn't moved. I set the still-steaming pot on the bedside table and said, "Try to have some when you have the chance. It will help you feel better in the morning. I also got some mung bean cakes as well, to soak up the wine."

"Wei," he murmured. His eyes were still closed, his knife still on the bed next to him, folded in lilies and vines.

I sat close to him. "What is it, my prince?"

"I am beginning to suspect," he said, in barely a whisper, "that you are not afraid enough of me."

His sigil glowed without warning. From its bed of flowers, the knife shot up and plunged itself into my chest.

38

RED

At first I felt nothing. I only saw the knife going into my body, like looking at a water-painting. The bloodstain on my chest grew like pomegranate blossoms, as red as everything else in the room—the curtains, the lucky lanterns, the azalea petals scattered across the bed and carpet.

Then the pain did come, and it came all at once and everywhere.

For a while I just lay there, gasping for breath. Red was fading to black. I tried to grasp at my throat, to open it and let more air in, but it wasn't working. Then my arms became tired, and I let them drop onto the sheets. There was nothing to do but stare at the ceiling, muraled with fearsome dragons, watching my vision darken. I did not cry, but only because I was too weak to do anything at all.

Wei, think.

It was hard, through the agony and the slow haze of my mind, but I forced myself to do it, *think*.

The wound in me had been made by a blade. I knew mending spells, for blades.

In the corner of my eye, I could see the movements of Terren's ward slowing. He was falling into a wine sleep. He would not notice if I traced a Dao mending spell on the ground, closed my wound, and saved myself.

But then what? I closed my eyes, imagining it. Terren would find out I was literate. He would kill me anyway.

I could mend myself and then run, just like Pima had. I could hide in the storerooms until I was well, and then find my way to the capital. I could keep running from Terren and his inevitable search armies—because he was definitely vindictive enough to go after me—and hope I made my way to Lu'an in time to warn my family, because he would definitely go after my relations too.

That would be unspeakably shameful.

And not only because I would have to tell my family I ran. I knew, by now, that Ma loved me enough to not want me hurt or killed. Besides, I was a girl; unlike Pima, I could be forgiven for trying to save myself.

No, this shame was a whole new kind of shame. It was the shame of knowing I had once been in the position to kill Terren and save the nation from a tyrant ruler. To change things, really change things, the way girls in villages only dreamed of—and knowing I had *run* from it.

I could not mend myself. I could not run away.

Despite the agony, the resistance in every muscle, I pushed myself up. My head felt like it was floating. I tore one of the curtains from its post and wrapped it around my chest, biting my lip to stop from crying out. Though it probably would have been fine even if I did scream; likely no servant would have come to check on me either way, assuming it was a part of the childmaking act.

I bound the silk as tight around me as I could, around the knife, and hoped it was enough to slow the bleeding. Then I leaned back against the bedpost and tried to focus on staying awake. I had only to make it until morning. Terren would mend me then. I knew he would.

I knew because I had not died immediately. Even drunk, he was still precise with his magic. He'd doled out his torture to Sima Zhen so carefully, during his selection in the Hall of Divine Harmony, avoiding her vital organs until the last possible moment to prolong her suffering; she had died only a few arm's widths from the gate. Terren could have sent that knife directly into my heart, but he didn't.

I knew because I still hadn't told him what I had been doing in the West Palace. If what I knew of him was correct, he was curious enough that he would not let me die before I did.

My mouth was full of the copper taste of blood, and it was gagging me. It was getting hard to breathe again.

But dying would not be so bad, a distant part of me thought.

The whispers of the Ancestors below—I could hear them now—were gentle. If I went to them, I was sure I would be welcomed warmly.

Larkspur was there. I could see her on the dawn hill, playing among the larches and wild poppies. My two older brothers were there as well—I could hear their voices—as were the ones who died after them, a boy and a girl, all laughing as they called after me—*Sister! Come join us!* Grandma and Grandpa, and the other elders in our village who came before us, they were all there too, smiles tugging their cheeks into a sunburst of wrinkles.

Dying would not be so bad. Instead of being among wicked princes, inside a palace full of those who wanted me dead, I would be *there*, among the mists, not scared. I could braid Larkspur's hair and chase her through the rice paddies for as long as I wished, and then I would be reborn again, in another place and another time, better ones.

But I could not, of course.

I could not die, because if I did, who would stop Terren from taking the Crown?

There were people counting on me now. The servants in the Cypress Pavilion, who were afraid but could not leave. Silian, who believed in me. Other people in Tensha who didn't even know my name.

And my family. My parents and my brother, and everyone in Lu'an who had given me a piece of their hope to put in my offering basket. In the beginning I had come to save them from the famine. Now I was going to save them from a wicked emperor as well.

All night, I refused the call of the Ancestors, over and over again.

When dawn came, it came slow and tired. I became dimly aware of Terren's blurry shadow over me, of a vague warmth around my chest. I smelled lilies. Then the knife became dislodged from my ribs and fell onto the bed, along with the blood-soaked curtain, and I knew he must have mended me.

"Get up," he said. "It is time to go on our wedding retreat."

I did not have the strength to move.

"*Get up*," he said again. Louder, angrier, more panicked.

I supposed I knew the reason for his panic. Terren might delight in hurting people, but he was strategic about it. He might be willing to torture a palace servant or a commoner whenever he wished, but he rarely harmed anyone of higher status without an excuse.

He would not be able to find an excuse this time. He could have killed me any other day and perhaps explained it away, but stabbing his bride half to death at his wedding? On a day sacred to both Heaven and the Ancestors? That was too much of an ill omen, even for a prince known to be cruel. If word got out, I had no doubt that superstition would turn almost all of Tensha against his leadership. Even a ruler as powerful as Terren could not easily deal with a nation in revolt.

He was pacing the room now, pulling at his hair. He seemed to know he'd made a grave mistake, one he would never have made while sober.

"Terren," I said, hoarse. "Calm down. Listen to me."

He stilled, though he was breathing fast.

"Fetch some servants. Tell them I've had too much to drink and need to be carried to our retreat. If anyone asks later, I will corroborate it." It hurt terribly just to speak. "That empty wine jar on the bed, put it beside me so it looks like I'm the one who finished it. Put my phoenix shawl on me so they will not see the knife's tear in my gown. Light some incense to cover up the smell of blood."

He was lucky that the room was already so red. The bloodstains were not visible unless you looked closely, and I knew Hesin would be able to deal with them.

What Terren did in the end, I never found out, since I fell unconscious not long afterwards.

When I woke up next, I was in the mountains, in the temple where we would spend our wedding retreat in only each other's company.

39

FLEETING FOOTPRINTS, LASTING CARVINGS

After the doctor's diagnosis, Maro started going to the tunnel with only Master Ganji and nobody else. The fewer witnesses, they reasoned, the less of a chance somebody would figure out the truth behind his illness.

It had been easy to cover up. Since Maro was much younger than the age Heavenly Fatigue usually struck, and he didn't have the more telling symptoms of confusion, nausea, or blood-cough, Doctor Shu's explanation for why he'd fainted in the tunnel—"the prince has simply overworked himself"—was accepted without question.

After all, he *was* overworking himself.

He was so tired that he hardly had the energy to keep up with his daily journal. His entries grew sparser. Some he had to fill in afterwards. Others were written by Terren; I recognized the calligraphy.

I imagined the way Maro must have lain in bed at night, eyes closed and exhausted, murmuring instructions to his brother in the room they shared by lanternlight.

"Make sure to note that we had fresh persimmons for supper," he might have said, one of the days. "That Governor Tun had sent them from Milong Province as a gift to us." Or on another, "Write down that I've hit a stretch of really hard rock. That I don't think I'll make much progress for a while."

Very rarely, when he had energy to spare, he would ask Terren to compose poetry with him. "Give me a line. I want to play 'dueling couplets.'"

"Okay."

"It better be good."

"Okay!"

It is easy to make fleeting footprints in the snow;
It is hard to make lasting marks in the stone.
Shall I dance ten thousand steps, unwitnessed?
Shall I make one carving, forever known?

Just like Hesin had said, Terren gained his magic while in the mountains, at the age of nine. It happened while Maro was at the tunnel. When he returned with Master Ganji that evening, he found the entire fortress in celebration.

Rice wine was being passed around like stories; bone flute music swirled in the air like snow. Colorful lanterns bearing the 刀/Dao sigil lit up ice and stone, and banners carrying the red azalea flapped defiantly against mountain winds. The entire imperial delegation of hundreds was laughing, feasting, or drinking.

And, at the center of it all, Terren.

Master Ganji's face had turned a dark mask of anger, but Maro could hardly contain his excitement. He even forgot his exhaustion as he dashed straight for his brother, nearly bowling him over with a hug. "Terren! I can't believe it! Why didn't you tell me earlier?"

It was the eunuch An Sui, one of Terren's advisors, who answered for him. "We did send someone to the Salt Road, but the guards turned us away. They said you told them not to disturb you for any reason, however important."

Maro laughed sheepishly. "Well, that's true." He then turned to his brother. "How do you feel? Do you like your new power?"

Terren started to reply, but his attention was promptly pulled away by General Wu. "Your Highness." The broad man fell to one knee before the second prince. "Heaven has been kind to us, that an Azalea son's power should be the exact one we need most. Please accept my pledge of loyalty." Behind him was a large crowd of military men, all waiting for a turn to speak with the dynasty's newest seal-bearer.

Maro was too tired to stay long. "I'll see you tonight," he told Terren, though he wasn't sure if his brother had heard. Then he pulled the hood of his cloak up and started back in the direction of his bedchamber. He wove through the bonfires, through clusters of men singing, celebrating, and reciting poems. They were roasting lamb skewers and frying savory pancakes over the fire, and the smoky smell of them made him sick. He had very little appetite these days.

Pieces of their conversation rose above the fire's crackle. "With the second son's power, will we finally vanquish the Lian?"

"At long last, we can take back the rebel provinces."

"Perhaps our armies will be as fearsome as in the days of the Shouyuan Emperor."

And then, far more insidiously: "His power is better than his older brother's."

Maro couldn't help but overhear the whispers. They were everywhere.

"The Yongkai Emperor values conquest and military achievement. Yet the crown prince has not made a dent in recapturing lost territory."

"What use is building roads when we have enemies everywhere?"

"Doesn't the first son seem a little weak? All he does when he returns to the fortress is sleep." A bout of mocking laughter.

Maro ducked his head as he sped up his walk. He was dimly aware that he could have them beheaded for the way they spoke—he was too young to issue the command himself, though he could tell Commander Remi or someone else with the authority. But what would that accomplish?

Everyone would think even less of him. *A prince who can't take criticism,* they would say, only more in private. *He is as despotic as he is worthless.*

And besides, he didn't want to kill anyone. Especially when they were right.

He crawled into his bed and lay there for a long time. He was tired enough that he just wanted to go to sleep, but the day was a momentous one. So eventually, despite the stone-heaviness in every limb and the ringing pain in his skull, Maro forced himself to sit at his desk and write in his journal.

He was still awake when Terren entered with a tray of food—steaming buns, cumin lamb skewers, and hot water that smelled vaguely of honey. "Master Len said you haven't eaten anything all night."

Maro kept his eyes on his journal. "Go away. I don't want to see you."

Terren put the tray on the desk, beside Little Sparrow, and gave him one of his kitten hugs. "You know, I'm really happy. About my sigil."

"Good for you."

"Because I can protect you now. Instead of always the other way around."

"I don't need protection."

"Family is for keeping each other safe."

"We're not a real family."

"And one day, when you're better, we can spar again."

"I'm not going to get better."

"You won't have to be mad at me this time, 'cause I'll play the game right."

"I'll always be mad at you."

"Maybe I'll even learn to use a steel sword!"

"Go away."

"I love you, Maro."

"Go away."

Little by little, the Salt Road crawled towards completion—but it was no longer what was top of everyone's mind. Instead, they were all speculating on what missions Terren would be sent on once a response finally came from the capital.

"I told you," Master Ganji said bitterly. "The Maple Pavilion has come to sabotage us. I did not think there could be anything that would overshadow the Salt Road, yet here we are. We should never have let that usurper and his advisors stay."

Maro kept his head down and worked silently. Whether there was fanfare around it or not, the Salt Road still needed to be built. The nation still needed his magic.

On the day the delegation from the palace finally did arrive, both brothers—along with the entire fortress—waited eagerly by the gate. It was near sunset, but heavy clouds had come to cover the mountains, and instead of a spectrum of brilliant colors there was only gray. The imperial messenger gave updates on shifts within the Great Clans, promotions and demotions of important officials, new memorials the emperor had stamped.

Then, an edict for Terren.

It was written in the pen of the emperor himself, detailing the second son's next mission. Terren was allowed to remain at Fallen Sun Pass until the completion of the Salt Road—I sensed that Hesin had done some persuasion work behind the scenes—but after that, he was to immediately ride to the occupied district of Tieza, in the north. It was as everyone had speculated: his first campaign would be against the Lian.

An army of seven thousand men would meet him there, along with martial artists from the Fog Enclaves and one of Tensha's best living generals, Cao Myn, the Evening Tide. It was going to be one of the most monumental campaigns since the Shouyuan era.

The entire fortress was abuzz with excitement at the news. Soldiers and military men were jostling each other to approach Terren or his advisors, asking if they would bring them on the mission. There had been no greater source of shame for Tensha in recent years than having lost Tieza-North; retaking it would be a huge step towards restoring the dynasty's glory. And everyone wanted a piece of it.

"This is our chance," Maro overheard one of Terren's tutors whispering to Lady Autumn. "If he is successful, he will not escape the notice of the emperor."

"He is already in the emperor's notice," she replied, a distant smile on her face. "The Dao sigil speaks louder than deeds."

"Even so," the eunuch An Sui whispered, "do you think it will be enough to tip the scales? Perhaps we need something more . . ." They went off to speak in private.

Maro pretended not to hear anything. He stood silently by the gates while everyone kept praising his brother, too tired and in pain to care. It was a feat to even keep his eyes open.

There turned out to be a message for him, too.

While everybody was still celebrating about Tieza, the herald placed a scroll in his hand. It bore the imperial dragon seal. Father's seal. Despite his overwhelming exhaustion, Maro managed to summon up at least a small tinge of excitement as he peeled off the seal and unrolled the letter.

After he read it, he stared at the paper for a long, long time.

Lady Sky, Second-Rank Concubine and Mother of the First Son, has died of an accident.

That was the entirety of it.

There was no expression of sympathy, no condolences, no acknowledgment of her long service in the Inner Court. No gratitude for raising a prince. Maro tucked the scroll away in his cloak, feeling like he was in a dream.

"... you can come with me," someone was saying to him. It was Terren, bouncing with excitement. "I'll make swords for the army, and you can make roads for them to march on. We can work together, take on the north side by side! What do you say?"

Maro blinked at him.

"Come with me to Tieza," Terren said again, throwing his arms around Maro's waist. "If we talk to Father together, I bet we can convince him. And once we're done with my campaign, I'll go with you on yours! We won't ever have to be apart again. We'll travel the country together, eat all the best noodles, play 'dueling couplets' a hundred times a day—"

"Let go of me," Maro said. He left his bewildered brother behind and walked, very calmly, back to his room.

That night, after everyone else was asleep, he left the fortress.

He went all the way to the end of the tunnel, pressed his hands to the leaf-covered wall, and started channeling his power. Stones rumbled and loosened, persuaded by Heaven's magic. Chrysanthemums bloomed into life from within nests of orange sparks.

If only he had worked faster, tried harder, been better, he could have completed this sorry road sooner. If he had completed it sooner, he could have gone back to the capital to see Mother. Maybe he could have stopped her from dying. And even if he hadn't, at least he would have accomplished something while she was still alive.

She would have known for certain he wasn't worthless.

He put his hand to the wall and kept channeling, harder than he ever dared before. Hot magic from Heaven mixed with his blood and pulsed straight into the mountain.

Maybe he could finish the tunnel early. That would be sure to make Father notice. And maybe everyone else would notice too, and see that he wasn't weak after all.

The stones kept rumbling, breaking apart, flowers bursting out of cracks in the ice. Their petals smelled like blood.

If he finished the tunnel early, he could go on his next missions early.

Widening the Grand Canal. Building roads to Ji Province. Rebuilding the harbor in Tian City. The nation needed him.

More stones breaking, more flowers, more blood.

His sigil burned hot like a fire. The nation needed him so desperately, yet he kept letting Father and everyone else down, just like he had been doing since always.

Why are you so worthless, Maro?

Why are you so worthless?

Why . . .

Maro.

Maro, wake up.

Maro, please wake up.

He blinked open his eyes and found that his vision was blurred. There was something wet all over his face. Blood. He could tell by the way it tasted in his mouth, copper and salt. He coughed and some more of it burbled out.

Someone was bawling. Terren. Maro had always hated how much of a crybaby he was.

The younger boy was kneeling beside him and dabbing at his mouth with a cloth. "You're finally awake," he said between sobs. "I didn't want to leave you until you were. Stay here, okay? I'm going to get Doctor Shu."

Maro's hand darted out and caught his arm. "You're not going anywhere."

If word got out about the Heavenly Fatigue, they would send Maro home. *Let him recover until he has the Crown,* they'd say, not knowing how much time mattered. Not knowing how badly Tensha was dying, how critical these years were.

Not knowing that if he went home, he might not even receive the Crown in the first place. Nobody wanted a weak and bedridden prince to inherit the dynasty. They wanted someone powerful and strong.

"But . . ." Terren whispered. "Doctor Shu said . . . he said you were running towards a cliff—"

"You will tell nobody about this. Do you understand?"

"But—"

"*Do you understand.*"

He flinched. "I'm sorry. Please don't be mad."

"What time is it?"

"I . . . I don't know. It's still night. Everyone's asleep."

"Good. There's still time to keep working." Maro wiped his mouth with a sleeve and stood. When he discovered that Terren's cloak was draped over him, he scrunched it up and threw it onto the moss. Then he took two steps towards the end of the tunnel.

"Wait, *Maro*." Terren clung to his leg to stop him from moving, but Maro shook him off easily. "Maro, please, stop." He tried again, this time clamping his arms across his waist, but he was littler—he had always been littler—and Maro flung him off like an irritating bug. He reached the wall, pressed his hand to the cold stone, and channeled.

"Stop it!" Terren screamed. He yanked at Maro's sleeve with just enough force that his hands left the wall, cutting off the flow of magic. "Please. Stop it. *Stop it*."

Maro imagined himself strangling him. Imagined his hands closing around that little throat, cutting off all that sniveling and screaming.

He didn't. Instead, he said, "I am the rightful heir, Terren. I do what I please."

"But . . ." He was crying so hard he could barely speak. "But I'm scared you're going to die."

Maro looked down at him with disgust. "Our father has done so much for this country, even in his sickness. The Shouyuan Emperor and Prince Han have lost their lives in these very mountains, in the campaign that won us the Fallen Sun Pass. You were born second, so you never learned the meaning of duty. You never learned that there is no glory without sacrifice. There is no greatness without suffering."

He turned back towards the stone and continued his work on the Salt Road. This time, Terren didn't stop him.

When he woke the next morning, everyone was standing around his bed.

Maro sat up, rigid with horror. Commander Remi, Master Len, Master Ganji, his advisors from the Dawn Pavilion—they were all there, their faces solemn in the stark morning sun. Behind them, wearing the gravest expression of them all, was Doctor Shu.

"Your doctor has informed us of your condition," Commander Remi said. He spoke very gently, as if Maro wasn't already eleven but a little baby. "We have already sent a messenger to the capital, announcing your intent to return. You will have the day to pack up your belongings, and then you will go home."

The horror, sheer and cold, clawed its way into every vein and every crevice in Maro's body. He couldn't even speak.

"At least let him finish the Salt Road," Master Ganji said, his voice iron. "There is not much of it left. The credit for building it must go entirely to the first son."

"No. We cannot take that risk. The crown prince is too important for us to lose."

"But Commander—"

"A crew will remain behind to excavate the rest of the tunnel. It will not be as permanent or as safe as what our prince would make, but it will do for now. After his recovery, he can return to finish it."

"*Commander.*" Master Ganji's fists shook with rage. "You are surely aware of the damage it'll do to our prince's already-tarnished reputation. They'll say he can't even complete his most important mission without help—*just like his first Blessing.*" He spun to look at Doctor Shu. "Tell them. Tell them he is capable of doing it!"

The doctor didn't even look at Master Ganji. Instead, he addressed everyone else around him. "The life of our prince is in imminent danger. He must stop using his magic immediately. He cannot finish the Salt Road."

The mocking whispers in the fortress turned into whispers of sympathy.

"No wonder he was so tired all the time," the men said. "Poor thing, so young and already so feeble."

"Is he even fit to inherit the throne? Strong enough to lead a nation?"

"Will we have another sick emperor, falling off his dragon, incapable of saving our dynasty?"

Maro hated these whispers even more.

Terren was hiding.

Maro went looking everywhere for him, and finally found him in one of the fortress's empty kitchens, huddled under a table. "You," he snarled. "You told."

He made a pitiful sound and shuffled further back.

Maro took a step closer, pushing aside the bench between them with a scrape. "You promised. *I trusted you.*"

"I was trying to protect you," he said in a tiny voice.

"Protect? *You ruined my life!*" Maro was shouting now, really shouting, the way he knew his little brother hated. But he couldn't stop himself. The anger burned as hot as coals, and it needed to come spitting out as flames.

"We're family. And family is for keeping each other—"

He squeaked with alarm. Maro had grabbed him by the collar with both hands and dragged him out from under the table. "Didn't I say I don't need protection? Only the weak need help, Terren! But I. Am. Not. Weak." He spat out the words like knives. "I am powerful. I'm going to be emperor one day. I'm going to command armies and send our enemies to their knees!"

"You never wanted any of that," Terren whimpered. Maro lifted him up by his collar and shoved him against the wall, as a warning, but he had the audacity to keep speaking anyway. "You might have everyone else tricked, but you never tricked me. I know you don't want to be emperor."

"I don't?" Maro said scathingly. "Says who?"

"Says you. That poem you wrote. *The wind, born only to run—*"

He hit him in the face.

Terren let out a small and terrified sound, and Maro resented it so much he hit him again. When he let go of him, Terren didn't even bother standing again, just stayed sprawled on the ground with his hands over his head like a coward. "I'm sorry," he begged, trembling. "I'm sorry ten times. I'm sorry a hundred times. I'm sorry a thousand times. I'm sorry—"

"I wrote that poem when I was six!" Maro screamed. "*Six!*" He kicked him in the stomach. "I'm not a boy anymore. I have my sigil. I'm grown. And I *want to be emperor!*" He kicked him again. "I want it because I worked all my life for it. Because I suffered for it. Because I'll be good at it." Another kick. "Because it's—my—*birthright!*" Three more kicks, the last one so hard it sent his brother skidding across the cold stone.

Terren had gone very, very still. He wasn't even crying anymore. The only thing he did was curl up as small as possible, as if trying to disappear from this world.

He had always been so pathetic.

"Maybe you should want it too," Maro spat, and left him.

They left the fortress at the same time. It was an angry sunset, like claws had torn apart the crimson sky beyond the Eriet Mountains' shadowed peaks. Lady Autumn stayed close beside Terren as they rode north, towards Tieza, towards greatness.

Maro went the opposite way.

40

TEMPLE IN THE CLOUDS

I spent the first few days of our retreat recovering. Aolian disciples, robed and masked in black and white, brought food to our remote cottage—plain rice, unseasoned meat, and an assortment of more teas than I could ever drink.

We were higher in the mountains than at the palace, and it snowed even more here, painting the pine branches white. The landscape outside the window scintillated with the color of funerals.

Lying on the bed, waiting for my chest to stop aching, I found myself far less afraid than before.

In Tensha, it was customary for new brides and grooms to spend a half month alone together at an Aolian temple. It wasn't practiced much in the villages—we could never have afforded so much time away from farm work—but it was mentioned often in the ballads, and so I had heard about the tradition long before the palace.

Aolian temples were scarce accommodations, with only hard beds and simple food. Even the use of seal magic was not allowed on its sacred premises. The idea was for the newlyweds to have two weeks to dedicate only to each other and their pledges. To reflect, pray to Heaven, practice worship to the Ancestors—and, of course, engage in the childmaking activity.

I remembered having nightmares and nightmares about the retreat with Terren. One night at a time was barely survivable. Two whole weeks of him, I had thought, would kill me.

But now, I was already recovering from a near-fatal knife wound. Now, he had already almost killed me. Somehow, that made me brave.

On the fourth day, I managed to sit up in my bed. Terren was not around; I guessed he was at the temple.

I wrapped my winter cloak around me and went to look for him. Every step sent a fresh pain echoing through my chest, a pain I ignored. Time was running out.

There wouldn't be an opportunity like this again. Not only did I have time with him alone during our wedding retreat, he was also cut off from his advisor. Hesin was far more careful than he was. Hesin would see through any moves I made, any falsehoods I told.

I needed to close in on Terren before we returned.

My boots were ankle-deep in the snow as I made the climb from the simple pavilion Terren and I shared, halfway down the mountain, to the temple at its crest. A layer of cold mist threaded through the ancient pines, which were twisted and bent with the burden of centuries. Through it all I could see the shadowed pagodas, plain and capped with snow.

Everything was quiet here. Aolian disciples in black and white walked through the courtyard with the silence and dignity of ghosts. For all I knew, there might actually have been ghosts among them; I would not have been able to tell. There were offerings of fruit and nuts laid out on the temple steps, for wandering spirits, though chipmunks and twittering snowlarks would come to share them.

I found Terren sitting cross-legged on a bridge, overlooking a pond. He was wearing his usual gray robe, sashed with azalea red. An open scroll was in his hand, and on it was a half-written poem that he seemed to have abandoned in favor of watching the carp in the water.

"Now that you are awake," he said without looking up, "you shall answer me. What were you doing in the West Palace?"

There were no Aolian disciples within hearing range, but even if there were, it would not matter. The disciples did not concern themselves with worldly affairs.

I seated myself beside him on the bridge, about three paces away, closer than I would have dared before. "If I tell you, will you kill me afterwards?"

"That would depend on what you tell me."

"I was spying on your behalf. I may not know much about the Outer Court, but I know your brother has been working to remove you from the throne. So I wanted to help. I befriended his wife on Mid-Autumn to learn, through her, of the West Palace's movements."

A puff of snow dropped from a nearby pine branch into the pond. Five or six carp, believing the ripples to be food, raced to the surface for a nibble.

"I don't believe you." He seemed like he was trying hard to put threat into his voice, but he only managed to sound tired.

"Why else would I risk my life to go to her? Certainly not so she can teach me nighttime techniques." I lowered my head, trying to seem embarrassed. "You of anyone know that what I said in front of Empress Sun was a lie."

He was quiet as he considered this. "How did you get Silian to trust you?"

"I told her I would help spy on you, for her. I told her that I found you cruel—which you are—and that I was frightened of you becoming emperor, so I would help Prince Maro rise to take your place."

"How do I know whose side you are truly on?"

I had prepared for this question. I made my voice hesitant, sheepish. "Because like everyone else in the palace, I want . . ." *Power.* I left the word unsaid—better he believed he was drawing his own conclusions. "If you inherit the Crown, I'll be empress. If Maro does, I won't. It is as simple as that."

He burst into laughter, a sound like knives scratching. "And here I was under the impression there was more to you. I had spent the past few days wondering what all that drivel on our wedding night was about, but it turned out to be something so mundane. So predictable." In the water, the carp dispersed again, darting back beneath clovers and water lilies. "Tragic, isn't it? Even the simplest villager cannot help but fall victim to the seduction of the palace."

I did not correct him. He could assume about me whatever he wished, so long as it helped me assassinate him.

"I will not kill you for it, then," he said, more to narrate a decision to himself than for my benefit. "Not yet, anyway. I have all the knives in the world, so I have no need for spies, especially not one who is a girl. But I am curious to see where this leads. At the very least, I expect to be entertained."

I hadn't realized how tense I had been until he had confirmed, aloud, that I would not die. I let my fists unclench from under my sleeves and said, "There's something I've been meaning to ask you."

He looked up sharply. Black eyes bored into me like coals.

Again, I had lured him in with curiosity. I wondered how few people in the nation dared to ask him questions.

"Your coronation," I said quietly, trying to make it seem like I was speaking from a place of concern. "I've been wondering all this time—why do it alone?"

By now I'd heard all the legends about the Taming of the Dragon, which all boasted of how dangerous it was, since dragons could not be tamed by literomancy. Princes had to rely only on the strength of their sigil magic and their allies.

In the beginning, when the tradition was still new, one in four seal-bearing princes perished in their attempt to take the Crown. It was only later that they became more strategic about it. They began using larger and more specialized armies, more intricate weapons. They recorded tactics and techniques to be passed to future generations.

But even so, the death rate was high.

One coronation had even killed *two* princes. Prince Arwa had been in the arena during his father's coronation, helping him tame the dragon using his own magic, out of filial piety. The dragon had ended up killing the son, and not even a month later, the newly enthroned Zhaowei Emperor had died of grief.

Terren made an impatient noise. "There is no shortage of people who want me dead. Do you think I am so foolish to let anyone in the arena while my ward is down?"

"But surely there are at least some you trust. Some who you are certain would support you."

"The privilege of being powerful, Wei, is that I do not need to rely on *trust*." He spat out the word like poison.

We sat in silence a while longer, and then he went to pray in the temple, unaware that he had been giving me material for his killing poem.

41

SNOWSTORM

There was a sunlit study attached to our accommodations, and it was there that Terren spent most of his days, reading and working on his Blessings, which he set aside for battlefronts, the House's stores, or far provinces. Sometimes he went up to the temple to pray—or, I suspected, to feed the carp; sometimes he took walks by himself alone, in the snow-drenched forest. He must have used those walks to find inspiration, because the moment he was back, he would pick up his pen immediately.

He did not hurt me much during our retreat. When he did, it was perfunctory. As if it was something he didn't want to do, like sweeping leaves off a footpath, but had to anyway. There was none of his usual creativity in his torture methods, no light in his eyes. He simply cut me, mended me, and was done with it.

The rest of the time, he ignored me, as if I did not exist at all.

He drank wine. Lots of it. He never did it within the limits of the temple—such indulgences were not allowed according to Aolian teachings—but every other evening, he would take a few jars of it to a quiet, shrouded cliff not far away. I knew this because one night, he did not come to sleep in our bed, so I went looking for him. I found him sprawled on the jutting rock, unconscious, right beside a steep plunge into the clouds.

I thought about pushing him off, but I knew the Aricine Ward would not let him die. Maybe it would sprout him wings like a crane's; maybe it would let him land softly like mist. Most likely, it would have stopped me from being able to touch him in the first place. In any case, he would wake up and cut off my head.

How unfair it was, I could not help but think, that the most wicked of us also got to be the most invincible.

Be patient. Wield the concubine's weapon. Instead of throwing him off the cliff, I brought him tea, the way a dutiful wife might have done for her husband. I hiked all the way up to the temple on the mountain, braving the still-throbbing pain in my chest, and boiled together ginger, pine bark, and honey. Then I brought it back to him, along with some plain glutinous rice wrapped in bamboo leaves.

He left the tea and food untouched, but since he did not punish me for it, I kept bringing them to him other nights too, especially nights he did manage to make it back to our quarters.

I felt like I was taming a tiger.

A violent, rabid tiger that wanted nothing more than to tear into my flesh. But if I kept bringing it treats, would it then begin to recognize me? Would it begin seeing me as a thing that could be trusted—even if it was powerful and did not need to trust anyone?

A few days before the end of our retreat, there came a blizzard. I happened to be at the temple when it started, and two Aolian disciples approached me.

"There have been omens pointing to it being an unusually large snowstorm," one said from behind their black mask. "We have seen a violet snake in the sky, and we have heard the whistling of the frost bunting."

"We suggest you take victuals back down to your quarters," the other said from behind their white one. "Enough for several days. It may become difficult to leave your room."

Terren was not awake for the storm's beginning. He had taken an overabundance of wine the night before and slept like a stone in his bed. I sat at the window alone, holding a warm cup of tea between my hands, watching the morning's light flurries transform into something angry and vicious. Something that battered at the ceilings and pounded at the windows, as if the sky were a beast screaming to be let inside. I could not even see the pine trees five paces from the window through all the blinding white.

I had read about snow like this in the books, and in Maro's journals, but seeing it in person for the first time was like seeing magic. I opened the door a sliver. Instantly, the wind came whooshing in, and when I held one hand outside, it filled with frigid white pellets within the span of a breath. I laughed, wishing I could take some home to show Bao.

When I woke up in the morning, on the second day of the storm, Terren was gone. He had left in such a hurry that hadn't even taken his winter cloak, which was still hanging near the door.

There were no footsteps outside—any he made would have been immediately buried under new snow—but I had a suspicion about where he'd gone.

It was a treacherous journey to the top of the mountain. I could barely see past my arm in front of me, and the blizzard kept stinging my cheeks, my hands, my still-aching chest. I lost myself in it twice before making it to the temple.

As I neared its courtyard, I spotted a faint silhouette.

"Terren," I shouted over the raging winds.

He didn't hear me.

I drew closer. It was only when I was three paces away that I could see him clearly: crouched by the shore of the pond, still in his bedrobes, holding a dagger. He was digging stiffly at the snow with it, but was making no progress. Every dent he made was immediately filled again by the storm.

He must have been out for a long time. The ice had already caked over him, his hair, back, and collar frozen white.

"Terren," I said again. The way he was acting, I was reminded of the scared child from Maro's story. "Get to the temple."

He did not acknowledge me.

"You're going to freeze out here." Did the Aricine Ward protect him from the cold?

He kept hacking away with his knife.

"Terren, the fish are *already inside*."

That made him finally look up.

"Come," I said. I threw him his cloak, but he didn't put it on. He just clutched it in his arms, as if he had no idea what to do with it, and stumbled dumbly after me. I led him through the knee-high snow for a cold forever, until at last, we were safe through the temple doors.

The summer he turned sixteen, Hesin had said, *he poisoned all the carp in the peach garden.*

I had believed it at first, because why wouldn't I? Terren had killed many things. He had killed many, many people. If someone came and told me he had slaughtered an entire city, I would not have questioned it for even a heartbeat.

But, importantly, he had *not killed those fish.*

It was the most surprising thing I had learned from Maro's journals, in one of the very last entries. I did not think I could ever write Terren's poem without it.

Inside the temple's stone doors, the loud of the storm had given way to a peaceful quiet. Several disciples were inside, copying classical texts with wooden blocks. Some of them knelt by the giant statue of Ao, a stone beast with eight legs and a mane like the sun. Others were offering incense to the statue of Li—a carved fish-creature with an eagle's wings and scales like shining moons.

Several large tubs, low and made of lacquered ceramic, were spread around the hall. Each was as wide as a table, and each held several dozen of the carp.

Terren stood beside one of them, staring numbly into the water.

"I was here at the start of the storm," I explained to him. "When I heard there was going to be a blizzard, I asked the disciples if I could move the fish indoors. They said the fish would be fine—they had survived many winters on the mountain before—but they did agree to help me in the end."

He didn't say anything, and at first I supposed he was having one of his quiet spells. Then it occurred to me that the cold might actually have hurt him. His lips were blue, his face gray as ice, his lashes still frozen with snow. Even the band of characters around him seemed to swirl slower than usual.

For a moment, I regretted bringing him inside. If I had left him out in the storm, maybe it would have killed him. I doubted his ward would have let him die, but still, I could not help but indulge in wondering *what if.*

I moved one of the braziers in the hall next to him so that its flames might warm him. Around us, the Aolian disciples carried on with their rituals, as if we were merely ghosts, not of this world.

"Why?" Terren finally said, breaking the silence.

I assumed he meant saving the fish. "I don't know," I answered truthfully.

Maybe it was because subconsciously, I knew he would want me to, and it was my own way of wielding the concubine's weapon. Maybe it was because the poem he'd written as a child had affected me—even the summary of it, as retold to me by Hesin in his story. *My life might be smaller than yours, but it is full of joy and worth living.*

Maybe it was how helpless they seemed.

"Even if they would have been fine outside," I said, as much an explanation to myself as to him, "I don't doubt that if they had a choice, they would have gone somewhere warmer. We were the ones who confined them out there, made them at our mercy, forced them to face the storm. So when the storm did come, I felt it was only our duty to bring them somewhere safe."

He fell back into silence. Sometime later, he finally seemed warm enough to hold a cup, so I brought him ginger tea. He removed the silver needle that he kept pinned in his hair and dipped it in the cup; his ward made him immune to poison, but likely he wanted to test my intentions.

When the needle did not turn black, he took a small and shaky sip and said nothing more.

42

A NEGOTIATION WITH DOVES

A temple shrouds itself in dense fog;
Nothing can burn here. Nothing is remembered.
If the sun also wearies like we do,
May it rest here, where all light is tempered.
—GUAN MARO, AZALEA DYNASTY, YEAR 628
(COLLECTED POSTHUMOUSLY)

After their separation in the Eriet Mountains, it would be another three years before Maro wrote again of his brother. It described a summer morning made mild by fog, which he had spent practicing with his cloud-staff deep in the Aolian temple. A staff was not a sword; each technique, ethereal and air-light, was designed not for combat but meditation. *Balance. Concentration. Detachment.*

"Your Highness," someone said, startling him.

It was a familiar voice, one he hadn't heard in many years. Maro dropped to the ground, lowered his staff, and turned to face the visitor. "Siming? It's good to see you!"

They went to share tea in one of the temple's many meditation rooms. Small incense pots of Ao and Li stared at them from the windowsill, and the room was redolent with pine smoke and sacred herbs.

Song Siming shifted uncomfortably. "I know that as part of your recovery, you are not to concern yourself with worldly affairs. But still, it would be nice if you showed your face."

Maro laughed fondly. "I am not even supposed to speak with you, let alone take off my mask."

"You're not subject to their rules. You are the crown prince, Your Highness, not a disciple!"

"That doesn't mean I don't observe their ways."

Siming lowered his eyes, presumably to avoid looking at Maro's draping Aolian robes, his white mask, the staff made of mystic metals tied at his back. "Then will it be hard convincing you to leave the temple?"

At once, Maro stiffened with alarm. Doctor Shu had ordered that he not be disturbed until he was fully recovered. If Siming had gone against orders, had ridden all the way here, there must have been a good reason. "It may not be," he said cautiously, "depending on what news you bring."

Siming cupped his hands around his ginger tea and spoke with urgency. Terren had spent the past three years in Tieza. He'd spent the beginning of it training in his magic, but by the end he had recaptured the contested northern region for the empire. Now he was advancing slowly eastward, a slew of military achievements following wherever he went. They called him the Winter Dragon.

"Now more than ever," Siming said, "everybody is speculating that His Majesty will switch his named heir. Not only that, they are *pressuring* him to. Some of the leaders of the Great Clans have been sending not-so-subtle messages in praise of the second son's achievements."

"I see." Maro stared at his hands. None of this came as a surprise to him, really.

"Your Highness, you know as well as I do how long his faction has been planning to overthrow you! I fear they will succeed imminently."

"Then let them."

"*What?*" Siming slammed his cup down so hard the tea splashed on the rug. "You're just going to give up the fight?"

Maro looked out the window. The temple was calm, the fog threading through the pines serene, his own heart steadier than it had been for years. His headaches still came from time to time, but it was nothing so ferocious as before. "My brother has always been smarter than me. Kinder. And his magic is what the nation needs. Siming, I've been thinking about it at length while I've been up here, and I thought, maybe I was never meant to fight him. Maybe it had only ever been someone else's fight, and I had been tricked into thinking it was mine."

The wind, born only to run.

"Kinder?" Siming echoed, incredulous. "Guan Maro, if you do not return and wrest political control back *immediately*, Tensha will fall into the hands of a cruel and vicious tyrant!"

Maro turned back to his friend, uncomprehending. "Tyrant?"

Siming's hand began to tremble. "You really haven't heard, then."

He told him everything, and it was all the same as in Hesin's account. Inside the palace, dead animals everywhere. Moonflower-rabbits with their heads lopped off, entire rooms full of dead pigeons. Servants punished left and right for minor wrongdoings, with flayings, or cut-off tongues, or knives through their hearts.

Outside the palace, in the battlefield, heads and severed limbs piling up like leaves in autumn. Blood flowing in the streets like rivers.

"No," Maro whispered. He felt like he was falling once again—into a chasm deeper than any he could have imagined. He tore off his mask and rode straight for the palace.

His council met that same afternoon. His tutors, friends, and old allies were all gathered in the newly inhabited West Palace. The parlor was still largely empty, but some servants had brought in pots of trumpet flowers from the now-vacant Dawn Pavilion, and they made it seem at least a little like home.

"You must not see him," Master Ganji said. "He's too dangerous."

"He's my brother," Maro said, bewildered. Part of him still didn't believe it. The boy who was scared all the time, who hid when there were loud noises, who had trouble even picking up a sword—how could he have turned into what Siming described?

High Eunuch Umei sighed. "We have sent four messengers to the East Palace already, Your Highness, in an attempt to negotiate. All we asked was that he fight more peaceably, to not harm innocents in his bid for power. In an act of remarkable irony, he killed all four."

Maro bit his lip. "But he would not harm *me*. Trust me on this." Nobody here knew Terren as deeply as he did. They did not know that Terren, not Doctor Shu, had been the one to evict Maro from his missions. And he claimed he had done it only to protect him.

Everyone in the room exchanged doubtful glances.

"If that is what you believe, you have not grown as much as I have hoped." Master Ganji's frown had only become more uncompromising over the years. "Maro, have I not warned you long ago that you are all that stands between him and the Crown? *Brother betrays brother; blood forgets blood.* All you need to do to find an example is look to your father, who—"

"With all due respect, Master Ganji, Terren is not our father." Maro was tired of the constant comparisons to those who had come before. "And neither am I."

It was a long walk to the East Palace, which was frightfully cold and decorated like a night-story. More swords than in all of the palace's armories put together bit into the air like icicles. Maro shivered as he entered, alone.

In its main hall, down many austere pillars, Terren sat high on a throne of lilies and blades. At his left stood Master Long, one of his longtime tutors; at his right was the eunuch An Sui. A dozen guards and armed personnel surrounded him.

"Brother," Maro said hesitantly. "It's me."

Terren did not look at him or speak. He kept his eyes only on the three dozen live doves in front of him, their pink feet tied to the branches of a fig tree growing out of the dais.

"You desire power. You desire my throne. That is . . . that is understandable." *Maybe you should want it too,* Maro had said in anger, all those years ago. Part of this, he knew, was his own fault. "But Terren, I beg of you, fight *me*. *Only* me. Don't drag the innocent into this. The animals, the civilians, the servants—leave them all alone."

Your veins are Tensha's flowing rivers, your beating heart its capital, your flesh its mountains and fertile valleys. Three years in the temple, while this was what had befallen the nation. How had Maro failed it once again?

Silence. Terren still did not look at him.

"Talk to me!" Maro cried in desperation. "Don't play at being stupid! I know you can understand every word I'm saying—"

The 刀/Dao sigil flashed. A knife floated down from the ceiling, stabbed straight through a dove's back, and came out the other end. Bird and knife sailed through the air to thump at Maro's feet.

For a moment, Maro couldn't even speak. Then his astonishment turned into hot fury. "Are you mad? How can you disgrace the ground our Ancestors live in like this? Behave so shamefully? You are a prince of Tensha, not a monster! I will not believe it, no matter how much you try to convince me otherwise!"

Thump. Another skewered bird landed near him, white feathers drenched with red blood.

"What happened to you in Tieza?" Maro whispered, his voice breaking. "Did you finally taste power, after obtaining your Dao seal, and you liked using it so much you couldn't stop? Did you finally feel strong, after years of feeling weak? Did you finally realize you could make others afraid, after years of being afraid yourself?"

Three more dead doves landed at his feet.

Panic and desperation pulsed against Maro's skull, making it hard to think straight. "Then *why?*" he choked out. "Is it . . . is it because I hit you?"

This time, a storm of knives. Flying down from the ceiling, running themselves through the rest of the birds. A moment later, Maro was pummeled with bloody feathers, wet entrails, lifeless beaks. He felt like he was going to be sick.

"Our prince is no longer in the mood for conversation," said An Sui, "and suggests you take your leave."

"My brother can speak for himself," Maro snapped.

"Our prince suggests you take your leave," the eunuch said, a little louder.

"I'm not leaving. Terren, *talk to me.*"

They had no authority to remove him, since he was the first son and heir. But, Maro realized with cold horror, they did have the authority to remove his brother. The eunuchs leaned in and whispered something to one another. A few moments later, guards stepped up to the dais and escorted Terren away, leaving Maro standing in the empty hall, ten thousand blades pointing straight down at his head.

It was much harder to get an audience with Terren after that. Whenever Maro went to the East Palace, he was always turned away with some excuse or another.

Our prince is away in the capital.

Our prince is in an important meeting.

Our prince is sick and resting.

The letters he sent were received but never replied to. Maro had no idea if it was Terren or his advisors denying him—or both.

43

LINGERING ATTACHMENTS

"The easiest way to stop him," said Master Ganji, during a council meeting in one of the gazebos on Thousand Lotus Lake, "is to kill him. No matter how we do it, the emperor will be enraged and suspect foul play. But all we need to do is ensure our prince is not blamed for it."

"I can take the fall," said Master Len. He was so old now that his hair was entirely white. "I have been Maro's swordmaster for a long time, so His Majesty will believe my treason. It has been an honor to serve the dynasty as long as I have, and it will be a greater honor to die for it."

To Maro's horror, everyone around the table began nodding. He stood hurriedly, hands balling into fists. "Nobody's dying for anything. We are not killing my brother."

"He is evil," said Master Ganji.

"He is family!"

"For you, *blood* does not mean family but country. Do you not serve Tensha first and foremost?"

It was all Maro could do to keep his breaths steady, to keep speaking like an adult and a peer. "Master Ganji, you know I do. I have served it my whole life. *With* my whole life." Those years building roads and waterways, those Fatigue-ridden months in the mountains—Maro could still taste the blood on his tongue. He would have done it all over again, if Tensha demanded it of him.

Master Ganji's black eyes were without mercy. "What would you give, to prevent the country from being ruled by tyranny? By blades?"

"I would . . . I would give everything."

"Then you will not let lingering attachments cloud your judgment."

Lingering attachments. Maro sank into his seat. His first instinct was to deny the accusations, to tell Master Ganji he was wrong. But he couldn't. Not when he knew with the marrow of his bones that they were true.

If it had been anyone else marauding across Tensha, killing everything in their way, he would have written the edict executing them straightaway. If it had been a favored advisor or friend who had tortured all those servants—even a friend as close as Siming, as Mei Yu—he would have raised the death-blade himself.

If it had been anyone—*anyone*—except his little brother, Maro would have done the right thing long ago.

"There is another way," he said, quiet.

Everyone's eyes fell upon him.

"We make sure he does not become emperor." His eyes swept the room, meeting the gaze of each of his advisors, allies, and friends in turn. "We play the political game and we win it. I am recovered enough that I can use my magic again, and I will resume my missions. The Grand Canal needs widening. The Aricine River needs new bridges. Tian City needs a new harbor. And the Salt Road needs to be finished properly. We are already seeing dividends from building the tunnel years ago, and there will be even more once we improve it further. All those things will contribute to our father's good opinion of our faction."

He was still not as good at speaking like an adult as he'd like, but by the nods around the table, he knew he was getting better at it. He turned next to the two leaders of the Song Clan and the Qi Clan. "While I'm on missions, we'll send part of our forces to the South Sea, to deal with the new piracy threat. We'll show my father that we do not need the Dao sigil to hold military strength." He then turned to High Eunuch Umei and Hai Vinda, the governor of Xilang. "Those of us who remain in the heartlands will focus on rallying allies and gathering support. Come up with policies that you think will please the Great Clans, promises you think I'll be able to fulfill. I am not convinced that as many people condone Terren's actions as it seems on the surface. There are likely more against him than we realize; it is only that they are too afraid to express their true opinions without a strong opposing force to rally with."

More nods. This time, Maro realized with pride, even his old tutor Master Len was looking at him with approval.

He thought everything had gone well, but after the meeting, Master Ganji stayed behind.

"If it comes down to it, if there are no other options, will you be able to do it?"

The tone of voice he used made Maro feel like a small child again, staring out at the trumpet flowers beyond his window, being struck on the cheek by a rod. There was no question what *it* meant. "If Heaven would truly force me to choose between my country and my brother, Master Ganji, then you already know what my answer will be."

For years, Maro proceeded with his alternate plan, playing the political game. Sometimes it felt like they were winning; sometimes it didn't. But with every new report of someone dead or tortured at Terren's hands, Maro questioned whether he had made the right decision.

Are their deaths my fault? he wrote, anguished. The maid Cilla who had spilled Terren's tea. The eunuch Tanse who had forgotten to bow to him. A citizen of Xilang who had happened to bump into his horse. All their deaths could have been prevented, if only Maro had let his allies kill his brother. *Lingering attachments—is my tutor right? Have they made me weak, unable to do right by Tensha, unworthy of looking my countrymen in the eye?*

Sometime amidst all the maneuvering and covert fighting, Isan came into his magic.

All of Maro's allies were happy about the third son's power. "It is not a threat to us," they told him, as the palace feasted and celebrated the 果/Guo seal. "It is not something the emperor would choose over yours. Terren remains our only enemy."

Isan was not in the celebration hall. As evening approached, Maro found him on the terrace alone, seated on the dragon rug behind the balustrade. "May I join you?"

The third son, ten years old, seemed surprised but delighted to see him. "Brother. Of course."

They sat next to each other, watching the nightbirds flit across the pavilion rooftops and the stars overhead turn slowly. The two of them had never been close. Though they had shared some years in the peach garden, the gap in their ages had been too large for them to play properly. But even so, something had compelled Maro to see him.

Tomorrow, Isan would be gone. Sent on campaigns of his own, as far from home as his brothers' had been.

"Do you know where you are going first?" Maro asked. "I assume famine relief, given what your magic is. Nama District has been hit hard in recent years, I hear. Tens of thousands of farmers perished just last winter."

"Father wants me near the old capital. He's prioritizing debt repayment—the Great Clans with businesses there are pressuring us to build them new vineyards and plum orchards. And after that, we're going to export apricots and golden loquats on the Salt Road, to replenish our treasury."

"Ah," Maro said quietly. "It makes sense. We have borrowed heavily in the years after Jinzha's reign."

They sat in silence for a while longer, then Isan yelled, "Look! Look! A burning star!"

Maro did; above them, a bright red streak cut across the sky and vanished.

"It's a good sign, isn't it?" Isan spun to look at Maro, eyes shiny with excitement. "On the day of my celebration, too! What do you think it means?"

Ten thousand stars in the sky, but only the burning ones made people pay attention. Maro smiled and squeezed his brother's shoulder. "It means you're worthy, Isan. That one day, you can become anything."

The time of no other options came the summer Maro turned eighteen, when Master Ganji called an urgent meeting. It was the first time the emergency signal had ever been used, and the entire council showed up thoroughly alarmed.

"We're out of time," snapped Master Ganji. "While you have been busy playing your little political game, Maro, our competition has been writing *the Aricine Ward*. And he is just days away from finishing it."

Maro's whole body went cold. The spell his tutor spoke of was the most legendary spell in all of Tensha. The one the Metal Scorpion had used to take down the First Emperor. The one that made its target *unable to die.*

If Terren cast the spell successfully, his path to becoming emperor was virtually guaranteed. Their father, who favored strength, was sure to name the more *invincible* of his sons heir—and even if he didn't, it wouldn't matter. Terren could simply seize the Crown by force.

And not one person would be capable of stopping him.

"I didn't even know that spell was real," stammered Mei Yu.

"It's real," said one of the black-robed literomancers in the room. "But it is widely regarded as the most difficult spell to write. Near impossible. Since the Metal Scorpion, it has not been done—and even the Metal Scorpion took a decade to compose it."

But Terren could. Without a question. It would have taken him years as well, to be sure, but he was good enough to write anything.

From the looks on everyone else's faces, Maro knew that they were all thinking the same.

"Are we sure he is writing it?" asked Master Len, white brows furrowing.

Master Ganji passed a paper around the room. "This is a copy of one of his verses. Look at it. Just look at it. Any literomancer with any competency can see it for what it is—and tell it is just a few lines away from completion."

He was right. It was not a long segment of the poem, but Maro recognized it like he would the shape of a dragon. And from the subtle hum of the paper, from the way it glowed hot, he could tell just how close it was to being completed.

And the diction. The rhythm of the lines. The flow. There was no question who the author was. Maro would have recognized his brother's poetry anywhere.

"Where did you get this from?" he asked, his voice shaky.

"Lady Autumn," Master Ganji replied.

"*What?*"

Everyone else seemed just as shocked. Terren's own mother, working against him? Things must have become truly dire in the East Palace.

"The window is short," Master Ganji said, bringing the meeting back to focus. "We *must* end him before he finishes the spell." When he said the last sentence, he looked directly at Maro, as if expecting protest. But this time, Maro had nothing left to say.

For the rest of the afternoon, the council discussed strategy.

"Poisoning won't work. The East Palace has silver needles and tasters in abundance."

"We can't break in with force either. His sigil is a strong one. We can't bring bladed weapons anywhere near him."

"Martial artists?"

"He'll gut them before they can even get close."

"Arrows, perhaps."

"Arrows are sharp enough that they are like blades. Perhaps he can manipulate those, too."

"I have never heard of him doing it. Maybe it's worth taking the chance."

"Then we must make sure there's no trace of the attack. The emperor cannot catch wind of this."

They were all thinking in the wrong direction. Maro stood, heart racing. "No, it's too risky." When everyone turned to him, he continued speaking. "We can't just attack based on blind speculation. We only have one chance to strike." If they didn't succeed, the emperor would punish the West Palace for their treason. The East Palace would redouble their defenses. There would not be another opportunity. "We need to be *certain*."

Silence. Then Master Ganji asked, "What do you propose, Maro?"

Maro met the eyes of everyone in turn. Allies who had supported him for years, who had given him trust and unquestioned loyalty. Allies who he would not let down. "I'll go. Alone. And I think I know how to get him alone, too."

The letter Terren finally answered contained just one line.

Want to play "dueling couplets"? I have the start of a poem.

44

LETTERS FROM AFAR

When I returned from my wedding retreat, there were letters waiting for me.

"Thousands of them!" Ciyi declared, pleased that his position of scribe had finally become important.

They sat stacked in my study, in the eastern section of the Cypress Pavilion. Ciyi had gone through them all in my absence. Most were formalities, ministers and other important men writing to express support and congratulations for the wedding. *May Tensha prosper under your reign.*

The letters came accompanied with gifts: jade necklaces, aged wine, a camellia bush in rare gold to plant in my garden.

"Now that you are officially wedded to the heir," Ciyi said, eyes narrowing into crescent moons, "everyone wants to be in your good graces. In their eyes, the fight within the Inner Court is now over. You are now guaranteed to be the next empress."

I picked up one of the letters, skimmed it, and set it aside. Again, I had the feeling that this was not really happening, that I had only dreamed it all. In my memories, the ministers were all of one sort, flush-faced and mean. Riding into Lu'an to collect taxes every year, beating anyone who could not make their payments with a cane. It seemed impossible that the same sort could have flowery words to say to me.

But not all letters were like those. I spotted, out of the corner of my eye, a letter that did not bear a seal, that was not addressed from a place I recognized. "Hand me that one," I said to Ciyi. "I would like to have a look."

He did, with some reluctance. I unfolded it and read:

Dear Lady Yin,

We write to you from Han Village. We have all pooled money to pay a scribe so that we may write this missive for you.

The famine has not been kind to us. The crops are failing, and we have lost several of the elders in our village and many young children. We have prayed to the Ancestors for help, and they have answered through you. When we learned our future empress would be a woman who is a farmer and a villager, that she would be one of us, we all hugged each other and shed many tears.

We write to you with hope in our hearts, that you would help speak with Prince Terren and the other Azalea sons to help us. The others in the palace may not care about people like us, but we know that you will.

There was a short list of requests at the bottom. They wanted two years of tax forgiveness from the emperor, so that the village might have reprieve from the famine. They asked for three knives from Prince Terren, to shear their sheep and cut vegetables. They wanted six pears from Prince Isan, so that each child in the village might try a piece.

They wanted me to persuade the Azalea House to send representatives to the nearest city, Wenning, next Near Year's to give out Blessings. *The children keep going every year,* the letter said. *They are always so sad when nobody comes.*

"Lady Yin." Ciyi peered at me closely. "Are you crying?"

If I was, they were tears of anger. All those blades hanging in the House like teeth, but not one could be spared for a village that needed it. All those pear trees growing all over the palace, so many that their fruit lay rotting on the ground for the sparrows, but not one could be sent to children who had never tasted pears in their life.

I set the letter aside. "Are there others like this one?"

There were. Many of them, all of the same nature, from Nangou and Liushu and Halfhill at Snake Bend. Places I had never even seen on a map, let alone read about in a book. They wanted a road from Prince Maro to shorten their half day's walk to the well; they wanted a small rainstorm from Prince Kiran to refill their dried-up rice paddies. They wanted famine relief. A few barrels of grain and rice from the storerooms near the capital. They wanted debt forgiveness or an apple tree from Prince Isan. They wanted some weapons, even rusted ones, from Prince Terren, so that they could defend against bandits.

It took me until morning, but I read every single one.

As I set down the last of them, Ciyi said to me, a little nervous, a little awed: "Do you know what they are beginning to call you? In the capital, especially, but places even farther away?"

"What do they call me?"

"*Rice Wife*. You see, you are the only peasant girl who has ever married the son of an Imperial House. You are the only one who has ever carried no emblem on Mid-Autumn's Parade, and given out only the most basic of foodstuffs. And there is an anonymous scribe in the capital writing about you, spreading your name. Lady Yin, you are becoming a legend."

An anonymous scribe, I thought. *Tel Pima*. The startled-looking eunuch with the braid. I could not think of who else it might be.

I wondered if the passage of time had helped erase the shadows of the past, or if his neighbors still saw him as a source of shame.

That evening, I began doctoring edicts.

After Terren summoned me, after he had finished his usual nightly ritual of threatening to hurt me, actually hurting me, and mending me, I lay beside him until his ward told me he was asleep. Then I rose and crept to his desk.

By the moon's light, I leafed carefully through his memorials. They were all long essays, written by ministers or officials to propose one course of action or another, that had been sent to him for his review and approval. If he stamped them with his imperial seal, they would be sent off to Hesin to be processed.

Rice Wife. Was that what they saw in me? It was not a title I would have chosen for myself. I could still remember that crippling sickness, that nauseating fire of pain, the first night Terren had summoned me. *Rice* was a way that he had, indelibly, hurt me.

But *rice* was also who I was, before the Azalea House. It was what I had sown in the terraces, with my family and the aunts and uncles of Lu'an, long before I knew the palace. *Rice* was warm meals and New Year's, and gatherings, and livelihood. It was how I had kept the seasons and counted the years.

I looked through the memorials already stamped, searching for changes I could make. Most of them were inane bureaucracy—requests from the Great Clans to enact regional policies, recommendations for scholars to court posts, judicial cases that concerned the lives of noblemen. But there were a few of them, only a few, that concerned the common people—ones that proposed famine aid, new infrastructure, or tax relief.

I kept my changes simple. Small enough to be beneath the notice of the House, but large enough to make a difference to its recipients. With just a few strokes of a brush, I could turn one year of tax breaks into three, one barrel of donated rice into ten. Having lived in Lu'an, I knew that even one barrel of rice could mean the difference between a child buried and a child laughing as she caught catfish in the paddies. Having lived in the palace, I knew that the same barrel would not even register in its treasury.

It was tempting to do more. I wanted to add the village names, from the letters, to the lists of places receiving aid; I wanted to write a whole memorial just for Lu'an itself, detailing all the things I wanted to give Bao and all the others. But although I might be reckless, I was not *that* reckless. I was not so arrogant as to think I could forge a minister's calligraphy. Hesin would catch me immediately.

But an extra brushstroke or two? That was both easy and not noticeable.

The safest thing to do, of course, was nothing at all. To lie next to Terren and stare at the ceiling, like I had done all the nights in the past, praying that he would not wake up and hurt me.

But the letters had reminded me that I was not that girl anymore. That I was in a position of power, even if I had a hard time believing it. They told me that there were those in Tensha looking to me, the same way that I had once looked to the Azalea House.

I had to stop thinking like a villager. I had to start thinking like an empress.

45

BUTTERFLIES IN JARS

For New Year's there were more than a thousand plates on the table. Spiced braised rabbit, salted duck egg, steamed crab with red claws poking out of their tureens: the cooks had brought them all to the empress's Hall of Even Temperaments. Giant bowls of soup, kept warm with lit candles beneath, filled the air with the scent of green onion and garlic. Wines of rice, sorghum, plum, honey, and lychee sat plentiful in silver vessels.

The entire South Palace was filled with lit lanterns and festive banners, with musicians and dragon-dancers. Everyone in the Inner Court was celebrating—lighting firecrackers, playing courtyard games, exchanging red envelopes.

Sometime midmorning, Wang Suwen surprised me by coming up to me. "May . . . may I speak with you alone?" When we stepped away from the group, her tone turned even more rushed. "My brother is the only boy in my extended family. The honor of my relatives rests entirely on him. But he has not passed the imperial exam and cannot find respectable employment."

I raised a brow. "Why are you telling me this?"

"Because you can do something about it." We were still in public, so she did not kneel, although she looked like she desperately wanted to. "Prince Terren has the power to grant him another attempt with just one edict, and you could whisper something in his ear while you bed him. I have always meant to do it myself, if I ever had a night with him, but . . . I do not think I will ever have the chance."

"I see." I swallowed a lump in my throat. How could I explain to her

that I could not help her, without revealing the true nature of my relationship with the prince?

"Please," she said in nearly a whisper. "My ba has been writing letters,
urging me to hurry. He had bribed many people for my place in the selection, for the sole purpose of helping his son. Our household is deeply in
debt. I am running out of time."

"I . . . I shall do my best, Lady Wang."

She gave a wan smile, dipped her head, and went back to the festivities.
I set the bowl I had been holding down, no longer in the mood for dumplings. Now I understood why so many of the concubines resented me. No
doubt they had all come to the Inner Court for a purpose just as urgent,
and I had—through no fault of my own—been their obstacle.

Maybe they even knew about Terren's cruelty. I had assumed, long
ago, that the city girls thought themselves invincible. But maybe that was
not true at all. Maybe they did know the risk, same as me, and had judged
that the gain was worth it. Maybe none of us had very much to give to the
world except for our bodies, and if being planted meant food on the table,
or honor for the family, perhaps that was our way of leaving our mark on
the dynasty.

Suwen was not the only one who came to me. Spurred on by my wedding, and possibly by the festive atmosphere of New Year's, Liru Syra also
pulled me aside.

"If you have a chance," she said, eyes darting about, "please ask him to
let the Liru Clan launch a strike against the Highlands. We control many
military men, but they are stationed as mere city guards in Anyang. They
hunger for glory and a chance to fight for the nation." Her words sounded
rehearsed, as if somebody had given them to her.

I wondered, idly, if Syra remembered our days in the Hall of Earthly
Sanctity. Her and Lily and Minma, sharing tea under a pear tree, mocking
me for wearing my sash on the wrong side. Those days seemed a lifetime
ago. "What will happen to you if this request is not granted?"

She lowered her head. "I do not know, Lady Yin. After I told my clan
I had only made third-rank concubine, none of my family has written me
back. I was hoping that with enough success in the palace, I would hear
from them again."

The last girl to speak to me was Qin Chen.

"My grandfather is the Magistrate of Dusu." She was nearly in tears. "For ten years, he has been wrongfully imprisoned. They say that he was corrupt, that he took a large bribe, but that's not true at all. He's the most honorable man I know. When I was little, he would not let me eat dinner until I had memorized a list of Aolian virtues."

"The Magistrate of Dusu," I echoed. I vaguely remembered seeing a memorial mentioning him, buried deep on Terren's desk. The prince received so many papers every day that some of them inevitably slipped his notice.

"As long as another trial is conducted, the truth will come to light. Our friends and family have enough evidence of his innocence. But"—her lip trembled—"the memorial for the appeal has not been approved for years. We . . . we have no idea why."

"I can help," I said, and marveled that it was, for the first time, true. It would be easy, too. I would not have to doctor anything. All I had to do was bring that one forgotten memorial to the prince's attention—slip it somewhere near the top of his stack—and I could free an innocent man.

"Lady Yin." Chen's smile was as true as any in Lu'an. "Thank you."

That afternoon, I finally found a chance to speak with the empress.

The firecrackers had made Prince Ruyi cry without end, and even his wet nurse could not calm him down. So eventually, Empress Sun sighed, set down her wine, and took him out to the gardens personally.

I followed her out and watched her try, unsuccessfully, to coax him into silence.

She looked up at me after a while. "If you are going to intrude in my gardens, at least have the decency to help me."

She must have been truly desperate if she was asking me. I took the tiny prince into my arms and rocked him the way I used to rock Bao when he was little, pacing gently around the garden and giving him little kisses on his forehead, his eyes, his nose. All the while, I sang him a song I knew from Lu'an. It was a wistful one, about a ghost-child who was lost in the rice paddies, looking for his way back to the Ancestors.

It took a long time for Ruyi to fall asleep. When I handed him back to the empress, she did not thank me.

"I take it you want something from me, Wei. Let me guess. You are here to talk about what I did during your wedding."

"No." I had about as little love for the empress as she held for me. There was one reason, and one reason only, why I would willingly speak with her, and that was to find material for my Blessing. "I wanted to ask about Lady Autumn."

In Hesin's account, she had hated her son. In Maro's, she had supported him wholly, even going with him on his missions. I guessed that the truth was somewhere in between.

Getting earnest words out of Terren might be one part of finishing his poem, but I knew that this part of it lay with the empress.

She barked out a humorless laugh. "I have not heard *her* name in a long time. Just as well you ask—I am about to visit the one you speak of."

We walked together, through the gardens. Ruyi remained asleep on his mother's shoulder, ignorant of the magnolias and plum blossoms dotting the sky above. Winter was already going away, chased off by the eager winds of spring.

"She was many things, Wei. She was beautiful and vindictive, charming and hateful, clever and ruthless. When she was in a room, everyone was looking at her, wanting to speak to her. The way she carried herself, it was like . . . like she was not a real person. Like she was someone who existed only in legends."

At first, I was surprised by how the empress spoke to me so freely. But then I remembered Hesin. The eunuch had been so eager to tell Jinzha's story, and that of his even more wicked son and grandson. Maybe some stories were like jarred butterflies, I thought, fluttering free as soon as someone broke the glass.

Or maybe she suspected the truth.

Maybe she had guessed that I was using it to write a heart-spirit poem, to kill her friend's killer, and this was her own way of helping me.

"All the same," the empress continued, "we could not help but like her. Autumn was very good to us, the girls in the Inner Court. She was selfless, generous, and made no enemies; whenever she had the opportunity, she helped the other girls get ahead. Even though she came in without a clan, without a distinguished name, she was beloved by all in the palace."

I had learned some of this already, just by asking around. I had heard that she was the daughter of a merchant, from Angkin City in Tieza—although the claims conflicted. Some said that she was not from a mercantile family but a family of herders. Some said that she was not from Angkin but farther north, near Besh.

"Is it true that she is from Tieza?" I asked.

"She has ties there, certainly. It was one of the reasons why she kept visiting the district, with her son, even after his military campaigns were over. But I do not know much about her past. She did not speak of it."

"You never asked?"

"I never felt the need to."

I had the sense that it was not quite the truth—that there was something she was holding back—but I did not press her.

We passed under an arch, into a new section of the garden. There was still some snow here, dotted with the fresh hoofprints of deer.

"Our generation of concubines was different from yours, Wei. In our time, Muzha did not spend all his nights with one girl, but rather spread them out, the way it's supposed to be. We were all in fierce competition for a slice of our emperor's nights. But Autumn did not play the game the way it was supposed to be played. She never competed with us. The emperor favored her very much initially, for her beauty and her charm, but unlike you, she never kept the favor for herself."

Perhaps that was another reason why the empress loathed me. Not only had I gotten my position completely undeserved, over her own niece, it must have also appeared like I was hoarding my nights with Terren, the way a mouse hoarded stolen rice.

"She whispered flattering words in his ear, on behalf of me, Qin Rong, and many others, to help get him to bed us. Not only that, she helped us perform for him. We were all so frightened, coming into the palace so young, but she was patient as she held our hands and talked us through the activity."

There was a waver of emotion in Empress Sun's voice. Until that moment, I had no idea just how much Lady Autumn had meant to her.

"When I received notice, for the first time, that I would spend a night with Muzha, I was so nervous I cried all afternoon. She came to my pavilion and stayed with me for a long time, calming me. She told me that it was fine to hate him, to resent him, to feel disgusted by him—she held all those feelings too. She told me that I should look at it as duty. *Men do difficult things all the time,* she said, *not because they like it, but because someone has deemed it necessary.* She was as young as I was, but you would never be able to tell. She knew everything. All the techniques, all the wisdom, all the secrets—and she gave it all away freely."

I thought of the way Lady Autumn schemed against Maro, in the Eriet Mountains. That version of her hardly matched the empress's account. "If she was helping her competition, does that mean she did not desire power?"

"Not at first." We were deep in the gardens now, in a grove of young maples with branches budding. The empress looked into the distance beyond. "But then Prince Terren came along, and something changed in her. I do not think she ever expected to have a seal-bearing son herself, but they say that once it happened, she immediately saw a path to climb higher. To use her son to become not only a concubine, not even worth a mention in history, but a mother to an emperor forever immortalized."

"'They say'?" I had not missed her hedging choice of words.

"That's what everyone believes. But I knew her well. I knew that the real reason she had become so ambitious was because she'd looked behind her and seen all that she had lost. For years, she had to service an awful, sickly man—a man who never saw us as people, only vessels to carry the dynasty's magic. Then she wasted the rest of her youth and beauty raising a son that she hated. A son that nearly killed her the day he dug his way out of her womb, bloody and hideous. In her eyes, if she did not keep playing and playing the game until she won, all that suffering would have been for nothing."

We reached the end of the path, behind a locked gate. There was a secret shrine tucked at the edge of the garden, under a maple so thick I could not wrap my arms around its trunk. Peonies and bright daffodils sprouted from the snow beneath its stone base. The empress must have hired someone to put it there, so that she could honor her friend.

"So it's true," I said quietly. "She really did hate him."

That timid and affectionate child, the one who wanted to heal and protect everything—nobody had loved him back. Not his mother, certainly not his father—and, at the end of it all, not even his brother.

"Can you blame her?" The empress lowered Ruyi into one arm. She cupped a hand over the sleeping infant's cheek, covering up his half-formed sigil. "When I do this, I love him more. When I do this, I am not reminded of who his father is. Of how afraid I was every night, when I was summoned to his bedchambers. When I do this, I can forget the way he lay in bed like stone while I serviced him."

I swallowed a painful lump in my throat. "Prince Ruyi is not even two years old. His Majesty must have been very sick when his last son was conceived."

A bitter laugh. "He was barely even conscious. The entire room smelled of sickness and strong medicine, of rot and urine. I was gagging when I entered. I tried to tell his advisors, many times, that maybe I ought not to do it with my husband in the condition he was in, but they would not let me leave until I was successfully planted. *The Azalea House needs more seal-bearing princes*, they insisted. So I took Autumn's advice from all those years ago, thought of it only as duty, and entered his bed. It took all night—and he was too weak to help me, so I had to do all the work myself—but in the end, I managed it."

If only Empress Sun knew how much we had in common. How much I also dreaded being called to my husband's bedchamber. How terrified I was whenever the call did happen. I might not have undergone the child-making activity like she had, but the fear, the helplessness, the enduring—they were all the same.

With her free hand, the empress fished a bundle of incense sticks and a fire-tube out of her pocket. "Help me."

I lit the incense and gave it back to her. She inserted the sticks in the snow, in front of the shrine, and, still cradling her son, got on her knees before the smoke. "You know what the most interesting part about that night was?" she said with half a smile. "He was murmuring *her* name the entire time."

The shrine did not have a full name on its stone. There was only one large character engraved—秋/Qiu, for *autumn*. Underneath it were smaller ones that described, briefly, her life.

FIRST-RANK CONCUBINE OF THE YONGKAI EMPEROR
THE VIOLET HERON TOWER
ANGKIN CITY, TIEZA DISTRICT

The Violet Heron Tower, I thought. It must have been a place important to her, if the empress had ordered it carved on her grave. Graves were
meant for the eyes of the Ancestors, and I knew they always told the most
important truths.

Staring at those stone characters, I could not help but wonder what
that place was, what secrets it held.

46

BEHIND BLADES

"Maro is out visiting the heartlands," said Silian, during one of our many covert night meetings in her pavilion. We met in a tucked-away pagoda, shaded by willows, sharing chrysanthemum tea on the shores of Thousand Lotus Lake. "He is meeting with influential people in the city, trying to get them to pledge their support. Here is the route he is taking."

She laid out a map on the table. It was annotated in red ink by one of Maro's strategists.

"Yunan," I read by a lantern's light. "Cloud's Landing. Mushenshan. . . ." I took notes on a roll of paper. "I'll tell Terren about Mushenshan, I think. That is a small city in terms of population, but it contains an important military base. I think Terren would want to wrest it back under his control."

There was a spark in her eyes as she nodded, a slight dimple in her cheek as she smiled. I could not help but remember my wedding night again, with the moonlight and the ormosia tree and the touch of her lips on my mouth.

As the spring winds became warmer and lusher, as snow melted into blossoms, Silian and I continued working together to gain Terren's trust. To give the appearance I was spying for him, she fed me information from the West Palace, so that I could turn it to the East.

They were little truths. Significant enough to get me closer to Terren, but not so much that it would harm Maro and his allies' overall efforts. From me, Terren learned that the West Palace was in talks with the historically neutral Jin Clan, and was able to send an envoy with a counterproposition. He learned that one of his armies had a spy in its ranks, and promptly sent his men to investigate. He learned that Maro was importing new and expensive medicine from the West, in an attempt to extend the emperor's life. That every week, the first son had been visiting their father in his bedchambers, holding his hand while he spooned it to him.

Against the medicine, Terren did not take any action.

"It will never work," he said with a derisive laugh. "To this day, Maro clings to the hope that our father only chose me because he was sick and drug-addled. He thinks that if only he can cure him, if only he can make him wake up with a clear mind, the emperor will take back his decision. My brother is even more of a fool than I thought."

Even so, the intelligence helped gain his trust. As he relied on me more, he hurt me less, both in frequency and in severity, until he seemed to have stopped entirely.

He even began to summon me during the day. He bade me accompany him during mealtimes, while performing prayers or rituals, on long walks in the Palisade Garden. He still did not trust me completely, nor did I think he even liked me, but at least he no longer felt the need to make me afraid of him. It seemed a change in the right direction.

It was a change that everyone else sensed, too.

The empress became more wary of me, his other concubines more ingratiating. My servants—with the exception of Hu and Wren—grew colder. They started turning their heads away from me when I neared, whispering about me the moment they thought I'd gone. They stopped inviting me to their meals and coming to my parlor to read.

"Do they actually believe I love him?" I asked Wren one night, frustrated.

She lowered her head. "Love, not so much. But there are other reasons you may choose to align yourself with a future emperor. You and I might know the real reason the two of you appear closer—but for everyone else, how can they tell whether you are one of us or one of them?"

Long after the other servants moved their lessons to their own pavilion, the elderly maid still let me hold her hand and teach her how to write.

"This is your name," I said. "Hu. It can mean *lake*, or *pelican*, or *fox*—or even other things, should you wish it." I wrote for her all the variations that I knew. "Hu."

"H . . ." She pointed at the paper, then pointed at herself. "H . . ." Her eyes welled with tears.

All night, by candlelight, she wrote those same characters over and over again.

Hu, Hu, Hu.

A poem of love, I thought, *for a man I hate.*

I continued my work on the heart-spirit poem. I added Maro's piece, from his journals—the love and the resentment, the pride and the envy; I added Lady Autumn's piece, from her description provided by the empress—her generosity and her ambition, her suffering and her hate. The tapestry of Terren's life was coming together, like a water-painting whose borders were becoming filled in.

The interior of it, I filled with Terren. As he had been before, and as he was now.

After Silian had encouraged me to use the concubine's weapon, I paid more attention. Though I wrote about his cruelty and his violence, I tried to see past them too. There was a person hiding behind all those blades, and if I wanted to kill him, I had to find him first.

He liked his tea very hot.

He drank it the way it came, whenever I was the one who brought it to him, but when he was making it himself, he would put a candle under his cup to keep the water near boiling.

He picked all the skin off his chicken, the century eggs out of his congee, the seeds out of his pomegranate. He did not pick the seeds out of his grapes, which he ate half at a time. He never ate fish. He brightened whenever a new shipment of pistachios came in from the West, delighting in the opportunity to use a sword to magick the more stubborn shells open. He still adored mung bean cakes.

He fidgeted when he was nervous. I would catch him opening and closing his fists under the table while reviewing some of his more troubling memorials. When he was in court, he did it under his sleeves so nobody could see. When messengers came, reporting urgent rebellion in

Ergou, he sent an army and Blessings to deal with it right away. But when a messenger from Sial Province came begging for relief from a mountain earthquake, he laughed viciously and told them to go to Maro.

Late nights, when he had the spare time, he played chess against himself. He did not move from his seat but instead rotated the board. Sometimes he made thinking noises, as if truly perplexed by his "opponent's" tactics. When the game was over, he was always more frustrated to have lost than pleased to have won.

One time, when we were walking in the Palisade Garden, he stopped before a plum tree. He brushed apart the flowers with an unsheathed blade, until he found a thrush's nest behind it, and watched the tiny fledglings inside for a long time. But then he noticed me observing him, and his expression darkened. At once, he cut up the birds, smashed up their skulls, and smeared their brains all over the ground, as if to show me.

He was cruel to most birds, but he spared the cuckoos, the sparrows, and the bee-eaters. He would kill most ground critters absently, as soon as he noticed them, but geckos and snails he never touched.

In mid-spring he found a rare species of snail on his balcony, its spirals huge and vibrant. It was the most genuinely happy I'd ever seen him. "Wei!" he called to me. "Get some pen and ink for me, quick. I must write a poem for it."

47

BURNING PAPER

Near the end of spring, my heart-spirit poem began to glow. It was night-time, and I was working on it in secret at my desk, when I caught a faint flicker.

At first, I thought it was the moonlight pouring in from the window. But the light from my inked characters did not stay still. It kept shifting, like a flame or something alive.

At once, I felt my heart soar. I felt like I was back on the hill in Lu'an, right after Grandpa Har had traced the Blessing, witnessing magic for the first time. It was an excitement too large not to be shared, and I called out to Wren. On nights I worked on my poem, if she wasn't in my bedchambers helping me with my lines, she was usually not far away. "Come look! We're getting close. The poem is glowing."

"Is it now?"

The voice coming from the darkness was not Wren's.

I spun around. There, standing not two paces from me, his face all sharp angles in the moonlight, was Yong Hesin.

He was pointing a knife at my neck.

I was sure my heart stopped beating then. Instinctively, uselessly, I grabbed the paper and hid it behind my back, as if removing my spell from view would make him forget what he had already seen.

His expression was tired, but his eyes were sharp. "For months, I have been telling him to be more careful of you, but he would not take my concerns seriously without proof. Now, it seems, I have proof." He extended a hand, the one not holding a blade. "Give it to me."

My throat had become very dry. I did not, could not, move.

"Give the poem to me. If you cooperate with me, I will talk him out of exterminating the rest of your relations. They might even receive some grave-money for your service."

Do something, I told myself. *Don't give up. Buy time.*

Everyone in the Cypress Pavilion, everyone in Lu'an, they were all counting on me to kill Terren. As long as there was still blood pulsing in my veins, I had to keep fighting, keep trying.

"Hesin, listen to me." I didn't need to feign the desperation in my voice. "You can still change your mind. You don't have to keep serving Terren."

My long bedrobes pooled on the ground. Hidden by the silk and the night's darkness, my foot moved.

"I serve the nation, Wei. I have already explained this to you."

"But how does helping him become emperor help Tensha? He's cruel, Hesin. Vile. Just because he is his father's chosen—just because he holds Heaven's Mandate—does not mean he is fit to rule."

Hesin's eyes burned into me. "That is the way this nation works. That is the way it has always worked. Now, give me the poem. Killing you here would violate the dignity of the House, but I will do it if I must."

"What if the Yongkai Emperor made a mistake?" I whispered. "Many believe he had only changed his heir because he was sick and not in his right mind. Hesin, have you really not once doubted? What if it was never meant to be Terren?"

His eyes never left me. "I watched Muzha write the edict with his own pen. And even if I hadn't, I *know* him. I have served him for over two decades. How could I not know what he would want for the nation? War is coming, Wei, even if many in the palace do not know it."

"Another war of conquest," I said, still trying to buy time. I put as much venom into my voice as I could, though my disgust did not have to be feigned. "A needless one. Lives will be lost for no reason other than pride and greed."

"You think this time it will be *our choice?*" A humorless laugh. "Who told you this? Your scribe? Gossiping maids, who have never once stepped outside the Inner Court? The House does not like people to know, but this war is inevitable. It is coming for us whether we are prepared or not. And there are far more of us than you'd ever know, who wish to be *prepared.*"

For a moment, I was so astonished I didn't know what to say. It was the first time Hesin admitted his support for Terren extended beyond the Mandate of Heaven. What he had told me before, about not being loyal to the prince, had only been half the truth.

"Since you will soon be dead, I may as well tell you everything." Hesin's voice was now more weary than angry. "The nation is not doing very well, Wei. Despite the appearances the House tries to make. The interest on our debts grows larger every year, and rebellions are blazing across the provinces. Unrest roils through the Great Clans while the palace busies itself infighting. Our enemies see our weakness, make no mistake. They have not attacked for one reason, and one reason only."

The Dao seal. They must have seen how the second son rained blades over the north and feared his strength. If Hesin was right, and Terren was the only thing keeping the nation from invasion, then it was a compelling reason *not* to kill him.

And if things weren't so dire, I might have given it more consideration. Perhaps a small part of me might have even doubted the path I had chosen, the vow I had made to Wren the night Pima nearly bled to death.

But it was too late now, by far. I had gone too long down my path, risked too much, experienced too intimately the depth of Terren's evil. There was absolutely no turning back.

And besides, I was no longer convinced Hesin *was* right. There was so much he had gotten wrong already. Why the branch had broken off the Century Peach. What happened in the Eriet Mountains. The poisoned fish, Taifong's death, the truth of why Terren turned against his brother. Hesin might have had decades of experience in politics, he might have served three generations of Azalea sons, but in the end, he was still only one man.

"That doesn't change the fact that Terren is wicked," I insisted. The hidden Blessing I was tracing on the rug, with the tip of my shoe, was almost complete. "The Dao seal does not sit the throne—the man bearing it does. A seal does not hold the title of emperor—a man does. You say you are loyal to Tensha, yet how can you let someone so evil write its laws?"

"Without the sigil," Hesin snarled, "there may not *be* a Tensha. Now, I will say it one last time. *Give me the—*"

His knife flew out from his hand and slammed into the wall behind me. A heartbeat later, I had pulled it from the wall and pressed it to Hesin's throat.

Orange sparks sizzled from the ground beneath my bedrobes, where I had drawn the spell, and more danced around the blade's hilt.

"Ah," he said, looking down at it calmly. "One of the prince's disarmament Blessings. I should have seen it coming."

I tightened my grip.

"But you forget I don't fear death, Wei. I have already decided, long ago, to go echo-step with the first prince I served. And this"—he made a gesture encompassing himself—"is what remains." He placed a hand over my trembling one holding the knife. "And besides, you know that I am not a fool. I would not have gone into your pavilion without contingencies. Terren already knows I am here, and if you kill me, he will know exactly who is responsible. A pity that I will not be around to talk him out of exterminating your family *then*."

With his hand over mine, he began prying the blade away from his neck.

I kneed him in the stomach. There was enough force in it to loosen his grip and send him sprawling to the ground. He was right about the killing, of course, but there were other ways of subduing him. I pinned him down with the weight of my body, and when he started to cry for help, I shoved a shoe in his mouth to muffle the sound.

He might be cleverer than me, more experienced than me, but he was not stronger than me.

He was old. I was young and raised on a farm, to do hard work. Even having been famine-starved my whole life, it was not difficult for me to overpower him.

The door swung open. Wren had arrived. With one look she seemed to glean the situation and helped me pin the struggling eunuch down. She shoved a silk handkerchief in his mouth to keep him silent.

"Keep holding him," I told her. "But don't hurt him."

I knew he had not been bluffing. If he was harmed at all in my pavilion, Terren would suspect me. It was not the only reason I didn't want Hesin harmed—he was still innocent, even if he was an enemy—but it was the reason I cared about more.

"What do we do?" Wren whispered. Her eyes went to my poem, still glowing faintly where I'd dropped it on the desk.

"We let him go. He's tried talking to Terren already. The prince won't believe him if there's no evidence." With Wren holding the eunuch down, I went to my desk, set down Hesin's knife, and lit a lantern. I took out each piece of my poem and, one by one, put them to the flame. I had spent long enough working on it that I knew it all by heart anyway.

The scent of burning paper filled the room.

After tonight, there would be precious little time. Days, if I was lucky. As soon as Hesin was freed, he would begin the investigation. He would turn over everything in the Azalea House, interrogate everyone, until he found proof to convict me. I did not think any of my servants or Ciyi would tell him anything—to avoid their own executions, if nothing else, since they were all complicit—but one of them might let slip something by accident. Or Hesin would chance upon a piece of writing I had forgotten to burn, or uncover one of my doctored edicts. He was bound to find *something*.

I had to disarm him—permanently—before he could scrounge up evidence against me. I had to get Terren to distrust Hesin before Hesin could get him to distrust me.

I finished burning the papers. We let him go. Then I went straight to the West Palace.

48

A FIGHT FOR DAWN

It was a stale morning, Maro wrote in his journal, about the day he met with his brother in the peach garden for the last time. *The blanket of mist covering the ground was as high as my waist, and the air hung so still that blossoms fell like stones.*

Terren was sixteen now, and grown.

Standing twenty paces away, across the bridge and on the other side of the pond, the second son had gained a new menace in his posture. Eight swords hovered in a ring around him.

"Brother," Maro said.

He did not reply or move.

"Why must you stand so far away? We are family, are we not?"

Silence.

Maro took a tentative step forward, towards the bridge. The peach garden smelled wetly of rotten blossoms and abandoned things. The cobblestones had gone unswept, the bushes wild and untrimmed, the pavilions into disrepair. Swallows dove in and out of the cracks in the pagodas' roofs, having made their nests among the wooden beams.

Anything that happened here, nobody would know.

"You left this back in the mountains." Maro made it to the middle of the bridge and set down the chest he'd been carrying. He hoped that Terren could not see his hands shaking. Somehow this was harder than diverting the Aricine River, worse even than the long months building the Salt Road.

Terren still didn't move from his shore, but his eyes drifted to the ornate tortoises carved in the mahogany.

Maro knelt next to the chest, trying to ignore the frantic pounding of his heart. "I've brought you something." He unclasped it, drew out a heaping plate of flower-shaped desserts, and set them onto the bridge. "Mung bean cakes. Would you like to share some with me?"

Terren's eyes narrowed, likely suspecting poison.

Maro had prepared for this possibility. He took one of the cakes and placed it into his own mouth, biting open the tiny antidote vessel that he kept in the corner of his cheek. He swallowed it along with the cake.

Serpent's Tongue. Master Ganji's voice echoed in his head. *A little-known poison, and nearly undetectable. It does not show up black on silver needles, and its symptoms are generic and indistinguishable from a common illness.*

So long as you get him alone, far from his advisors and food tasters, you will be able to kill him.

Terren still looked suspicious, but there was confusion in his expression now, as if the situation had deviated from his predictions.

"Remember?" Maro made himself smile. "When we were really little, you could never reach the banquet tables. I used to have to steal these for you. Every time I gave you one, your whole face would light up. You would look at me like I was a hero, and I would feel . . ." He had gone back to his journals to remember what it was like, to have a brother he loved so dearly. "I would feel important. Enough. Like I could do something right, even if I had to be a disappointment to everyone else."

Terren still didn't move, but the blades at his side wavered where they were suspended.

"I also brought our oakwood swords." Maro took them out from the chest and set them onto the bridge, next to the cakes. "In case you wanted to spar. I don't think I can win against you anymore, but it was never about who won. I think you knew that too."

"I use steel now," he said.

They were the first words Terren had spoken to him in years, without going through his eunuchs. Maro felt his throat suddenly tighten, unbidden.

It's progress, he told himself. The West Palace didn't have much time left. The Aricine Ward was almost completed, and Terren had all but secured the throne. The future of Tensha depended entirely on whether Maro could gain his brother's trust.

But why couldn't he be happier about the progress?

"You promised a line," Terren said, into the silence. There was no humor in his voice.

"I have it." Maro drew the last item from the chest: a scroll inked with half a quatrain. He held it out for Terren.

If he wanted it, he would have to come closer to get it.

Terren eyed the scroll. For a brief moment, Maro thought he saw a spark in them, the same one he always had as a child before a game of "dueling couplets." Then it was gone. His swords followed him as he took seven slow steps forward, until he was halfway over the bridge. He seated himself across from Maro, on the wood, just close enough to take the end of the scroll but no closer.

He unrolled it in his lap, eyes flickering as he read the words.

> *From one branch, two azaleas blooming,*
> *Fighting for a piece of the dawn.*

"I admit the metaphor is a little transparent." Maro managed a small laugh. "But this is just one poem. We can write many more together, starting today, and they will be even better than this one." It wasn't true, of course. If everything worked as intended, this would be their last. Maro pushed the plate towards him and said, "Here, have a mung bean cake as you think."

Terren set down the scroll and eyed the sweets, but did not reach for any. "You didn't bring me here just to play 'dueling couplets,' I presume."

"No, I didn't."

"Say what you came here to say, then." There was impatience in his voice, mixed with cold contempt. "Tell me I'm stupid, shameful, and a disgrace, and be done with it. I'll kill some birds and we'll part ways."

Maro took a deep breath and met his brother's eyes. "I'm not here to condemn you this time. I'm here to apologize."

That caught him off guard. His swords jerked once in the air before righting themselves again.

I'll gain his trust, Maro had told all his allies, *until I manage to kill him.*

"Over the years, you've said sorry to me a hundred times, maybe a thousand. Even more, if we count the times you said multiple sorries at once. But I have never once said it back. I want to say it now. Terren—I'm sorry."

He had gone as stiff as ice.

"I'm sorry I kept myself from you, after you wrote your first Blessing. I should have brought my books to the garden and let you teach me how to write mine, but I was too proud and wanted to do it all alone." Maro took a deep breath. He didn't know why, but it was getting harder to speak. He forced himself to anyway. "I'm sorry that I stopped playing with you, after our father's birthday banquet. The world wanted us to be against each other, and I was young and foolish enough to listen."

Terren was still silent, but his bottom lip had begun to tremble.

Keep going, Maro told himself. *The fate of the nation is at stake. The Aricine Ward is days away from being complete.*

You must kill him before he becomes unkillable.

"I'm sorry for how I treated you in the mountains, too. For being mad at you. For telling you to go away. For thinking you were weak because you couldn't raise a steel sword, because you couldn't fight the way I could, when you were brilliant in so many other ways. I'm sorry for shouting at you when you told Doctor Shu about my condition, when you were only trying to keep me safe."

Now he was shaking all over.

"And I'm sorry . . ." Maro could barely get the words out now. "I'm sorry for hitting you. Even though I knew that it would break us, that it would make me no better than everyone else, that it would scare you away from me forever. I have regretted it for years and years, and it hurts every time I think about it, and if I could do my whole life over it would be the first thing I changed."

The knives around Terren shivered and fell, clattering onto the bridge. He suddenly looked very fragile, the way he had when he was still tiny.

"And because of that, I wasn't there for you afterwards," Maro whispered. This part was not planned, but the words wanted out anyway. They forced themselves—dragging, stuttering, limping—out of his throat. "After we were separated in the mountains, I didn't protect you like I should have. I . . . think I know what happened to you in Tieza. You fell off a tree, didn't you? A big one, bigger than either of us had ever seen, and I never asked you to show me, and I'm more sorry than I can express in words."

Terren was crying now. Two big tears dribbled from his cheek to his chin. "Maro, turn me . . . Turn . . ."

"Turn you?" Maro prompted gently.

The words came out with a heaving sob. "Turn me into a fish."

Beside them in the blossom-covered water, the carp played joyfully, knowing nothing.

"Or a flower." All the azalea bushes lining the garden, their plumage vibrant even through the pale mist. "Or a peach tree. You're good at spells, aren't you?" His voice was as brittle as a crumbled leaf. "If you're really sorry, then turn me into something nice."

"Terren," Maro said softly. He felt close to tears himself. This wasn't supposed to happen. He wasn't supposed to—

"Or, at the very least, turn me little again." He wiped his eyes with a sleeve, and stared at the plate of mung bean cakes. "Little enough that all I wanted to reach for was the banquet table. When all I knew to desire was a sweet cake. And even if everyone punished me, or yelled at me, or hated me, at least back then I didn't know why. If you can't turn me into a fish, at least turn me little."

The younger boy lifted one of the flower-shaped cakes and cupped it in both hands, preciously, like it was a beautiful snowflake that could melt at a moment's notice. For a long while, he stayed hunched over it, tears dripping onto the bridge as he cried quietly. Then, with shaking hands, he moved it to his lips.

"Terren, don't!"

The next moment Maro wasn't thinking anymore. His hand flew out, of its own accord, and knocked the cake out of his brother's grasp and into the water. Then he shoved the entire plate off the bridge too.

Terren looked up, startled.

For a while, they just stared at each other, breathing fast. Then Terren let out a strangled cry and rushed to the side of the bridge. He leaned over the railing, eyes bulging as he watched the carp pick at the felled cakes with their big, circular mouths. "No," he wailed. "What have you done?" He grabbed for a stick nearby, found one of the toy swords, and began tracing a panicked Blessing on the bridge. Two of the fish were already floating on their side. A third, spasming, was beginning to turn belly-up.

"Help me save them," he shrieked. "Maro, *help me*—"

An arrow struck Terren in the leg.

Maro didn't see it until its tip had already come out his brother's thigh, red. Terren cried out and stumbled backwards, right as four more arrows came flying towards him, but he was paying attention this time and sent his swords darting back to deflect them. Another volley of arrows, another deflection, Terren gasping in pain as he made for shore.

"What . . ." Maro finally reacted enough to look up, and that was when he saw all the archers. Camouflaged amidst the peach trees, squatting on the roofs of the pavilions, perched atop the garden walls. Someone darted out of the trees and grabbed him. Mei Yu. He pulled Maro out of the way, into the shelter behind a tree, just as another volley of arrows met Terren's knives.

"What's going on?" Maro cried, panicked. "The plan was for me to meet him *alone.*" He tried to wrench himself out of his friend's grasp, but a second set of hands found him and held him tight.

"Master Ganji was worried you might not go through with it," Song Siming said, soothingly, as if speaking to a small child, "so he had us prepare a backup plan."

"Don't worry," Mei Yu chimed. "You at least helped distract him. If you hadn't, we would have never gotten that first shot in."

Rustle. Swish. Maro twisted around the tree and watched in horror. The next volley was as dense as rain, far more arrows for Terren to fend off with just his swords. But he didn't die. The arrows never reached him. Before Maro even had time to blink, Terren's sigil had begun gleaming—bright as a bonfire in the mist—and then the arrows were *changing course* midair, curving around him, thumping harmlessly into the blossoms and peat.

With the arrow still in his leg, he was half running, half crawling towards the garden's gate. The archers kept shooting at him, but he redirected almost all the arrows with his sigil magic; the rest clattered off a shield, made from crude swords, that he had somehow grown out of the ground.

He was getting away.

Several fighting men were giving chase on foot now, desperate not to let the second son out of their grasp. But they were failing. Terren might be slow, he might be injured, but he had all his weapons and now he also had the *arrows*. With every flare of his sigil he sent them flying back by the dozen, and nobody could get remotely close to him, not even Master Len—especially when an arrow went into the old swordmaster's skull and came out the other end.

Maro started to scream, but Siming shoved a cloth into his mouth. "Quiet, Your Highness. We can't let the rest of the palace hear."

They didn't catch him in the end.

They cleaned up the arrows afterwards, the swords, to cover up the attempted treason. Any blossoms stained with blood they swept away.

"The fish?" someone said. The entire pond was floating with dead carp, their bodies bent at stiff, horrifying angles. "It will be suspicious if the pond is emptied."

"Leave them," Master Ganji said. "Even if someone notices, they'll just assume it was Terren who killed them."

49

CONDEMNATION

Worthless.

Maro knelt vigil for Master Len all night, the thousand candles around him burning in sorrow, in anguish, in condemnation. The old swordmaster was the closest thing he'd had to a father. A real baba, the kind they spoke of in the stories about afar.

He cried all night. Ugly tears, built up over the years between the Eriet Mountains and now, tears that he had never let himself spill because he was a prince and supposed to be brave. By dawn, when Master Ganji arrived, Maro's chest hurt so much he could scarcely breathe.

"This is your fault." There was no forgiveness in the tutor's iron voice. "If only you did your duty, you would not have to mourn him."

"I won't fail you next time." Maro's words came out a choked whisper. "Forgive me, Master Ganji, Master Len. I won't let you down again."

"There won't be a next time. The East Palace will not give us another opportunity to strike. Maro, it's over for us. If the dynasty ends in flames, it will have ended with you."

He was still in mourning when Hesin came to see him that evening. He had little energy left to speak to the eunuch, with all his shame and crushing grief, but at the end of the day, Hesin had played a role in raising him. Maro, who still felt filial piety towards the eunuch, received him in the West Palace.

It was a mistake.

The eunuch's friend Taifong had just died—brutally—and he was redirecting all that fury at Maro. *We had spoken in private*, I recalled Hesin saying, *but Terren must have found out about our conversation somehow. The next day, I found Taifong's body in front of my office, cut into twenty pieces and arranged neatly so that they caught the sunlight.*

"Do something," Hesin said scathingly. "Your brother has killed my colleague of twenty years. Your father might not care, but I know that you are the kind of prince who would protect the innocent."

Do something. Maro wanted to laugh. All those campaigns to gain his father's favor, all those covert political maneuvers, an attempt to poison Terren only yesterday. The years of failure, the heartbreak, the grief. *Hesin, you have no idea.*

He turned to face the moonlit lake outside, so that the eunuch wouldn't see the anguish on his face, the redness still rimming his eyes. He had to remind himself that it was all intended, that the succession war was meant to be covert. Hesin, who served their father, would not—should not, if Maro and his allies had maneuvered correctly—have known the truth.

"He is not my brother any longer." Words that didn't sound like his own. "Do not call him that."

Lingering attachments were what had killed Master Len. Maro would never forgive himself for it. There would be no more *lingering attachments* going forward. Best to see Terren as only a monster or a force, to be hunted, put down, extinguished.

They exchanged a few more words. Hesin said more things in anger. Maro said some more words to placate him, words he hardly remembered. Then, after the eunuch was gone, he sent for Siming.

"You killed Taifong," Maro said, tiredly. It was barely even a question. He had trained with Song Siming since they were boys, and he knew him well; it was the exact kind of depraved thing he would do to get ahead.

Siming was unrepentant. "Our failure in the peach garden called for desperate measures, Your Highness. Hesin is our emperor's most important advisor, and it is critical that we have him on our side. I had hoped that killing one of his colleagues—and framing Terren for it—would turn Hesin against him. And it worked, didn't it?"

Maro buried his head in his hands. "Another innocent person dead. Siming, are we really that much better than the East Palace?"

Siming laughed darkly. "Look at us. Look at the state of the succession

war. Look at what happened in the Palace of Everlasting Spring just yesterday. We are long, long past the point of playing fair."

If I am a star, Maro wrote that night, *then let me burn.*

*Let me burn and burn until the whole empire is devoured, along with all
its corruption, its villainy, its rot. Let me burn and burn until this night is not
remembered, nor this year, nor this dynasty, until even history is buried in ash.
And then maybe green things would grow again.*

The journal entries ended there.

50

NOBLE CAUSES

Silian was in her nightgown, in a gazebo on the Thousand Lotus Lake, practicing a Northeastern song on her mandolin. She looked so assured, with her white hair radiant in the moonlight, like there was nothing in the world she was afraid of.

I wondered if Maro ever hurt her.

Maybe it was only normal for a husband to hurt his wife. Maybe it was like how parents hit their children. The good ones did it to teach a lesson, the bad ones because they felt like it. Back in Lu'an, I had never seen Ba lay a hand on Ma, but maybe he only did it when I was not looking.

Silian lowered her mandolin as I approached. "I was not expecting you tonight, Wei."

Even as anxious as I was, the way she looked at me still made my cheeks heat. "The heart-spirit poem that Maro wrote," I said, trying to remain focused. "May I see it?"

Something in my voice must have alarmed her, because she took me to his study at once. She watched me copy a segment of it onto a scroll as I explained my predicament and my plan to counter it.

"You seem frightened," she said. "Are you worried your plan will not work?"

I sucked in a breath, stole a glance out the window at the lantern-lit waters. "Yes, very. And . . ." My voice came out quiet. "And I'm also worried it *will* work. Yong Hesin is innocent. I do not wish him harm. All he has ever done is serve the nation dutifully, even if it meant attaching himself to princes he hated. He definitely doesn't deserve . . ." I shuddered even imagining what Terren might do if I successfully convinced him of Hesin's treason.

Either way, someone was going to have to be on the receiving end of knives.

"He is far from innocent," Silian countered. "He has made no shortage of ruthless decisions, in the name of serving his nation."

It was true, but hardly justified what I was about to do to him. "Silian, I will become no better than the rest of them." Qin Rong, whose false accusations had nearly destroyed Maro's reputation. Empress Sun, whose gambit during my wedding had nearly killed either me or Maya. Song Siming, who *did* kill Taifong, gruesomely, just so he could frame Terren for it and turn Hesin against the East Palace.

All those insidious lies, told only for political gain—and now I was about to do the same.

"Is it necessary to be better?" At that moment, Silian's smile had become as sharp as the empress's. "Remember: our cause is noble. So many more innocents will die if we let the second son become emperor. Whatever the cost, you must survive to kill him."

"Everyone believes their own cause is noble."

"Then may everyone do what they must to win."

I hid the copied verses somewhere I thought Hesin might find them and asked Wren to keep checking on them. The moment they went missing, I asked Ciyi to send a message to Terren. *I cannot bear to spend another day without you,* the message said. *If I do not see you at once, I shall weep so hard I go blind.*

He was sufficiently alarmed when he received me in his tower. "What is it, Wei? Something urgent again?"

"I went to visit Lady Song in the West Palace." I put a stammer in my voice, as if I expected the news was something he didn't want to hear. "But before I met up with her, I saw . . . I saw Hesin there, speaking with your brother."

He instantly stiffened. "When was this?"

"Two nights ago, after supper."

"Two nights ago? He told me he was going to *your* pavilion."

I lowered my head and said nothing, letting the silence be an implication.

His breaths quickened. "What were they discussing? Did you hear?"

"Yes, some of it. They were walking around the lake, and I could not get close enough to catch it all. But I think . . . I think they're looking for a way to depose you through me. They want to come up with enough evidence that I am literate."

If a prince's wife was found literate, it would be grounds for him to be deposed. The idea was that if he couldn't even keep his own wife in check, how could he keep an entire nation in order? Usually, any accusations of literacy would be verified through an exam, but with enough proof—especially if it was brought to light by the prince's own advisor—the exam could be bypassed.

"I don't believe you," he said quietly. But beneath the sleeve of his dragon robe, I saw his hands opening and closing into fists. He was nervous.

"Hesin mentioned he had doctored some of your memorials to frame me. In a simple way, a way a woman might have done. Since I am the only one who sleeps with you, I am the only other person who has access to your documents. Any changes to them will be evidence directly pointing to me. They plan to bring them to the public."

His eyes narrowed. He went to the door, threw it open, and summoned one of the servants waiting outside. "Go get some of my old memorials," he said to the young and frightened-looking eunuch. "The ones I stamped and sent to Hesin to process. I want to see them."

As soon as the door was shut again, I said timidly, "There is another thing."

His head swiveled to me.

"Prince Maro"—I winced, as if I knew saying his brother's name would enrage him—"is helping him fabricate evidence. He was saying that I would not learn to read without a strong motive. They mentioned . . . a heart poem. Something like that. I saw Prince Maro giving him a piece of paper."

Terren was pacing the room now, his ward swirling frantically around him. "No. It can't be. It *can't be.*" He grabbed at his hair. "Hesin is loyal. He has served me since I was sixteen, running council for me all this time. If he wanted to betray me, he would have done so long ago. Why *now?*"

"Perhaps . . ." I looked at my feet, trying to seem too afraid to speak my mind.

He spun towards me sharply. "Spit it out already. You have been spying on my behalf for months, and you choose this moment to lose your speech?"

"Perhaps he is afraid of being replaced," I said in a tiny voice, and immediately flinched as if I expected him to hurt me. I was getting good at this.

He understood my implication at once. "Ah, of course. He sees that I am relying more on you now, and does not like sharing his control of my affairs." His anguish was plain on his face. "After he came to serve me, I killed or deposed all my other advisors. I allowed him to be my only ally for years, and now I see that it was a mistake. The moment he sees me listening to someone else, he finds me compromised and plots to remove me." A bitter laugh. "Perhaps he has never been loyal to the nation at all. Perhaps it has all been a front to gain power. Perhaps that was all he ever wanted, same as everyone else in the palace, and I was a fool to have assumed him any different."

My chest felt heavy. Somehow, this seemed the cruelest part of my scheme—this making of an honest man into a villain.

At least when Siming killed Taifong, the eunuch had died true to himself. But with Hesin, nobody would know the depth of his loyalty. His stories would only ever paint him as a lying and power-hungry traitor, if his stories were told at all.

"I wonder what my brother promised him to switch sides. Even more than what he was getting from me?" Another laugh, even more bitter than the first. "Or perhaps Maro didn't need to offer him much at all. Hesin has always liked him more anyway, ever since we were children. Just like everyone else."

He went to his wall, plucked a glass jar of wine from his shelf, and downed it all in one drink. Then he let it fall to the ground with a deafening shatter.

This time, my flinch wasn't feigned.

"Although, there *is* another possibility." His sigil flashed, and all the pieces of the glass sharp enough to respond shot up in the air, spinning until their tips pointed at me. "There is the possibility that you *do* know how to read, and that Hesin is onto you. That you knew he was coming with evidence against you, so you have come to me first."

My mouth went completely dry, my heart pounding furiously. "Terren, I—"

"But I don't think that's the case." He let the glass pieces clatter to the ground again, looking satisfied that he had managed to frighten me. "If you knew how to read, you would not have been lying in bed after our wedding night like a butchered rabbit, bleeding out from that knife wound in your chest."

If you could read, I knew he must be thinking, *surely you would have used one of my Blessings to mend yourself.*

A knock on the door interrupted us. It was the young eunuch, returning with a crate of memorials.

Terren drew a few scrolls from the crates, unrolled them, and read them. His expression became darker and darker, sigil flickering with increasing malevolence.

"Go fetch my advisor," he said to the servant, and this time, there was enough anger in his voice to make even me shiver. "Tell him I wish to discuss . . . poetry."

After the servant scurried off, he opened another jar of wine.

My heart raced even faster. Very soon, I would find out if my plan would work. So far, everything had been going my way, but only because Hesin was not present to defend himself. As soon as the eunuch arrived, he would be able to talk to Terren, explain his own side. And Terren could . . .

I watched as he drank his second jar of wine, staring at the moonlit valleys outside his tower's window. Terren could conceivably figure out that I had set Hesin up. He was certainly clever enough to.

Clever, but not always rational. I knew him well by now. I knew that sometimes, he was not a person so much as a monster, one with only violent intent and drunken anger. When Hesin came, he could win with reason—but only if Terren listened to it.

I couldn't let that happen. Tonight, I needed him to be a monster.

I said, "You didn't kill her."

It was an abrupt change of topic, and he spun towards me with rightful suspicion. "What are you talking about?"

He hadn't killed the carp. He hadn't killed Taifong. He had killed many, many people, done many wicked deeds, but he had not done *everything* he had been accused of.

I voiced a suspicion I'd had for a long time. "Your mother. Lady Autumn. Everyone believes you killed her. But you didn't, did you?"

He dropped his jar.

It fell onto a rug this time and didn't break; instead, rice wine poured out its opening, drenching the bottom of his floor-length gown.

He blinked. Then he blinked again. "I . . ." His breathing had become fast and shallow, his eyes unfocused. "I . . ."

Ten long heartbeats passed, and he was still standing frozen in the same position, utterly incapable of speaking.

I was honestly shocked. I had intended to get a reaction out of him— insinuate that Hesin had killed Lady Autumn to get his post, if my guess was a lucky one—while fishing for truths to write my poem. But I had not expected anything near this extreme. For a while I could do nothing but stand there, watching the quick rise and fall of his chest, his hands clenching on nothing.

"Wei," he finally croaked out. "Give . . ."

He couldn't finish his sentence, but I knew what he wanted. I went to his wine shelf and handed him a jar, which he finished very quickly. Then he gestured for another one, which I also gave him. He slid against the wall and sank to the ground, hugging it like it was the only thing keeping him alive.

The wine was helping. He still wasn't breathing right, but two more jars later, he seemed almost normal again—the meanness in his eyes having returned and redoubled—except for the fact that he was really, really drunk.

There was knocking. Hesin had arrived.

When I opened the door, the eunuch's eyes burned into me with hate. His eyes narrowed even further when he took in the scene—all the shattered glass and spilled wine, the prince huddled on the ground under the windowsill with more empty jars next to him. The entire room reeked of fermented rice. "Wei, what have you done?"

I looked up at him innocently. "I don't know what you mean."

"You are so impatient for him to die, it seems, that you will not even wait to finish your poem. But don't you know? Wine cannot kill him. Once the Aricine Ward is cast on someone, the only thing its wearer can die of is old age."

"Poem?" I pretended to be hung up on that word.

Hesin scoffed and held up the piece of paper in his hand. "Recognize this?"

I widened my eyes with feigned terror, which made him look at me with contempt and turn to Terren. "Your Highness, it is a good thing that you summoned me. I was just about to come to you with proof that your wife is literate. She has been writing your heart-spirit poem."

"Is that so?" Terren slurred. "Or have you realized that Wei is onto you, and are coming to me with evidence against her first?"

"Your Highness," Hesin said, baffled.

His laugh was dark with menace. "Never mind. Say your piece, Hesin."

"Perhaps we should hold this discussion tomorrow instead, when you are of clearer mind."

"No. Now." He made an incomprehensible gesture. "I want this resolved tonight."

Hesin looked as if he was about to protest, but at last took a deep breath and spoke. "Two nights ago, I discovered Lady Yin in the middle of writing a heart-spirit poem. She burned it before I could seize it as evidence. But she has not managed to destroy all of it. It took me a while, but I found a piece of it in her storerooms."

He placed the paper on the table, but Terren did not move from his wall. "The spell you speak of is a complicated one. You expect me to believe that a girl—an illiterate village girl, at that—is writing it? You could not think of a single more plausible lie?"

"It is not a *lie*," Hesin said, sounding frustrated. "What I have here is definitely a heart-spirit poem—I have confirmed it with a palace literomancer. And Your Highness is one yourself, so once you read it, you will see it for what it is right away."

Terren's face was a mask of anger. He tried to get up but fell back to the ground. He summoned an unsheathed sword from the ceiling and, using it as a walking stick, finally made it to the table.

He unrolled the scroll in front of us. The more he read, the greater his fury. His sigil flickered like a caged flame, and when he spoke, there was so much menace in his words even I shuddered. "Hesin, you are getting older. Your game is off."

"I'm not sure what—"

"This *is* a heart-spirit poem. The calligraphy *does* look like an amateur's. I'll give it to you: this piece of evidence could have fooled the public. But you are delusional to try it with *me*." The danger in his voice was raw, his sigil afire, the blades hanging from the white wisteria ceiling beginning to rattle. "I have read a thousand poems by him. I have written a thousand more *with* him. Yong Hesin, did you really think I wouldn't recognize a poem written by *my brother?*"

Hesin stared at him. Then he looked at me. I could tell the exact moment he realized he'd been set up. "Your Highness," he said with a new franticness, "calm down and listen to me. Wei did this. She orchestrated this meeting. She has been working with the West Palace—"

The eunuch cried out in pain. One of the knives from the ceiling had shot down and cut cleanly through his elbow, cleaving off the hand with the 忠/Zhong scar. It landed on the ground with a sickening *thump* as Hesin fell to his knees, stump dripping blood onto the dragon rug.

"*She?*" Terren bellowed. "You think a stupid, illiterate *woman* could get her hands on my brother's writing? That she is capable of *orchestrating?* Tell me, eunuch, just how long have you been colluding with Maro?"

Hesin gritted his teeth and met Terren's eyes. "Don't be a fool. Wei deceives you. She once confessed to me that she hates you. If you just *think*, for even a moment—"

A scream tore from the eunuch's mouth. Another dagger had stabbed into his bloody stump, burying itself in his flesh all the way to its hilt.

"Knives cannot be fools," Terren spat. "Swords do not know the concept of hate. A sharp enough edge does not fear being deceived, and a strong enough weapon does not need to *think* to win."

"Please," Hesin gasped through his pain, his face a sheen of sweat. "Terren, *your life is in danger*—"

The dagger twisted. The eunuch shrieked with agony and collapsed onto the ground, spattering droplets of blood everywhere.

"No, it is not." Terren looked down with disdain at Hesin's limp body.

"Crown or no Crown, I am the most powerful man in the nation. Nobody can contest me. Not one person in the world can hurt me."

Guards came and dragged the old eunuch away, leaving his severed hand behind. As soon as the door was closed, Terren sank to the floor and buried his head in his sleeves, shaking uncontrollably. I just stood there, unable to take my eyes off that hand.

It became hard to breathe.

First I had cut off a tongue, and now I had cut off a hand. And I was not even finished. If someone told a younger version of me about the Wei who lived in the palace, that little girl would have been disgusted.

51

REWARD

He wasn't there when I woke in the morning. That was my first hint that something was wrong. The second was when Wren did not come to walk me to my pavilion, so I had to make my way back alone.

It was a gray day, the rain falling light, barely more than mist on the back of my neck. It made the Cypress Pavilion blurred, so at first I did not see all the carnage. When my foot bumped into Teela's head, I thought I'd hit a rock.

Then I looked down and saw her eyes, blank. Her neck ended in a bloody stump. I blinked. There was a blood trail next to it, and I followed it to find her organs strung up over the branches of a nearby cypress, like ornaments.

My breaths came very, very slow. My heart might have stopped beating.

Aron, the old gardener, was the next body I found. His corpse hung limp over an azalea bush, blood still smeared over the cobble paths; the rain was too light to have washed it away. Not far away lay Mo, the storyteller. Gutted. Like a fish. Duan the bookkeeper. Fern the scullery maid. Rinan the cook. More heads. More bodies. Feet and limbs not attached to torsos, open hearts. Aunt Ping, so disfigured I did not recognize her at first.

It smelled like the butcher's stall at the wet market.

I should have screamed, cried, fallen onto my knees. But I was stone, not alive. I dragged my feet towards the rear garden. I found Lin Wren. Lying between two cypress roots, her crane-colored dress in tatters. Seven swords skewered her body. One hand was still twitching.

Beside her, in the wet leaves and mud, sat Terren. Staring out into the rain.

I wanted . . .

I stood there, trying to gather my thoughts enough to decide what I wanted. I took one slow breath, then another, then another, and then I decided that what I wanted was to make him hurt.

I wanted to take a knife and cut him open. Slowly, hair by hair. I wanted to pour acid on him between each cut until I heard him scream.

I wanted to burn him with a torch. Again slowly. I wanted to melt off that wicked face one drop of flesh at a time.

Then, when he was on his last breath after all the cutting, the burning, I wanted to thrust my hand into his ribs. I wanted to dig my nails into his pulsing heart and squeeze it until it burst—with an ugly, underwhelming whimper.

Suddenly it didn't matter how many tongues I cut off. How many hands I severed. How many people I pushed out of my way. It did not matter how high a cost I had to pay, so long as it resulted in the thing in front of me *dead*.

Wren's hand twitched again. She was beyond help, but still alive, still suffering. I went to her, pulled one of the swords out from her torso, and plunged it into her skull.

She stopped moving. Dark blood oozed down her face, as slow and thick as syrup.

Terren looked up, calm. "Wei, I was angry last night. Very much so. But I am not angry anymore."

My head turned to him. I was glad for the rain-shawl I was wearing and the gray mist between us, because I could not hide the look of hatred on my face even if I tried.

"Besides, *someone* had to be punished." He said it like it was self-evident, a given. "It couldn't be you this time, since you were the one who helped me. And it couldn't be that traitor eunuch. He is already barely clinging onto life as is, in his prison cell, and torturing him more would only kill him. I think he would be glad to die, since he once tried to go echo-step with Jinzha. I will not give him the kindness of release." He gestured at the cypress trees around him, strewn with bodies and organs. "So I came here. To punish, to make myself not angry anymore, but also to reward you.

Hesin probably has spies everywhere in my court, including your pavilion. I figured I would clean it up on your behalf, as a gift for helping me."

I stared at him.

"Don't worry. They are only servants. I will find you new ones. Better ones."

I kept staring at him.

He tilted his head. "Wei, are you mad at me?"

Mad.

Mad.

I was *this close* to taking two steps towards him and throwing my hands around his throat. He would not see it coming at first, but once he had time to react, he would summon his knives and stab me with them, over and over, until my grip loosened and my body thumped onto the mud. But it wouldn't matter, because I would die knowing how the pulse of his neck-blood felt against my palms, and it would have all been *worth it*.

I didn't, because his ward would never let me touch him.

And because—somehow, even now—a small, buried part of me still remembered the poem. The heart-spirit poem. The ballad of love. If he killed me, I would never get to finish it. And if I didn't finish it, he and all his knives and violence would become emperor. Kill more people. Make more places than just the Cypress Pavilion smell like the butcher's stall.

I had clawed my way into Terren's good graces. I had gotten rid of Hesin, my opposition. The way to kill him now was completely clear. I could not give in to my anger. I could not let Wren and everyone else die for nothing.

I had to keep him believing I was still on his side.

Keep him believing I was still that dutiful bride I pretended to be on his wedding night, who got on her knees and spoke of a village girl's dream. Who spied for him. Who loved him.

"Not really," I said. My mouth tasted like ash.

He must have still sensed that I was upset, because his sigil flickered with agitation. "You didn't like that."

"Not really."

"Then what would you like?" He seemed genuinely puzzled. "As much as I find you contemptible, you still helped remove a traitor from my court. I wish to reward you."

"It's fine, Terren. I am your wife. I am only doing my duty."

"Wait. I remember." He brightened as he picked himself up, not bothering to brush off the mud and leaves still stuck everywhere to his gown. "You want tuition for your brother to go to school. You told me our first night together, more than a year ago. And you want food sent home to your village of Lu'an—because the famine has torn it apart."

He had no right to say the name of my home.

"That should be easy enough for me to arrange." He nodded to himself, as if pleased. "In addition, I will allow you one month's time away from the palace, so that you can deliver the gifts personally. Wei, will that do?"

He kept looking at me, as if expecting me to thank him, or smile, or even acknowledge him, but I had used up all the kind words I had left in me and could not.

At last he seemed to bore of me and went away, leaving me with Wren's cooling body and the muted rain.

52

A NATION BEAUTIFUL AND WOUNDED

It rained for a few more days, each as cold and gray as the next. Each new day, new servants trickled into the Cypress Pavilion. Their faces held the blankness of strangers, not the warmth of friends. I did not bother to learn any of their names, except for the head attendant, Mi Yung, who kept hovering about my parlor, rearranging furniture.

Not here, she said anxiously. *Nor here. The mandarin plant cannot be next to the east window. The mirror must not face the rear door.*

Who was your attendant before this? She has gotten the spatial harmony all wrong.

She spoke a lot, and hurriedly, and I wondered if she was afraid. I wondered if she thought that by invoking the right superstitions, she could find logic in what had no logic, and avoid being skewered like her predecessor.

Ciyi and Hu had been the only two Terren spared in his killings. The scribe had been appointed by me personally, and the elderly maid had no tongue. Neither, the prince must have reasoned, were likely to be Hesin's spies.

I did not see either of them much, and when I did, Ciyi spoke as little as Hu did.

At last, when the sun clawed its way feebly out of the clouds, it became time to go.

My traveling party stood ready in front of the Cypress Pavilion, along with several carriages full of provisions, which were draped heavily with red azaleas, both real ones and the painted ones on the Guan emblem.

Ciyi and Mi Yung rode on either side of me as we left the palace's grand gates and descended the valley, towards home.

Home. The thought was tempting.

I wanted to see Ma again. I wanted to go back to the tiny room we shared, with the bamboo mats and the leaking roof and the old incense, and put my head to her warm chest, and have her run her fingers through my hair. I wanted to see Ba again, to feel safe with his strong arms around my shoulders, and be able to forget the palace even existed.

Uncle Gray, and Grandpa Har, and Aunt Lien, and the Rui sisters. I wanted to visit them all.

I imagined myself knocking on the Rui door personally, delighting at the sisters' surprise as they noticed my cartload of gifts and hands full of red pockets. *You were right,* I would say. *Myrna's milk really was fresh and sweet, and it really did please Prince Terren. And now look at all he has given us in return.*

Bao. I wanted to hug Bao again, most of all. There was little left in the world that could lift the stones from my heart, but his squealing laugh was one of them. When I went home, he would climb onto my shoulders, and then I would give him a prune—maybe two—and tell him all the stories.

I had so many stories.

Did you know, I imagined myself telling him, *that there are eight palaces, six hundred pavilions, and two hundred and forty gardens in the Azalea House? Have you ever heard of cats with holly leaves for fur, or larks with pine needles for feathers? And the dragon, it is real too. I have seen it in the sky myself.* And his eyes would have gone so wide.

But a much larger part of me knew the truth: I could not go home.

As we arrived at the end of the palace road, where it split off into a fork, I told my carriage driver—a sharp-nosed eunuch with hardened cheeks—to halt. To Mi Yung, I said, "Take half the provisions south to Lu'an, and bring a few servants and guards with you. If anyone asks after me, tell them I am well." I could not help but remember Ma holding my hand and weeping that night, terrified that Prince Terren would hurt me. "Tell them that I have never slept anywhere so comfortable, nor eaten so much. Tell them I am very happy."

She blinked with surprise. "Will you not go yourself, Lady Yin?"

"I will meet you back in the palace in one month's time," I said, in a tone that left no room for negotiation.

Even though I had fulfilled my original purpose, of bringing gifts back and helping Bao go to school, I had a greater one now. I was no longer a villager but a future empress. The Rice Wife. Even if those roles would no longer be mine after I killed Terren, I still felt the weight of their duty. I would perform them until the very end.

There were others looking to me now—Han Village, Liushu, Halfhill at Snake Bend. The letters sent to me had been from all over the country, places that were not on maps or mentioned in books. They were all counting on me to ensure the next emperor who sat the throne was a kind one—not one who rained down knives and suffering with his amplified Dao magic.

I had to finish my poem. I had to kill Terren. Even if it broke me to pieces, knowing that the road I was traveling was the one that led me farthest from my family.

Wait for me, Ma, I thought, into the darkening sky. *Ba, things will be good again. I promise.*

After Mi Yung was gone, I took the other half of the servants, supplies, and horses, and rode straight for Tieza.

We traveled anonymously. We stripped the carriages of their flowers and Guan banners, of anything that identified us as from the House, and draped blankets over our horses to cover up their leafed manes. I put on a less extravagant silk dress, Ciyi donned the purchased uniform of a city magistrate, and my servants exchanged their shining red livery for the more mundane armor of hired guards. To anyone we passed by, I would have looked like the mistress to a wealthy official from the capital, traveling with him on an imperial errand.

"Why the north?" Ciyi grumbled from inside the carriage we shared, fidgeting with the flaps of his scholar's headdress. He was evidently not used to wearing one.

Tieza. The district where Terren had fought, the place named on his mother's grave. Something had happened to him there, I was certain. Something so awful, so unprecedented, that it had turned him from the timid and loving boy he had been into the monstrous thing he was now.

"To delight our prince," I replied without emotion. "He had fought in Angkin City many years ago, as a youth, and he told me once he left something there. I want to bring it to him as a surprise."

He crossed his arms, his frown deepening. "Prince Terren's edict spells out, very clearly, that our destination is Lu'an. What if he kills me for letting you change course, just like he killed all your other servants?"

He was terrified, understandably. The morning after Terren had massacred my servants, I had found the scribe huddled behind a potted mandarin tree in my parlor, shivering like a cornered mouse.

"Ciyi, I told you already. As long as you remain loyal to me, he won't hurt you." I repeated the words I had said to him then. "Our prince holds me very dear now—everyone in the palace can see it. He will not harm anyone under me unless I let him, and I have told him specifically to spare you."

He seemed to untense a little at the assurance, though he still looked extremely upset. "Why," he muttered under his breath, though not so quietly I couldn't hear him, "did I ever agree to teach you to read?" He crossed his arms and stared sulkily out the window, as if a great injustice had been done to him.

I had told many lies that day to get him to crawl out from behind that tree, lies so wicked that a year ago, I would have shivered at them. I had told him I was the one who bade Terren kill all the servants.

They know how to read, I had said, *as you know. And I've grown paranoid that they might use their literacy against me.* My mouth had been ash as I spoke those lies, but I was already getting used to the taste. *Now that Hesin turned out a traitor, who knows how many more are hiding in the palace? In this political climate, it is much better to be safe.*

I'd seen it in Ciyi's eyes—the disbelief, the fear, the disgust. Even someone as dishonest and power hungry as he was had judged me ruthless beyond redemption. But it didn't matter. I had to convince Ciyi that I had Terren under my control. If I didn't, he might decide to betray my literacy to the West Palace—and pray that the invaluable information would lead to his pardon. Teaching a woman to read might be an unforgivable crime, but there was a tipping point where it actually became *safer* to plead mercy from Maro—however unlikely that mercy came—than to risk being slaughtered serving under Terren. I had to make sure we never reached that point.

Besides, having Ciyi be afraid of me was assuring. A thing I'd grown to like. I had discovered that there were few things dependable in the Azalea House, and fear was one of them.

As for Terren, I was not that worried. I had an idea about how to explain why I had gone off to Tieza. It was a dangerous one, one that would have never worked before—but our relationship had changed over the past few months. It might work now.

We rode night and day. Our horses held the magic of the House, and they ran fast and tirelessly—but even so, there was no time to lose if I wanted to make it to Tieza and back before month's end. If everything went smoothly on the road, I would still only have two days in Angkin City, the base of Terren's military campaign and his mother's childhood home. Two days to scavenge for the parts of himself he had left there.

The nation, I was surprised to find, was still beautiful.

Jinzha's rule might have wounded Tensha, but as I looked out the window, I saw that it was still the breathtaking country the poets of the early Azalea Dynasty wrote about with such tenderness. Just like in the ballads, the hills stood lush and mist-shrouded, the rivers flowed jade green. Wild geese flocked high in the sky.

It was easy to see why all those men had fallen in love with it.

But the farther away from the capital we got, the more obvious the famine became. The land might still be green, the flowers of early summer still abloom, but almost everything edible was dead. The mulberry trees stood wilted, the soybeans dried. The fields of wheat stretched on ghost-pale. Sometimes I spotted people standing in them, and they were all so thin their clothes fluttered loose around their bodies.

The first village we passed by, I tore my eyes away from my curtain, unable to look. I didn't want to be broken by the sight of sick grandfathers, or mothers with sunken eyes, or little children toddling about with visible ribs. I didn't want to see the holes in their roofs, swallowing the light of the languid sun.

But then I started forcing myself to look, because not looking felt even more wrong. When I sat in my comfortable carriage, full and swathed in soft silks, not looking felt like forgetting. When I returned to the palace, where the banquet tables were stacked high and the pear trees drooped heavy with fruit, I wanted to remember places like these.

We gave out what we could. I told Ciyi to calculate what provisions we could spare—food supply, clothing, shoes without holes—so that we could pass them out to the villages. When the recipients asked who to thank, I named the Rice Wife. I told them the story of a girl who grew up on a farm, one who had somehow survived to marry the crown prince. "She is the one who sponsored my husband's mission," I would tell them, and Ciyi would nod and play along.

It was not out of egotism that I told them this. I had been thinking of all those cold New Year's mornings, when nobody had come to give any Blessings. I was remembering the night on the hill, when the spark went to Bao's heart, and everyone—even for just one night—had believed greatness was possible. I was picturing all the letters I had received after my wedding retreat, asking things of the House nobody would have dared ask before.

It was important, I now viscerally understood, for one to believe. That far away, in the capital, behind impenetrable palace walls, where there lived magic and unimaginable power, there was at least one person who cared about them, who thought of them. When I named the Rice Wife, I had only told those villagers what I wished someone had once told me.

It was near Tieza that I wrote my first Blessing.

We had taken a winding back road through Torun County. Beside an old river, under old larches, I had spotted a field of graves. Dried buttercups, valerian, and wild asters lay at their bases. In the traditions of Lu'an, it was customary to pay respect to the dead we passed, to appease their ghosts, so I sent Ciyi and my servants away and visited them.

Only a few graves had names on them. Presumably, only a few families could afford a scribe to translate names into written characters, and when they did it was mostly for patriarchs or eldest sons. Even fewer held descriptions, to tell their lives' truths. I bowed to each of them in turn.

Under one of the unnamed graves, someone had laid a little doll. It had hair made of yarn and a dress woven from old cotton, and an inked smile under round, black eyes.

Something about it made me stop. I stared at it for a long time, until the sun had begun to set a poppy red. And then all the grief, sorrow, and bitter anger accumulated over the years came pouring out at once.

When I carved a poem into the soil, it was for that nameless girl at first. But soon it became also a song for my sister Larkspur, and my two eldest brothers, and the children who came in the middle. A song for Ba and Ma, and for my village, languishing in the famine.

For Pima, unhappy and ashamed in the capital. For the other eunuchs, brought to the palace young and frightened. For Hu, the maid with the cut-off tongue. For all the servants in the Cypress Pavilion, who had once told each other stories by the fire but were now just as silent.

For everyone else in Tensha who were not in books, or memorials, or poems.

Let the suffering be over. There has been so much of it, enough of it. Let there be no more.

As I traced those characters on the ground, the Ancestors saw in them truth and emotion, and they vanished with a flurry of sparks.

My eyes stung as I stood again. Nothing had happened, but I had known it wouldn't. The Blessing I had written had not been for now but the future; the Ancestors had told me so. In two years, perhaps three, the wheat fields would turn golden again in the perimeter all around Torun. The mulberry trees here would once again bear fruit.

By then, I would be gone. Nobody would suspect the spell had come from me. But perhaps some little girl would stumble upon the doll, where the magic had begun, and see that its eyes had become full of light. And perhaps, even without anyone telling her, she would believe that anything was possible.

A Harvest Song, I thought into the setting sun, having decided on a title for the poem I was already beginning to forget. It was the spell I'd wanted to write from the start, when I had first decided to learn how to read. Now, more than a year later and far from home, I had done it.

53

THE WINTER DRAGON

The famine had not affected everywhere equally. Though in many parts of the country, it showed itself like blisters and festering wounds, in others, one could hardly tell it was there. The palace was one of them; the capital, another.

And—twelve days north of either—Angkin City.

It was so much busier here than I had ever imagined. The most populous city in the Northwest, Angkin was nestled between wind-flattened hills and a younger section of the Aricine River, still turbid with mountain silt. Across it yawned a stretch of unending meadow. The city sat on the route connecting the rest of the country with the Caeyang Corridor—and, as of recent years, the illustrious Salt Road—and the sounds of commerce and trade boomed like firecrackers.

"Come buy, come buy!" cried a girl laying out silver tureens on a rug; a bearded merchant beside her waved me over to look at his assortment of jewelry and sparkling hairpins. "I'll beat his price," a bull-faced vendor claimed from across the street, but her attention was promptly pulled away by a wealthy foreigner draped in velvet.

Buskers vied for space in street corners, trading flutesong, poetry readings, or character divinations for coppers. Street-food vendors lined the entire bank of the river, offering pan-fried dumplings, spicy pulled noodles, and sizzling lamb skewers on grills. Standing here, amidst the crowd of thousands, I could not help but remember my childhood dream—the one of rickety wagons, and thin but dependable horses, and sundries.

"Look for the Violet Heron Tower," I instructed my servants, while I stayed behind to scout.

There were dragons everywhere in this city. Ice-gray and ferocious, they were carved into statues, painted on banners, and engraved over arched gateways. Some held a sword between their teeth; others bore a red-painted 刀/Dao on their foreheads. A few held bouquets of white lilies in their claws.

The Winter Dragon, I thought.

Since Terren was the one who liberated the city from their occupiers, it was unsurprising that they would celebrate him here.

Through Maro's testimony, I had learned that Terren had spent many years training here, honing his magic while forging weapons for Cao Myn's army. I knew that he'd used Angkin as a base for the country's assault north, to retake Tieza-North from the Lian.

From Empress Sun, I had learned that his mother had ties here. His beautiful, vindictive, and cruel mother, who had wanted to win more than anything because she'd looked back and seen how much she'd suffered.

Lady Autumn, I thought silently, into the cool northern summer, *what happened in Tieza?*

Why did your son stop breathing, that night in his tower, the instant I mentioned your name?

Not long after, one of my servants returned. "Lady Yin, we have found the place you're looking for."

Built into the sides of a hill surrounding the city was an elaborate, gold-and-violet pagoda. At its gates hung an ornate sign with three characters, spelling out the name of the building. *Violet Heron Tower.*

I heard the music before I even entered the building. Vibrant, sensual music, full of beckoning erhu instruments and entreating zithers. I left my servants and guards and crossed the arched gate alone, still disguised as a scholar's wife, to scout for truths to feed my poem.

The tower was eight stories tall, open in its interior so that I could see each of its lantern-hung balconies. From the side of it facing the city, I could see the sunset pouring in from outside; from the side built into the mountain, there shone only yellow lantern light. A giant waterfall poured from the top floor, out the mouths of two white jade dragons, to plunge steaming into a pool at its base.

There were guests bathing there, between half-submerged statues of painted herons. Dancing girls barely as old as I was, dressed in scant but shimmering costumes and carrying little dishes and wine in bejeweled glasses, giggled as they draped themselves around half-naked men. The men had no silk clothes on to announce their high status, but their plump, well-fed cheeks and carefree smiles made their wealth obvious.

My stomach twisted at the sight of all that flesh. It was not hard to guess that this was one of the pleasure houses I'd heard so much about. A place where the childmaking act happened not for a purpose but for entertainment.

I could still feel the echoes of that deep and horrible pain, that night in the bamboo forest. Of the doctor's warm and inquisitive hands the next day, wandering across me.

"Pretend your work in the capital does not exist," one of the girls drawled, curling herself over one of the men. "You'll get wrinkles if you keep worrying about official affairs."

Another had one of the guests' fingers on her cheek. "I'm very good at keeping secrets," she said playfully, and gave the fingers a kiss. "Your family at home will never know my name."

The way the pleasure girls acted made me sick. The dainty way they spoke, like petals unfurling, the deliberate gentleness of every brush of a lip, every touch of a shoulder—I could tell they had been taught to perform, just as I once had.

Not only did she get him to bed us, Empress Sun had said, *she also helped us perform for him.*

She knew everything. All the techniques, all the wisdom, all the secrets— and she gave it all away freely.

"What are you staring at?"

I started and spun around. An older woman, glaring, had marched over to me with her hands on her hips. She was in her fifties, maybe sixties, but was dressed even more extravagantly than the younger girls. Her face was powdered even whiter, the pin in her hair even shinier.

"Are you the owner of this place?" I asked.

"The exit is that way," she said, her voice deep and hoarse. She pointed past the pool—past the bathing guests, the potted indoor bamboo and cherry trees, and the water-painted murals of poetry and mountains—at the arched gate. She must have seen the way I was looking around and known I was not here to spend money.

She *was* the owner, then. "I am here to inquire about someone you may know. Lady Autumn." I had planned to search the place on my own, but perhaps she could help me.

"Did you not hear what I said? Get out. You don't belong here." She waved a hand at a pair of heron-masked guards standing by one of the pillars, who started advancing towards me.

A year ago, I might have ducked my head and scurried away, like Ma had once taught me to do. But now I stood firm. Perhaps my heart was heavier now, and it did not move as easy.

"I do," I told her. "I belong here." *This country*, I had decided long ago, *this dynasty, they could also belong to people like me.* I produced an imperial writ from my sleeve.

She immediately paled. The guards reached us, but blinked with confusion when their mistress got onto her knees and bowed. "Aunt Ahma," one of them said, "who is it?"

The owner could not read, but she must have recognized Terren's dragon seal. "This is Lady Yin Wei," she said. "Wife to Prince Terren, the Winter Dragon, and the Second Son and Heir of the Azalea House. She is our future empress."

After that, Aunt Ahma was much more amenable. She welcomed my entire party—including my servants waiting outside with the carriages and wagons—with a grand and plastered-on smile.

"You are all welcome to enjoy the establishment," she said, in a voice genial but edged with nervousness. "Whether enjoying the baths in public, or taking one of our best girls in private." She gestured behind her, at the pleasure workers who were dancing or plucking at zithers, at the men who were bathing, feasting, or composing poetry.

Or rather, *had been*. Everyone in the tower had stopped to stare.

My servants and guards, having been recognized, were no longer anonymous. When they had come in, it had been bearing the banners and striking red livery of the Imperial House, flooding the tower with the scent of azaleas, and lush capitals, and spring.

For a moment, the only sound in the tower was the waterfall.

Then everyone was scrambling to kneel. The pleasure girls, the servants, the guards. Even the naked men in the pool threw on a robe hurriedly and prostrated themselves on the marble floor, all muttering, "May you live a thousand years."

It surprised me that I was pleased.

In the palace, I had never really felt *powerful*. I had been derided by the other concubines, subverted by the empress, and tortured by the prince. Even still, I was at his complete mercy. But out here, as far north as Angkin City, my position mattered. With it, I could get anything I wanted.

Now I understood why this vile thing, this thing that we could not even hold in our hands, this *power*, was something women and men fought so viciously for. Now I had tasted it for myself, and it was as sweet as peaches, as wine.

I left my other servants to enjoy the establishment, as Aunt Ahma had put it, and followed her into her office to speak in private.

One way or another, I was going to find the whole truth.

54

OFFERINGS

The owner's office was on the top floor: a small space lit by a sea of flat yellow lanterns and filled with plush furniture, each embroidered with threads of gold. One side was covered by a large window, overlooking the waterfall and the baths eight stories down. I could see, not hear, the naked men below.

Aunt Ahma was fidgeting with her hands. "You are here about Lady Autumn, Your Highness?"

"I am here about the prince. But we can start with her."

She was afraid of me. She hid it well, but her posture was shifting, uncomfortable. Her gaze flicked back and forth between the violet herons— real ones, killed and dyed and posed midflight—hanging from the ceiling. "I'm afraid I don't know anyone by the name of Autumn. There are many pleasure houses scattered about Tieza and Caeyang, to serve the merchants of the Salt Road. If it's a pleasure girl you seek, you ought to visit the Jade Tortoise Tower down the street, or Scarlet Crane the city over, or—"

"Don't worry." I leaned my elbows on the lacquered table between us, pushing aside little plates of sesame candies, pumpkin seeds, and dried dates. "I will not hurt you or punish you, so long as you tell the truth."

"Your Highness, I—"

"*So long as you tell the truth,*" I emphasized.

She wiped at her forehead with a handkerchief, which came away white with powder. "She . . . she was here before the war. Back then, it was simply another tribute house—one of the many places along the border where the nation offered Tenshan girls to Lian men, to make them cease their raids."

Offered. As if girls were currency, or a plate of sweet gao.

We'll set up tribute houses at the northern border to broker peace, Hesin had said, when he'd told me about how he and Muzha stabilized the dying nation. Back then, I had not known what he was talking about. I hated that I knew now.

"She was nine years old when we bought her. I don't remember most of the girls sold to the Violet Heron Tower—there were so many of them, sold by desperate families in droves, and they never lasted long—but I do remember her. How could I not? She had such bright, discerning eyes. You took one look at her and knew immediately that she was special. I remember thinking, if someone that brilliant had been born in a different time, a different place, she could have held the world in her hands."

There was something catching in her hoarse voice. Fondness, perhaps—or regret.

"Her true home, family, and name we never knew. We only called her Qiu'er, after the season in which we received her. *Autumn*. She came in a wagon packed with girls, but the bright maple leaves from the journey had somehow chosen only her hair to tangle in."

I imagined it: a little girl with bright eyes, on a crisp, cloudless afternoon, looking up at the twin heron gates leading to the tower. The place where she would be *offered*. She must have been so frightened, to be so far from her home, away from her family and everything she knew.

She must have been relieved, too. In this place, she would not have to be hungry anymore. In this place, there were soft beds and roofs that did not leak. In this place, there was music and laughter and dancing. And even if she couldn't read, she could at least kneel next to murals of poetry while she endured the offering and feel a part of something lasting.

"But someone that special," Aunt Ahma continued, "could never have been content with a life as a pleasure girl. I should have seen it. How hungry she was, for something more—power, wealth, a place in history. Anything. I should not have been surprised when, the year the Yongkai Emperor put out a search for concubines, she stole a tremendous amount of money from my tower and vanished. She had only been fourteen, a year younger than the age of eligibility, but of all the lies she must have told to get into court, age would have been the least of them."

I knew that feeling. Standing in the city square of Guishan, among all the candidates with painted brows and sturdy shoes, at once terrified and desperate and hopeful.

I wanted to reach into that long-ago scene, of that young girl riding in a carriage to the palace, and take her away. To beg of her to turn back, to stay far from the Azalea House, to save herself.

But I was hardly in a position to judge her, when I had dreamed those same dreams myself.

Aunt Ahma picked absently at a pumpkin seed. "I didn't hear from her for a long time. Not until the war. The Violet Heron Tower might have been a tribute house before, but while the Evening Tide's army was here, the House repurposed it to be a place for soldiers to enjoy, to keep morale high. It was only after Prince Terren liberated Tieza-North that we converted it to a moneymaking establishment—a pleasure house, a luxurious one, to serve the wealthy traders doing business with the West."

"When she came back during the war," I said, "did she bring her son with her?"

For a moment, she froze. But she gathered herself very quickly and said, "Yes, Your Highness. It was dawn and empty when she returned, just me sweeping the floor. When she showed up at the door"—she gestured out the window of her office, at the bustling entrance far below us—"I was tempted to have her immediately executed, for stealing all that money. But then I noticed she wasn't alone. Her arm rested firm around the shoulders of a beautiful little boy, maybe nine or ten years old. A scarf was wrapped over his cheek. When Qiu'er unraveled it, a House Seal gleamed red and fierce, and it was then that I realized she had made it to the Inner Court after all. And not only had she made it there, but she had also become mother to a prince. The very prince who had come to Tieza to liberate us."

"She brought him here for the childmaking duties," I said, more a statement than a question. A vicious kind of hate was beginning to roil in my veins. Some part of me must have realized this truth long ago, but had refused to think about it until now.

He had been not much older than Bao. Bao, who had begged me to take him to Guishan on New Year's, who had been delighted when I'd saved him a sweet prune. The more I thought about it, the angrier I became.

I still remembered vividly all the nights Terren had refused to plant me. How, even on the night the rumors came and he had no other choice, he still couldn't bring himself to do it.

Don't touch me. I'll kill you.

"... Yes. When Qiu'er spoke to me, it was with a practiced sweetness she must have learned in the Inner Court. *Aunt Ahma, how would you like for one of your girls to become mother to a seal-bearing son?*"

"And you agreed." I wanted to strangle her.

"I . . . I was enticed by the possibility. If one of the pleasure house girls gave birth to a prince's son, it would have been a boon for everyone. The girl would find herself suddenly in the notice of the capital and its court, and the resulting fame would have paid dividends for the Tower."

It was true. Prince Kiran, the fourth son, was born outside the palace; I had heard his mother, and the fishing village she was from, had received an abundance of gifts for her contributions to the nation. I even knew her name—Liu Sacha. I knew the names of few women who were not part of the palace, but I knew hers.

"What did Lady Autumn get out of this?" I asked, struggling to keep my voice even. "Was it revenge? Did she hate her son that much?"

For the first time, Aunt Ahma looked baffled. "Is it not obvious, Your Highness? Prince Terren might be heir now, but he had to fight a long and harrowing succession war for the position. Back then, Prince Maro had everything in his favor. Not only was he the eldest, with tradition on his side, he also had formidable allies among the Great Clans and a slew of accomplishments for the nation. And don't forget his crowning achievement: right when Tensha needed it most, he had built the Salt Road, almost in its entirety." She shook her head. "Even if Prince Terren managed to find success retaking Tieza-North—and that was far from guaranteed back then—it still would not have been enough. But if he managed to father a seal-bearing son as well? That would almost certainly push the emperor to name him heir over his brother, knowing the dynasty would be secured for yet another generation."

My incredulity must have shown plain on my face, because she hurried to say, "Don't worry, Your Highness. We treated your husband very well. He quite enjoyed it."

"Did he?" I said dryly. *Turn me into a fish,* he had sobbed to Maro, the day Maro had tried to kill him. *Or a flower. Or a peach tree.*

If you're really sorry, then turn me into something nice.

"Of course. They always enjoy this kind of thing." I could have sworn Aunt Ahma started shaking then—and she shoved her hands immediately under the table to hide it. It was like she knew she had done something horrible, and was afraid of me finding out just how bad it was. "We built him a custom chamber just for him, one fit for a prince. We filled it with the most luxurious silk, gave him the best girls, and hired the best apothecaries to stoke his magic. Of course, we were never successful"— she forced out a laugh—"but it was certainly not for lack of trying."

I wonder if the pleasure girls wept for him or for themselves, or if they viewed it only as duty and did not weep at all.

"I want to see it," I said, standing.

"Y-Your Highness?"

"The chamber. The one you built for him. You claim you treated him well, so I wish to see just how well."

It was the last place I wanted to visit, the place that had made Terren so broken. But those years that he had spent in Tieza, missing from Maro's and Hesin's accounts—I needed to know what they were like, so that I could finish his poem.

She was sweating now, and dabbed at her forehead again. "Your Highness, the prince has not been here since he was sixteen. His chamber has not been used since then. It is . . . it is bound to have collected dust over the years."

I said nothing, just looked at her, wielding silence like a weapon.

I did not even have to wait two heartbeats before she drew in a shivery breath and said, "Of course. I shall take you right away."

It was down a long corridor and nestled deep in the mountain, so it had no windows, but it was filled with red lanterns. Aunt Ahma lit them one by one, and by their blood light, I could see an enormous plush bed, several lacquered desks, murals of classical poetry, a dragon rug, and a fireplace that tunneled somewhere deep into the stone walls. A few child-sized night robes hung on one wall.

It smelled of stale, long-ago incense.

The chamber had once been decorated with plants—potted bamboo, figs, and ancient cherry trees lined the walls—but they were all shriveled and dead.

I had no idea why she was afraid to show it to me. It was as luxurious as she claimed and completely innocuous.

Or perhaps it was the innocuousness of it that made it so wrong. One could give a prince the best silks and the best incense, but making him perform the childmaking duties against his will was *still* a cruelty.

I thought of the fear on the other concubines' faces, the New Year's they had come to me for help. How terrified I had been myself that first night, curled up against the cold walls of the Cypress Pavilion, awaiting my planting. The act may not have been magic, but it was often just as terrible.

I walked around the room, examining the bed, the furniture, the art on the walls, memorizing the texture of the velvet curtains for my poem. The whole time, Aunt Ahma stood by the door, looking like she wanted to bolt the moment I allowed her. When I reached the fireplace, which was full of ash, I spotted something shiny within it that caught the flickering lantern light. I searched for something to fish it out and found a pair of golden tongs, sitting on the mantel. I picked them up— and paused.

The tongs were not ordinary ones. They were forked at one end, with three metallic prongs branching out from its center.

I had seen that pattern before.

That night I had begged Terren to plant me, I had managed to loosen three buttons on his gown before he'd stopped me. They had exposed a conflagration of three-pronged scars on his chest. *As if a bird made of fire had trampled all over him*, I recalled surmising.

I looked up at Aunt Ahma standing by the door. "Remember what I said about the truth?" There was no threat in my tone, but my words must have been threatening enough. She immediately burst into tears.

"It wasn't me," she sobbed, and fell onto her knees. "It was her, it was Qiu'er, never me. I never did anything. I never—"

She stopped speaking when she found me next to her, pointing a blade at her forehead. I had plucked it off my ceiling in the Cypress Pavilion before leaving.

If there was anything that I learned in the palace, it was that knives were more convincing than words. Aunt Ahma hadn't listened to words, so I had little choice but to pull out a knife.

"The truth," I said, and let its tip press into her skin.

The truth was, for seven years of his life, the young prince had been brought to the Violet Heron Tower. For seven years, his mother and Aunt Ahma had worked together to arrange the childmaking duties for him and teach him how to plant his seeds.

Arrange was the word Aunt Ahma had used, but what she really meant was *force upon.*

Teach him was what she'd said, but what she really meant was punish him—violently—when he couldn't manage it.

He cried in the beginning.

In the beginning, they had to physically drag him into the room for his duties. Several girls had to hold him down while he kept crying and kicking and screaming. He grew calmer as time went on. He stopped resisting and took his treatment silent and still. Sometimes he asked for one of his toys to hold. They interfered with the act, so they did not always let him, but sometimes Lady Autumn was in a generous mood and indulged him.

The treatment lasted from when he was nine to when he was sixteen, the year she had died. It was more intense for the first few years, when he was still in Tieza for the war, almost every day; after that, it had been a few weeks at a time, whenever he had a break from his campaigns or his obligations in the palace.

Lady Autumn had known how badly she was hurting him. She just hadn't cared. *We have done our duty for the nation already,* she would say to excuse it. *It is his turn to do his.*

Aunt Ahma had found the enterprise profitable, so she had not cared either.

The shine in the fireplace was Niu Niu. When I fished the object out, I saw that it was a petrified snail shell. Most of it was covered in soot, though a few of its crystal spirals were exposed. I could only imagine that Tiger and Little Sparrow had been in that fireplace too, their fur and wood having caught fire much easier.

"Why did you have to burn his toys?" I asked Aunt Ahma, not kindly.

I was tremendously angry at her.

It was not a burning anger, one that would have made me want to cross the room and throw her against the wall, but a cold one. A frost-anger, an anger that permeated so deep it made me too numb to do anything, except perhaps step out of my body and marvel at it.

And it was not only because of the unforgivable cruelty of what she had done to a child—which was worth more than that kind of anger by itself—but the unfathomable shortsightedness of having done it to *Terren*, a prince, who held the magic of blades and the power of dynasties.

A thousand people like me could die and the world would not stop turning, but breaking one person like him could break a nation.

Aunt Ahma was still shaking, even though she no longer had a blade pointed at her head. "No," she sobbed. "It wasn't me. I didn't burn the toys."

"Then *who*?"

"He did." Her voice was barely a whisper. "One day—it was just after he'd liberated Tieza—he came here, finished his duties, went to the fireplace without a word and . . . and threw them in. He didn't even stay to watch them burn. I guessed he had finally grown out of them."

I wanted to kill her, I really did. I went as far as to imagine how warm her blood would be on my hands when I sank my knife into her skull. But I had told her I would not hurt her or punish her, so long as she gave me the truth—and she had, in the end, even if it had been a hard road to get there.

I left her soon afterwards, having gathered everything I needed from the Violet Heron Tower. I did not want to be in that place a moment longer than I had to.

When I stepped outside its arched entrance, into the cool summer night and the gentle murmur of Angkin City's commerce, I found a ghost.

55

SPEAKING WITH GHOSTS

The ghost was perched atop my carriage, which was still parked in front of the Violet Heron Tower. It was a sparrow the size of my palm, sitting in a bed of azaleas and glowing faintly. I recognized it immediately as something not from this world.

A ghost bird. Just like the ones I had seen everywhere in the palace.

It cocked its head at me and fluttered off. Suspecting that it would lead me somewhere important, I left my servants and followed it outside the city, across the Aricine River, and into the surrounding meadows, where fireflies played.

I was right. There was a ghost boy there. About nine or ten years old, kneeling among the wildflowers. Even without the red seal on his cheek, I would have recognized him. He looked just the way I had pictured him from all the accounts, small and wide-eyed and timid.

He was doing something with his hands. Making a sword. His sigil glowed as he brushed his palm across its side, leaving a red-hot trail wherever he touched.

"Terren," I said.

He did not acknowledge me, since he could not hear me.

I had seen quite a few ghosts before. My grandmother one summer in Lu'an, so hot the rice paddies misted into the sky, and the snowless winter after that, my two eldest brothers. For a few days after her death, Grandpa Har's wife had stayed behind to wander the village, and we had followed her as she drifted from door to door as if to say her final farewells. Ghosts were harmless, I knew, and rarely stayed long.

But I had never seen the ghost of someone still alive.

I seated myself next to him and watched him for a while. I was still angry, but not at him. I was angry at Aunt Ahma and Lady Autumn, and at the real Terren, who had tortured me and slaughtered my friends. But for the ghost boy in front of me, I could summon no such blame.

"I think I understand now," I said, though I knew my words could not reach him. "You were frightened, and hurting, and nobody had ever shown you a different way to be. So, you began hurting others. Maybe you wanted us to feel as you did. Maybe you wanted to frighten us, so that we would keep our distance. Maybe you didn't even think about it. You had learned that suffering was normal, a part of life, and so it hardly seemed remarkable to do it to others."

He continued his work. With a child's hand, he molded the sword into something sharp, new white flowers blooming with every stroke.

"They sent you to war so young. Young enough that you were still learning what the world was like. But the world they showed you was full of bloodshed and pain."

I thought, strangely, of the way Bao went to the stall selling glazed hawberries on New Year's. His eyes had been wide with longing, but he had not asked for one, because the world we had shown him had no money in it, no sweetness, no berries. Children were clever. They learned quickly.

How many weapons had they made him forge? How many battles had they bade him fight? How many people had they forced him to kill?

"The Aricine Ward," I continued. "Maro and everyone else, they think you've written it to make yourself strong, so that you can become powerful enough to seize the throne." Discovering that ward was why the West Palace had decided they were out of time, why Maro had met him in the peach garden that last time to kill him—why the carp in the pond had been poisoned, why arrows had rained from the sky. "But that wasn't why, was it? You only wanted to protect yourself, to make yourself invincible. You spent years writing the most difficult spell Tensha had ever known— not to fight your brother, but for the far simpler reason of making sure nobody could hurt you again."

Another flash of his sigil, another brush of his hand. His friend Little Sparrow fluttered onto his shoulder, watching him. It was taking him far longer to make his sword than I was used to. His movements were still uncertain, like it was something he was only beginning to learn.

I fished into my pocket, found the shell I had taken from the Violet Heron Tower, and set it onto the grass. "Here. I believe this belongs to you."

He did not take it, because he could not see it.

An idea struck me. I looked around and found two large rocks in the meadow. I set Niu Niu on one of them, and, using the other, smashed the shell until it broke into pieces.

It worked. Terren's head jerked up. His face lit up with unbridled joy as a ghost snail appeared, shimmering, from between the crystal pieces. He crawled over to it, took it into his arms, and nuzzled his cheek against its shell.

Then he looked up, and his eyes landed on me.

He blinked.

He reminded me so much of an older Rui Dan, from my village. In spite of my anger, hatred, and grief, I could not help as my mouth tugged into a smile. "Pretend I'm not here, all right? Keep doing what you were doing before. I wish only to keep you company for a while, and then I will be on my way."

He resumed his work, with two of his friends keeping him company. I seated myself next to him, on the summer grass, and pulled out paper and ink to work on my spell. Around us, the scene had changed. *A battlefield.* Gone was the summer scent of earth and pollen, replaced by hot winds of blood and copper ash. Gone were the fireflies, replaced by smoke and flames. A towering mound of finished swords had appeared behind Terren, swallowing him in its shadows.

There were more ghosts.

Ghosts bearing both Tensha's banners and foreign ones. Crowding around us, whispering. Standing on hills of corpses, stray weapons, broken shields. Some wore armor, tasseled helms and lamellar; others were clearly civilians, their clothes plain and stained with dirt. Some still had swords buried in their bellies or arrows in their hearts. Now I knew where men aimed on battlefields.

They all seemed so afraid of him, the berth around him so wide.

Was he the one who killed you? I could not help but wonder. *Or was it the war, our enemies, our country?*

It was almost completely dark, except for the ghosts and the fire, and, across the distant river, the lantern light of the city.

And my poem. I had already rewritten the verses I had burned, and the characters were glowing once again. I added a few more lines, from what I had learned in the Violet Heron Tower, and then, watching the ghosts, I added a few more.

As I was finishing up to leave, I was surprised to find someone looking over my shoulder.

"I thought I said to pretend I'm not here," I told the ghost boy, in the same tone I would have used to tease the village children.

He glanced again at my poem, and then he used his freshly made sword to carve a few hurried characters in the earth. When he was done, he stepped back and presented it to me—shyly, with his eyes on the ground.

I stared at the words he had written. "Is this for me?"

He lifted his head but did not speak.

It was a verse. A verse to fit my poem. And it was far better than anything I could have come up with.

He truly was brilliant. Even having studied all those classics, I had seldom come across words as expressive and heartfelt as his. I copied them down, and then I met his gaze. "Terren, thank you."

His eyes widened. Then he ducked his head, as if embarrassed, and went to hide behind his mound of swords. I bid him a gentle farewell and made back for the palace.

At the Azalea House, there were imperial guards waiting for me at the gates, weapons drawn and expressions grave.

"Lady Yin," they said, as soon as I dismounted my horse. "You are to come with us."

56

TEST OF TREASON

They would not tell me what my crime was as they marched me to the palace's prison, Heaven's Worship—only that it was treason, something I would be executed for. All afternoon I paced around the ledge of my confinement, mind spinning, trying to figure out exactly what my crime had been.

Confinement was not quite accurate. The prison was built into the side of a mountain, each cell a ledge, and the only thing *confining* me was a stomach-twisting drop on three sides, far enough beneath me that I could not see individual trees. Even the Aricine River curving away below was no larger than a finger's width.

The wind at this altitude was ferocious. Even the ancient pines growing out of the cliff face had to submit to it, bent and trembling like the meadow grasses in Tieza. I huddled in the alcove of my cell, trying not to shiver as the cold penetrated my cloak.

The order to arrest me could not have come from my husband. That much was certain. Although I had been nervous about facing him—and the inevitable confrontation about my visit to Tieza—I knew he would not jump straight to executing me. We were familiar enough by now that he would at least talk to me first.

Besides, he would never go through all this bureaucracy, not in ten thousand years. He would put a sword in me, maybe two—and if my crime was severe enough, play cruel games with me until I died more slowly—but he would not do something as impersonal as having *guards* throw me in prison.

Had one of the concubines finally found an opening to oust me? Had the empress come up with a new way to have me dead?

The third day of my imprisonment, two Azalea guards came to get me. They brought me to the main hall of the East Palace, the Hall of Divine Harmony, the same place my exam with the doctors had taken place nearly a year ago.

There were more people in attendance this time. There was the usual coterie of courtiers and ministers sitting between the pillars, but also officials who had ridden in from afar. Their huge banners announced places beyond the heartlands, places I only recognized from maps. Now that I was no longer Terren's betrothed but his wife, I supposed my trials had become even more of a spectacle.

As the guards dragged me to the front, I caught a glimpse of Terren, standing at the far side of the hall, alone. But unlike last time, when he kept his thoughts masked, his face now was a dark cloud of fury. His sigil flickered fast with agitation.

What reason was there, I wondered, for him to be so angry he could not even hide it?

A violet-robed magistrate stepped to the front, passing by the empress, Maro, and the rest of the princes. "We will now conduct a test of treasonous intent, devised by Heaven," he announced in a sonorous voice. "It will help determine whether a woman, like Lady Yin, is tainted in her heart. If she is, then the Ancestors will punish her with pain. If she is innocent, she will remain unharmed."

Several helpers laid down three large scrolls before me and gave me a long elm branch. "Choose one of them to copy," said the magistrate, and waved a magnanimous sleeve.

I clutched the branch as I blinked at the scrolls before me.

They were Blessings. The two on either end were as the magistrate had described: pain-inflicting spells, meant for torturing prisoners. The third had no effect. Another girl would have to pray to Heaven for guidance, but since I could read, I knew immediately which was the correct choice. *If she is innocent, she will remain unharmed.*

But at the same time, something wasn't right. Why hadn't they told me what I was accused of? Why did the empress, surrounded by a crowd of Sun men, seem almost smug?

Why was Terren so *angry?*

I glanced up at him again, standing in the back behind those hundreds of men, fidgeting with his hands. Whatever crime I had been accused of, it must have implicated him as well. And while that had been the case last time, he'd had Hesin then, and the eunuch would have been able to calm him, and—

Wait. I recognized that anger.

It was not the contemptuous one Terren had displayed at the empress, during our wedding; neither was it the pitying one he often showed me. It was pure, raw, and unbridled, the kind he had displayed the night I'd convinced him of Hesin's treason. The night I'd made him believe the eunuch was working with Maro to get him deposed, by fabricating evidence of my literacy.

This was not a "test of treasonous intent" at all. It was a literacy test.

With enough evidence, an exam might not have been needed. But in the absence of it, the House needed to make certain.

I lifted the elm branch with a shaking hand. I did not copy the third spell, the safe one, but instead traced one of the torture spells. I traced it in the uncertain, unpracticed way that somebody who didn't know how to read might have done, copying the way I had seen Grandpa Har draw that Blessing on the hill.

Not even three characters in, the pain came for me. Shuddering spasms that shook my entire body, making it hard to keep my grip on the branch. I actually did drop it once, but the magistrate just looked at me and said, "Keep going," and I fumbled to pick it up again.

When it was over, he swapped out the spells for three different ones. "Again."

I chose another torture spell. This time, the pain was even worse. It was like every capillary in my body was set on fire, every vein a devouring river of flames. I bit my cheeks and squeezed my eyes shut to keep from screaming, but that had the added effect of making me pause writing. The moment the branch stopped moving, the magistrate kicked me with a boot and said, "Keep going," and I forced my eyes open and completed the spell.

There was a third round after that—I chose the safe one this time, since it would look suspicious if I never got lucky—and then on the fourth, I did scream, I couldn't help it anymore. The pain was that unbearable. It was like nothing I had ever, ever felt before.

I kept writing. There was a fifth round and a sixth. Blood dripped out of my nose and my mouth, making scarlet spatters on the floor. A seventh, an eighth—every time I finished one, the magistrate immediately put out three new ones. I felt my body weakening over time, my mind slipping. At some point I fainted. When I woke again, shaking on the ground, there was a fresh set of spells for me to choose from.

"Again," said the magistrate, without emotion.

I supposed they needed to push me to my breaking point, in case I really *was* literate and hiding it. I wrote another spell.

"Again."

Every part of me begged for the agony to be over. If I confessed I was literate, and I'd been plotting to kill Terren, and that I was not actually an empress but a villager who was worth nothing, knew nothing, maybe the pain would finally, finally stop.

I picked up the elm branch and kept writing.

One humid summer when I was nine, maybe ten, I had spent an entire day weeding the rice terraces without break. It had been an oppressively hot day, with no clouds to hide the sun, and I had been tired and so, so thirsty.

So I plopped myself in the paddy, hot water soaking my trousers, and threw a big tantrum. For a long time I screamed and kicked at the reeds, complaining of the heat, and the mosquitoes, and my hurting hands, hoping that Ba would come and tell me I could go inside and rest. But he never did.

When the sun was halfway down, and at last I wiped my eyes and looked up, I saw that Ba was still working silently. He had not even lifted his head up once.

I would never forget the sight of him, hunched over in the haze of heat, pulling up clumps and clumps of sedges. While I had been sitting there feeling sorry for myself, he had been working hard, enduring, suffering.

At nine years old, maybe ten, I had learned the price we must pay to live.

I kept writing. The pain kept coming.

And coming.

And coming.

And—

What happened next I was not aware of at the time. It was only afterwards that Mi Yung and Ciyi filled me in.

Everyone had been pretty sure I was about to die.

The exam had been going on and on, the magistrate ordering more and more rounds. Blood was leaking from my nose, mouth, and ears. I wasn't breathing right. I had just finished a spell—the fourteenth, by Ciyi's count—and the helpers had been about to put out another set, when Terren said from the back of the room, "That's enough."

The magistrate looked up, annoyed. "Your Highness, we are in the middle of conducting a sacred exam."

"She has done fourteen rounds of the test already. Is that not enough proof for you?"

"A Heavenly trial cannot be aborted."

"It can if I say it can."

"That is not how that works."

"If she keeps going, she will die." Despite how quiet Terren's voice was from where he stood, his anger seemed to shake the entire room.

"She is only a concubine."

"She is my empress."

The magistrate heaved a deep sigh and shook his head. "Whatever she is, I am still a representative of His Majesty the Son of Heaven. I do not answer to your commands, only those of the emperor himself. And seeing as he has not given the order—"

"My father?" Terren threw his head back in a laugh, and it was wild and not held back. "That half-dead creature lying like boiled radish in his bed? Tell me, when was the last time he has given *any* order? The last time he was even coherent?"

The murmuring crowd was stunned into silence. Nobody spoke of the emperor like this. Not even a prince. Not anyone, not *ever*.

Even the magistrate was too shocked to respond.

Terren used the silence to take echoing steps forward, down the length of the hall, to stand not two paces from the magistrate. He might have been shorter, but there was no question which of the two men was more dangerous. "My father is as good as dead. He will never wake up again or regain the ability to overturn his decision to name me heir. Tell me, Magistrate—does that not mean *I* am effectively emperor?"

"Impudence!" the magistrate screamed. "Treason! Guards, take him!"

The imperial guards stationed along the perimeter of the hall started to move, but immediately froze when the knives on the ceiling began to rattle.

Everyone else became equally still.

Terren looked with pity at the magistrate, whose eyes had begun bulging. The magistrate's head spun around wildly before his gaze settled on Maro, who was sitting among a group of his own allies. "Prince of Roads," he said, desperate. "Do something. You heard what he said."

Maro needed little prompting. He stood, hands in fists, and as he spoke his voice shook with rage. "Even you are not above Heaven, Terren. You might have disrespected your post, the Azalea House, the whole country—but speaking ill of the emperor is the *highest level of treason.*"

"I spoke merely the truth."

"True or not, those words were a crime."

Terren kept looking at him, a dark fire burning in his eyes. "So punish me for it."

Maro stared at him, but didn't move.

"Punish me for it," Terren repeated, louder. "What are you waiting for?"

There was enough hate in the first son's eyes to end dynasties, but still he didn't move.

"I thought you were honorable." Terren sounded almost disappointed. "Patriotic. Pious. Yet you would let *the highest level of treason*, as you say, go unpunished."

That finally incensed Maro into motion. He threw himself at Terren, but he had not made it two steps forward when he was forced to halt. In the time it took to draw breath, the ten thousand swords in the ceiling had dislodged themselves from the lichens and were now swarming in the air. About a hundred of them hovered around Maro, restricting him from moving; the rest were flying everywhere else around the room. A few people started to scream, but quickly stopped when they found a blade at their throat.

"It is not a crime," Terren said through his teeth, "if nobody can punish me for it."

The swords pressed lower and lower onto Maro until he was forced onto his knees, his head down, his body hunched into a humiliating posture of subservience. He was shaking violently, and his face was twisted with loathing, but he did not speak further.

This seemed to satisfy Terren, because he now stilled the rest of the swords and turned them all to the magistrate. "Any other objections?"

The magistrate's face was completely white. He did not look capable of speaking either.

Terren laughed without humor, then spun to face the Orchard Palace and the men in blossoms, his suspended swords spinning with him. "Isan. Perhaps you would like to help our magistrate out." When he was met with silence, he turned his attention and blades to Kiran and his Southeast Palace, to his sailor friends all averting their eyes. "How about you, little brother? Perhaps you would champion for resuming his precious trial." None of them so much as looked at him.

His eyes flicked to the pillar closest to him. "Sun Ai." He took a few steps towards the empress, who was trembling as she clutched Ruyi tight against her. "Surely you have something to say. You always do."

He lifted her chin with the edge of a floating knife, and she squeezed her eyes shut, let out a tiny gasp, and did not speak.

He made a sound like a laugh and let her go. Then he swept his eyes across the rest of his audience, all in varying shades of terror. "Well, then. It seems that we are in agreement. *I* am the emperor. And as emperor, I declare the trial over."

57

DUTY AND SHORTCOMINGS

I woke to the cry of an enormous gray cuckoo, perched on my window-sill. When it spread its wings, its flight feathers were almost translucent against the summer sun. *Bu-guu*, it mourned. *Bu-guu, bu-guu*, like a haunting ghost.

It flew off somewhere into the canopy of cypresses.

I wasn't dead, I was somewhat surprised to discover. I knew this because it still hurt everywhere, my body still searing with a flame-river of pain.

Mi Yung in her blue dress came to my bedside to bring me medicine and watery congee. She had to spoon it all into my mouth, since I could not move at all, and the whole time, I could not stop thinking about how little she had in common with Wren.

She only managed a few spoonfuls before my eyes closed and I sank back into the darkness.

Sometimes imperial doctors came by. Sometimes the other concubines did too, presenting little gifts, flowers, and trinkets. Almost none of my other servants came to visit—they were all strangers, after all—but during nights, Hu would sit by my bed, silently holding my hand while we listened to birdsong and the rustling of summer cypresses.

Once or twice, I would wake to find a pot of ginger tea at my bedside table, with a candle under it to keep it boiling hot.

"How is my village doing?" I asked Mi Yung, when I was able to speak again.

This whole time in the palace, I may have been occupied with my own survival, but that did not mean I didn't think of them often. I missed home with a terrible, constant ache—an ache that was not noticed when there were more pressing pains, but when everything was calm again, on a day like this one, it was there waiting for me.

She sat on the rug next to my bed. "It's . . . bad, Lady Yin. I will not mince words. Everyone is thin. Everyone is suffering."

That did not surprise me. The past year of famine, I knew based on the reports I'd read, and my own trip to the north, had been particularly hard. "Tell me."

"The rice harvest last year was three-quarters of the year before, according to reports. Central taxes were overall lower, but officials in Guishan District had levied even larger local taxes. It was all under the table, but there was nothing the villagers could do about it." At my growing anger, she only shook her head. "Last year, there were even some deaths. The first few people I asked would not give names, but I kept pressing until I got a report."

"Tell me."

"Lien Ina has passed away, of an infection brought on by hunger. Her husband followed not long after, since she had been his caretaker. Shu Monshu fainted last summer in the rice terraces, during a heat wave, and drowned in the water. Two newborn infants did not make it—I believe they were of the Tong family and the Gray family. And, there was a boy, seven years old . . ."

I went ice-cold.

No. Not Bao. It couldn't be.

For a moment, my heart stopped beating. A thousand memories flashed at once. Bao giggling as he splashed in the paddies while my family worked. Bao hiding behind me by the bonfire, muffling the sounds of his crying with the back of my shirt, while Grandpa Har told an especially scary night-story. Bao on New Year's sucking on that sweet prune. Bao staring bug-eyed when Prince Isan's Blessing went to his heart, when Ba had told him he would grow up to become a great man. Bao clinging to my legs, on the day I was to leave for—

"...named Rui Dan," said Mi Yung.

Oh.

For a long time, I just sat there in silence, my mind blank with relief. I had forgotten that Bao was not seven anymore, he was nine; two birthdays of his had passed unnoticed in the year and a half since I'd come to the palace.

And then I thought, what an absolute monster I was. To learn of a child's death and have the audacity, the sheer depravity, to be *relieved*.

"I told them," I choked out—and maybe I was laughing, or sobbing, I didn't know, it was all becoming the same. "I told the Rui sisters that Myrna's milk was not for me. I told them to keep the goat for Dan, so that he could grow up lively and strong ... I told them but they wouldn't listen ..."

Mi Yung said a few more things. She told me how happy my parents had been to see all those apples and barrels of soybeans. How Bao had squealed and jumped for joy when he learned he was going to school. How the Rui sisters had still been grateful in the end, because they had received money enough to buy medicine for their ailing father. But I could not stop thinking about how Rui Dan was dead, dead, dead, just like Larkspur, just like the Cypress Pavilion, just like the pig at the wet market, just like a lot of things.

Soon, I was well enough again to work on the heart-spirit poem. Late one night, I was making final edits and additions when I heard footsteps outside my door. Heart hammering, I shoved it under my pillow just as Terren opened it.

He seemed surprised to find me awake. "Wei, I was just ..."

I waited for him to finish his sentence, but he didn't. I sat up in my bed and faced him. "The tea left on my bedside table. Was it from you?"

"No," he said, too quickly. He was awful at lying. I had not realized it until that day. If he wanted to be even a little more convincing, he ought to have said something like *What tea?*

Perhaps since he had gained the Aricine Ward and become invincible, he had never needed to lie.

For a while we just looked at each other. We had not had a proper conversation since he had saved me from my exam, since I had returned to the palace. Since I had spent an evening with his ghost in the meadow, writing poetry among friends and fireflies.

Since he had slaughtered almost the entire Cypress Pavilion that misty morning. Organs and cut limbs strewn everywhere in the mud, blood staining the cobblestone. Wren's hand still twitching when I found her.

I didn't know what to say to him.

I already knew what I would *do*—which was throttle him, if his ward would ever let me—but as for what to say, I had not the first clue.

"You shouldn't have done it," I managed at last.

"Done what?"

"The treason you committed against the emperor. At the trial." Even for Terren, those words had been too much. I had never known him to lose control like that, in a way that could turn the whole nation against him.

"They were about to kill you."

"You should have let them."

He gave me another one of his glass stares, the way he did whenever he thought I was being stupid. "I'm the only one who gets to take your life."

It might have been the most romantic thing he'd ever said to me, and I was startled into bitter, self-pitying laughter. Then I started coughing, because the pain came like a dagger between my ribs. It was a while before I recovered enough to speak again. "The level of treason you committed, the House will not let it go. Word will spread and all the Great Clans will turn against you. They will band together and overthrow you."

At that, he actually smiled. He took a few steps inside until he was facing the window, with its lush summer cypresses and warm winds just beyond. "You know, I'm beginning to suspect they won't." My confusion must have shown plain on my face, because he said, "Hesin used to tell me the same thing. *Be careful, Your Highness,* he would always remind me. *Watch yourself, and rein in your cruelty, lest even your allies betray you and destroy you.* It used to frighten me, quite a bit—the threat of everyone rallying behind Maro, marching into the East Palace, and ending me. But not anymore. After I had gotten rid of that traitor eunuch, and that annoying buzzing in my ear was gone, I finally began to think for myself. And I thought, maybe they won't do such a thing after all."

Two cuckoos chased each other just under the eaves. He watched them absently.

"It is true that if the whole nation worked together, it could defeat me. Even the combined army of six or seven of the biggest clans could overpower my blades and my ward. But that's the thing. I don't think they are going to do that, *work together*. The Sun Clan hates the Jin. The Wang can't stand the Nian. The Qi and the Miao have been fighting for control of the southeast coast for centuries. The Shangtze Coalition might hate me, but they hate Maro more; Salt Road imports have destroyed their near monopoly on ivory.

"And don't forget what I have done for the north. You've seen those dragon statues; you know already what they think of me. Do you think the herders in the mountains care whether a prince calls his father *boiled radish*? Do you think wheat farmers would pick up their scythes, make the long march to the capital, and storm the palace in defense of the emperor's dignity? The north is too far away to care what happens here. But war, occupiers, liberation—that is close enough to home to matter."

Dragon statues. I sat up straighter. So he already knew I had gone to Tieza.

Maybe that was why he'd saved me. He wanted me to explain myself, did not want me to die before I could. But then I remembered the tea he had been leaving on my table, and I thought, maybe not. Not entirely, anyway.

"You see now." He turned back towards me, a twisted smile on his face. "Nobody will challenge me. Nobody is brave enough—or foolish enough—to stand up to me. You and me, Wei, we can rule together for as long as I live. Our enemies will fear us, and the nation will kneel for us, and nobody in the world can ever hurt us." The Aricine Ward flashed. His smile vanished. "So long as you give the explanation you owe me."

It was time for my lie. A lie that would never have worked before, but might work now.

One that was—as far as all my lies went—surprisingly close to the truth.

"It's simple. I went to Tieza because I knew you had left a piece of yourself there." He stared at me blankly, but I kept speaking. "During our wedding, I pledged to you, *care*. I knelt before your bed that night and told you that I wished to stand at your side. To love you. And I could not do so, not truly, without finding it."

Half a year ago, he would have drawn knives at this. Now he just looked at me tiredly. "You have a roundabout way of speaking, Wei. Just tell me straight. What did you find?"

"The Violet Heron Tower."

"Ah." He was far more serene about it than I could have predicted. "Beautiful place, is it not? Quite a few poets frequent there."

"I know what they did to you. How they made you fight. Your mother and everyone else—"

He cut me off almost immediately. "I cannot imagine you learned anything new. You are already well acquainted with my shortcomings—the best acquainted of anyone alive. I can only imagine you went to Angkin to spite me. To take pleasure in knowing precisely how deep those shortcomings go. Tell me, did it please you to know I had been undutiful even then?"

Shortcomings. *Undutiful.*

My mouth fell open. Did he really see Tieza as his own failure?

"Terren," I said uncertainly. "What they made you do, it was not your duty. The burden of empire is not a child's to bear."

He blinked. "Of course it is. I am a prince with magic, and it is my duty to spread it. The House only needs more seal-bearing sons, so that the dynasty can become glorious and lasting."

They were words given to him, not his own. I knew him well enough to know he would never, not in ten thousand years, speak that way. "Terren—"

"And if I had been stronger, less of a coward, I could have succeeded." His breaths were coming faster now, his hands clenching and unclenching into fists. "And maybe Father would have named me heir sooner and there would not have been a fight for the throne. And maybe Maro would not look down on me and hate me. And maybe Lady Autumn would not be dead. It's my fault. I couldn't manage it. All the other princes, they sacrificed so much for the country, but I—"

"*Terren.*" All at once, I had tears in my eyes. I had no idea where they had come from. "What your mother did to you was cruel, and needless, and evil, and it was *not your duty.*"

They were the first words I had said to him, since I had begun writing the heart-spirit poem, that had not been for my survival or to gather material for it. They were earnest words.

He was shaking now. Sigil flickering like a wild flame. "Say one more word," he said, burning and dangerous, "and I'll kill you."

"She failed you. They all failed you. Everyone who knew what was happening to you—"

"*I'll kill you!*" he screamed. "Did you not hear me?"

"—but had not done a thing to stop it, because they saw you as not a person but a vessel carrying magic."

He was breathing very, very fast. A knife had appeared in his hand.

"They were wrong, Terren. *I* was wrong. You are a person." A monster, yes, but a person. "You deserve to be safe."

"I mean it," he whispered, lip quivering. "I'm going to kill you."

"They should have protected you."

"Don't think I won't do it."

"You deserve to be safe."

"*Say one more word—*"

"You deserve to be safe."

The knife flew across the air and slammed into the wall, missing my neck by a breath. Terren let out a choked sound, threw his hands over his face, and ran.

58

CHASING AWAY MONSTERS

He was gone by the time I made it outside—my injury slowed me—but even so, it did not take long to find him.

When I passed the Palisade Garden, I noticed that it was missing its swords. Normally, there were thousands of them, half-buried in the ground, but they were all gone.

I unhooked a lantern from the eaves of a nearby pavilion and ventured into the cold fog; where the light shone, ghost cuckoos cried out with alarm and scattered back into the dark. It was deep into the garden that I found the swords: arranged densely in a giant dome-shaped cage, held together by their own weights, a dense tangle of lilies, and Dao magic.

"Terren," I called.

When no answer came, I grabbed one of the swords by the hilt and pulled. It came away with some resistance, a tiny *ting* breaking the night's quiet. I worked on prying more away—cutting myself several times in the process—until I had created an opening to the dark center of the cage.

By the red light of my lantern, I could see him. Curled up against one side, very small, his head buried in his knees. He was crying. I could tell by the way his shoulders shook.

"Terren, it's me."

No answer.

I crouched beside him in the small hollow, the way I had done with the boy in the meadow. "May I keep you company?"

No answer.

"I'd like to tell you a story, if you would hear it. It's one that my Ma used to tell me."

Silence. Not even the stirring of grass in the wind.

"There was a year, before I was born, in which many animals in Lu'an had vanished. Hens and ducks and rabbits, and even the milk goats had not been spared. It had been a desperate summer, a summer when the sun seared the land so dry the catfish were cooked alive right in their holes."

I kept my eyes on him as I did the telling.

"Nobody knew why, except for an old man who came from the village over. He walked in a stooped shuffle, and his skin held many wrinkles, so we knew he was very wise. He told us that there was a fox spirit who lived in the hills. He said on dark nights, when even the stars were not visible, it would come out hunting; that was why our livestock disappeared.

"Everyone was infuriated. As you can imagine, our village was already suffering from the famine, so this loss was not small. We knew we had to drive the demon away before it could do more damage.

"We tried to set traps for it, the way we might trap a wolf, but the demon was not of this world and could not be contained by normal materials. We tried to lure it with meat and lay ambush in the shadows, but the demon was devious and avoided it. Ba and Uncle Tam even tried going up the hill, to chase it away with sickles, but they could not find it. You know what did work in the end?"

He said nothing, so I answered my own question: "We worked together, all of us, as a village. We picked a clear, windless day, and then we gathered all the scary things we could find. Torches and kites, pots and wood-drums, leftover firecrackers from New Year's. We went to the hill. Everyone—from the children to the elderly—clapped and yelled and stomped our feet and told the demon to go away *or else*. And, well, it really did grow afraid. It left our village for good, and from then on, no livestock was ever taken again."

I finished the tale. The summer remained silent, except for the call of an owl, very far away. The fog hung cold in the darkness between us.

For a while Terren was so still that I thought he hadn't been listening, but then he said, his voice small and broken, "Why did you tell me this?"

I honestly didn't know. There was no point to it, except that I wanted to take his mind somewhere else, a place where people were good. "Because these are the stories I grew up with," I said, wishing I was more articulate. "Because they are lovely and I like them."

"Demons are not real. Anyone who has spent a day in school or read a book knows that."

"Then good thing I have done neither."

"If there was any truth to what your ma told you, then it was probably road bandits who took your livestock. There were lots of them, in the early years of the famine."

I had suspected as much already, having read the histories by now, the memorials, the records. "Perhaps. But I like my version better."

At last, he lifted his face from his sleeves and wiped furiously at his eyes. His voice was still broken as he said, "I should have you beheaded for seeing me like this."

It was another flat attempt to get me afraid of him—or perhaps merely a force of habit. But I knew the threat did not have his heart behind it. "Is that so?"

"Beheaded and worse."

"Terren, it is not a weakness to be seen."

There were no knives between us now, no fear, not even enough distance for a sparrow to spread its wings. I looked into his eyes, and though they were older and meaner, there was no question they were the same ones as on the boy I'd seen in the meadow. I looked into them and I saw him.

Maybe it *was* possible to love somebody that one hated.

Maybe, buried heart-deep, I really did love him. Not the kind of love a wife shared with her husband—that was not possible, after all he'd done to me; I might have borne no scars, but my body still remembered—but the kind of love one human could not help but feel for another when they had to pry away blades to find them.

I did not know what else to call it, if not *love*.

"Wei." Something in my words had made him start crying again. "I'm . . . I'm lost."

"Don't worry. I'm here."

"Will you hold on to me?"

I was taken aback. "Will it help you?"

He didn't answer, only cried harder, shoulders shuddering with every heaving sob. I put a gentle arm around him and brought him close, and his face fell wet onto my shoulder like he could hold it up no longer. "I don't know anymore," he gasped into my gown. "I . . ." He was crying so hard he could barely speak. "I don't know . . ."

He never managed to articulate what it was he didn't know, but I knew his meaning. *I don't know how much suffering is normal.*

How much was ordinary, expected, the price we paid to live.

How much was created by us, needless.

I didn't blame him for not knowing. I didn't think I knew either. I did the only thing I knew how, which was to sit with him in silence and hold him tight, the way Ma used to do for me. I let him pour his gasping sobs into my shoulder, each one like his whole body was fighting for air. They were the rawest, most heartrending sounds I had ever heard come out of a human. "I don't know . . . I'm lost . . . I'm lost . . ."

He had done many evil deeds, I thought, but he had not done *everything* he'd been accused of. He might have been a monster, but not all the ugliness in the world was his fault.

I held on to him as the night turned around us, as the dim flame of the lantern brushed our wall of knives and outlined the small shape of him in red. At last, when the sky was beginning to lighten through the lattice of our cage, he finally seemed to run out of those sounds. And he whispered, so quietly I almost didn't hear him, "I did do it. Lady Autumn. I killed her."

Then he told me how it happened, and the words he spoke were earnest ones.

59

THE RIGHT PATH

He never left the peach garden that day.

As he was running from the arrows, under the cover of mist, he had passed by one of his usual hiding places. An azalea bush, near the gate. He had thrown himself under its leaves and waited, breathless, for the men with swords to pass him by. His leg throbbed terribly. There was an arrow still stuck in it. Arrows were not quite blades, and even if he could bend them in the air with his sigil, he had not been able to mend a wound caused by one.

For days he hid there, while the sky battered the garden with cold rain, huddling in the scent of blood and wet earth. He would have hidden there forever, except on the fourth afternoon, when the sun finally broke through the clouds, someone found him.

"Come out." A woman's voice, as melodic as larksong. "Everyone thinks you're somewhere deep in the East Palace. But I know all your hiding spots." The voice was accompanied by footsteps. Every snap of a twig made his heart leap to his throat.

Hungry, soaked, and still hurting, he tucked himself smaller inside the shadow of his bush. He sent a silent wish to the Ancestors that she wouldn't notice him.

But the Ancestors did not listen to his prayers. They rarely ever did. The footsteps came closer.

I did not know if it was some new form of literomancy, or the more simple magic of good storytelling, but as Terren told his tale, I found myself no longer in the sword cage, holding on to him. I was right there, in the peach garden, in the body of that boy, cowering under the skin of his scars, living by the beat of his heart.

"I was not going to come looking for you, you know. But Hesin asked me to speak to you, to guide you onto the right path. And how could I refuse him? I am your mother, after all."

The footsteps stopped right in front of him. From under the rain-slicked azalea leaves, he could see shoes, narrow and silk-soft, barely peeking out beneath a maple cloak.

He held his breath, tried to disappear.

"Seven years," she said. "Seven years since you went to the mountain with him and learned he was dying. Seven years since you've begun writing that spell to make him invincible—behind his back, because he would have never allowed it if he knew. And you were *so close* to casting it on him."

If he stopped breathing entirely, he thought, maybe he could turn into wind. Nobody could see or catch the wind.

"A few more days, and you would have finished the most powerful spell in the world. A few more days, and you would have given it to our enemy." Her voice was still kind, but it was tinged with disappointment, the way a drop of poison could turn a cup of honeywater bitter. "If I had not intervened, you would have ruined everything we've worked for."

He tried it. He tried squeezing his eyes shut, becoming wind.

"But you are very lucky that I was looking out for you. That before you could cast it, I have shown you the truth. I have shown you who he really is." The shoes stepped aside, squelching in the mud. Beyond them, in the distance, he could see the pond. It was full of dead fish. "Look. Look for yourself what he has done, the lengths he will go. He understands what you can never seem to grasp: that the right path is the *winning one*."

Maybe it was really working. Maybe he really *had* become air, and she would stay here only a brief while, become bored with him, move on. Maybe—

"But don't worry, my beautiful son. Soon you will understand this too. Your mother is here, after all, to guide you."

Without warning, the bush shielding him parted. The harsh afternoon sun intruded inside his shelter, stinging his eyes. A pair of hands seized him. As they pulled him out, the arrow in his leg snagged on a branch. He screamed in pain, but the hands kept pulling. They dragged him out, across the wet earth, until his face fell beside the silken shoes.

"Kneel."

He coughed out a clump of rotten blossoms, bitter with mud and rain, and pushed himself up. His wounded leg felt like water. Next to him sat a large crate made of lacquered sandalwood. He did not know what was inside, but he instinctively didn't like it.

"Look at me."

Trembling, he raised his chin.

Terren never described what she looked like. I pictured her as only a blur—a tower of shifting shadows under that maple cloak, not real.

"He is willing to do anything to win," the shadows said. "Trick you, betray you, kill you. He is even willing to murder *fish*." The voice was like lullabies, like warm hugs from when he was little. He could not reconcile it with the pain. "But your weakness is that you have never been able to do just that, *anything*. Over the years, your advisors and I have told you, over and over again, to go for his throat when nobody is looking. Yet three days ago, when you had the chance, did you take it?"

A shoe pressed down on the arrow in his leg, sending a searing wave through his body. He gasped as his vision darkened.

"It's still hard for you, isn't it? You can hurt almost anyone, kill almost anything—but as for the ones you've tricked yourself into thinking you love, it's still so hard. But don't worry. We'll work up to it. We'll practice."

The hands unclasped the lid of the crate. Inside was water and a golden carp the size of a kitten. There was a rope hooked in its mouth, making it bleed. One hand lifted it out of the water, and it thrashed in the air, fins stiff with its pain. The other pulled out a knife.

He made the mistake of letting out a sob, which made the shoe press down on the arrow harder. The sob turned into another scream of agony.

"Make a cut," she said, still in that lullaby voice, and threw the knife on the ground in front of him. "Consider it an act of mercy, if it helps you. These palace carp were never meant to survive long anyway."

He wanted to become a tree. He wanted to be grass. He wanted to be the clouds and the daylight, that little ant crawling among the wet blossoms. He wanted, most of all, to become air.

"One cut, and there will be no more lies. No more betrayals. No more poisoned fish or arrows in your leg."

It hurt so much he could barely think. With whatever bit of magic he could scrounge, he lifted the knife, and it hovered in the air, shaking.

"One cut, and the future of the dynasty will be decided. Everything will be over. You won't have to fight any longer."

He let out another sob—he couldn't stop it from coming out. He was exhausted, and still hurting, and the fish was suffering so much, dangled like that.

"One cut, and you will become the most powerful in all of Tensha. Nobody will be left to contest you. Not one person in the world can hurt you."

The carp's thrashing was feebler now. It was dying.

The shoe stepped down into the arrow. It broke with a *snap*. He collapsed onto his side, gasping for breath. It took everything he had not to pass out from the pain.

"One cut, and you will be safe again. No more hurt. No more fear. Just one cut, my beautiful child, and you will become—"

Heir, was what she likely meant to say.

Free, was also possible.

Wind, was how he liked to imagine it.

He would never know for sure, because he finally did make a cut. And then the voice and the shadows, the hands and the shoes, they all went as silent and still as the fish.

Seven years.

Seven years since you've begun writing that spell to make him invincible.

How arrogant I had been to assume I'd known the whole truth—when I had heard it from Hesin, when I had heard it from Maro, even when I had gone in person to Tieza. How foolish I had been to have believed I could write Terren's poem without once speaking with him, without hearing his testimony from his own mouth.

That night, after I'd returned to my pavilion, I added one final, crucial verse to my love poem. Then I summoned my messenger.

"Tell Lady Song it's done," I said.

"What's done?" Ciyi asked, out of habit, but he knew better by now than to press me.

He left to deliver my message, leaving me in my empty parlor, with my killing spell safe under the floorboards, its characters glowing hot like the Archer's nine shot-down suns.

60

SUMMER CICADAS

A week later, Silian invited me to visit the West Palace, using the summer solstice celebration as an excuse for us to meet.

At the wisteria arch leading to the Thousand Lotus Lake, a soft floral aroma and two polite but wary maids greeted me. "Welcome, Lady Yin."

Their wariness made sense: I might have been here twice before, but those visits were covert. This was the first time I had been here as an actual guest, and during daytime.

The West Palace looked different in daylight. The lake seemed even more endless, the near end of it bobbing with gentle lotuses, the far end vanishing only in a distant haze of peaks. Gazebos, walkways, and bridges crowded the shores, reflecting in the clear water. They were already filled with guests. Men and women, all dressed in shimmery silks and vines, holding silver wine vessels and conversing over the strum of zithers.

A distant sort of sadness settled heavy in my chest. I had never once seen Terren's palace this full. I had never seen it anything other than empty.

Silian wove her way through a bridge full of fan-dancers to greet me. "Lady Yin," she said genially. "You look magnificent today, like a real empress."

"Where can we talk? There are too many people here."

"Not yet." She smiled and took my arm. "Let us first enjoy the solstice."

It was hard to think of anything but the paper hidden in my sleeve, and Terren's imminent assassination, but I followed her into one of the gazebos to join the dozens of courtiers already there.

Within the circle of the crowd, two child eunuchs unjarred a fist-sized cicada each onto a table. There was a green one and a red one, their bodies covered with moss and little leaves, their wings clipped so that they could not fly away.

"I've consulted the stars," said one of the observers, "and my money's on the green one."

"Pffah," rebuked another beside him, red-faced with drink. "Your amateur astronomy is nothing compared to tradition. Even the youngest children know that red is the luckier color."

The two cicadas scuttled about the arena, which had been carved with Tensha's mountains, valleys, and rivers, ramming their heads against each other until one of them stopped moving. The crowd went wild—with excitement or frustration, depending on which way the betting had gone. Coins clinked as they changed hands. Even Prince Maro, who was mid-conversation with a courtier on a bridge not far away, glanced over to see what the commotion was about.

I did not think I was meant to feel sorry for the cicadas, but I did. The little eunuchs scooped the wingless cicadas back into their jars.

"My turn!" One of the younger men, white-haired and grinning wide, cracked his knuckles and stepped forward. He had his own jar with him, with an iridescent cicada rattling inside.

The crowd cheered his name. "Nobleman Song! Nobleman Song!"

"The son of the Song patriarch," announced someone with enthusiasm. "Who will be worthy enough to challenge the likes of *him?*"

That turned out to be a literomancer from Dusu District, with a cicada as black as his robes, and the crowd went even wilder. "A renowned literomancer against the heir apparent of a Great Clan," someone exclaimed. "A match even Heaven would pause to watch!"

Amidst the excitement of the crowd, I turned to Silian. "Which one is your husband's tutor? Can you introduce me to him?"

She raised a brow. "Tutor?"

"Master Ganji." I was curious to know what he was like in person, after having heard so much about him from the journals.

"Oh, him. He passed away two years ago, of illness."

I was not sure why the fact made me feel so empty. "He won't get to see Maro's coronation, then."

She gave me a strange look. "No, I suppose he won't."

As the afternoon went on, there was more entertainment, more feasting, more performances. Silian made me try cold noodles drenched in sesame oil, cucumber salad spiced with vinegar, and sweet watermelon and hibiscus wine.

At last, when the shadows began to draw long, and the men had become distracted with drink, Silian waved me towards the bridge leading to Maro's study, removed from the rest of the festivities.

It looked different than it had at night. By the light from the setting sun, I could see how far the view of the lake stretched, full to the horizon with lotuses. The bookshelves by the window looked larger, as did all the blooming chrysanthemums. The dragon kite on the wall looked smaller.

"Now that you've had enough fun that everyone is convinced you are a real guest," Silian said, closing the door behind us, "it is time to talk business. Do you have it?"

"I do." I pulled out the piece of paper from my sleeve, and the light from its characters spilled across the entire room.

She took it, eyes widening with awe. "I have never seen a Blessing so bright before, and that is including the ones I have seen my husband and his colleagues write. He will be joining us in a moment, by the way."

That surprised me. "He knows?"

"He has to. He must prepare himself to undertake the coronation himself once Terren dies. But I only told him a few days ago, after I received news of your success; any earlier and, as I said, he would not have believed us. When he sees your writing"—she ran a fond hand over the glowing ink—"he'll know it for what it is. He'll have no choice but to believe us then. Is this the whole poem?"

"It's only a section," I said truthfully. Even after working with her for the past half year, even after all the gentle evenings we'd spent sharing tea, I could not let myself trust her entirely. To bring the whole Blessing—and give the West Palace complete possession of it—would have been foolish. If I had, nothing would have stopped them from seizing it and leaving me with no leverage.

Besides, it was *my* love ballad, my killing spell. Terren's life was mine to take. I may not have been qualified to judge whether he should die, but those who had not written his poem were surely less.

The door swung open.

I spun around and it was him, the first son. Prince Maro, with his sweeping white-and-gold robes, his curtaining black hair, his Aolian cloudstaff tied to his back by a ribbon kept looped around his neck.

I knew him.

That was the strange thing—I *knew* him, even though I had never once spoken to him.

In the process of composing a poem for his brother, I had also, by necessity, found Maro. I had known him when he was a child and willful; I had known him when he was a youth and dutiful. I had known him even later, as he maneuvered politically against the East Palace, in a desperate bid to save his brother and the nation both.

I knew his strengths; I knew his flaws. I understood how much of the stories I'd heard about him—of his honor, his virtue, his piety—were true, and how much were only exaggeration. I admired him for some of his deeds. I begrudged him for others.

Perhaps that was what it meant to be heard through words. He might not know the first thing about me, but I knew *him* well enough to judge him.

I had spent an entire harrowing year trying to make him emperor. It was only fair that I got to.

"Lady Yin." Maro gave me a polite bow. "My wife has told me about your literary achievements."

"Your Highness," I replied. "May you live a thousand years."

Silian gave the piece of my poem to him. He took the paper, brows furrowing just slightly as he skimmed over the verse. I saw something like disbelief in his expression—as if he had not actually thought I would be able to do it, write a heart-spirit poem as a girl and a villager—but then it was gone.

"Yes," he said, nodding to himself. "This will work."

He gave it back to me, and I felt a weight vanish from my shoulders. I had already known it would—I'd felt the heat under my pen after all, seen the radiance of the characters—but part of me had not let myself believe it until I'd heard it confirmed by a real literomancer.

"Cast it during the coronation as you have planned," he said, efficiently, "and I will see that you are well rewarded once I become emperor. I bid you farewell." He turned to leave.

Silian looked as surprised at his sudden departure as I felt. "Do you have to go so soon, my love? It is summer solstice, a holiday. Surely you have some time to spare, today of all days. And besides, we have an honored guest." She gestured at me.

"I have my filial duties to attend to. Silian—Lady Yin—please accept my apologies."

We watched him go, bewildered. His golden-white robes swept the carpet as he crossed the room, aglow in the waning light of the sunset.

"Maro," I said, before I could stop myself.

He paused at the door.

"He did it for you."

That quiet, extraordinary child, who had suffered so much for so long—he had never once thought to save himself. Even as they forced the childmaking duties upon him, even as they punished him with vicious beatings and threw him into the flames of war, he had only been thinking of protecting his brother—his family—his burning star.

The boy who had once saved him from his tree.

"Until the day you poisoned the fish," I said softly, "he was never against you. Until the day you tried to kill him, he had never stopped trying to save you. Seven years, an impossible spell, a poem wrung out of love— Maro, he did it for you."

"Then he has learned nothing," Maro replied without emotion. He opened the door and left us.

That night, the world began to rumble.

I felt it first under my feet. Then I heard it: in the rattle of porcelain bowls on the shelves, the rustle of cypresses outside my pavilion. Far in the sky, a fiery rend had been ripped out of the night, and from the tear fell hundreds of red burning stars.

"What . . ." I began to gasp out, as panicked shouts erupted from the courtyards, the gardens, the nearby pagodas. Then I saw it. The Crown of the Azalea House, roaring as it shot up into the sky, its dragon body thrashing and frenzied and untamed.

It could only mean one thing: the emperor was dead.

61

WHITE

They ruled the emperor's death an illness. There was no evidence of foul play or poison, the imperial doctors declared; it was only natural and a long time coming.

But still, there was something strange about the timing of it. Strange and frightfully convenient.

The emperor was sick, Hesin had said, *but even so, it could take years or decades for him to finally die and pass down the Crown.*

It could have happened any other time—years before or years after. So why, I could not help but wonder, had it happened the day I took my poem to the West Palace?

Maro, I thought, *have you shown me who you really are?*

The funeral and coronation were scheduled very quickly after that—the funeral just two days after the emperor's death, the coronation right after. Time was of the essence. There was still an angry red tear in the sky and an imbalance between Heaven and the Ancestors. Until the dragon was tamed and a new emperor was enthroned, the nation would remain vulnerable.

The scent of ash and burned things hung in the air.

There were even more people present at the funeral than had been during my wedding, all dressed in ghost-white. I could see the full scale of the event from where I sat on the top terrace, overlooking the square before the Hall of Heavenly Supremacy. Even the bonfires below me were white, enchanted to burn much hotter than usual.

Servants and eunuchs busied themselves burning items for the emperor to enjoy in his afterlife: coins and silver treasures, silk gowns and porcelain plates, scrolls of classics and poetry, water-painted murals, ivory game sets, bamboo flutes, wooden zithers. They burned spells too, contributed by his sons and the nation's literomancers, their glowing characters vanishing as they were swallowed by the white flames.

They even burned an army of soldiers and horses, carved from sandalwood, so he could be well protected in the spirit world.

"You may now perform your kowtows," said the Minister of Rites, who stood close to me.

I knelt beside the princes, Silian, and the empress, on a carpet of lilies and white chrysanthemums. The emperor's casket was here, elevated on a carved-gold dais that was adorned with dragons.

As we performed our rituals, I glanced over at the first son.

Silian had told me that he'd been importing medicines from the West. To save his father's life, she'd said. Every week, he had been visiting him in his bedchambers, spooning them into his mouth while holding his hand.

I have my filial duties to attend to.

That was the last thing he'd said before he left us that night, the night he'd found out I had a working heart-spirit poem. The night he'd confirmed that Terren would be killed during his coronation, and that *he* would be the one inheriting the throne.

That same night, the emperor had died.

"It is nearly time to send His Majesty on his way," intoned the Minister of Rites. "Who volunteers to go echo-step with him?"

Serpent's Tongue. Undetectable. Its symptoms indistinguishable from a common illness.

It must have been so easy for him. Slipping it into the medicine he was already giving his father, during one of the many visits he was already making. And nobody would suspect him either. Terren was heir, not Maro, so there would have been little motive for Maro to want the emperor dead.

"I will," said a voice from the crowd below. Li Panya, one of the emperor's loyal generals and oldest friends, who had fought for him during the Azalea Civil War. As the man made his way up the steps to the top terrace, I kept my eyes on Maro.

The first son showed no emotion on his face—no grief, no regret, no satisfaction. It was like he had done something only routine, like building a road or widening a canal.

I understood why he'd done it. The longer the fight for the throne went on, the weaker and more divided the nation. The longer the Crown remained unridden, the longer its power went unused and wasted. Maro murdering his father would only allow him to begin stabilizing the dynasty sooner. Any one of them would have done the same.

But still, I could not help but judge him for it.

Perhaps it was unfair, my judging. Perhaps it was only because I had heard the stories—both from others and from his own pen—and knew he was supposed to have honor and integrity. He had once believed he could rule a nation while keeping both, and perhaps it was the *once* that bothered me most.

We are long, long past the point of playing fair, Siming had said. But the people we told legends about were supposed to be better than us.

Li Panya reached our level and knelt next to the casket. "Where my dear friend and benevolent master goes, I follow," he declared, and drew his sword. He sliced himself from the base of his neck down. The sword had not even made it to his stomach before he crumpled and collapsed next to the casket, red blood staining pale lilies.

There were a few more volunteers. Guards and loyal servants, and two eunuchs who had been with the emperor since he was a boy. They all gave themselves up in this world, for the honor of continuing to serve him in the next.

Women were forbidden from going echo-step. The journey beyond the grave was perilous, it was said, and only to be endured by men. Forbidden too was anyone bearing a seal, since their magic was too precious to not be used in this world, but Maro, Isan, and Kiran volunteered anyway. Even knowing they would be denied by the minister, they got onto their knees and asked to accompany their father.

Terren did not bother. "I shall not be a willing participant in theater," he said privately to me, from where we stood a few paces away. He had been doing that more as of late—confiding his political opinions to me. I supposed he had not been able to do that with anyone since Hesin's departure, and even so, I suspected he had not been quite as forthright with his former advisor. "Do you think any of my brothers truly wish to die? The pretense is more insulting to my father's cold body than if they had not gotten on their knees at all."

I kept my eyes on the carpet. I understood his way of thinking—I really did. But at the same time, I could not bring myself to agree.

If I was really his wife who loved him, if I really wanted to help him become a better emperor, I might have advised him differently. *Terren,* I might have said, *don't you know? Sometimes pretense is everything.*

For the people who have never stepped foot within the palace walls, I might have told him, *rumors are all they have. For those who live a thousand li away, who have never seen your face, stories are all they know. For the little girls in villages, far from the capital, all they have of you are pieces others give them.*

Terren, don't you know? Sometimes fiction is more important than the truth.

But I was going to kill him tomorrow, so I said nothing.

The last of the volunteers slew themselves on the terrace. Priests burned the bodies along with the casket and the flowers, and the pillar of flame was so tall it reached all the way to Heaven.

62

A QUIET DEATH

After the rituals came a period of mourning. The important guests were directed inside the Hall of Heavenly Supremacy, much like the day of my wedding. Fan-dancers drifted in ghost silks through the pillars, which were decorated with grief poetry on sheer banners. Little boats of rice cakes, white gao, and corpse-colored tea were set out for the guests, who spoke quiet words in praise of the deceased emperor.

"He has rescued the country from the Yonghuan Emperor's corrupt reign. The dynasty would not have survived without his sacrifice."

"He has built the Salt Road during his reign and liberated Tieza-North. These deeds will surely go down in history, as poems."

"He has fathered five healthy sons—all but guaranteeing the continued prosperity of our dynasty."

Amidst the chatter, the empress found me standing alone, by a far wall, and fluttered her way over to me.

"How happy you must be," she said pleasantly, "that you have succeeded in taking my place. My husband is dead. Your husband will soon be emperor. Congratulations, Wei—you have won." She was wearing the proper mourning colors instead of her usual gold, but her smile was still painted in sharp vermilion.

I gave her a dignified bow. "I was not aware that there was any *winning* involved, Your Majesty." The empress did not know that soon, I would not be a part of the palace at all. I had given thought to what I would ask of Maro, once I had cast the heart-spirit poem and helped him become emperor. I was going to ask to go home.

"There will always be winning and losing," she said lightly, "so long as not all people are born equal."

"You know, I talked Terren out of killing you."

Her surprise was immensely satisfying. I had said what I did out of a childish desire to alarm her, to flaunt my power, and it had worked.

It was true. After our night in the Palisade Garden, after I had told him the story about chasing away monsters, he had visited me several more times—without enmity now, without barriers between us. Sometimes it was to share a meal, sometimes to walk under the plum trees, sometimes to teach me how to play chess.

And we'd exchanged more earnest words, held several more earnest conversations.

One of them had been about who to punish. *Someone*, Terren had insisted, had to pay for the allegations of my literacy, since they'd almost caused my death and his deposition.

"There was an investigation of where the accusations came from this time, the rumors that led to my literacy exam. We have not found anything, but it does not take much deducing to see that they have come from you. Terren was so angry he'd been ready to storm into the South Palace and slit your throat." He really would have. He was certainly fearless enough now that he would have done anything, killed anyone.

"But you stopped him?"

"It took a long time, and it was not easy, but I managed to calm him down and talk him out of it."

She barked out a laugh. "If you are so sure that I was the one who started the rumors, and caused you such agony during your exam, then why bother to save me?"

"Because death is irreversible. Because while I believe it was you, I am not certain enough to feel worthy of passing the judgment. Because you are still the empress, and the matriarch of the Sun Clan, and your death will mean unrest for the nation." I glanced at the giggling toddler far behind us, playing chase with one of the empress's eunuchs. "Because Prince Ruyi is still young and needs a mother."

"I see," she said, and gave an odd sort of smile. "Well, it was a good thing you did. Because it wasn't me."

I could not believe she was denying it, even now. "If not you, then who?

Who has the right motivation to threaten both me and Terren? Whose allegations, besides yours, would even be believed?"

She looked at me with pity. "Wei, I had gained such a high opinion of your cleverness, after that stunt you pulled at your wedding. But now you quite disappoint me. If you only looked around you with your eyes open, even once, you would find the answer to your questions." She went off to join her clan again, leaving me in the shadows at the edge of the grand hall, bewildered.

I looked around me. My eyes fell upon Terren's other concubines—Jin Veris and Kang Rho sharing wine; the Qi Clan sisters, whispering about something under a potted cherry tree; Wang Suwen, trying to gain a political edge by speaking the emperor's praises to the chancellor. None of them had anything to gain with a move that harmed Terren.

It could not be any of the men in the room either, who were sharing solemn tea to commemorate their former emperor's life. Since their business remained with the Outer Court, since they had little contact with me, any suspicion they had of my literacy would not be taken seriously.

So then, it had to be—

Song Silian was standing by one of the pillars, her arms hooked around Maro's as he spoke with a literomancer. I watched her for a while, almost curiously, like she was a creature in one of Grandpa Har's night-stories. I wished I could summon anger, but truthfully, I was not even that surprised.

During the preceding months, in which I had grown closer to Terren, everyone had noticed. Those months must have frightened her so. *What if Wei really has fallen in love with her husband?* she must have wondered. *What if she has decided that killing him is too hard?*

What if she wants to be empress after all?

After our wedding, everyone in Tensha knew that she was my teacher and we were close. If she came forth with allegations of my literacy, they would not hesitate before ordering an exam.

And had she succeeded with her plan—had I not identified the "test of treason" as a literacy test, or had I given in to the pain—it would have been a far more efficient way of achieving her goal. She might have taken her chances with me and my poem, but she had never stopped searching for other ways to win. *There are no altruists in the palace.*

I should have been angry or shamed. A younger version of me might have heated at the thought of being betrayed by someone I'd once considered so beautiful, someone who had used the concubine's weapon on me and made me stupid.

Instead, I only felt lost. I had been so certain. So certain I needed to kill Terren, despite the necessity of the Dao seal, and make his brother emperor in his place. That hope had been the one thing that kept me stubbornly surviving, my one path of light within the House's darkness and corruption. But now Maro had murdered his father for power, and his wife had almost killed me for the same. And now, for the first time, doubt was creeping into me, and it was icy and dangerous and *terrifying*.

And I thought, maybe Terren was right. Maybe it was easier to tear everything down, because then there would have to be no decision at all.

At the very least, there would be nobody left to judge me wrong.

"Wei."

It was him. Dressed in a flowing white mourning gown, a dragon pin of frost jade threading through his hair. Terren seemed almost nervous as he said, "May I speak with you outside? Alone?"

We went to the terrace outside the hall, overlooking the square. The summer was everywhere in the Azalea House, verdant through the walkways between the pavilions. Even as the ash and smoke lingered in the air, and the fiery tear split the sky, the winds did not stop bringing in new leaves.

"What is it, my prince?"

He leaned against the balustrade. "If I die tomorrow, I should not like such a grand affair for my funeral." His voice was unusually quiet and strained.

It had not occurred to me that he could be *scared* about his coronation until that moment. Nervous, perhaps, but never scared. I was shocked he even thought about his own mortality—he wore the legendary Aricine Ward, after all.

Perhaps it was his father's death that prompted this. Or perhaps it was just how imminently his fight loomed. Tomorrow, he was going to have to face the dragon, and he was going to have to face it alone.

"Terren, you are the crown prince. Holding a large funeral for you is tradition."

"You saw what those thousands of people did in front of my father. All the fanfare, all the ceremony—the charade, the theater—I can't stand it. I loathe to think of people pretending they mourn me when they do not, or praising me when they detest me, or remembering me as kind when I was wicked. I cannot bear the thought of anyone offering to go echo-step with me when they do not mean it." His voice wavered with real emotion, real fear. "Wei—if I die tomorrow, I beg of you, don't let them make a spectacle of me in my death. I wish to die quietly, just as I am."

"I will do my best to convey your wishes."

He deserved that much from me at least, if I took his life.

He nodded, seemingly assuaged. "There . . . there is another thing. I have hidden a stash of my Blessings. Dao spells, twenty thousand of them, for the House to use in the event of my death."

That surprised me, but not overly much. During one of our first nights, in his bedchamber, I had watched him write three Blessings in almost no time at all. I had not thought it unusual at the time, but now I realized that such velocity must not have been typical. His exceptional talent for literomancy must have allowed him to contribute to the House's stores and still have plenty left over.

I thought of Muzha having hidden away his 鹽/Yan Blessings, to use after he won the Azalea Civil War. It was not so much of a stretch to imagine Terren had done the same.

"I have never told anyone where. Not even Hesin. Not even Lady Autumn, back when she was still alive. But in case I die tomorrow, someone must know."

"And you would like it to be me." Someone of the Inner Court, who shouldn't even be able to read them.

"I do not know who else I would tell." His voice was pained. "I may kill people, but I am not so evil I would murder a dynasty. The country has many enemies, and it has become over-reliant on my seal for its military power. I fear for its survival without the Dao sigil. The Blessings will help at least a little—and if I should die tomorrow, turn them over to my brother as you see fit."

He leaned in and told me where he kept them.

On the balustrade, above a nest of lilies, his fingers laced over mine.

"And if you don't die tomorrow?" I looked up at him. "If you should survive and become emperor?"

". . . I don't know. I have never thought that far."

His mother, his tutors, his advisors—they had only ever taught him to think of the fight, not of what to do after winning it. "Surely you have at least decided on your era name?"

He shook his head. "I do not think I will choose one. It has always seemed presumptuous to me, to take on an era name—as if one has the right to decide what one's own reign will be like." He looked out at the torn-apart sky, over the rooftops of the House's beautiful pavilions to the haze of valleys beyond. "Let the nation decide what to say about me, what to call me. Let the people decide their own truth."

That night, I went to my servants' graves.

The emperor's funeral had heightened the connection to our Ancestors, so it was a good time to remember others who had passed. And anyway, I wanted to visit them. I needed them.

Deep in the cypress grove, by the servants' quarters, stood their twenty-two graves in a bed of moss and wildflowers.

I burned incense and presented gifts for each of them in turn—a bamboo flute for Teela, hydrangeas for the gardener Aron, a crane-colored dress for Wren. I put down baskets of dates and mandarin oranges for everyone. I set down a pot of tea for Aunt Ping, because I could still hear her scolding me—*Hot water is good for the bones, heh? You young people don't know how to take care of yourself . . .*

When I was done paying my respects, I stood before all of them and confessed, into the humid darkness, "Tomorrow morning is the coronation. I am no longer sure whether to kill Terren or let him live."

It should have been an obvious choice. To kill my torturer, to avenge my friends and the rest of the nation, to prevent a violent ruler from ascending the throne and the warlike Dao power from being amplified—to not let knives rain from the sky again, anywhere, *ever*—that decision should have been so easy. Most people would not even have to think about it.

But I was not most people, I was petty and vindictive. And I did not want to hand over the position of empress to a person who had betrayed and almost killed me. If I assassinated Terren, it would make Maro emperor and Silian empress, and the thought of the two of them running the nation I could not bear.

"I hate her," I spat into the night. "I hate her husband a little too, if I am honest, though I do not really know why."

Oh, wait, I did. I hated him for the same reason I hated all of them, ever since I was a little girl. Walking half a day to Guishan every New Year's in hopes of receiving Blessings, being disappointed over and over again. I hated him every time there was no meat on the table for celebrations, and every time I had to bury a sibling from the famine, and every time Ma fell sick because she had given her share of rice to her family. I hated him before I'd even known him, and knowing him only disappointed me more.

"And besides," I said, quiet now, "I want to be empress."

It was true. I did.

I had not wanted it in the beginning, had perhaps loathed even the thought of it. But I had tasted power now—albeit because it was shoved into my mouth—and I had found that its taste was sweet. Those bathing men in Tieza, scrambling to put on robes to kneel for me, they had pleased me greatly. Aunt Ahma's stammer as she addressed me, it had pleased me greatly. The alarm in Empress Sun's eyes, when I told her I had stopped Terren from killing her, that had pleased me most of all.

Was it a weakness to desire it?

Perhaps, but I was no worse than the rest of them.

I took a deep breath, my gaze sweeping across the quiet graves, bathed in smoke from the incense I had placed at their bases. "All the same, it is hard to imagine myself letting Terren live. Forgiving him would not be fair to you. To any of you—everyone he has ever hurt, everyone he has killed. It is true, he has suffered, but if everyone who suffered became monsters, the world would be overrun with them."

I remembered how my heart had stopped beating, that bloody, rain-misted dawn. I remembered how barely I was able to hold back from throwing my hands around his throat, just so I could feel the pulse of his neck-blood. I *still* wanted to, but that was not practical; one could not always get what one wanted. Killing him from afar would have to do.

"So tell me," I asked of those who had come before me, because without their wisdom, I was going to get it wrong. "Tell me what I must do. The fate of a dynasty is in my hands, but they do not know I am just a girl."

The cypress grove stayed silent, except for the gentle rustle of leaves. A nightingale crooned from somewhere amidst the canopy.

Then, movement behind me.

I spun around to find Du Hu, the elderly maid with no tongue, standing at the edge of the grove. I had no idea how long she had been here for. She must have had the same idea, to visit the graves on the day of the emperor's funeral.

She held Wren's scarf in her hand, the one that she had been mending for a long time. No, not mending, embroidering: she had woven a beautiful display of orchid-wrens onto its silk. She draped it around my neck—I had not realized I was cold until she did—and with a cypress branch, traced a few characters in the earth. An answer to my question. Wisdom that she had accumulated over her long life, that she had been waiting for a chance to share.

Remember who you are doing this for, and you will not be lost.

If I had a granddaughter, that is what I would tell her.

63

TAMING OF THE DRAGON

The wind on coronation morning was relentless. It was as if the sky, itself torn, hungered to tear everything else apart as well.

Overnight and with stunning efficiency, the House had transformed the square in front of the Hall of Heavenly Supremacy from a white place of mourning to a bustling arena for the coronation. From between a sea of gray clouds, the angry rip in the sky bathed everything in red: the banners bearing the 刀/Dao sigil, draping from every rooftop and balustrade; the tapestries of past princes fighting their own dragons, billowing ferociously from the eaves; the cymbal-bearers, the auspicious bronze lion statues, the ten thousand guests crowding the balconies and the perimeter of the arena below.

It was hard for me to comprehend the sheer scale of the event. It was a scale greater than any I had seen before, even after having spent so long in the palace. Greater than the Selection Day, than my wedding, than even the emperor's funeral.

I was in my usual seat, on the dragon rug on the top level of the terrace, my phoenix shawl wrapped tight around me. A guarded tent around me shielded the House's most important people from the wind. A cadre of Sun Clan men, the empress, and Prince Ruyi sat in a far corner; Prince Kiran, Prince Isan, and their advisors took up another. Closest of all, not ten paces from me, was Prince Maro, Silian, and a scattering of West Palace men. Servants wove between us, pouring chrysanthemum tea, refilling plum wine, and setting out small plates of dates, soft candies, and cut fruit.

Terren was beside me on the carpet, behind a table carved with dragons. He did not eat anything, though he did take a few sips of his tea. The hand holding his cup was shaking.

"You'll be fine," I said to him, tritely. The heart-spirit poem I had memorized swam in my mind, truth and emotion hungering to be freed.

He stared into his cup. "Of course I will. I am very powerful."

It struck me that this was possibly going to be the last time I spoke to him alive. I searched for something meaningful to say, but could only find another platitude. "Terren—good luck."

He met my eyes. "Wei . . ." He paused, as if also searching for meaningful words, then—for all his prowess in poetry—settled on something equally mundane. "Thank you."

A gong shuddered through the square.

It was time.

Terren took one last sip of his tea, set it down, and stood. His loose hair and plain gray robe billowed behind him as he made his way down the red carpeted stairs, from the top of the three terraces to the enormous square below. He brought just eight swords with him—perhaps opting for finesse rather than quantity—which floated beside him as he left us, around the swirling Aricine Ward.

All around the balconies, underneath the 刀/Dao banners and blazing torches and auspicious lanterns, the crowd of men leaned in eagerly to watch. They were all chattering excitedly, or perhaps nervously; it was impossible to hear their words over the roaring of the wind. Everyone seemed to know that no matter what happened today, the fate of the dynasty was about to change irrevocably.

It took Terren a long time to reach the bottom of the steps. It took him even longer to cross the square to reach its empty center. An area large enough to fit the entire Palisade Garden had been cordoned off from the onlookers by imperial guards, and it was in the middle of it that he took his place.

He looked so small.

In all the tapestries around us, displaying past coronations, the princes were accompanied by rows of specialized swordsmen, martial artists, and archers; more often than not, there were trumpeters, flag-bearers, and heralds carrying strings of firecrackers. In some eras, there had been bridges and platforms custom-built for maneuverability; in others, the armies had horses or armored elephants to carry them. But in this era, this coronation, there was only Terren standing in the vast and wind-battered square. Alone.

"We begin the Taming of the Dragon," the Minister of Rites announced from close to me. There was no chance the people at the bottom could have heard him over the wind, but the words were standard; and anyway, a group of servants carrying a banner on the opposite balcony announced the same thing in written characters. "We gather here to witness the coronation of Prince Guan Terren, the Winter Dragon, The One Who Cannot Die, and the Second Son and Heir of the Azalea House. May Heaven above and the Ancestors below watch after our dynasty."

"May they watch after our dynasty," the crowd repeated.

"Summon the dragon!"

Cymbals crashed as dancers wearing vivid dragon costumes marched around the perimeter of the square; pillars of flame each as tall as three men flared from the terraces all around. Terren himself traced a summoning spell on the ground with a sword, and the moment the Ancestors drank it, the tear in the sky ripened and reddened, and a deafening roar shattered the nation.

Hurling down from the tear was the dragon. The Crown of the House. First a dot, then larger, then larger still, until the whole length of it landed rumbling on the cobble amidst a storm of dust.

It was the first time I had seen it so close. It looked even more ferocious than all the depictions of it I'd seen, on the murals and tapestries and carvings scattered around the House. The pictures all showed sharp teeth, fierce claws, and a long, serpentine body, but the Crown was even more formidable in real life. Formidable and—I drew in a breath—*beautiful*. It was a rich, majestic shade of red, with golden horns and a forest-colored mane. White salt crusted between its scales like cloudfoam.

"Seal the arena!" cried the minister.

The dragon-dancers stepped aside, and then two dozen literomancers took their places around the square's perimeter. They traced a spell in unison, and Terren did too, giving his own words to use as the focus of the Blessing. A moment later, a transparent, cylindrical barrier erupted from the ground just before the literomancers' feet and stretched all the way to Heaven. It was barely a glimmer, unseeable unless one squinted, but I knew that it was magic strong enough to protect the spectators from the coming battle between prince and dragon.

And to protect Terren from assassins, I thought. In a moment, he would have to take down his Aricine Ward—for the dragons accepted no literomancy in the taming process. In a moment, he would have to become vulnerable again.

But the barrier, impenetrable by arrows, daggers, or ordinary spells, would protect him from anything coming from outside. Anything— except for a heart-spirit poem.

"Begin the ceremony!" the minister shouted, as another gong shattered the square.

Terren, with one of his swords, cut the chain of white characters swirling around him. The Aricine Ward broke for the first time. It first loosened like a ribbon, then coalesced into the outline of a white tiger, then finally vanished into air. And, just like that, The One Who Cannot Die became as killable as the rest of us.

He raised all eight of his swords and made his way towards the dragon.

From hidden under my shawl, I raised my pen.

64

THE PRINCE AND THE CROWN

Terren attacked first. He kept two of his swords near him and sent the rest of them hurtling into the dragon's body. It shrieked viciously as it thrashed in the air. The knives burst out the other side of the dragon, reversed directions, and sailed back for a second strike.

But they never reached the dragon, because the dragon struck back.

One claw—and it was the size of a house—knocked the swords out of the air; another crashed down towards Terren. He leapt away in time, just barely, and instead of his bones it was the earth beneath that was crushed. Dust and broken cobble spewed from where the claw had landed, making it impossible to see. But from the earth-haze under the dragon's shadow, a red sigil gleamed like a sun, and the knocked-away swords straightened in the air again and arrowed towards the Crown.

Around me, on the three layers of terraces wrapping around the arena, men cheered: a thundering sound that rose even above the howl of the wind.

The back and forth continued. As my uninked pen moved under my shawl, I watched as Terren wove his swords in and out of the dragon like sewing needles; I watched as the dragon lashed back at him with claw, tooth, and tail. The beast was vicious and merciless in its fury, and I now understood, without the slightest shred of doubt, why the coronation was so dangerous. Each slam of its claw could have crushed five or six swordsmen; each slam of its tail could have thrown twenty archers into the air. Each gnash of its teeth could have torn into the armor of a war elephant and turned it to pulp like a mulberry.

But Terren was, without a question, its match.

Some of the dragon's attacks he dodged, but the rest he parried with the sheer strength of his sigil magic. With the flat blade of one sword, he could hold back a claw; with two, crossed, he could beat away a lash of its gigantic tail. No wonder he only needed to bring eight of them.

I had known Terren was powerful, of course. I had heard his tales of conquest in the north, and I had witnessed, in person, the way he could command ten thousand knives at once. But even so, his power astonished me. Watching him fight the dragon—in a way that trembled sky and rumbled earth—was absolutely spectacular.

"He's really doing it," exclaimed Wang Suwen in awe, from the terrace below where I was sitting. The other concubines around her cried their agreements.

"If our prince defeats the dragon alone," Liru Syra shouted excitedly, "he will be the first in all of history!"

Under the cover of my shawl, my pen continued to move subtly on the carpet. In the space hidden between where I was seated and the table, I traced one character at a time.

The West Palace was seated not ten paces away. From their midst, Silian watched me closely, with her tea cupped in her hands. There was a conspiratorial half smile on her face, as if she still believed we were working together. Maro was in deep conversation with his friends and advisors, but I did catch him glancing my way occasionally. Both of them, as they witnessed my hand move only slightly, would believe I was still writing the heart-spirit poem. The poem that, once finished, would cross the barrier, find its way to Terren, and kill him.

A series of devastating *booms* thundered from the arena. The dragon—now bearing a hundred, perhaps a thousand, blade wounds—was thrashing violently, thwacking its body against the barrier. *Boom. Boom.* Salt poured out of the holes in its body like bonedust, scattering in the wind like a sandstorm, blanketing the ground in white.

Somewhere in the dust was Terren. I could not see him at all.

Remember who you are doing this for, and you will not be lost. I had thought about it the night before, and had made my decision. The decision to let him live.

It had not been an easy one. It was possibly the hardest I'd ever made in my life. I had been fantasizing about his death for one and a half years, ever since the first night he had tortured me. And every time he had cut me, drowned me, choked me, stabbed me, or hurt one of my friends, the fantasies had only grown more vivid. The satisfaction and catharsis of finally ending his life—they had been such difficult things to relinquish.

And there was the matter of Tensha's future, too, under the reign of the Dao sigil. That had been a hard image to stomach. To picture Terren's power amplified a thousandfold, to have war and conquest become his legacy—that frightened me to no end. To think of cities pulverized by knives, the way that so many had been during the Winter Dragon's northern campaign—that was absolutely terrifying.

But, I had bargained with myself, *maybe it doesn't have to be that way.*

Maybe there did not have to be war, or conquest, or pain. Because I would be Terren's empress. Because I was going to sit on the throne next to him, keep close to him, guide him onto a better path. Not the right one—that was overly ambitious, even for the best of us—but at the very least, a better one.

I had not become *so* wicked in my heart that I had stopped believing people could change. If a gentle child could turn into a monster, I thought, then surely a monster could become gentle again.

You and me, Wei, we can rule together for as long as I live.

An earth-shaking crash. The dragon had fallen onto its belly on the near side of the arena. Salt had flooded the entire arena by now, dusting the smashed cobble in a coat of white—and I was reminded of the snow on my wedding day. Still more was pouring out of its myriad knife wounds, as if the entire, unmoving length of it was a punctured sack of flour. Amidst the settling dust, I spotted Terren again, limping towards the felled dragon. Seven of his swords were still around him; he used the eighth as a walking stick. His gown was tattered, his forehead covered in blood, and his back scored by a giant, raw slash. But he was still alive, had still won.

"*Wei.*" Silian had come to my table, her expression panicked. "It has been long enough by now for you to have cast it, has it not? Terren has subdued the dragon. He is going to tame it soon. We are running out of time!"

Around us, everyone else was too busy watching the arena to hear us. Their cheers were lost in the raging wind.

I slipped my pen back into my sleeve, stood to meet her eyes, and smiled. "No, *you* are."

The characters I had been tracing on the ground were not my heart-spirit poem. They were not even poetry at all. They were just random words, words to make it seem like I was still going through with the plan.

At first she looked confused. Then the implication hit her, all at once, and her lower lip trembled with rage. "Have you forgotten who you are? That night we met on Mid-Autumn, you were so afraid. So desperate. You were practically begging me to work with you, to help you kill the evil man you were bound to, to prevent him from seizing the throne with his blood-thirsty hands. Have you changed so much since then? Have you been so *seduced* by power?"

My smile never faltered. "Silian, you say it like it is a bad thing."

I had thought it through the night before, and I understood now. Power was not always evil, the pursuit of it not always selfish.

Being able to help one's family, one's village—that was power.

Having enough provisions to dole out to starving farmers in the north—that was power.

Holding the authority to question the wicked owner of a pleasure house, to seek out the truth, to protect the innocent—*that* was power.

Remember who you are doing this for, and you will not be lost. What Silian didn't know was that my decision to spare Terren was not so that I could become empress. It was for me to become the Rice Wife. Someone in the palace who understood—viscerally—what it was like to languish in the famine. Someone who could answer letters from places not on maps, and change edicts, and write spells to turn blanched wheat fields golden.

The expression of shock and betrayal on Silian's face, at that very moment—that was *also* power. I broke into a grin. When Maro narrowed his eyes at us from where he was sitting beside his men, I grinned even wider.

Maro, I thought, *how does it feel to have fought so long for nothing? To have betrayed your brother—and murdered your father—for absolutely noth-ing?* It was a wicked thought, and it delighted me to no end. I was going to be laughing about it for years.

The crowd roared louder with excitement, and we turned back towards the arena. Terren had made it to the wounded dragon and was kneeling before its head. He produced a small silver dagger from his sleeve, plunged it into its snout, and kept his hand around its hilt. A moment later, his sigil flared; a river of brilliant red light flowed from his palm to the dagger to the Crown. He was really doing it. He was really about to tame the dragon all by himself.

Then, piercing above the cheering, one of Kiran's men screamed, "The Crown is still awake!"

The dragon's tail moved slightly. Terren, focused on channeling into the dragon, had not noticed. The shouts of excitement turned to shrieks of alarm, and a moment later, the tail whipped up with the speed of arrows and *slammed* into him.

He was thrown across the arena. A terrifying distance, bouncing across the salt-smeared ground. When his body at last rolled to a stop—all the way on the opposite side of the square—he did not get up. His swords, which had been hovering midair, all dropped to the ground like stones.

"No," I gasped.

Silian started to laugh—a vulture's shriek. "Perhaps the nation did not need to rely on a lowly village girl after all. Perhaps the coronation itself shall be what kills the tyrant prince. After all, he is stupid enough to take on a whole dragon by himself." The way her smile twisted her face then, I could not fathom why I had once admired it. Why I had once believed her afraid of nothing. "Stupid, also, is anyone depraved enough to support him. Did you really think the world could allow someone like him to live? Evil never wins in the end, Wei. Even children know this."

With those last words, she went back to join those of the West Palace. I just stood there, too petrified with horror to speak.

Beneath the terrace, Terren was still sprawled on the ground, not moving.

The Crown bellowed, then raised itself—with great difficulty—onto its four claws. Its vicious eyes fell on the prince, splayed out on the far side of the arena, and it began to move towards him with slow, rumbling steps. I couldn't breathe.

Terren, don't die.

Not now. Not like this.

The West Palace already knew I had betrayed them. If Terren did not manage to tame the Crown, and it passed to Maro, I would be the first person the new emperor beheaded.

The dragon was close enough that the steam from its nostrils billowed the prince's hair. It reared back, then *threw* its head forward, jaws snapping—

But not around Terren. He stopped it just in time, fast enough that I barely caught it happening: three of the swords on the ground shooting underneath the dragon's chin, *lifting*—with a flare of the 刀/Dao sigil— the dragon by the bottom of its head, high enough that when the jaw did snap shut—a colossal snap that shook the balustrades and rattled the plates on the tables—it caught only wind. And the swords didn't stop there. They kept rising, and rising, until the dragon was near vertical— then they *flung* it back, and the entire enormity of it sailed across the air and smashed against the literomantic barrier with a sky-shattering *boom*. The shock of it made an entire section of the balustrade crumble away, startling the men who had been leaning on it.

The dragon slid down the side of the barrier like it was glass. It landed on the ground and lay still. Even its wounds were hardly leaking salt anymore, as if whatever store within it had run out.

The audience rioted with awe and cheer.

On the far side of the arena, Terren tried to push himself off the ground—and collapsed immediately. He tried again, and managed to make it onto his knees but no further. There he stayed. Hunched over, with his head hanging, blood dripping onto his tattered gown and the salt-dusted arena.

He must have been exhausted beyond belief. That last use of magic— the one strong enough to *hurl a dragon across the arena*—must have taken everything he had. If something like it had been easy, he would have done it much sooner.

But he has still won, I thought, even as I felt my palms sweat. *He is still to become emperor. The fight is already over, the dragon subdued. He only needs a moment to gather his strength, and—*

"Prince Maro is going in!" someone from below shrieked.

I rushed to the balustrade with everyone else and looked down. They were right. Amidst the chaos, the first son—in his gold-and-white splendor—had found his way to the arena. He was pressing a palm to the literomantic barrier, and his sigil—of roads, of tunnels, of *passageways*—burned like the sun. And then a moment later, he stepped through with a ripple, as if all that magic was only a curtain of water.

With cold horror, I remembered what he had pledged to Master Ganji after his failure in the peach garden. *I won't fail you next time. I won't let you down again.* Maro never had a chance to make good on that pledge— not until now, when Terren was on his knees, with his ward down, so gravely injured that he could not even stand, let alone defend himself.

65

A BEATING HEART

Everyone was shouting in alarm now; the wind, already relentless, became even more frenetic. The tapestries flapped precariously, the torches sputtered out, and Maro kept walking calmly across the empty arena towards his brother, stepping over salt and scales, crushed stone and blood.

Terren could not even lift his head. His sigil flickered feebly from where he knelt, summoning his swords. But only two of them responded to his call. And even then, they only stayed in the air a moment before falling to the ground like dead things.

"He's going to kill him," someone in the crowd screamed.

He really was. I watched, uselessly, as Maro reached Terren, closed both hands around his throat, and lifted him off the ground.

The despair I felt then was like being buried by a mountain. It was over. It was truly over. Terren was going to die, and Maro was going to tame the already subdued dragon and become emperor. And because I had betrayed Maro, because I had not cast the heart-spirit poem as planned, he would—

I sucked in a breath. *Wait.*

The heart-spirit poem.

My pulse was racing. I all but sprinted back to the tent. My section of the terrace had been abandoned; everyone had poured towards the balconies on the far side of the arena, where the brothers were, to be closer to the action. *The heart-spirit poem.* I tore out my pen and started writing on the rug, frantic, one memorized character after the other.

In my periphery, I could see Terren struggling in his brother's chokehold. His mouth was open as he gasped for breath, and his face had turned an alarming shade of red. He tried again to summon his blades—刀/Dao sigil flickering like a dying flame—but his magic must have been spent entirely. The swords stayed motionless on the ground. Weakly, he pried at the hands around his throat, but it was no use. Maro held firm.

I had very little time.

The heart-spirit poem was developed in the early Ash Dynasty, Ciyi had once told me, *as a potent derivative of the more commonplace healing spell.*

A spell that can find its way directly to the heart.

Maybe it did not have to be a killing spell. I scribbled down one hurried character over another, line after line. Maybe finding someone's heart did not have to condemn them to death. Maybe it could, instead, give them *life.*

I would not even have to change my poem much. Everything was already there. I needed only to change the framing of the truths I had already laid bare—add a few characters, imbue it with my new intention—and then it would tell another story entirely. A story not of tragedy or suffering, but of joy, of love.

That little prince on the bridge, hadn't he healed the carp in the same way? His first Blessing, born of instinct and simple empathy, had been an ode much like this one. Even as young as he had been, he had still taken one look at a small life and seen not its suffering but its exuberance.

Do not assume that I dream of greatness.

Do not assume that I wish to be reborn in a different time or a different place, in a different life.

I wish only to admire the blossoms in this one.

The screams in the crowd were getting louder. The audience of ten thousand stared in horror as Terren's already feeble struggling became even weaker. Soon he stopped resisting entirely. His hands dropped limp to his sides.

My palms were sweating so much that I almost dropped my pen.

See him, I begged the Ancestors, as I scrawled more and more characters onto the rug. *See him and find his life worth living. See all of him.*

Terren, very little, squealing with delight after Maro stole a cake for him from the banquet table. Terren and Maro sitting on the pagoda's roof, legs dangling in the spring wind, playing "dueling couplets" where no grown-ups could hear them. Terren sneaking into the Dawn Pavilion, standing on tiptoes to reach the windowsill, helping his brother write his first Blessing.

Ma-ro! Catch it! Catch it in a poem!

Terren with his brother in the mountain fortress, watching the sunrise spread vibrant over the titan hero, the dragonhorse, and the demon king. Terren in the cold room they shared, hugging each other as they cried about the burning star. Terren in the moss-covered tunnel, after Maro had fainted, wrapping his own cloak around him to keep him warm. Terren hiding under the kitchen table, knowing his brother was going to be furious—but having told on him anyway, to save his life.

I'm sorry ten times. I'm sorry a hundred times. I'm sorry a thousand times.

Terren in Tieza, even amidst all the war and suffering, writing the Aricine Ward. Perhaps in his military base, by daylight; perhaps in his luxurious Violet Heron chamber, by firelight. Laboring over the most difficult spell known to history, for seven long years, to save his brother from reaching the edge of his cliff.

It was a love poem after all. The heart-spirit poem I was furiously writing—it really was a poem of love.

The prince was not moving anymore, except for a few grotesque convulsions of his body. But Maro kept his hands around his throat anyway, no doubt wanting to play it safe. After he had failed the last time, the time that had caused one tutor's death and the other's condemnation, he must have wanted to take no chances.

Only a few verses left, I thought desperately. *Terren, stay with us.*

It was not just his love for Maro that I wanted to show the Ancestors. There was more of it he had given away. Love for his nation, even if it was more understated than his brother's; *I am not so evil I would murder a dynasty.* Love for his friends, who had been with him for so many years; I had not forgotten how he'd tucked Little Sparrow under his cloak to keep her warm, or the shining joy on his face when he was reunited with Niu Niu. Love for literature, one that was lifelong; as long as I'd known him, he had not stopped reading or composing poems.

Ancestors, do you understand now? This is his story. His true story.

Even after he was grown, he had not stopped giving it. I had witnessed it myself. In the temple, braving a snowstorm, hacking away at the ice; the attempt to bring the carp somewhere warm had been futile, but the love had been true. In the Palisade Garden, parting plum branches, just so he could watch the fledglings play in their nest; in the Tower of Mental Tranquility, on his balcony, writing an entire poem for a snail he had chanced upon. A creature so small most would not even have paid attention.

Wei, get some pen and ink for me, quick!

All of it had already been in my poem. But could the Ancestors see it my way?

As I finished the last stroke of my Blessing, my heart beating fast, Maro let go of his brother. He must have decided he was dead enough. Terren crumpled to the ground and stayed there, among the salt dust, like a broken toy.

The crowd screamed with horror. The wind tore mercilessly at the banners. Even the bent pillars of flames seemed to be crying out with agony, though I knew that flames could not make a sound. But somehow, even through all the uproar, the chaos, the loudness, I could still hear my frantic heartbeats.

Thud. Thud. Thud.

And yours, Terren?

Underneath those gray robes, inside the cage of your chest, is there still a beating heart like mine?

Can it still hear me, if I sang it a love ballad?

Maybe not. He was not moving at all.

Maybe it was too late. Maybe he had already left us, becoming air.

My body felt strangely heavy as Maro turned away from him and made for the felled dragon. Now the audience was rioting, but not just with horror—amidst cries of outrage, there were also cheers, and applause, and tentative celebration. A few fights had broken out. I could see men shoving each other on the crowded balcony opposite me. The events of the coronation must have been so unprecedented that nobody truly knew how to feel; the nation had become a beast that did not know what it wanted.

There was no response from the Ancestors to my poem. No sparks on the rug beneath me, no warmth under my pen, nothing. Terren remained small and motionless in the arena. The wind tugged at his hair, his torn sleeves, as if in a futile effort to wake him. Even his sigil was not glowing anymore and had gone as black as charcoal.

So it was over, then. There had been no heartbeat after all.

Perhaps I should have felt disappointed. Afraid for my own life, maybe. Or, at the very least, I should have tried something else in desperation or panic. Instead, I just sat there silent, feeling like I was very far away.

I felt, strangely, like someone else had lived the events of the past year. Like someone else had been chosen to be Empress-in-Waiting. Like someone else had been enduring those horrid nights, and learning to read in secret, and piecing together truths for her spell. It felt like someone else's eyes, not mine, staring down at the arena. Watching Maro make it to the dragon and kneel in front of its head and put his palm to the scales between its glass eyes. Someone else seeing him channel his magic, sending his red light into the Crown, persuading it to amplify his power of 路/Lu, of roads.

Then I blinked, because I realized I actually *was* far away. I was not just imagining it.

Part of me was still on the terrace, in my body, under the tent, but another part was—

There. Inside the arena, as a spark. A spark right inside Terren's heart. I could feel its warmth around me, the embrace of its pulse. The spark became brilliant light, and the light flooded the entire ground of the arena before I could take a breath.

And then I saw—with the part of me still on the terrace—the arena transforming. Transforming into an orchard. Soft grass unfurling from amidst the scattered salt, trumpet flowers bursting out of the cobblestones against the crushing wind. In another span between breaths, trees sprouted, grew, and blossomed—pear and apricot, and cherries, and sweet peaches, turning the dry air lush and fragrant.

And amidst them, a little fish made of golden light sprang into life, tail wagging as it wriggled among their trunks.

A Fish That Swam Among Trees. That was the title I'd given my poem.

Maro must have sensed the change in the air. He stopped channeling, stood, and turned.

With the part of me inside the arena—the part that lived inside the little fish—I saw Terren's eyes open. I watched him summon his eight swords back to his side and use one of them to push himself to his feet.

66

BUILDING BRIDGES

Maro crossed the distance between them until they were seven paces apart. As he faced his younger brother, the tail of his elegant white-and-gold gown billowing behind him, the first son looked almost serene.

Terren, in contrast, was battle weary, blood drenched. His gown blew tattered in the wind, his hair wild and scattered with salt. But the Blessing, I was relieved to see, had healed him completely. Even the gash on his back had closed.

"I did not know you could cross the barrier," he said.

Maro's voice was just as calm. "I did not know you could come back from the dead."

A wind brought down a shower of blossoms from the canopy above, red pomegranate and pink cherry and white pear.

To my surprise, they said nothing more. It was the first time they were alone with each other in so many years. With no advisors in their way, no tutors, no mothers, no allies. Alone, with a literomantic barrier between them and the world, they were as tucked away as they had been on the golden roofs of that pagoda, where no grown-ups could ever hear their secrets. But where I had expected honest words—if ones that were tense and hate-filled—there was only silence.

Maybe they knew each other so well that words were not needed.

Maybe they had grown so far apart, there was nothing left to say.

Up on the terrace, the audience of ten thousand clamored in shock and bewilderment. With the part of me in the tent, I could hear their cries:

"How is the Winter Dragon still alive?"

"Which literomancer has healed him?"

"What kind of spell *was* that? To have sprouted all those trees . . ."

Everyone—the guards, the servants, the clansmen, the concubines—was rushing back to my side of the terrace now, to get closer to the brothers and the dragon. Since they could not see from inside the arena like I could, they all jostled for a prime viewing spot around the balustrade, trying to catch a glimpse of the princes through the gaps in the canopy.

Silian was the only one who knew it was me. When she returned with the West Palace men under the tent, she gave me a look so vicious that I could not help but feel vindicated. There was nothing she could do now. The spell was already cast.

There was nothing anyone could do. The fate of Tensha rested entirely on the two brothers.

From within the arena, Maro moved. I saw, through the eyes of the little fish, as he loosened the ribbon tied around his neck, drew the metal staff from his back, and let it expand to its full length.

When he charged, it was so quick that I didn't see his cloudstaff thrusting forward. Not until it hit metal—Terren had crossed his eight swords into a star-shaped shield. *Prang.* Maro used the momentum from the clash to leap back. He pivoted on the grass and struck from a different direction, again lightning quick. Terren shifted his star of swords to parry. *Prang.* Maro kept up the assault. He ran at him, over and over again, relentlessly—dashing at his side, bouncing off the tree trunks to attack from behind, sprinting across the leaf-heavy branches to strike from above. *Pring. Prang. Pring.*

The wind pummeled the trees, shaking down a rain of blossoms and leaves.

Above the arena, the sky glared red.

At first, I was worried for Terren. I had never seen Maro fight before, but from the first strike he made, I had known immediately that he was competent. More than competent. He made it seem easy, the way he darted under the canopy like wind, cloudstaff barely a glimmer under Heaven's red light. *Balance. Concentration. Detachment.*

But it soon became apparent that it was not even close. Not when his opponent was the Winter Dragon, who had commanded armies and ended wars. The more time went on, the more obvious the differences in their ability became. Each of Terren's parries were effortless. Perfunctory. He had not moved from where he stood—or struck back—even once.

Maro noticed, too.

He stopped his flurry of assaults and landed on the grass, lowering his staff. "Are you afraid? Are you so much of a coward that you would simply stand there, refusing to fight me?"

Terren lowered his floating shield of swords, but said nothing.

"Or perhaps you are so arrogant you think you can win without striking."

Now there was something new in Terren's black eyes. Pity.

Maro seemed to catch it as well. He nodded to himself, as if making a decision. Then he turned and walked away.

Maybe he was going to do the sensible thing. Leave the arena the same way he had come in, get to safety on the other side of the barrier, preserve himself. Even if he missed the one opportunity to kill his brother—the one time the Aricine Ward would ever come down—it didn't matter. He could still go back to the West Palace, to his wife and his allies, and live a long life as a prince if not an emperor. He had enough supporters that he could absolve himself of his treason, enough influence to still maintain significant control in court.

And even if his brother ruled with iron swords and bloodied the nation with war, it was *still* better for Maro to live. Surely he could see that. If he lived, he could at least be Terren's opposition, could at least check his cruel whims with political plays of his own. And even if Terren did manage to break the nation, Maro's own economic power could at least help bandage its wounds.

Maro, do you see? I thought, holding my breath. *Or are you still caged by love of your own?*

Ever since he was young, he had known one truth above all: that his veins were Tensha's flowing rivers, his beating heart its capital, his flesh its mountains and fertile valleys.

What would you give to prevent the country from being ruled by tyranny? By blades?

I would . . . I would give everything.

Twenty paces away, Maro stopped. Then, without warning, he spun around and slammed his cloudstaff onto the ground.

The earth cracked. Not just cracked, *split*—within the span of a heartbeat a canyon had formed, as deep and wide as the height of two men, starting from Maro's staff and spanning all the way to the edge of the arena.

Terren didn't even have time to react. His eyes widened a sliver right as the ground beneath his feet fell away, and the next moment, the chasm had swallowed him whole.

Maro wasted no time. Brilliant red magic poured from his body into the staff, from the staff into the earth, forcing the canyon to close like the jaws of a dragon. Chrysanthemum flowers bloomed in yellow bouquets on its walls, beautiful even through the salt and broken earth.

But the canyon could not close completely.

As the little fish hovered above Terren, I could see, through its eyes, as he wielded the flat of his swords to push back the walls. Four and four. His own sigil was agleam, his breathing quickened, his open palms to either side trembling with the effort of holding back solid stone.

Maro was shaking too. He grimaced as he pushed harder, forehead shiny with sweat. A thin trail of blood appeared at the corner of his mouth. They struggled for a long time at a stalemate, earth against steel, 路/Lu against 刀/Dao—and then Maro changed his strategy.

First his sigil dimmed and flared again, and then the water came. Erupting out of nowhere, it surged down the canyon like a ravenous beast.

Terren's eyes flicked to the oncoming torrent, and then his own seal flared just as bright. He raised an open palm. A twisting spiral of swords burst out of the stone floor, forged from nothing, hundreds of blades interlocking as they lifted him out of the canyon. As the newly formed river rushed beneath him, he stood safely above the water on a crest of steel and lilies.

Maro's expression darkened.

With a poisoned scowl, he sent a bridge hurtling towards Terren—bricks swathed in yellow flowers arcing out across the river—but Terren lowered the crest of his sword-spire to evade it. Maro threw two more bridges over the canyon, three—no, four—but Terren rode his swords like an iron serpent and dodged them all.

"Fight me," Maro snarled between attacks. "*Fight me*, damn you!"

Terren glanced down at him and said nothing, only kept evading. There might have been a hint of disappointment in his eyes, or perhaps it was still only pity.

The crowd had become positively feral. I doubted any of them had seen anything so spectacular—two princes battling each other with their sigil magic, in a way that shook earth and Heaven—and their cries of alarm, excitement, and outrage seemed a confirmation. But even so, I was not sure how long the spectacle would last. Terren's power was no less than remarkable, I knew, but I was less certain whether *Maro* could keep up his assault.

The West Palace seemed to share my doubts.

"Someone stop him," Silian begged from where she was sitting with her husband's men. "He's going to die if he keeps going like this." She shook Song Siming's shoulders in desperation, but Siming shook his head in resignation. Mei Yu only sat frozen in horror, along with the rest of Maro's advisors.

Maro changed his strategy again. With a flare of his sigil, he summoned a river to catch Terren in its torrent; as the water rushed towards the canyon, Terren leapt off his swords and onto solid ground in time to dam it—with a fresh wall of interlocked blades, like a great wing erupting from the ground. The river broke around it. Became a roaring waterfall as it crashed into the canyon. Maro attacked from a new direction, sending a fresh river hurtling towards Terren; but Terren raised his arm across his body and the wing folded, like an immense gray owl's, to block it once again. The water slammed into the blades so fiercely its spray reached all the way to the treetops.

River after river, dam after dam. Before long, water was flooding the arena. Lashing against the wind, washing away leaves and rubble, dissolving salt.

And the dragon woke.

Perhaps because its belly was now drenched in salt water, ankle-deep; perhaps because of the way the earth rang with each burst of blades. In any case, one glass eye had slid open.

"No!" Silian screamed. "Get out of there!"

But it was useless. Maro couldn't hear her. And even if he could, I was not sure he would listen. His 路/Lu sigil was burning, burning like a sun, as he slammed his staff down again, this time summoning a road. Cobblestones paved themselves, like a carpet unrolling, a gray wave making straight for his brother. Terren erupted a second wing of swords from the ground, crossing it with the first to block. *Smash. Crack.* A spray of rubble smothered the white blooms of new lilies.

It went on and on. Roads and rivers, bridges and canyons, Maro somehow improvising his seal magic into one he could do battle with, Terren defending with equal ferocity. Maro built bridge after bridge in an attempt to reach his brother; Terren blocked every last one of them with knives. In no time, the arena had turned into a frothing, furious landscape of spitting stone and hurling water; and the trees fell crashing, and the sky shook, and the earth broke.

The light in Maro's seal was sputtering out.

After he sent yet another flood of water towards Terren, he doubled over to catch his breath, wiping at the blood pouring from his mouth. Then he slammed his staff back onto the ground, his sigil glowing again, but almost instantly it extinguished.

Maro swayed, clutching his chest.

Terren lowered his shield of swords and leveled his dark gaze at his brother.

Another feeble flicker of the 路/Lu sigil. Another attempt to summon magic. But it still wasn't working. Maro leaned heavily on his staff, coughing uncontrollably, blood flecking his soaked white-gold robes. And then a shadow fell over him.

Terren's eyes flicked up to meet the dragon looming over Maro. Maro noticed at the same time. He took a few stumbling steps away, but he was far too weak to be swift—and the Crown swooped down and snapped its mighty jaws. When it rose again, both the first prince and a chunk of the arena were gone.

The crowd fell into a horrified silence. It dragged on for first one heartbeat, then another, then another. Then, all at once, bits of chewed rock and viscera fell from the sky like someone's nightmarish idea of rain, and Silian—along with everyone in the West Palace, the tent, and the terraces below—screamed and screamed.

A piece of entrail—or brain, or heart; it was hard to tell—landed on Terren's cheek. He peeled it off, looked at it with disgust, and flicked it to the ground.

"Good night, Maro."

67

BLOOD AND SALT

Terren subdued the dragon quickly and unspectacularly. It had already been near its end—its strike at Maro had been a desperate one, a dying thrash—and after only a few quick sword maneuvers, it slammed into the near side of the arena and fell limp next to the barrier.

Then it was over. Maro was dead, the dragon felled. Everything was decided.

The audience did not cheer. Witnessing a prince's death—and not the one they would have expected—seemed to have stunned everyone into solemnity.

I left the tent behind and began making my way down the long, carpeted steps, passing by torches, the tasseled statues of fortune lions, the flapping 刀/Dao banners. The summer winds—which did not seem to be blocked by the literomantic barrier—carried the scent of salt and ash. Nobody stopped me. I was as close to being empress now as Terren was to being emperor.

As I passed the second layer, I overheard some of the ministers still trying to figure out exactly who had cast the Blessing, exactly what it was.

"It must be a heart-spirit poem. I do not know what else can penetrate that barrier."

"No—can't be. That is a killing spell, not a healing one!"

"Will the Crown forgive the prince his use of it?"

Terren waded through the foaming, ankle-deep water to the dragon, the little fish following him as a golden glimmer. He knelt by its snout and sank the silver dagger into its scales. Red rivulets of magic glowed bright as he began his persuasion once again. Let the Dao power be amplified. Let the coming reign be one of blades.

Probably, I thought, in answer to the literomancer's question. The dragons accepted no literomancy in the taming process—and there hadn't been any. The spell had not been used in the fight against the Crown, but to save Terren from Maro. And in any case, it had been cast by someone outside the arena.

I reached the bottom of the square, stepped past the hushed audience, the imperial guards, and the literomancers, and put my hand to the barrier. It felt like nothing, not even glass. But my hand could not move past it at all. I was reminded of how the Aricine Ward had stopped me from touching Terren, the night the rumors came and we had tried to bed each other.

The little fish wriggled its way from beside Terren towards my hand. Terren's eyes followed it. Without taking his hand off the dragon, he used a floating sword to trace a quick spell on the ground, releasing his part of the barrier spell. A moment later, the air in front of my hand rippled. He had let me in.

I had predicted he would. In coronations past, the princes always had allies in the arena with them—the ones who survived, anyway—to cheer them on as they claimed the Crown. Terren might not have brought any allies with him for the fight, but that didn't mean he had none.

He might be hesitant about trusting anyone, but he had no reason anymore not to trust *me*. He had already died. I had brought him back, given him life. If I had any intentions at all of harming him, he surely had reasoned, I would have just left him lying on the ground, broken.

As soon as I stepped through, the little fish dug its way into my heart and vanished, and I knew it was at that moment the crowd of ten thousand learned what Terren already knew.

"Wei," he said with a laugh. "I felt it. I *felt* it. I felt your heart inside mine . . ."

It was a strange laugh, a laugh I was not used to—one that was entirely devoid of menace, that held only joy.

From the dagger he was holding, still more magic was pouring into the Crown. I knelt next to him in the frigid water and held his free hand while the salt wind battered us. I could barely hear anything outside. The barrier must have muffled all sounds, shutting out the world.

"Why didn't you tell me?" Terren asked, still with wonder. "That you were writing a poem to help me with my coronation?"

"If I did, would you have allowed it?"

"Unlikely." He laughed again. He also looked as if he was about to cry.

And, as I took in the sight of him—exhausted and drenched, water slicking his hair against his sigil—I thought I knew why. All his life, people had only ever hurt him, maneuvered against him, wished him dead. For someone to *heal* him must have been so unprecedented that he could not possibly have been prepared.

"Did you frame Hesin, then?" he asked after a while.

"No," I lied. "He really did betray you."

He considered this, then nodded. "Tell me everything, but only after this is over. Not now. I am very tired." A pause. "I am also happy, for once, and I wish to remember this moment untarnished." More red magic flowed from him into the dragon, hot. The water beads on its scales began to steam.

The dragon was changing. The last of its salt crust was vanishing like snowmelt. Its red scales lengthened, became more muted in color, grew sharper, until each one of them was a knife capable of cutting flesh. The change had begun near Terren's dagger at its head, but soon spread all the way down its body, until the entire length of it was steel gray and as reflective as a thousand mirrors.

The Crown had turned over to blades.

Dimly, distantly, from beyond the barrier, came a wave of tentative cheering from the crowd.

The sky was not red anymore. The heavy gray clouds had broken, too. Bright sunlight poured through with Heaven's approval, reflecting off the chopped water and the dragon's scales.

Terren removed the dagger from its head and stood.

For a long time, he just stared at the Crown, as if he could not even believe he had managed to succeed. Then, all at once, it seemed to hit him. His fists shook as his eyes glittered. "Wei," he called to me breathlessly. "I did it. I . . . actually did it."

Then he said, louder, more confidently, "*I did it.* Look! There's proof!"

He pointed to the dragon with a sleeve and grinned, near overflowing with joy. And then his lips began to tremble and he made a choked sound, and then he was still grinning but also bawling his eyes out. "The dragon . . . it's over . . . it's over . . ."

I stood, dabbed at his cheek with a sleeve, and said, "You don't have to fight any longer," which made him shake his head a little and laugh through his tears. Then I put a hand over his and began gently prying his dagger away. "You won't need this anymore."

He resisted me, but not as much as I thought he would. The moment it left his hands completely, he began to shake and cry even harder. It was like he did not know who he was, if not someone who held a blade.

"What now?" he said, in a voice small and utterly lost.

I took a step towards him in the water, close enough to feel his breath on my cheek.

His eyes widened. He understood.

And I could tell the idea terrified him. He had gone completely rigid, though his hands still trembled. The fear on his face was so raw that for a moment, I almost regretted what I was about to do—what I *must* do.

Terren. Do you trust me?

Three heartbeats passed, maybe five. Then he nodded to himself, took a deep breath as if to gather his courage, and leaned in. A tear rolled down his shining Dao seal as the gap between us closed, and closed, until there was no room for even the wind, and he had touched his lips to mine.

"Wei," he whispered. "I was lost, but then you came bearing a lantern."

The world melted away entirely as I focused on the prince. I sensed his breaths calming as the moment dragged on, saw his expression becoming more peaceful under the wind-stirrings of his damp hair. He kissed me tentatively at first. Then he found his courage after all and kissed me harder, blood and salt. And maybe he was laughing a little, I didn't know. All I knew was that the moment he closed his eyes was when I stabbed him in the heart.

"Good night, Terren."

NOTHING

I held on to him as he died.

I stood in the sun-glittered water as my torturer sagged into my arms, and his blood seeped warm into my gown. He was lighter than he looked, or perhaps I was stronger than I thought. Stray hair billowed over his still-wet cheeks, and his eyes fluttered shut, like a child giving in to dreams.

We were all so foolish in the end, I thought. *So foolish and so, so wicked.*

Leaves and blossoms drifted in the water and swirled in the sky around us; mutilated roads and forests of twisted blades stood among the bones of what had once been trees. It was remarkable, the things we made.

I was sorry I killed him. I was even more sorry for the girl who would have been empress, the girl who held the power of dynasties, the girl who could have been anything.

With her husband's death, she had become nothing.

I wondered if, in the poems and the ballads and the history books, they would mention her name—if they would mention that she was a rice farmer from Lu'an, that she was sister to bright-eyed Bao, that she had once danced with her village under a sky full of lanterns—or if they would simply write *Guan Terren was murdered by his wife*, and let that be the truth.

THE GREATEST NATION

It took only a day before the new emperor visited.

I was pacing my cell in Heaven's Worship, high up in the mountains, when Isan came. I spotted his dragon coming at a distance as it unraveled itself, above bent pines and steep valleys, towards the ledge where I was confined. The sight surprised me. I had imagined he'd be busy sorting out the dynasty affairs after his sudden and tumultuous coronation. Still, it pleased me that I was important enough to see so immediately.

The Crown of the Azalea House was near bursting with fruit. Its scales gleamed the bright orange of persimmons, its horns the jewel shade of plums, its eyes apricot gold. Its mane and bristling spine had transformed into verdant branches, which each hung so heavy with kumquats, hawberries, and mandarin oranges that I could not guess at how it stayed aloft.

Isan stood on its head, holding one of its horns; he directed it until its giant eye floated parallel to the ledge I was confined on. They brought with them the scent of orchards, sweet wine, and long-ago fancies.

Once, I had been so intimidated by him. That crowded New Year's, in Guishan, I had held my breath as he had stepped out of his carriage, too busy staring at his House Seal to judge his appearance. Now he merely appeared like a person.

"Why?" was the first word out of his mouth. "After you healed him?"

I went towards the edge of the cliff. It was the closest I'd ever been to the third son, who wore a gown of pink-and-gold blossoms—gold, I supposed, because he was now emperor. He looked little like his older brothers. His mouth was more innocent than Maro's, his eyes not contemptuous like Terren's. His 果/Guo seal shone a riper red than either the 路/Lu or the 刀/Dao, the red of jujubes and hawberries.

As I neared him, he took a step back. He stayed close enough for us to speak, but not close enough for me to reach out and stab him. Possibly he was afraid of me.

"Why do you think?" I replied, a little disappointed he had not already figured it out. Perhaps I had gotten too used to Terren's cleverness, and had gained unreasonable expectations for his successor.

Isan went quiet for a moment as he pondered. Then he said, "Because Maro died."

"Yes."

The choice between Terren and Maro might have been difficult—so much so that I'd spent the entire coronation's eve agonizing over it—but the moment Maro had died, Isan became the next in line to receive Heaven's Mandate. And it had not even been a question then, to choose between knives and something so gentle, so necessary, as *fruit*.

And even if I had to give up becoming empress, even if it meant I would lose all the power I'd tasted, it had *still* not been a question. I would choose it over and over again. I would choose it in this life, and the next, and the next.

Isan shook his head sorrowfully. "You are very foolish, Wei. You may think you have done the right thing, but what do you know? A girl like you, having been raised in the rice fields and confined to the Inner Court—you have no idea what the world is really like. The nation has many enemies."

"Does it?"

"It will not survive long without my brother's power."

"Won't it?"

"Why do you think so many have supported him, despite his villainy?" He sounded exasperated. "By killing him, you may have murdered a dynasty."

"Murdered a dynasty," I echoed, and laughed softly. They all cared so much about these things, didn't they? "You say it like it is an unspeakable crime, Isan. A greater evil than killing a child. But dynasties are not real. They are made up. Fiction."

It was him who didn't know anything.

It was the officials of the Outer Court, with their soft faces and shaven chins and bee-eater robes, who had no idea what the world was really like.

Had they seen how the country lay bleeding in the famine, had they seen the rice paddies dried and the wheat fields blanched, had they seen the babies curled dead next to their mothers or buried a sister on a hill with their own hands, they would have known the truth. And it was not conquest, not glory, not *blades*.

Truth was simpler. It was warm bowls of rice on the dinner table, enough for everyone, not only young sons who were still growing. It was families sleeping in the same room. Villagers working together, staving away demons or something worse that plagued them. It was suffering. It was enduring. It was living.

Isan, I thought, *you have no idea. No idea how hard it is, living.*

It is not something you can learn from inside the palace walls.

And if it meant we had no swords to defend our borders, so be it. If it meant the Cividí would come raiding the West, so be it. If it meant the Lian charging in from the north, and retaking Tieza, and all the other territories, then let them. Maybe they would be better rulers. Maybe they would not allow us to starve. And if it meant provinces rebelling and the dynasty crumbling like dust, if it meant emperors and thrones sinking into the ashes of history, if it meant Tensha, with all its culture and commerce and glory, becoming only a distant memory, then let them, there was nothing so awful about oblivion.

It could be the greatest nation in the world, the most magnificent empire there ever existed. But if it could not keep its own children safe and fed, was it really something worth fighting to save?

Isan's expression was pained. I could tell he was still thinking hard about how to rescue his new era. Possibly he was imagining selling his magic on the Salt Road. Shipping crates of apricots and pears across icy oceans. Possibly he was making the calculus of which provinces to cede first, to ensure the capital and the heartlands could still be defended.

It is just like the first years of Muzha's reign, he might have thought to himself. Maybe he was even thinking of making sons to help him.

I let him agonize over it a bit longer before putting him out of his misery. "Do not worry, Isan. Your brother has left you Dao Blessings to defend your new nation. Twenty thousand of them."

His chin jerked up as his body sagged with relief. "Twenty thousand . . . ?"

I waited. A moment later, he seemed to finally register my implication. His eyes became alert, his tone that of cautious negotiation. "What are your conditions?"

"There are four."

"Speak them. But do not make them unreasonable."

"One: you use your amplified power strictly for famine aid, at least in the beginning. Not to export and replenish our treasury, nor to appease the Great Clans. Your debt to them can come later. Your people come first. We will start with Nama District and South-Ulan, the places that have been hit the hardest, and we'll move northeast from there. If you perform to my satisfaction, I will release your brother's Blessings to you—as I see fit, over time."

"That is reasonable, and truth be told, I was planning to do similar. But you do not have to speak so harshly with me, Wei. We are negotiating. You need not *coerce*."

"Two: I am absolved of all my crimes. Reading, literomancy, stabbing a prince in the heart. Anything else I have missed naming. I walk free, back to my village, and every household in Lu'an gets an annual stipend from the palace for perpetuity. My brother, Yin Bao, gets free admission to the imperial academy."

"Agreed."

"Three: Terren gets a quiet burial. Nobody attends except for you, and Kiran, if you believe his regard for his brother is genuine." I thought about it some more and said, "And Yong Hesin, if the eunuch should wish it."

It surprised him, but he said, "Agreed."

"Hesin walks free too," I added. It had not been one of my original conditions, but now that I was thinking of him, it felt only right to include it.

"He already does," Isan said, and it was my turn to be surprised. "One of the first things I did after my coronation was ask him to be my advisor."

"And he said yes?"

"Not at first. To be sure, he said he was tired. He wished to go echo-step with Terren. But I managed to convince him to stay. I told him that the nation is in crisis and needed someone with his experience to put it to order."

"An unkindness," I said quietly, feeling a twinge of pity for the eunuch.

"A ruler cannot always afford kindness. What is the fourth condition, Wei?"

I lifted my chin and met Isan's eyes. My last request was going to be the most difficult of them all. "It concerns Terren's remaining concubines. Tradition would dictate that they go home with gifts. But . . ."

Wang Suwen and her brother who needed employment. Liru Syra and her clan that hungered for glory. Zou Minma, from Guishan, who dreamed of becoming mother to a prince.

A dream she had clung to so feverishly, I was sure, because it was the only one she had known how to dream.

"But should they wish it, they shall be permitted to stay in the palace's Inner Court. Should they wish it, they may learn how to read. And if they should further wish it, they may even practice literomancy."

If I had learned anything during my time in the palace, it was that if we wanted to send Blessings home—to our families, our villages, our clans— the only way was to write them ourselves. And even if it meant confining ourselves to the Azalea House, even if we had to endure being called to an emperor's bedside and being planted for a son, at least our cries would now be heard.

Isan's stare burned into me, brows furrowed, lips downturned. It was easy enough to forgive one girl for her literomancy, but to endorse it for many was nothing short of heresy. By accepting my last condition, he would be going against hundreds of years of law and tradition. A move that would no doubt make him many enemies in court.

A necessary move, I thought.

To grow a tree was not easy, the wait until it bore fruit long. But if the seed was not planted in the first place, nothing would ever grow.

And there was nowhere better to plant a seed, I knew, than the fertile soils of the palace. A place lush despite the famine, strong despite the wars, constant even over generations of empire changing hands. A lot of things began at the palace.

The silence between us stretched ripe and long.

At last, he said, "Agreed."

70

HOME

It was evening when I left the palace through the side entrance. The stars hung gentle overhead as the nightbirds whistled a familiar song. The branches waved with blossoms. Even the crisp mountain air came to tussle at my hair, its own kind of farewell.

A horse with a summer mane stood waiting for me. Next to it a red carriage was parked, containing what little belongings I had chosen to take. An assortment of pretty gowns, some headpieces I had grown fond of, some powder, blush, and eyebrow ink. I had finally learned how to paint my face properly, and was excited to teach the Rui sisters. The remaining space was filled with bags of haw candies, mung bean cakes, sweet gao, and other treats for the village children.

With the reins tight in my hands, I cast one last glance at the Azalea House. At its striking vermilion walls, its beautiful pillars inscribed with poetry, its ornately curved eaves. A soft stirring whispered in my heart; it really was a place worthy of the stories.

After today, would I remember it well? Would I remember the silk in its chambers, the cold lattice of its windows, the wet of its courtyard grass under my feet—or would the red palace become only a distant dream?

The gates clanged open, startling me.

A eunuch, old and white-haired, appeared at the entrance. One sleeve leaned on a cane; the other hung loose like a ghost's.

"Hesin," I said. I could not guess at what business he wanted with me.

"His third son emperor, Wei. Not his second nor his first. Muzha could never have predicted this outcome."

There was no resentment in Hesin's voice. No anger for my framing him, no loathing for my causing him to lose his hand. I supposed he had practice with not *resenting*. He had served Jinzha, whom he had disapproved of, then Muzha, whom he had deemed wicked, then Terren, whom he had despised.

I wondered if Hesin had paid a large enough price for his misdeeds. I wondered if *Jinzha* had, joined by all seven of his sons and now two of his grandsons. Had whatever he borrowed from the future been repaid? Was he swimming under the moonlight again, wherever he was, laughing as joyfully as he had in life?

And Muzha . . .

"Who did he really want on the throne?" The question came out unbidden. It did not matter anymore, but searching for answers had become something of a habit. "Why did he change his heir so suddenly, just last year?"

The emperor naming Terren, in one of his last coherent moments, was what had prompted the selection in the first place. My becoming Empress-in-Waiting, the prince's wife, his killer—everything had followed only after.

To take on our enemies in the north, Ciyi had once led me to believe. But now I was certain it was not that simple. Truth in the palace, I had learned, was rare and doled out only sparingly.

Hesin's expression turned grave. "He always meant to make Terren heir. Always. Ever since the night we heard about the second son's sigil: a military one, one that can conquer nations. *Hesin*, he told me in private, *now I will finally be worthy*. He had always been so ashamed while he was alive, of how the borders of Tensha had shrunk during his reign instead of grown. *With the amplified Dao sigil fighting for my legacy*, he told me, *I will finally become immortal in the ballads*."

"But he did not name him heir then."

"No." Sorrow creased the lines on his face. "He wanted to wait until the last possible moment. He did not want his sons to know it was decided."

I remembered Maro leaning his cheek on the windowsill, dreaming of leading the nation with integrity, with pride. How hard he had worked for Tensha. How he had bled for it. And Terren, too—the war, the suffering, all those broken years in Tieza. None of it had mattered.

Are you so sure the emperor will keep you as heir? Hesin had snapped at

Maro once, the night Taifong had been killed. The eunuch had known, all those years, what lay in wait for them at the end of their road—even as the princes themselves remained oblivious.

A cruelty, perhaps. But I was no longer in a position to judge.

"He wanted them to fight," I said quietly.

Hesin nodded. "Would the West Palace have worked so desperately to build those roads, if they never believed they had a chance? Would the East Palace have fought so hard for Tieza, if everything was already decided? Muzha was not a good man, Wei, but he was clever. *Put a mountain before a man*, he once told me, *and if he is worth anything, he is certain to climb it.*"

A silence followed. I could hear the warbling of two wrens, playing in the leaves above.

"Do you have remaining business with me?" I asked Hesin, because he had not yet said what he'd come to say.

"Emperor Isan has asked me to be his advisor."

"Yes. He told me."

"My first piece of advice to him was to take you for empress."

I was so shocked I let go of the reins. "After I killed his brother?"

"It was not hard to convince him, Wei. The nation is in turmoil after the coronation. Power and capital flow loose. The clans who were backing the two eldest princes are rioting. The civilians are afraid. What we need most during this time is stability—and the emperor knows this too." When I kept staring at him, he said, "You are already the Rice Wife. What you did at the coronation only helped add to your legend. To kill the wicked heir and bring fruit to the nation—many people are already praising your name on the streets of Xilang. And besides"—he met my eyes now, speaking earnestly—"who better to put on the throne than one who has already given it up?"

It was true. On coronation's eve, I might have chosen Terren, to make myself empress and to become powerful. But the moment a better path came along, I had given it all up without hesitation. Power might have tasted sweet, but it was also easy to let go of, once we remembered who we were doing it all for.

"But I will not force you," Hesin said. The compassion was back on his lined face, the compassion I had first seen that foggy morning in the Palisade Garden, when I had told him my truths, when I had listened to his. "I told His Majesty Isan that it must be your choice, and your choice only. I will not bind you to a man against your will a second time. For your sake, and"—he gave half a smile, the first sign of humor I had seen on the old eunuch—"for the peace of the nation."

Bind against my will. If I accepted, then I would wed yet another stranger, one who likely resented me. I would be trapped in the Inner Court once again, with all its politics and intrigue and never-ending schemes for power. There might be poison. There might be rumors. There might be the childmaking duties. I would have to relearn the aphrodisiacs, the pressure points, the patterns of the moon.

The choice was an obvious one. Marriage, after all, was only a means.

I gave one last glance at the path that led to Lu'an, and went with the eunuch back to the palace, back home.

It took me a few days until I made my place in the Orchard Palace comfortable. The Rice Pavilion's parlor had already been filled with fruit trees when I moved in—apples and pears growing out of peony rugs, pomelos hanging from the ceiling rafters, blossoming plum branches arching over the doorways. But over the past few days, my servants and I had busied ourselves making it our own. We hung blades everywhere. Rusted and shiny, new and used, ones with wooden handles and ones with leather grips. We hung them from the ceiling, dangling from the branches, and fastened to the walls, until the room smelled not only of ripe fruit but new steel.

Even the throne Terren had made for me had been moved to my new pavilion. Forged initially from a cold twist of swords, it soon caught the magic of the Orchard Palace, and became draped with mandarin blossoms, berries, and wild peaches.

When it was finished, I invited all the women in the palace for a feast. All except for Song Silian, who had fled the palace and returned to her clan. I hoped I never saw her again.

"Your Majesty!" Second-Rank Concubine Wang Suwen came rushing in excitedly. Her jeweled hairpiece clattered as she gave me a deep bow. "May you live a thousand years."

"May you live a thousand years!" declared Noble Consort Kang, who had arrived with her own maid in a dress littered with daisies.

My servants had already set up my parlor with full tables—skewered meats, egg soups, sliced melon, and hundreds more small dishes—but the visitors came bearing even more gifts. Jiang Rovah had brought in lucky buns, filled with sesame and sticky lotus paste; Jin Veris had brought her clan's signature golden plum wine. "Each jar can sell for up to a thousand coppers," she bragged, to absolutely anyone who would listen. Sun Ai—now the Dowager Empress—had brought in lotus wraps in bamboo baskets, each tied neatly with a piece of yellow string.

"These are my favorite!" Li Ciyi exclaimed to me, as he unabashedly swiped two more of the wraps into his sleeve to save for later. "Now that I am chief eunuch to an empress, I must dine like one too."

Not everyone had decided to stay. Some of the concubines, like the Qi Clan sisters or Chua Yan, had decided to take the gifts and go home. Qin Chen, whose grandfather the Magistrate of Dusu had finally been freed after ten long years, had gone back to reunite with her family.

In the end, there had been seventeen from Terren's Inner Court who chose to remain.

We feasted, and an opera girl came in to sing a famous piece for us—"Pity the fish, confined to its pond . . ."—and then came time for the first lesson. Tables were set up with blank scrolls and brush pens, and soon the aroma of lit candles and ink filled the room. Scholars in headdresses came in to teach, and Ciyi finished chewing his lotus wrap and went to join them. "Reading need not be daunting," he said, his eyes turning into crescent moons. "The characters are not random . . ."

It was not only the concubines receiving the lessons. Any servants they wished to bring with them were also permitted to learn. Mi Yung, my head attendant, sat next to a twelve-year-old maid who served under Third-Rank Concubine Liru Syra; one of the old eunuchs from Ni Mara's pavilion shared a pot of ink with my senior maid, Du Hu. Tel Pima—my former scribe I had rehired into the palace—was tutoring two buoyant little eunuchs under a pomelo tree. One of them was tugging at his braid.

Even the toddler prince Ruyi was present, though not as a student.

He was crawling under the tables, in pursuit of an ivy-cat, while everyone else studied. "Cat," he squealed between fits of giggles. "Cat cat cat cat cat."

Then the gate creaked open. Another woman bearing the last name Sun had arrived.

Sun Jia did not look at me as she entered. Her scowl was gone, her head hunched. There were lines on her face that had not been there before. But when she approached Wang Suwen's table, Suwen did make room for her and offer her an inked brush. Her hand closed around Jia's as she guided her into writing her first word.

I watched them from my cold throne, of fruit and blades, while reviewing one of Isan's memorials. The emperor had not given me the authority to stamp them myself—we were not at that point yet; we might never be—but I was allowed to annotate them and give my opinions.

The one in my hands was from spies near the northern border, reporting enemy movement. War was encroaching. The Lian, the Cividí, the island nations, the rebel provinces—they had sensed a weakness after Terren's death, and were now going for the nation's throat.

Maybe we would win against them. Maybe we would lose. Maybe the whole empire would be burned to the ground, and new green things would grow in its ashes.

I added my notes, then signed it with my name. Yin Wei.

Wei—but not the character for *tail*, or *end*, or *last*. The same sound in the Tenshan language could have many meanings. Now that I could read, I could choose the one I liked best, so when I signed my name, it was with the Ancestors' word for *greatness*.

71

AIR

From one branch, two azaleas blooming,
Fighting for a piece of the dawn.
The roots lie rotten, the leaves die weeping;
Come night, all the flowers are gone.
—GUAN TERREN, AZALEA DYNASTY, YEAR 631
(COWRITTEN WITH GUAN MARO; COLLECTED POSTHUMOUSLY)

It was a bright dawn, unusually cold for summer, when I went with Isan to bury his brother. Only a slight breeze stirred the pines and the larches. There was a sunrise, but it was gentle instead of spectacular, a thin haze of pink over the far mountains.

We were a small party. Isan and I led the way, with Kiran and Hesin following at a distance. A few guards and servants had come as well, to accompany us and to carry the casket.

"Do you mourn him?" I asked Isan, as we walked uphill under the quiet canopy.

"I mourn Maro, but you did not kill him."

I nodded. There were still questions I had not had the opportunity to ask until now. "Why did you go to Guishan to help your brother with his selection?"

Isan kept his eyes on the trail ahead. "Partially as a front to give famine aid. I had heard many places had been hit hard, and seen the selection as an excuse to use my magic to help."

I remembered all the fruit trees he had grown in Guishan—grapes and hawberries and pears. I remembered the Blessing that had grown a peach tree in my village. "And the other part?"

"To make my own bid for the throne. My advisors pointed out that Maro and Terren had long been maneuvering in the capital and among the Great Clans, and competing with them here was useless. They suggested

I take a different strategy—to gain the goodwill of the people, to angle for popular support. When the chance to tour the cities arose, they told me to take it."

It did not disappoint me to hear it, as it might once have.

My final question was one I had been meaning to find the answer to, ever since I first arrived at the Azalea House. "My brother received a Blessing from you on New Year's. It was a spark that went to his heart. What was it?"

"Oh, that." He actually flushed a little. "That was . . . nothing."

"Nothing?"

"Nothing useful, at least. When I was preparing my Blessings to give out, there were only so many useful spells I had—I do not have the same gift for literomancy as my brothers did, you ought to know. But I still wanted the firecrackers stuffed full and the people pleased. So I improvised. I put in what I could. Small pieces of magic, not much, but I hoped the recipient would find value in them all the same."

For instance, I thought, *a spark that inexplicably chose a child.* One which showed that even an impoverished villager could be destined for greatness. I remembered Bao's bug-eyed excitement, the hushed silence from the villagers, Ba standing up and declaring his son would grow up to change the world.

Yes, I thought, but did not say aloud. *There had been value in that Blessing after all.*

Isan—thank you.

Not long after that, we crested the peak. Little alpine flowers dotted the mountain in yellows and blues, and wild grass shivered with life in the breeze. The valley stretched out green and lush beneath us, cradling the Aricine River, and it all seemed a gentle assurance that the world went on turning, even when we were not around to see it.

We laid the bamboo casket down on the soft earth, lit some incense, and knelt before it. As I performed the funerary rituals, I glimpsed his ghost.

The boy I had met in the meadow appeared not ten paces away, slightly aglow, and there was a tiny, timid smile tucked between his cheeks.

Nobody else seemed able to see him. Isan, Kiran, and Hesin were all finishing up their rituals, heads down, a few paces away.

"Terren," I whispered, and stood.

The boy's smile widened, just a little. Then he did something that astonished me. He clasped his hands together in front of his heart, palm over fist, and bowed deeply. A Tenshan gesture of respect, deference, and gratitude.

I did not hesitate before returning it. We stayed that way for a long time, our heads facing the green grass beneath us, our hearts beating in sync.

Thud. Thud. Thud.

When we rose again, something pulled his attention to the side.

The ghost of a second boy had stepped out of the dawn, only a bit older. The glow of his sigil was gentle. The instant they laid eyes on each other, Maro let out a little gasp and threw his brother into a crushing embrace. And the way he held him, so *tightly*, with his cheek buried in his hair, it was like he never, ever wanted to let go again.

They did let go in the end, but only because they had somewhere to be.

Behind them, even more friends had appeared. I could see a wooden bridge arcing over a pond, brimming with hundreds of shining carp. Behind it, a peach garden sprouted into life, its endless branches ripe with summer fruit. Bee-eaters played about the canopy, and under their shade, holly-cats chased each other's tails. At the back of the garden stretched a giant tree, next to a golden, thousand-tiered pagoda, and it plunged so high into the sky I was sure they would have to spend a whole lifetime climbing it.

In front of it all was a white tiger, life-sized, sitting on her haunches as she licked a paw. Niu Niu shimmered from beside one of her ears, and Little Sparrow hovered above them both, whistling a beckoning song.

Terren's smile was not shy anymore, it was beaming. Maro straightened the collar of his brother's gown, put a gentle arm around his shoulder, and began leading him to the summer garden—perhaps to spar, perhaps to play "dueling couplets," perhaps simply to run around. They did not look back.

After they crossed the bridge, all the ghosts vanished, and there was only air.

Not long after, the Ancestors took him. Below me, vines curled over the bamboo crate and white lilies bloomed from the cracks in the wood. On one of the soft petals, a tiny ant crawled. The sight was comforting. The country might not forgive people like us, but at least the Ancestors still could.

ACKNOWLEDGMENTS

When I was younger and writing my first books, by myself, I was self-conscious about not being able to fill an acknowledgments section. It turned out that I didn't need to worry, because those books with empty acknowledgments sections didn't get published anyway. It was only after I'd stopped going at it alone and started inviting others onto the journey that my writing career truly began, and I am immensely grateful for everyone who chose to walk with me.

The first thank-you goes to my fearless agent, Jennifer Azantian, who dreamed bigger for this book than I could ever imagine. A heartfelt thank-you to my brilliant editors—Monique Patterson and Mal Frazier—who believed in this story enough to make it better. To the team at Bramble, including Jim Kapp (production manager), Jessica Katz (senior production editor), Shawna Hampton (copyeditor), and Jen Edwards (interior designer), Sarah Weeks (publicist), and Isa Caban (marketer). Working with you has been the biggest joy and privilege.

A heartfelt thank-you to my brilliant editor in the UK, Brendan Durkin. To the team at Gollancz, including Bethan Morgan and Grace Barber (editorial), Jess Dryburgh (sales), and Rachael Lancaster (art), Javerya Iqbal (marketer), and Tom Hill (publicist). I cannot express how lucky I feel to work with such a fierce and passionate team. To Alba Arnau Prado and the foreign rights team at Mushens, and all the publishers and translators abroad, my sincerest gratitude for bringing this story to more readers than I ever thought possible.

Thank you to my book-loving friends and earliest readers—Amit Rao, Gard Von Appen, Matthew Gilmour, and Curtis Graham—who saw this manuscript when it was the book equivalent of scribbles and ensured that "ways" would be felt. To my wonderful beta and specialized early readers—Santiago Márquez Ramos, Wenqi Zou, Sander Shi, Justin Kwon, Ash Howell, Kristi Heath, Greg Tarlin, Tzeyi Koay, Victoria N. Shi, Xuexing Tao (Dad!), and Tara Rayers—thank you; this is a better story for having had your eyes on it.

Much gratitude to everyone whose ideas, feedback, or encouragement has touched the book in a small or large way—Ben Baxter, Thais Afonso, Kyle Nix, Russ Nickel, Donald McCarthy, Erik M. Johnson, Chris Balliet, Elizabeth Hawxhurst, Gaby, Dana Sweeney, and Chris Campbell. To Marlee Roth, dear friend and cheerleader. To the Taos Toolbox class of 2023, for believing in this story first. Much gratitude to Nancy Kress and Walter Jon Williams, whose generosity has touched so many aspiring writers' lives. To Jeanne Cavelos, for your warmth and wisdom in navigating the publishing seas. To all the friends and instructors at Viable Paradise—in particular Max, Scott, Teresa, and Sherwood—for a formidable community I will forever feel lucky to be a part of. Much gratitude to Ms. Palumbo and Ms. Schwartz, who believed in me when I was a much younger writer, still writing about mice bombing asteroids.

A special thank-you to dear friend and writing partner Kathryn Wolterman, who brought all our stories to the fourth dimension. To dear friend and writing partner Kayla Green, and most beloved of alpha readers, who taught us all an inexplicable appreciation for bears. To all of the Enchanting Pros, whom I offer the "light" kind of cheers.

Last, but never least, to Jackson, who was here through the highest and the lowest, from the beginning to the end, thank you.

ABOUT THE AUTHOR

SHEN TAO immigrated to Canada at an early age and grew up inspired by both Chinese and Western stories. She has wanted to be a writer for as long as she can remember. *The Poet Empress* is her first book.